# 論文寫作要領

第4版

Essentials of Successful
Thesis Writing

林隆儀 著

五南圖書出版公司 印行

# 李序

　　林隆儀博士是本人同鄉，久聞其名，最近這幾年見面後，互動頻繁、倍感親切。故鄉有此優秀人才，學有專精、成就非凡，與有榮焉。

　　林博士在企業界服務三十多年，歷任總廠長、企劃處長、行銷處長等要職，貢獻公司，經驗豐富。在職期間積極追求進步，獲得公司高層的賞識，特例給予公假進修，先後在中興大學、臺北大學取得企業管理碩士、博士學位，堪為在職進修的最佳典範。轉任教職後在學術跑道上發揮所長，現在真理大學管理科學研究所擔任行銷領域專任教職，擔負傳道、授業、解惑的重任。以林老師的專業背景與實務歷練轉任教職，不僅是學生們的福氣，也是學校的榮耀，更是學界的光榮。林老師為人謙遜、治學嚴謹，視指導學生寫作論文為一種樂趣，課暇之餘都在關心學生論文寫作，都在修改論文，短短幾年下來所指導的學生中已有五名考進博士班深造，更令人激賞的是這五名博士生中有三位是EMBA畢業學生。

　　誠如林老師所言，論文寫作是一門非常專業的學科，也是一種非常實用的方法。然而學過研究方法的學生，不一定可以順利地展開論文寫作工作，卻是普遍的現象。在做研究、寫論文方面，各校的教學安排與要求不一，有些學校在大學部就開設「研究方法」這門課，有些則到研究所都沒有開這門課。綜觀學生寫作論文最大的盲點在於不知該寫些什麼，以及不知該如何寫，平常又怯於請教，甚至不敢主動面見指導教授。為了突破這種學習障礙，林老師經常在思考編寫一套簡易可行的論文寫作方法，好讓初學者得以迅速進入寫作情況，將視寫作論文為畏途的心態，轉換為一種喜悅與成就感，於是自行編寫講義，傳授論文寫作要領，鉅細靡遺，傾囊相授，所指導的學生都在「知其然，亦知其所以然」的薰陶之下，順利完成論文寫作。

　　林老師把企業務實的做法帶進校園，將顧客第一的理念在校園蔓延，在新的跑道上創下豐碩的成果，堪稱學界不可多得的良好案例。欣見林老師將手頭上的講義彙編成《論文寫作要領》一書，將全書聚焦於「要領」，輔之以「實例」，分享指導經驗，嘉惠更多學子。本人敬表感佩並謹做推薦。

國立聯合大學校長　李隆盛

九十九年三月

I

# 方序

　　我們常說理論與實務是有落差的，將理論用於實務中，說起來簡單，真正的執行是困難的。

　　在企業界服務了超過三十年的林隆儀博士，就是這樣一個成功的例子。自臺北大學博士班畢業，從企業轉換跑道到學校服務，在真理大學管理科學研究所擔任行銷領域相關課程的專任教職，開始讀書、教書、讀論文、寫論文。如今他在指導研究生撰寫論文之餘，完成了這一本《論文寫作要領》，更是讓我十分佩服。

　　論文寫作是研究所畢業的要求之一，故大多開有「研究方法」這門課，一般安排在一年級，以便讓研究生知道如何開始進行研究。我個人也在研究所任教多年，認知到這門課對剛考進研究所的學生而言，常有摸不著頭緒的感覺，甚至部分在職的同學認定這是學界的八股文，常有排斥的心理。如何循循善誘、提綱挈領，在不知不覺中學習到論文寫作的重點，是需要高度技巧的。

　　林隆儀教授能將其這幾年編寫的「論文寫作要領」及「論文寫作技巧」講義，寫成《論文寫作要領》一書，使研究生迅速進入情況，不再視寫碩士論文為苦差事，是學界的大功勞一件。

　　我與林隆儀博士曾在臺北大學一同學習、一起研究，看到有這樣的一本研究方法的書可以出版，實在是與有榮焉。

國立臺北大學商學院院長　方文昌
九十九年三月

# 四版序

　　論文寫作歷程是一條漫長的路，對大多數人而言，也是一項嚴峻的考驗。要走的路雖然漫長，而且有一定的規範與門檻，不是人人都熟悉的工作（功課），但是只要用心學習，按照指導老師的教導與指點，按部就班，循序漸進，確實可以完成，無庸置疑。

　　撰寫一篇碩士論文，或許比較容易，通常在兩年的修業期間內都可以完成，然而要創作一篇博士論文，由於要求的門檻比較高，需要考慮更多因素，通常必須投入更多心思，花費更長的時間，才能順利完成。無論是完成碩士論文或博士論文寫作，通過口試那一刻的喜悅，總是令人畢生難忘。作者和臺北大學企業管理學系蔡坤宏教授，共同指導的臺北大學企業管理學系博士生商懿勻，去年（2021）六月二十九日通過論文口試，耗用多年，投入心思，辛苦有成，取得博士學位，學生心中的喜悅，溢於言表，不言可喻，身為指導老師，與有榮焉，同享喜悅。

　　去年（2021）十月間，五南圖書出版公司主編侯家嵐小姐告知，「論文寫作要領」第三版即將售罄，計畫要出第四版，要我準備資料。這一本聚焦於「寫作要領」，輔之以「寫作實例」，定位為「論文寫作工具書」的著作，旨在指引論文寫作方法與要領，鼓勵學生不再視寫作論文為畏途，而是可以輕鬆愉快，循序漸進的一門功課，此一信念受到很多讀者的認同與肯定，洛陽紙貴，不脛而走，心中喜悅，油然而生，倍感欣慰，更增添作者無比的信心。值此修訂新版之際，審慎增列部分資料，充實本書內容，回饋及感激眾多讀者的肯定與支持。

　　學術論文所蒐集到的資料，經過資料整理及統計檢定結果，獲得研究結論，通常需要加以討論，這是碩士論文比較欠缺者。討論旨在檢討統計檢定結果，研究假說獲得支持的原因與意義，或是沒有獲得支持的原因與解釋。沒有獲得支持不用緊張，也許這是更重要的研究發現。本書第四章研究結果與發現，摘錄及增列商懿勻博士論文中的一段綜合討論，將三個實驗驗證結果列表逐一討論，一方面分享讀者，一方面做為討論的實例。

　　在職學生常會選擇自己服務的產業或公司，採用個案研究方法撰寫論文，因為對個案研究方法及寫作要領的瞭解有限，缺乏理論基礎，欠缺邏輯原理，以致寫作過程陷入一團迷失，甚至無以為繼，時有所聞。本書第三版增列第六章「個案研究實例」，摘錄作者在產業管理學報發表的個案研究實例，受到在職學生的喜愛與肯定，獲得許多迴響。為澄清個案研究的意義、方法與要領，第四版增列部分資料，希望有助於讀者對個案研究的理解與應用。

本書第八章附錄，安排有作者指導學生所寫的「論文寫作心得」，已經安排兩篇，以現身說法的姿態，以拋磚引玉的心情，寫出他們撰寫學術論文的歷程與心得。第四版邀請新科博士商懿勻，提供一篇論文寫作過程的點點滴滴，分享她的寫作心得。

林　隆　儀　謹識
2022年元旦

# 三版序

　　論文寫作是一門非常專業的學科，一般人若不是對其感到陌生，就是認為高不可攀。會寫文章不等於就會寫論文，這是千真萬確的事，尤其是學術論文規範特別嚴謹，特別講究格式，要求特別多，不像一般人想像那麼容易。所以學校都會開設指導論文寫作的相關課程，教導學生寫作論文的基本方法與要領，不僅要達到校際統一，甚至要和國際接軌，方便閱讀、溝通與交流。

　　本書《論文寫作要領》問世以來，獲得廣大讀者的喜愛與肯定，心存感激之餘，仍不忘與時俱進，充實內容，回饋讀者的鞭策。其間第二版曾經做了部分修訂，增加部分實例，再版新書上市不脛而走，獲得更多迴響。這一本聚焦於精簡實用的論文寫作工具書，獲得喜愛與流傳，增添我不少信心。

　　去年暑假應臺灣科技大學科技管理研究所邀請，為高階科技研發碩士在職專班（EMRD）學生開設「學術論文寫作」課程，就是因為這本《論文寫作要領》而結緣。今年再獲邀請於暑假期間繼續開設此一課程，深感榮幸、心存感激。有機會和我國高階研發菁英們研究學術論文寫作，何嘗不是一件高興的事。

　　近年來質化研究方法受到重視，尤其是質化研究方法中的個案研究方法，廣泛被應用於各種領域的研究，有些領域或學系主張採用個案研究方法寫作學術論文。但是學校教導研究方法時，卻很少有系統地介紹質化研究方法與個案研究方法，以致讓初學者常常「只知其一、不知其二」，不知如何著手。

　　質化研究方法和量化研究方法的方法論雖各異其趣，但是基本的研究設計、研究程序、資料蒐集方法、問卷設計、研究發現的管理意涵、研究限制、後續研究建議等寫作要領，並沒有太大差別。然而質化研究所要求的門檻更高，研究設計的構思，所需投入的時間與分析方法，需要有更高瞻遠矚的策略思維、更周詳完整的研究設計、更高明的研究能力，才能寫出一篇好的論文。因此，研究過程比量化研究方法所需要的思考時程更冗長，而且無法利用電腦程式執行資料分析。質化研究方法以文字描述事物現象與特徵為主，無法像量化研究方法採用具體數據，檢定及證明研究變數之間的關係。儘管如此，質化研究方法在社會科學領域締造了觀念上與理論上的貢獻，功不可沒。

個案研究方法屬於質化研究的領域，看似簡單，實則不然。事前的研究設計扮演關鍵性角色，初學者或功力不高的研究者，常誤以為只要選擇一個個案，約定訪問對象，確認訪問時間，照表操課的進行訪問並蒐集相關資料、整理資料，然後提出報告，大功即可告成。殊不知這樣的報告常常淪為走馬看花式的「參訪報告」，頂多只能算是粗淺的「訪問報告」而已，距離學術殿堂所要求的「學術論文」非常遙遠。

本書第一、二版以介紹量化研究方法為主，透過大樣本資料，利用科學統計方法檢視研究變數之間的關係。近年來質化研究有逐漸受到重視的趨勢，尤其是有些學術領域的論文主張採用個案研究方法，以致許多人對質化研究產生濃厚興趣，很想瞭解質化研究或個案研究的特質、實施方法與要領。

為滿足讀者及學生的需求，正值本書第三版修訂之際，特別增加一章「個案研究實例」，以實例解說的呈現方式，並以作者在《產業管理學報》所發表的個案研究實例——「臺灣中小型家族企業生產技術發展之研究：自販機製造業金雨公司之個案研究」，逐一說明個案研究進行程序及其要領，以及介紹個案研究方法的意義、特性、程序、優點與缺點、實施方法與要領，回饋讀者的鞭策與期待。

林隆儀 謹識

2019年5月12日（母親節）

# 再版序

　　寫論文是研究生求學生涯中最大的挑戰，因為論文寫作是一門新課程，也是一門相當專業的學科。學術論文和一般文章的寫作方法大不相同，擅長撰寫一般文章的人，不見得可以撰寫優良的學術論文，尤其是初上研究所的學生，對論文感到非常陌生，心中往往存有不知所措的茫然感。論文是什麼？該寫些什麼？題目從何而來？到哪裡蒐集資料？需要用到什麼統計方法？如何下筆寫？要寫到什麼境界？有什麼規範可供遵循嗎？這一連串的疑問一直困擾著研究生們。

　　研究所雖然開設有「研究方法」這門課，教導研究生們論文寫作的相關知識與方法，並且有「指導教授」面授論文寫作技巧，但是對毫無寫作概念的學生們而言，除了茫然之外，仍然還是一片茫茫然。修習研究方法課程時，大部分學生都尚未身歷其境，不瞭解這門課的效用與重要性，以致普遍都學得不是很精通，等到開始著手要寫論文時，總覺得沒有學好，又不得不上路，而有不知如何下筆的感慨。

　　從企業界轉換跑道，在研究所擔任專任教職，指導研究生很自然成為我的重點工作，十幾年累積下來，共指導過五十一名碩士生，其中有七人考上博士班深造，同時也共同指導一名博士生。我一向鼓勵學生用心寫作論文，並且要求寫到可以發表的境界，指導的學生們也都非常投入，不但順利完成寫作，而且都有在國內外學術期刊發表論文，學生們感到非常有成就感，也令我感到無比的欣慰。

　　前一陣子將指導論文寫作的一些心得，寫成《論文寫作要領》一書，從寫作「要領」的角度切入，輔之以「實例」印證，分享初學者。新書出版後獲得許多迴響，令我非常感動，也因此增添我無比的信心，尤其是在崇右技術學院經營管理研究所兼課時，分享論文寫作要領，學生們受益之餘，要我在書上簽名留念，因為人數多，逐一簽名有點費時，於是特地製作一張精美彩色卡片，上面寫著「有緣相逢學術大殿堂，知識分享期盼再成長」，請學生們貼在書上，共同勉勵。

　　學生們回饋的寶貴意見中，大多認為書中針對寫作方法與要領的提示相當清楚，而且非常實用，最感迫切者莫過於「如何寫」的課題，因此建議多引用實例，增加臨場感。正值本書再版之際，本著廣納建言的初衷，決定在研究變數的重要性、變數之間的關係、變數衡量方法、觀念性架構、抽樣方法與樣本數的決定、問卷設計方法、假說檢定的階層迴歸分析、研究發現的管理意涵，分別加入新的實例，並且將參考文獻做更新與修正，期使本書更迎合初學者的需求。同時增加一篇作者發表在期刊上的新論文，一併提供參考。

林 隆 儀 謹識

2015年10月10日

# 作者序

在企業界服務三十三年之後，轉換跑道到學校服務，在真理大學管理科學研究所擔任行銷領域相關課程的專任教職，和學生們一起讀書、學習、研究，寓教於樂、傳承經驗、貢獻所學，其樂融融。本著「演什麼、像什麼」的信念，這幾年來教導學生學習新知，蒐集與補充實際案例，指導研究生撰寫論文，成為日常生活的重心，也是惕勵自己的重要功課。

企業經營和學校運作不僅生態環境不同，工作內容迥異，使命也各異其趣。在企業界服務算是起步得早，得有機會接觸企業經營各領域的工作，歷練各管理功能的運作。轉換到學術跑道則起步較晚，堅信「只要有開始，永遠不嫌晚」的道理，秉持嚴謹的態度、認真的信念、務實的精神、平實的作風，在教學中找尋樂趣、在傳承中貢獻所學，在指導學生中感受到欣慰，短短幾年來所指導的學生，已有五人考進博士班深造，甚感喜悅。

論文寫作是一門非常專業的學科，也是一門很實用的方法。研究所大多開設有「研究方法」這門課，而且大多安排在一年級上學期，有系統地教導學生做研究的基本方法。這門課對剛考進研究所的學生而言是一門嶄新的課程，學生學起來常常有摸不著頭緒的困惑感，一方面是因為尚未接觸到論文寫作的切身課題，沒有辦法體會這門課的重要性與實用性；另一方面是因為進入研究所之後，課業繁重、時間緊湊，忙得不亦樂乎，無暇專注於這門新課程，等到開始著手寫論文時，才發現研究方法學得不夠深，寫作功夫練得不夠精，不知從何開始、不知如何下手，於是普遍都有「書到用時方恨少」的感慨。

指導研究生寫論文是我這幾年的重點工作之一，深深感覺到要使學生迅速進入情況，順利展開論文寫作工作，確實不是很容易，於是經常在思索論文寫作應該有一套簡易可行的方法與要領，消除學生學習與寫作的盲點，引導學生輕鬆愉快地寫作論文。在這種思維與教學需求之下，乃編寫有「論文寫作要領」及「論文寫作技巧」講義各一套，指導學生按部就班的進行寫作。配合每星期的Meeting，面授機宜，詳細解說這些要領，讓學生們知其然，亦知其所以然。從面授中瞭解學生理解及體會的程度，掌握學生的寫作進度，發覺學生寫作的問題點，然後逐一協助解決。幾年下來欣見這兩套講義發揮功效，學生們學會應用這些要領，順利完成論文寫作。所指導的學生絕大多數都在二年級下學期開學前後就完成整篇論文初稿，甚至有在二年級上學期期末就完成論文寫作並準備發表者。

　　兩年多前就有學生建議把這一套方法寫成一本書，與更多學生分享。當時確實有點心動，幾經評估，總覺得資料蒐集還不夠完整，整體構想也不夠純熟，幾次都因此作罷。講義經過多次增修之後，覺得資料蒐集及時機都逐漸成熟，乃決定以講義為藍本，開始著手寫成一本書。本書定名為《論文寫作要領》，定位為「引導論文寫作的工具書」，以淺顯為經、以實用為緯，聚焦於要領、輔之以實例，以幫助初學者迅速進入寫作狀況為目的。全書按照一般學術論文的章節結構順序，逐一介紹各章節的意義、原理、功用、內涵，以及該寫些什麼、該如何寫等要領，輔之以作者所發表論文的部分實例，期望幫助初學者更容易掌握寫作要領，順利完成論文寫作。書後附錄附有兩位指導學生現身說法所寫的兩篇「論文寫作心得」，以及作者所發表的三篇論文全文以供參考。

　　本書得以完成，首先要感謝真理大學校長吳銘達博士、前校長葉能哲博士的厚愛與鼓勵，讓我在新跑道上順利向前走。感謝真理大學管理學院前院長兼管科所所長莊忠柱博士（現任淡江大學管科所暨經營決策學系教授）的相知相惜，讓我得以貢獻所長及指導學生寫作論文。藉此機會要感謝我的指導學生們充當我的忠實顧客，讓我暢所欲言的教導「論文寫作要領」這一套方法，也因為你們的優異表現，讓我與有榮焉。

　　全書定稿之後，承蒙國立聯合大學校長李隆盛博士、國立臺北大學商學院院長方文昌博士惠賜序文，鼓勵與加持，銘記在心、謹致謝意。同時要感謝五南圖書出版公司副總編輯張毓芬小姐的督促，使我將講義寫成書的構想得以實現。最後要感謝我的家人給我的支持與鼓勵，讓我得以專心做我的工作。

林隆儀 謹識
2010年春節

# CONTENTS

# 目錄

# 第一章
# 緒論

## 一、前言

　　論文寫作是一門非常專業的學科，也是一種很實用的方法。學生寫報告、做專題，需要懂得寫作方法；經理人寫報告、做簡報，需要熟悉寫作技巧；研究生寫論文、發表文章，更需要熟練寫作要領與技巧。論文寫作要領與技巧具有一般性與普遍性，各個階層、各個學科、各個領域都派得上用場。論文寫作可以透過科學方法，配合有系統的教導與傳授，可以利用邏輯的思考與學習，學得論文寫作的方法與訣竅。

　　論文寫作這一門專業的學科與方法，既重要又實用，自不待言；但是平時教導與傳授的卻極其有限，即使是大學的課程，也不一定會開設這一門課。通常都到研究所才正式安排有「研究方法」這一門課，開始教導學生有關論文寫作的基本方法與技巧。論文寫作對研究生來說，是一門新的課程，學生學起來往往有點摸不著頭緒的感覺與困惑，究其原因，一方面是尚未接觸到論文寫作的切身議題，所以不瞭解這一門課有何重要性、有何實用性；另一方面是上了研究所之後，學生發現課業繁重，平時要準備功課，蒐集資料，參與課堂討論，又要上臺報告，期末要寫報告、交報告，忙得不亦樂乎。一般學生對「研究方法」這門課普遍都不是學得很專精，雖然修過這門課，但是總覺得充滿生疏感；到了一年級下學期或二年級上學期，開始要著手寫論文時，才恍然大悟，深深體會到真的學得不夠深、不夠精，於是普遍都有「書到用時方恨少」的感慨。

做任何事情都有其方法與要領，寫文章也不例外。寫文章有其基本的方法，寫一篇好的文章也有一定的原則與脈絡可循。學術論文的寫作更嚴謹、更嚴肅，國內外皆然，因此有一定的規範與方法。有一定的方法，才能達到相當的水準；有一定的規範，才容易進行溝通。「工欲善其事，必先利其器」，無論是初學者或熟練寫作的人，都需要熟諳論文寫作的要領與技巧。

本書定名為《論文寫作要領》，主要是從介紹實用寫作要領與技巧的觀點，輔之以實例解說的方法，深入淺出的論述論文寫作方法，幫助初學者儘速進入論文寫作狀況，協助學會論文寫作方法的學生，熟能生巧，更上一層樓，寫一篇更好的學術論文。同時也幫助一般讀者理解學術論文的結構及寫作要件，瞭解好文章的一般特徵，學會欣賞及評析學術論文。

## 二、論文是什麼？

「論」者，寫作文體之一也，以科學、邏輯、理性的方法，主觀或客觀論述個人的創見、思維、見解、觀念、意念的文章。「文」者，由優雅的字句所組成的篇章，用於表達個人的意思。質言之，「論文」者，以科學、邏輯、理性、客觀的方法，所寫成的論述性文章也。

論文是研究結果的呈現，尤其是學術論文，沒有研究，就不可能有論文呈現；研究沒有獲得有意義、有價值的成果，也不可能有好的論文發表。研究工作有一定的方法、一定的規範，無論所採用的是探索性、描述性或因果性研究方法，都需要遵循既定的研究方法與規範。此外，寫作過程中尚須兼顧研究倫理，嚴謹、審慎的設計，理性、務實的執行，而後將研究結果做完整、完美的呈現。

　　論文寫作和一般的作文有很大的差別，即使是一般作文也有寫作的方法，無論是採用三段論法或五段論法，只要有靈感、有構想，就可以運筆如飛、暢所欲言；只要思慮清晰、文筆流暢，要寫一篇好的作文並非難事，例如學生參加聯考，短時間內即可完成一篇作文。但是學術論文的寫作就不是這麼單純了，寫作一篇好的學術論文需要考量的因素很多，例如需要有周詳的規劃、需要有嚴謹的設計、需要有正確的方法、需要有務實的執行、需要有最完美的呈現，這些都屬於方法論的課題。

　　論文寫作到底是屬於科學的領域，或是屬於藝術的範疇，這是一個耐人尋味的問題。廣義的科學是指用精密可靠的方法，以虛心誠實的態度，所求得有系統、有組織，而且可以實驗的一切知識。科學應用在學術研究，則是指以有系統的實證性研究方法所獲得之有組織、有系統且正確的知識（林萬益、林清河，2002）。一般而言，科學的要件有三，包括：(1)可以用理性的、邏輯的、客觀的、系統化的方法加以處理及解釋者；(2)可以根據同樣的方法加以複製者；(3)可以有系統的加以傳授者。Feigl（1958）針對「事實」的科學提出科學的要件，他指出科學必須具有五項標準，即客觀性、可靠性、精確性、系統性、全面性。

　　藝術對自然物及科學而言是指，凡為人智巧所成的一切製作，而且具有審美上的價值者。藝術本身具有獨立的價值，不受任何問題的影響；而審美眼光言人人殊、各異其趣，藝術價值對每個人也各有不同的意義。從管理的角度言，藝術的特徵包括管理者在制定決策及解決問題時，除了應用科學方法之外，還必須依據個人的直覺、經驗、本能，以及洞察力、判斷力、創造力，也就是創作藝術的功夫，每個人都各不相同；欣賞藝術的意境，每個人也都有很大的差異。

　　再對照論文的寫作，舉凡論文題目與論文結構的構思、理論基礎的建構、研究方法的設計、研究過程的執行、資料分析與解釋、研究結論的呈現、管理意涵的提供、研究建議的提出，都需要符合科學精神、引經據典、客觀務實、詳實論述、清楚交代，提供後續研究者具有參考價值的指引，這一部分顯然是屬於科學的領域。論文寫作過程中有些部分需要發揮個人創意，例如題目的構思、實驗方法的設計、抽樣對象與抽樣方法的設計、資料分析方法的選擇、文章結構及文辭的表達、圖表呈現方法的規劃、論文可讀性的修飾等，充分發揮個人的直覺、經驗、本能、洞察力、判斷力、創造力等功力，有助於使論文達到更完美的境界，這一部分顯然是屬於藝術的範疇。由此可知，無論是研究工作或論文寫作，都需要兼顧科學精神與藝術造詣，因此，論文寫作既是一門科學，也是一種藝術。

一篇好的論文，通常具有許多特徵。不同領域的論文，其特徵可能略有差異。一般而言，一篇好的論文至少應具備下列特徵（林隆儀，2005）：

1. 科學精神，理性研究。
2. 符合邏輯，條理分明。
3. 理論深厚，基礎穩健。
4. 引經據典，資料可考。
5. 言之有物，內容精緻。
6. 觀念新穎，見解獨到。
7. 推論適中，循序漸進。
8. 務實研究，著有貢獻。
9. 管理意涵，應用價值。
10. 文辭清晰，交代清楚。

論文寫作涉及研究程序的步驟，完成一篇論文需要一段時日，絕非臨時抱佛腳可以竟全功。論文的參考價值與貢獻，取決於寫作的優劣；瞭解論文品質的評估準則，有助於指引研究者寫一篇優質的論文。Fox（1958）指出，評估論文品質有下列六項準則：

1. 研究問題及研究目的界定清楚。
2. 詳細說明研究程序，以便後續研究者可以照著此一程序進行研究。
3. 審慎而嚴謹的規劃研究設計，以便獲得客觀的結果。
4. 誠實報告研究設計的缺失，估計這些缺失對研究成果的影響。
5. 使用適當的資料分析方法，充分揭示資料分析結果與重要意義。
6. 研究結論應以研究發現為基礎，並以具體數據佐證之。

# 三、論文寫作程序

論文寫作程序是論文寫作方法中很重要的部分，瞭解這些程序的內涵及其重要性，以及每一個步驟的寫作要領，可幫助研究者按部就班，循序漸進地寫一篇完整的論文。反之，忽略寫作程序，不按牌理出牌的寫作，所寫出來的可能淪為雜亂無章的作品，能不能登論文之堂也可能令人質疑。

論文寫作的程序可以區分為構思階段、文獻探討、研究設計、執行調查與實驗、分析與報告等五個階段或步驟，如圖1-1所示。這五個階段環環相扣、互相呼應、逐一進行、一氣呵成，每一個階段都是論文寫作成功的關鍵因素，也都各有其要領。本書為方便討論起見，將這五個階段依序分別討論。

## （一）構思階段

包括構思論文題目及思考研究目標。構思論文題目應往前追溯自研讀核心文獻資料，用心思考，把研究構想轉換為可以進行研究的題目。思考研究目標屬於廣泛方法論的課題，包括所要研究的問題、動機、目的，所要研究或實證的範圍與所要採用的方法、發展初步觀念性架構草案、研擬研究假說草案等一連串的工作。

## （二）文獻探討階段

包括回顧相關文獻，以及瞭解所要實證的產業背景。此一階段所要做的功課是蒐集相關文獻及產業背景資料，接著精讀所蒐集的文獻與資料，摘錄文獻與資料的重點並予以消化，整理成論文所要參考的文獻資料，作為建構論文之理論基礎。然後根據文獻探討及產業背景資料，將上一階段所研擬的論文題目、觀念性架構、研究假說，做必要之修正。這一連串的功課需要花費很多時間與精神，需要有耐心與恆心、儘早開始、務實執行。

## （三）研究設計階段

包括確定研究方法（探索性研究、描述性研究、因果性研究）、選擇資料蒐集方法（初級資料、次級資料、質化方法、調查方法、實驗方法）、發展研究設計細節（變數操作性定義與衡量方法、抽樣方法與決定樣本數、設計調查問卷、設計實驗方法、資料蒐集方法、資料分析方法）、進行問卷設計，以及問卷前測與修正問卷等工作。此一階段為整個研究的核心工作，需要審慎思考、嚴謹設計、力求完整。

## （四）執行調查與實驗階段

此階段就是根據前述各階段的規劃與設計，實地執行初級資料蒐集、調查與實驗等工作。此一階段需要堅持理想、務實執行，落實整個資料蒐集工

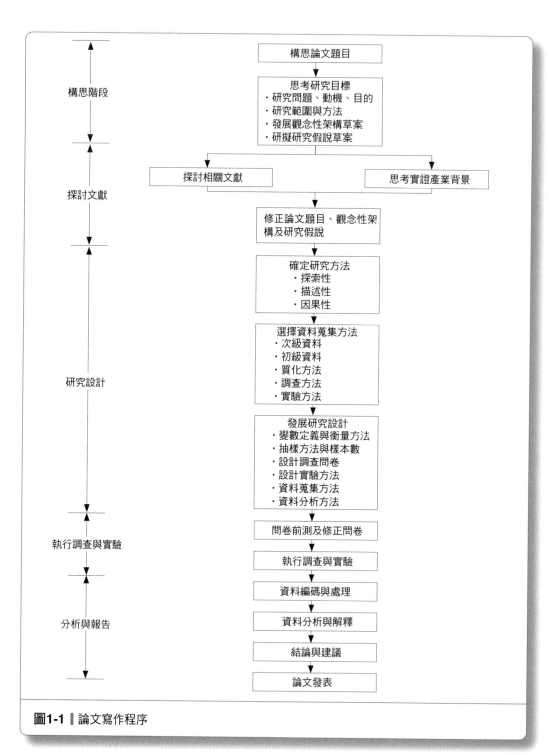

**圖1-1** ▌ 論文寫作程序

作，使整個研究因為蒐集到正確且具有代表性的資料，而提高參考價值。

## （五）分析與報告階段

包括資料編碼與資料處理、資料分析與解釋、檢定研究假說、撰寫研究結論、交代研究限制與建議，以及發表論文等工作。此一階段需要選定資料分析方法，確定統計檢定工具，以研究發現為基礎，提出管理意涵與實務意涵，突顯研究的貢獻與價值。

# 四、構思論文題目

題目是一篇論文的主題，也是整篇論文的靈魂，在寫作過程中扮演舉足輕重的角色。論文題目是在揭示研究什麼，精準地傳達整篇文章的主要概念，因此必須做到直接、簡潔、明確、容易理解、具有強烈吸引力的境界，讓閱讀者一目了然，一望即知文章的重點，進而作為是否繼續閱讀的判定依據。

論文題目需要合乎幾個重要原則，包括：(1)題目不宜太大；(2)題目必須適合做研究；(3)精準地指出要研究什麼；(4)指引研究設計的方向；(5)副標題的適當應用。

論文題目不宜訂得太大、太籠統。掌握小而美、巧而精的原則，才容易做到單點直入，寫得深入、寫得有內涵，突顯差異化的效果。所訂的題目必須適合研究，適合研究才有意義，有意義的題目才有研究的價值。論文題目必須清楚指出所要研究的是什麼，精準的呈現研究變數及其關係，而且題目不宜太冗長。題目是整篇論文的核心，具有指引研究設計的功能，隨後的研究設計必須和題目相互呼應，根據題目來發展研究設計。

構思論文題目比想像中要困難的多，初次寫論文者往往摸不著頭緒，儘管在這裡花費了好長一段時間，仍然不得要領，陷入空轉。尤其是曾經有過工作經驗的學生，往往試圖把工作職場的某些想法當做論文題目來研究，經過費盡心思、再三思索之後，向指導教授請益時，經指導教授解析後才發現，職場的構想不一定可以直接作為論文題目。因為職場上的某些想法或公司的做法，要當做學術論文題目來研究，需要經過一番轉換，轉換後或許可以進行研究，也有可能仍然不適合研究，這就是論文寫作為什麼需要有指導教授指點迷津的原因。

眾所皆知，良好的論文題目要有創新性、要有吸引力，然而初學者最感棘手的問題，莫過於如何找到可以進行研究的題目。在構思論文題目時，有幾個來源可供參考：第一，可以針對有興趣或想要研究的方向，搜尋最近幾年的相關研究，從中理出可能的題目。第二，可以參考國內外學者的後續研究建議，找到適合的研究題目。第三，以國內外相關研究為藍本，增加或改變研究變數與構面，發展出新的研究題目。第四，可以在研究變數間加入中介變數或干擾變數，發展出新的題目。第五，採用不同的研究設計與資料分析方法，也可以發展出可行的研究題目。第六，改善他人的研究缺失，也是找到研究題目的好方法。

構思論文題目的要領，是在思考及研讀核心文獻時，先將所想到的可能題目一一寫下來，經過幾天或幾星期的沉澱之後，再拿出來檢討、修正與精煉。每一次檢討與修正，都會有不同的見解，也會激發不同的新構想。經過幾次的檢討、修正與精煉，並持續向指導教授請益，所構思的論文題目就會逐漸成熟。例如：「議題行銷的社會顯著性、活動持續度與執行保證對品牌權益的影響」、「臺灣石化產業外包策略與外包管理對製造績效的影響」、「表演品質、服務品質與顧客滿意對顧客忠誠的影響」、「名牌服飾消費價值與消費者涉入對仿冒品購買行為的影響」，都是把醞釀許久的構想轉換為值得研究的題目，而且都把題目寫得清楚、簡潔、有力。

副標題的適當應用，可以發揮畫龍點睛的效果，不但可以精簡論文題目，同時還可以明確指出研究的產業或使用的研究方法。例如：「不同聯盟型態之下經濟誘因與信任之相對重要性——以臺灣清涼飲料產業為例」、「郵寄問卷調查無反應偏差改善方法之效果——Meta分析」、「The Influence of the Country-of-Origin Image, Product Knowledge and Product Involvement on Consumer Purchase Decisions: An Empirical Study of Insurance and Catering Service in Taiwan」，也都把論文題目呈現得很清楚。

# 五、研究背景

論文的第一章通常都安排從「緒論」開始。緒論的內容及寫作要領有四項，包括描述研究背景、點出研究問題、說明研究動機，以及指出研究目的。

論文的開場白通常都從描述研究背景開始。研究背景主要是論述寫作這篇論文的發想經過，以及所要實證的產業背景，從中發現值得研究的問題。論述發想經過與描述產業背景，必須引經據典，引用相關文獻及政府或產業統計資料，提高文章的可讀性與可信度。

## 【實例】
### 「不同聯盟型態之下經濟誘因與信任之相對重要性——以臺灣清涼飲料產業為例」研究背景實例
（林隆儀、黃營杉、吳青松，**2004**）

……近年來臺灣清涼飲料產業〔註1〕產生革命性的變革。首先是進入障礙大幅降低，新的競爭者紛紛加入，參加飲料公會、協會等產業組織的廠商由民國七十九年的38家，到民國九十年有78家（民國九十八年有117家），這些眾多公司競相爭食此一約420億元的市場產值〔註2〕（民國九十八年約為450億元），以致競爭局勢年年升高。其次是行銷通路環境大幅改變，現代化連鎖零售通路當道，如便利商店、超市、量販店等紛紛崛起，清涼飲料品透過其銷售的比率逐年提高，足可左右清涼飲料品的銷售。第三是消費者購買習慣不斷在改變，而且改變的速度非常快，嘗新試鮮的心理愈來愈顯著，以致品牌忠誠度有逐漸相對降低的現象。清涼飲料業者為掌握此一迅速改變的消費趨勢，無不努力開發新產品，例如：民國八十八年總共開發435項新產品、民國八十九年共推出459項新產品〔註3〕（民國九十八年有292項），試圖滿足消費者的新需求，於是清涼飲料的產銷走上多種少量的現象愈來愈明顯，結果造成投資龐大、重複投資、設備利用率低，甚或設備閒置的現象屢見不鮮。

策略聯盟的觀念近年來在國內普遍受到重視與接受，清涼飲料業者在降低成本（Saffu and Mamman, 2000；Devlin and Bleackley, 1988；吳青松，1996）、分擔風險（Saffu and Mamman, 2000; Contractor and Lorange, 1988）、功能互補（Saffu and Mamman, 2000; Contractor and Lorange, 1988）、迅速進入市場（Contractor and Lorange, 1988）等多重考量下，認為策略聯盟是提升競爭力比較簡易可行的一種途徑，不但無須成立新的事業體，亦不涉及股權的轉移〔註4〕，在現行經營環境下不失為最佳的選擇方案，於是紛紛興起合縱連橫的策略聯盟。

臺灣清涼飲料產業的策略聯盟並不複雜，以產銷功能互補的外包式（Outsourcing）〔註5〕策略聯盟為主。由於生產技術進步迅速，產品包裝材料推陳出新的速度也快，清涼飲料業者在自行籌設生產線趕不上市場需求的情況下，紛紛尋求委託代工生產，例如：臺灣可口可樂公司、家鄉公司、維他露公司等。有些業者在市場拓展不易的情況下，為提高產能利用率，乃萌生為他廠代工生產的念頭，例如：久津公司、名牌食品公司、泰華油脂公司等。除了委託生產的合作型態外，銷售活動的聯盟也屢見不鮮，例如：黑松公司與統一超商合作銷售杯裝100%藍山咖啡、家鄉公司與統一超商合作銷售果汁產品、名牌公司與福客多超商合作銷售礦泉水等。此外，委託生產與委託銷售混合也是常見的聯盟型態，例如：可口可樂公司與雀巢公司合作產銷雀巢檸檬茶、久津公司與聯合利華公司合作產銷立頓紅茶等。在供需雙重衝擊下，功能互補型態的產銷策略聯盟環境於焉形成。

以往有關策略聯盟的研究，大都把焦點集中在經濟交換因素的考量，例如：Dyer（1997）、Contractor and Lorange（1988）、Dwyer and Oh（1988）。晚近許多學者主張從社會交換觀點看策略聯盟，例如：Kogut et al.（1992）、Gulati（1993）、Eisenhardt and Schoonhoven（1996）、Tsai（2000）。單一理論在解釋策略聯盟現實的現象時，難免有其偏頗與不足之處，明顯可見的是沒有一個單一理論可以單獨解釋策略聯盟過程的複雜性（Spekman et al., 1998）。例如：涉及經濟因素的交易成本理論認為，策略聯盟的主要目標是在追求經濟利益，特別重視合作契約關係與聯盟夥伴的理性行為，由於過分強調合作夥伴的經濟誘因，因而忽略了合作夥伴之間尚存在有感性的社會關係。涉及信任的社會交換理論認為，策略聯盟是一種關係導向的合作行為，主張以道德義務來規範企業之間的合作行為，認為公司在進行資源交換的過程中，所須履行的義務與可能獲得的報償，往往無法事先確定，此時，組織間的信任與依賴，就成為組織進行社會交換的基礎（Hallen et al., 1991）。它所重視的是聯盟夥伴所建立的長期合作關係，由於過分強調社會關係導向，反而忽略了交易成本理論下追求經濟利益之理性因素的現實。

〔註1〕：清涼飲料係指不含酒精的飲料，我國貨物稅條例第八條正式稱為「清涼飲料」。清涼飲料有多種類別，按SIC Code／CCC的分類，主要類別從2202.10.00.10-8到2202.90.90.99-6等23種類別。

〔註2〕：依據經濟部統計處、臺灣區飲料工業同業公會統計資料顯示，以及黑松簡訊第106期，民國八十九年臺灣清涼飲料產業的市場產值約有420億元。

〔註3〕：臺灣區飲料工業同業公會統計資料，黑松簡訊第106期。

〔註4〕：有些學者認為策略聯盟包括權益型與非權益型合作，本文所稱策略聯盟是指非權益型合作而言。

〔註5〕：「Outsourcing」一詞有譯為「外包」者，也有譯為「委外」者。本文的研究對象為臺灣清涼飲料產業，有關價值活動的聯盟，該產業均使用「外包」一詞，因此本文亦採用「外包」一詞。

**【實例】**
**「學校行銷策略與學校形象對家長選校決策的影響──知覺風險的干擾效果」研究背景實例**
（林隆儀、李明真，2010）

　　……學校組織具有較為穩定保守、鬆散結合的組織特性，故因應環境變革的能力及整體競爭力均較為薄弱（張明輝，2002）。因此在學校經營上，若能引進企業行銷的觀念，運用行銷策略，將正面積極的學校資訊，有效地讓家長與社區民眾知悉，有助於學校跳脫傳統的思維，促使學校組織轉型，將是學校組織經營與管理突破現狀的一條蹊徑，也是學校組織在經營上找出另一條出路與活水的最佳途徑。

### 1.少子化趨勢之衝擊

　　臺灣在過去農業時代，家中需要人丁幫忙種田，會將小孩視為生財工具，並將養小孩當做是投資與儲蓄。當時的社會觀念是「多子、多孫、多福氣」，且有「養兒防老」的價值觀。但隨著農業時代的結束，進入工業時代後，城市都市化的結果，造成社會功利主義的盛行及扶養小孩的成本增加，養小孩的經濟價值（對父母而言），則較農業社會大幅下降，政府也因社會型態的轉變而鼓勵家庭實施「兩個小孩恰恰好、一個也不嫌少」的家庭計畫（張憲庭，2005）。

　　從工業時代進入現代科技時代，經濟的發展及社會快速的變遷，反而讓許多人感受到撫養子女是件沉重的負擔，而有「養老防兒」的觀念。近年來，隨著就業機會萎縮、失業率攀升、薪資卻持續降低之下，大家對於社會及生活充滿著不確定感，年輕人對經濟前景普遍感到不安，覺得生活愈來愈辛苦，組成家庭及養兒育女形成了一種經濟及心理上的壓力與負擔，自然更不願意生育（陳美君、吳俊秀，2006）。

　　臺灣過去四十年來，中小學入學教育是屬國民義務教育的一環，採學區制，學生來源應是穩定且入學人數是可預測的。但根據內政部戶政司統計資料顯示，自1980年出生人數從41.4萬降至2000年30.5萬人，2008年更已降至19.8萬人〔註1〕，少子化的趨勢已逐漸衝擊教育各階層。國內學齡兒童人數遽降，98學年度後預估國小減班合計將近一萬班〔註2〕，且少子化衝擊也將延伸到國中，未來國中小減班、裁併校案例也將增加（張憲庭，2005）。

　　每個家庭的子女數一旦逐漸減少，在「望子成龍、望女成鳳」的心理期待下，每個父母都希望給子女最好的栽培。因此，人口結構出現少子化型態，使得父母會更加重視小孩的教育，儼然已是目前不可忽視的社會現象。

## 2.家長教育選擇權之行使

　　教育選擇權（School Choice）或稱為「學校選擇」，是指在義務教育階段，家長有為其子女選擇就讀學校的自由與權利（吳清山、黃久芬，1995）。教育選擇權的概念，源起於1950年代美國經濟學家佛利曼（Milton Friedman）的觀點，期望經由自由市場的競爭原則，透過「教育券」的實施，改善公立學校品質低劣的窘境（黃建忠，2004）。國內家長教育選擇權的觀念，起始於行政院「教育改革審議委員會」，於民國八十五年成立，全力推動教育改革，期待藉由教育體制的轉型，在自由化、多元化、民主化、適性化的發展之下，將臺灣的教育朝向國際化的目標前進〔註3〕，而明訂家長教育選擇權，就是為了因應教育市場化的改革所產生的教育政策。

　　受到少子化的衝擊，各學校理應都有面臨年年減班的壓力，但民國八十八年「教育基本法」公布後，保障了家長有學校選擇權及事務參與權。家長教育選擇權的確立，所衍生出教育市場化、分權化、專業化及績效化等理念，將我國的教育帶入另一個嶄新的時代，但也充滿了許多競爭與挑戰（許朝信，2001）。越區就讀早已存在於各國中小學，尤其國中時期正值叛逆期，家長往往更會花心思去瞭解、比較，選擇校譽、學習效果良好的學校，而以遷戶口方式來就讀其理想的學校。因此，黃乃熒（2000）指出，家長教育選擇權能夠規避低品質的教育、調整價值體系、促進學校辦學績效等功能。

　　近來「寶貝兒女一個」已成風氣，多數家長因小孩少及生活水準提高而頻頻行使教育選擇權，在整個教育環境走向市場化、競爭化的趨勢下，對公立學校造成的衝擊尤甚。目前在臺北縣國民中學，已有部分公立學校因少子化而減班，但也有部分公立學校卻逆勢增班，這樣的教育生態已逐漸形成。

## 3.行銷策略運用在學校經營

　　Kotler and Levy（1969）發表一篇名為＜行銷觀念擴大化＞（Broadening the Concept of Marketing）的論文，提出有關非營利機構行銷的基本觀念，認為行銷是一種廣泛的社會活動，其範圍不應限定於一般商品（黃俊英，2002）。Kotler and Fox（1994）更將行銷策略應用於教育組織中。

　　近二十年來，臺灣在政治民主化、經濟自由化、社會多元化、科技發展快速化之下，使得教育面臨愈來愈多的挑戰，教育改革也在眾人期盼下推動。為使教育組織能提升自身的競爭力，追求卓越並提升教育品質，教育部要求各公立國民中學校長，研究引進企業經營理念及行銷策略，推廣並宣傳自己學校特色的可行性，並納入校務評鑑中。行銷概念的發展，由商業機構擴大到非營利機構，乃因應而生。行銷非僅適用於營利性的企業，同時也適用於非營利性的個人或組織（黃俊英，2004；Kotler, 1969）。因此，將行銷觀念應用在教育組織，視教育為市場，學校擬定行銷策略以達成永續經營，有其重要性（許舒翔、周春美、沈健華，2002）。

　　將企業行銷運用在學校經營，其理念與做法是目前臺北縣公立國民中學校長遴選及校務評鑑的一項重要指標〔註4〕。然而，各校推行幾年下來，臺北縣97學年度85所公私立國中，呈現出17所公立國中穩定地增班，28所公立國中卻持續減班中〔註5〕。因此，如何有效地執行學校行銷策略，提升學校形象，以影響家長選校之意願，在少子化的衝擊及家長教育選擇權呼聲高漲的此時，已成為創新學校經營的重要議題。

---

〔註1〕：中時電子報，〈養不起　去年新生兒跌破20萬〉，2009 chinatimes Inc. com
〔註2〕：教育部統計處，2009 www.edu.tw/statistics/content.aspx?site_content_sn=8869
〔註3〕：教育改革總諮議報告書www.ey.gov.tw/public/Attachment/
〔註4〕：臺北縣教育局校長遴選聘任及任期考評作業要點（民國九十八年四月二十四日修正）
〔註5〕：臺北縣教育局學校資料https://esa.tpc.edu.tw/

# 六、研究問題

　　研究問題是要明確地指出研究試圖要解決的問題。釐清研究問題，才知道需要蒐集什麼資料，也才知道如何進行研究。要指出研究問題，需要從回顧文獻著手。研讀過幾篇核心文獻之後，通常都會有一定的理解與心得，也會發現某些問題有待進一步釐清，這些有待釐清的問題經過審慎思索，通常都會形成很有價值的研究問題。

　　發現研究問題最重要的要領就是回顧核心文獻，用心精讀、確實消化，發覺及釐清研究問題，並予以具體化。研究問題具體化，有助於設計可以解決問題的研究方法。初學者之所以無法明確地指出研究問題，主要是沒有研讀相關文獻，就急著要寫「研究問題」。不瞭解「研究問題」的意義、不瞭解發覺「研究問題」的方法、不瞭解寫「研究問題」的要領，又缺乏相關的資料與題材，當然就無法寫出明確的「研究問題」了。

---

### 【實例】
### 「服務品質、品牌形象、顧客忠誠與顧客再購買意願的關係」研究問題實例
（林隆儀、周佩琦，2010）

　　……服務競爭時代，企業成功的關鍵因素在於服務品質。Reichheld and Sasser（1990）指出，客戶與企業往來的時間愈長，對企業的獲利愈有助益。維持高品質的服務水準是維持銀行競爭優勢的必要條件，專業服務與不斷提供創新的產品與環境，是促使顧客再度光臨及建立顧客忠誠的主要動力，而提高服務品質、品牌形象與顧客忠誠，進而激起顧客購買意願，已成為企業經營與獲利之重要指標（簡永在，2002）。

　　因此，如何確保並提升服務品質，一直是金融服務業最重視的議題之一。雖然我國已進入服務經濟的時代，但服務品質大都從生產的立場去思考如何提升服務品質、改進服務傳遞過程，而缺乏從滿足顧客需求的角度去慎思，因此，很難實現「以客為尊」的最高服務原則。服務品質中，人員的服務態度最為人所重視，如果服務態度不佳，會直接影響顧客滿意度，甚至造成企業出乎意料的損失。Diener and Greyser（1978）的研究指出，約有30%～90%不滿意的客戶不會再購買同一品牌的產品，可見不滿意所帶來的抱怨成本及品牌移轉，對企業的傷害至深且巨。這是一個值得服務業深思的問題。

## 【實例】
## 「The Influence of Corporate Image, Relationship Marketing, and Trust on Purchase Intention: The Moderating Effects of Word-of-Mouth」研究問題實例
### （Lin and Lu, 2010）

... In respect of the tourism industry, Internet marketing has been widely applied, and the competition is getting more and more serious. Thus, it's most important for the internet travel agency to build up a good corporate image and better apply relationship marketing to enhance the trust of customer. As more consumers are relying on word-of-mouth (WOM) to evaluate products, WOM has been playing a persuasive role in influencing consumers' purchase decisions.

By June 2008, the number of cable broadband network subscribers in Taiwan had reached up to 4.70 million and the penetration rate of Internet applications had hit 44 percent.[1] The brisk development of the Internet has brought new changes in the business model and marketing strategies for the tourism industry. As the tourism market flourishes, and the competition among tour agencies becomes keener, the highly efficient online marketing has turned out to be the most widely used marketing tool. While making e-commerce transactions, buyers do not have face-to-face contact with vendors and are not able to take a substantial look at their products. Thus, it becomes more important to establish mutual trust (Turban et al., 2000). When it comes to doing online business, tour agencies have begun to realize the importance of trust as a core issue as e-commerce transactions are characterized by high uncertainty and distrust.

Corporate image helps consumers obtain a better understanding of the products offered by specific corporations and further mitigate their uncertainty while making buying decisions (Robertson and Gaitgnon, 1986). As a result, establishing the corporate image of a website dealing with travel transactions becomes even more important. More than three-fourths of online buyers indicate that their buying decisions regarding tour packages depend on the information offered online. Therefore, online tour agencies have to face the influence brought by word-of-mouth among customers. Although word-of-mouth among customer plays an important role in modern business situation. There is a little bit difference in the importance between online and offline consumer. Online customer do not face-to-face with the vendor, word-of-mouth is more important for online consumer than offline consumer.

_____

1. "Innovative Information Application Project" developed by FIND of Institution for Information Industry/Dept. of Industrial Technology, MOEA.

## 七、研究動機

　　動機者，引發人們採取某種行為的原因也。質言之，動機是指人們採取某種行為時，內心所抱持的目的。人們做任何事，採取某種行動，背後都存在著一個或幾個動機，做研究、寫論文也不例外。

　　研究動機是指為什麼要進行這一項研究，為什麼要寫這一篇論文，為什麼要選擇這個題目。撰寫研究動機的要領是要從Why Study的角度思考，冷靜、審慎、務實的自問，為什麼要選擇這個題目來研究，然後清楚、明白、精準的回答這個問題所得到的答案，才是真正的研究動機。

　　撰寫論文第一章時，研究者感到最困難的就是寫研究動機。動機是心理學上一個很重要的名詞，看似簡單易懂，然而卻又存在幾分抽象，不容易表達，初學者往往抓不到要領，以致標題寫的是「研究動機」，所寫的內容卻是南轅北轍，不是不知所云，就是停留在描述「研究問題」階段；不是陳述毫無關係的內容，就是撈過界限的寫到「研究目的」。

　　要檢視研究動機是否寫得很精準，其實並不難，除了掌握上述要領之外，進一步比較所寫的「研究問題」、「研究動機」與「研究目的」即可分曉。這三個標題顯然各不相同，所寫的內容若是很相近，甚至寫得一模一樣，就一定有問題，而此時的問題通常都出現在「研究動機」這個環節。「研究問題」、「研究動機」與「研究目的」是三個不同的議題，而且是必須區分得很清楚的標題。

## 【實例】

## 「不同聯盟型態之下經濟誘因與信任之相對重要性——以臺灣清涼飲料產業為例」研究動機實例

（林隆儀、黃營杉、吳青松，**2004**）

　　……本研究主要想回答一個問題：廠商決定採行策略聯盟，在既定聯盟型態之下，考量策略聯盟決策因素時，經濟誘因與信任的相對重要性是否有差異？

　　為回答此一問題，乃引發了本文的第一個研究動機。臺灣清涼飲料產業的策略聯盟實務已經做得很多，經查閱相關文獻，發現尚未有人針對此一主題做過深入的研究，因此乃引起本文的第二個研究動機。

## 【實例】

## 「The Influence of Corporate Image, Relationship Marketing, and Trust on Purchase Intention: The Moderating Effects of Word-of-Mouth」研究動機實例

（**Lin and Lu, 2010**）

　　... Previous literature mainly focused on the influences of corporate image on consumers' purchase intentions (Grewal, Monroe, and Krishnan, 1998; Solomon, 1999), while few study have discussed the influence of corporate image on consumers' trust. Geiger and Martin (1999) suggested that the Internet plays a decorative and informative role most of the time. Few enterprises use the Internet to establish and maintain relationships with customers. Although many scholars had published papers on relationship marketing or corporate image in the past, few explored both at the same time. This is the first motivation of this paper. In recent years, the development of word-of-mouth communication in marketing has mainly been analyzed from the perspective of human contacts (Silverman, 1997; Derbaix and Vanhamme, 2003). Previous literature on word-of-mouth was dedicated to the influences of factors on consumers' adoption of word-of-mouth (Duhan, Johnson, Wilcox, and Harrell, 1997), the influences of other marketing information on consumers (Bickart and Schindler, 2001), and motivations for consumers to carry on word-of-mouth (Henning-Thurau et al., 2004). These studies were oriented to the broadcasting of messages and the influences on consumer behavior, while few took word-of-mouth as a moderating variable between the influences of trust on consumers' purchase intentions. This is the second motivation for this study.

## 【實例】
## 「議題行銷的社會顯著性、活動持續度與執行保證對品牌權益的影響」研究動機實例

（林隆儀，2010）

　　……目前國內實行議題行銷的企業正日漸增加，大多數的研究都把它歸類為企業的行銷手段之一。但從消費者角度觀之，議題行銷不啻為企業提供給消費者慈善誘因，激起消費者以助人行為之決策模式決定參與，而此助人行為之決策模式則涉及了消費者個人對議題是否有責任認知。因此議題選擇的出發點，本質上是否應立基於符合消費者的期望，而對品牌權益有顯著的助益，需要進一步研究，此為本研究的動機之一。

　　晚近許多企業實行議題行銷都有朝向長期性的趨勢，Barnes and Fitzgibbons（1991）亦認為企業透過與非營利組織長期合作的議題行銷，可以改善及提高企業形象。然而，企業是否對議題採取長期性觀點，會影響消費者對議題行銷活動之評價，尤其是以長期觀點評價企業的品牌權益，更有可能因為企業對議題所付出的長期承諾，或隨著時間經過不斷付出努力而有所收穫，因此，企業實行議題行銷的持續度值得深入探討，此為本研究的動機之二。

　　許多消費者對企業結合愛心的行銷手法，往往抱持懷疑或不信任的態度（黃俊閎，1995）。因此，企業在推行議題行銷時，若能同時消除消費者對企業所承諾的事項是否確實履行之疑慮，掃除消費者因此而產生的負面觀感，進而獲得消費者的信任，對企業藉實行議題行銷，創造品牌權益，應可提供有價值的建議，此為本研究的動機之三。

## 八、研究目的

　　目的是指人們意念中想要達到的境地。具體言之，目的是指人們採取某種行動所要達成的終極目標。研究目的就是研究者執行一項研究計畫，所希望達成的最終目標。

　　論文寫作過程中指出研究目的比較容易，其中的要領是從What Study的角度思考，根據所設計的觀念性架構圖上所標示研究變數之間的關係，逐一寫出所要達到的具體目的。最簡單的方法就是順著觀念性架構圖上所標示研究變數之間關係的線條及箭頭，逐一寫出所要證實的關係。

---

**【實例】**

**「不同聯盟型態之下經濟誘因與信任之相對重要性——以臺灣清涼飲料產業為例」研究目的實例**

（林隆儀、黃營杉、吳青松，2004）

　　……本研究試圖提出一個兼具有經濟交換與社會交換的觀念性架構，主要目的有二：其一為探討策略聯盟型態，以臺灣清涼飲料產業為例，探討外包式策略聯盟的型態，一者，試圖填補過去文獻只提到外包是策略聯盟的一種模式，未深入探討其型態的部分空隙；二者，提供後續研究者有可供參考的資料。其二為研究不同聯盟型態之下，廠商在考量策略聯盟的決策因素時，經濟誘因與信任的相對重要性是否有差異。

---

**【實例】**

**「議題行銷的社會顯著性、活動持續度與執行保證對品牌權益的影響」研究目的實例**

（林隆儀，2010）

　　……基於上述研究背景與動機，本研究的目的在於：(1)比較企業選擇不同程度的社會顯著性議題，對提升品牌權益效果的差異。(2)研究企業實行議題行銷時，不同程度的持續度，對提升品牌權益效果的差異。(3)比較議題之社會顯著性與活動之持續度的不同組合，對提升品牌權益效果的差異。(4)探討企業實行議題行銷時，有無執行保證，對提升品牌權益效果的差異。(5)研究議題之社會顯著性與有無執行保證的不同組合，對提升品牌權益效果的差異。

# 九、摘要

摘要，顧名思義是指摘錄要點。學術論文摘要的寫作要領是要正確、明白、精簡的寫出研究什麼，指出研究對象，說明抽樣方法與樣本代表性，所採用的假說檢定方法，以及研究發現與結果。

由上述要領可知，摘要通常都等到整篇論文完成之後才撰寫，文字的鋪陳必須確實做到簡潔、精準，讓閱讀者很快就能夠瞭解這篇論文在研究什麼、採用什麼方法、研究結論有何貢獻與參考價值，然後再決定要不要繼續研讀詳細內容。

學術論文題目頁的編排順序，最先出現的是論文中英文題目，其次是作者中英文名字，第三是中英文摘要（包括關鍵詞）。由此也可以看出，論文摘要在整篇論文結構中的重要地位。

論文摘要是一篇論文中最精華的部分。既然稱之為摘要、精華，就不宜贅字連篇，更不適合長篇大論，通常以300字至500字之間最適當。關鍵詞字數的要求，各學校及期刊各異其趣，研究者必須遵守學校或期刊的要求。有些期刊的要求更嚴謹，規定一篇論文的摘要不能超過300字，所以，投稿時務必詳細研讀各期刊的要求。

摘要最後一項要件，是必須寫出論文中所使用的關鍵詞，通常以五個為限。關鍵詞的目的是在指引本篇論文所屬的領域與方向，方便學術及研究機構收錄，也方便讀者搜尋與查閱。

**【實例】**
「**The Influence of Corporate Image, Relationship Marketing, and Trust on Purchase Intention: The Moderating Effects of Word-of-Mouth**」摘要實例。
（**Lin and Lu, 2010**）

**Purpose**-The main purpose of this study is to investigate the influence of corporate image and relationship marketing on trust, the impact of trust on consumer purchase intention, and the moderating effects of word-of-mouth between the influences of trust on consumer purchase intention.

**Design/methodology/approach**-Consumers of an online travel agency in Taiwan aged over 18 were taken as the research sample. Primary data were collected through convenience sampling. Regression analysis was used to test the hypotheses.

**Findings-**The main findings are as follows: (1) Corporate image has a significantly positive influence on trust, and commodity image has the most significant influence on trust, followed by functional image and institution image. (2) Structural and financial relationship marketing has significantly positive influence on trust, and structural relationship marketing has greater influence on trust compared with financial relationship marketing. (3) Trust has a significantly positive influence on consumer purchase intention. (4) Positive word-of-mouth has a moderating effect between the influences of trust on consumer purchase intention.

**Research limitations/implications-**Limitations of this study: (1) The data obtained in this study only reflected the correlations and cause and effect among the variables studied during a specific period of time. (2) This paper only focused on tour agencies. (3) Consumers who used only the most popular online tour agencies were selected. Therefore, the samples might involve some bias. The implication of this study include: (1) Different types of corporate image will have different levels of influence on consumer trust. (2) There is a need to support the previous study that relationship marketing has a significantly positive influence on consumer trust. (3) The moderating effects of positive word-of-mouth between the influences of trust on consumer purchase intention must be examined. (4) The influence of trust on purchase intention must be considered.

**Practical implications-**(1) The study findings reveal the need and importance for a company to improve corporate image continuously. (2) The study indicates the need to emphasize the use of critical relationship marketing. (3) Realize the nature and importance of the moderating effect of word-of-mouth.

**Originality/value-**The value of this study is combine theory an practical and finding four management implications and three practical implications.

**Key words** Corporate Image, Relationship Marketing, Trust, Word-of-Mouth

**Paper type** Research paper

**【實例】**
**「服務品質、品牌形象、顧客忠誠與顧客再購買意願的關係」摘要實例**
（林隆儀、周佩琦，2010）

……本研究旨在探討服務品質、品牌形象、顧客忠誠與顧客再購買意願的關係。選擇臺北市銀行產業財富管理部門往來的顧客為研究對象，以向我國15家金融控股公司購買金融產品的顧客進行抽樣調查，採用人員指導的問卷訪問法蒐集初級資料，發出470份問卷，回收有效樣本428份，有效樣本回收率為91.06%。採用迴歸分析及層級迴歸分析檢定研究假說，研究結果發現：(1)服務品質對顧客忠誠有顯著的正向影響；(2)品牌形象對顧客忠誠有顯著的正向影響；(3)顧客忠誠對顧客再購買意願有顯著的正向影響；(4)服務品質對顧客再購買意願有顯著的正向影響；(5)品牌形象對顧客再購買意願有顯著的正向影響；(6)顧客忠誠在服務品質對顧客再購買意願影響中具有部分中介效果；(7)顧客忠誠在品牌形象對顧客再購買意願影響中具有部分中介效果。

關鍵詞：服務品質、品牌形象、顧客忠誠、再購買意願

# 十、結語

如前所述，論文第一章除了呈現論文題目之外，接著必須精準的描述研究背景，點出研究問題、說明研究動機、指出研究目的。至於研究流程或程序、研究範圍與限制等，則不適合編排在第一章。

研究流程或程序，是在指引論文寫作的程序與步驟，屬於一般性的論述，是放諸四海皆準的原則。每一篇論文的寫作程序與步驟都相同，每一位研究人員的做法也都大同小異，因此建議研究流程與程序無須特別在論文中贅述。

研究範圍屬於研究設計的範疇，研究者必須在論文第三章中詳實交代，所以建議無須在第一章就急著交代研究範圍。至於研究限制，主要是要指出整個研究設計，以及執行過程中所受到的某些限制，以致使整篇論文出現有不完美的現象，這是研究人員表現自我檢討、謙虛為懷的態度，屬於研究倫理的領域，需要完成整個研究工作、完成整篇論文寫作之後，再來檢討與交代。通常都把研究限制編排在論文第五章研究限制中，因此建議第一章無須重複交代研究限制。

# 第二章
# 文獻探討

## 一、前言

　　文獻探討也稱為文獻回顧，目的是在蒐集及探討、整理相關文獻，建構所要撰寫論文的理論基礎。

　　文獻（Literature）是指以往的學者所創作的相關典籍與資料。所謂「相關」，是指我們所參考的文獻與所要研究的領域或題目有密切關係者。而文獻探討（Literature Review），就是在回顧學者最近所做的相關研究，檢閱產業的相關研究報告、檢視公司經營的相關資料，以及瞭解政府相關單位所公布的最新資料。這些文獻與資料對論文的寫作太重要了，對研究者而言亦十分珍貴。

質言之，文獻是既有的相關資料，只是分散在不同的地方，研究者必須設法找出所需的相關文獻，詳細研讀、摘錄重點，尤其是掌握學者的研究發現與結論，瞭解這些文獻研究設計的來龍去脈，然後說明如何將文獻應用到你的研究及論文中。

初次撰寫論文的人對文獻探討不僅感到很陌生，而且會有一種迷惘、不知所措的感覺。文獻探討的目的為何？功用何在？為何要探討文獻？撰寫論文時，文獻有何重要性？文獻探討到底要寫些什麼？如何寫？沒有探討文獻會有什麼後果？這一連串的問題，一直困擾著初次撰寫論文的人。

文獻探討是要呈現論文撰寫者引經據典的功夫，回顧他人發表過的相關論點、觀念、見解和看法，並加以消化，而後有系統地加以整理。除了做邏輯、合理的呈現之外，最重要的是要建構成整篇論文的理論基礎。因此，文獻探討貴在廣泛探討、深入回顧、引經據典、精準論述、豐富呈現，整理成足以支持你所要撰寫論文的理論基礎。

論文者，論述性的章篇、論理性的文章也。論文的寫作要廣泛的探討文獻、引經據典，合乎邏輯的建構理論基礎，然後根據作者的特定思考法則與方法，完整且精闢的論述學問、見解、事物、現象、因果關係，進而提出自己的創見。論文寫作是一門非常專業的學問、一種非常嚴謹的研究方法，也是一種極為實用的寫作技巧。

文獻探討的重點在於回顧各研究變數及其構面的相關文獻，而且必須和第三章（研究方法）觀念性架構中所揭示的研究變數及其構面相呼應，也就是各研究變數及其構面，都必須做廣泛、適切、深入的探討。

寫作論文時所參考的文獻，分散在各種期刊、書籍、創作之中，通常可區分為核心文獻（Core Paper）與相關文獻（Related Paper）兩大部分。前者是指所回顧的文獻和你所要撰寫的論文題目比較接近，或所使用的研究變數與構面相近、甚或相同，足以精準、有力的用來支持及建構論文的理論基礎者；後者是指所探討的文獻和你所要撰寫的論文題目，雖然沒有像核心文獻那麼接近，但是有著密切相關，可以用來支持及建構論文的理論基礎者。撰寫一篇論文所參考的文獻中，總是會有幾篇核心文獻可供參考，這幾篇核心文獻的參考價值最高，建構理論基礎的功效最強，因此必須仔細且深入的探討。至於相關文獻的精準度雖不如核心文獻，但是其參考價值仍然不可忽略，尤其是在強化文獻廣度方面的貢獻厥偉。

文獻探討顧名思義是在回顧他人的文獻，藉助他人的研究結果來建構你所要撰寫論文的理論基礎，也就是要站在巨人的肩膀上，以便看得更高、更遠、更深入，將相關思想、論點、見解、看法發揚光大。既然是探討他人的文獻，就必須忠於原著、務實呈現，不宜加入太多個人的見解，以免有失真或偏誤之虞。尤其是引述他人針對某一研究變數所下的定義、分類、衡量方法等嚴肅的課題時，更需要充分掌握忠於原著的原則。探討文獻的一般要領是在研讀他人的文獻之後，摘錄要點、勤加消化，然後用自己的話語有系統地寫出來。

文獻探討的第一個要領是必須兼顧所探討文獻的廣度與深度，因此需要掌握「古今中外」原則。也就是說，當代最新的文獻需要探討，年代較久的文獻也不可遺漏。尤其是有些屬於該領域的經典文獻，年代雖久遠，卻絲毫不減其參考價值。同時所探討的文獻也必須中文、外文兼顧，亦即國內學者的研究成果要探討，國外學者的文獻也不可偏廢。

文獻探討的第二個要領是要優先探討他人發表在期刊上的文章，儘量避免直接參考他人的原始論文。發表在期刊上的論文通常都經過期刊的審稿機制，由兩位以上匿名審稿老師嚴謹審查，符合期刊所要求的水準才予以刊登，因此參考價值比較高。原始論文雖然也經過指導教授的精心指導，並經過口試委員的認可與肯定，但是到底還是屬於尚未發表的論文，其參考價值自然就不若發表在期刊上的文章堅實有力了。

文獻探討的第三個要領是將預定要探討的各研究變數分別建立檔案，然後在研讀相關文獻的過程中，將有助益的文獻內容或資料摘錄，並放到對應的研究變數檔案中，如此隨著研讀文獻的累積，探討的內容就會逐漸豐富化。當文獻探討累積到某一程度時，再回過頭來針對每一變數所探討的內容與資料，做一番整理、增刪、修飾與精煉，完成文獻探討的工作。

文獻探討的第四個要領是確實掌握「相關」原則，僅止於回顧並納入和你的研究有關的文獻即可，不相關的文獻就不要納進來了。回顧不相關的文獻不僅會浪費很多時間，而且無助於論文寫作，殊屬不當。

第五個要領是要探討及引用原著者的第一手文獻，確認徹底瞭解之後才引用，避免轉述錯誤或過度解釋，甚至誤用文獻。有些論文所引用的並非第一手文獻，甚至引用已經轉手多次的文獻，結果不僅造成文獻失真的現象，甚至使文獻的意義嚴重走了樣。

初次撰寫論文者對於文獻探討到底該寫些什麼、如何寫、要寫到什麼程度等課題，往往感到很陌生，以致不知如何著手，遲遲無法動筆。本章將闡述論文寫作中文獻探討的要領與方法，包括研究變數的定義、研究變數的類型／型態／分類／構面／種類、研究變數的相關理論、研究變數的特徵與重要性、研究變數的應用、研究變數的衡量方法、回顧研究變數之間的關係，以及所探討文獻的綜合評析等，提供給初次撰寫論文的人參考。

# 二、研究變數的定義

闡述一項理論或觀念時，最有效的方法就是優先明確定義之。因此在進行文獻探討時，一開始就必須先就研究變數的定義做明確的交代。研究變數經過明確定義之後，界定該變數的意義與範圍，可清楚的指引寫作的方向。

同一理論或觀念用在不同領域，常有不同的定義。論文中所使用的研究變數也有這種現象，不同的研究者對同一研究變數可能有不同的定義。在你的論文中所使用研究變數的定義，可能和他人的定義相同，也可能和他人的定義不同。例如：投資報酬率（Return on Invest, ROI）就有許多不同的指標與定義，有總資產報酬率、使用資產報酬率、淨資產投資報酬率、固定資產報酬率等，不一而足。因此在探討文獻時，首先必須回顧他人對某一研究變數曾經下過的定義，而且要引經據典的回顧多位學者的定義與看法，避免只探討一、兩位學者的定義，這樣才不至於陷入以偏概全的泥沼中。

例如：在探討競爭優勢的相關文獻時，回顧Michael Porter的相關文獻與著作，勢必不可避免；在回顧行銷觀念的相關文獻時，探討Philip Kotler 的相關文獻與著作，亦勢必不可或缺。同理，在回顧企業社會責任時，參考Peter Drucker的相關文獻與著作，則是第一首選；在探討品牌策略的相關文獻時，若遺漏Kevin Lane Keller的文獻與著作，就會留下不完美的遺憾。

研究變數的定義是一種非常嚴謹的解釋，也是一項很嚴肅的議題。所謂嚴謹，是需要有公信力及可信度的文獻支持。因此，回顧研究變數定義的要領之一，就是儘量探討及引用著名學者或權威人士所下的定義，這樣才能突顯定義的權威性與可信度，也才可以突顯你所撰寫論文的參考價值。所謂嚴肅，是指著名學者或權威人士針對某一研究變數所下的定義，必須完整且忠實的呈現，不宜斷章取義，更不能扭曲定義，以免定義失真，影響後續程序所要引用的意義。

例如：Kotler and Keller（2009）將行銷（Marketing）定義為一種社會和管理的過程，個人與群體可經由此一過程，透過彼此創造、提供及自由交換有價值的產品與服務，以滿足其需要與慾望。他同時將行銷管理

（Marketing Management）定義為是一種理念、商品、服務概念、定價、促銷及配銷等一系列活動的規劃與執行過程，經由此一過程可創造交換活動，以滿足個人與組織的目標。Griffin（2006）將產品創新（Product Innovation）定義為改變現有產品或服務的實體特色或功效，或創造新品牌的產品或服務。Belch, Lutz and Mackenzie（1983）認為廣告態度（Advertising Attitude）是指在特定展露情況下，對於廣告刺激所反映的喜好與否的傾向。

又如許士軍（1990）將管理（Management）定義為人們在社會中所採取的一類具有特定性質和意義的活動，其目的為藉由群體合作，以達成某些共同的任務或目標。黃俊英（1997）指出廣告訴求（Advertising Appeal）是指在廣告訊息中所強調的產品利益，不僅把產品利益清楚表達出來，也能把自己與其他競爭品牌做區隔，展現其不同的特色，讓消費者心目中留下深刻的品牌印象。司徒達賢（2001）認為策略（Strategy）是指企業經營的形貌，以及不同時間點間這些形貌改變的軌跡。

探討研究變數定義的另一項要領，是除了找出著名學者或知名人士所下的定義之外，還要發揮「整理」的功夫，不只是片段式的呈現所蒐集到的定義，而是要把這些引用自不同學者或文獻的定義，做有系統的整理，穿針引線的整理成更具有可讀性的文章，整理成更有意義的文獻、整理成更有參考價值的文獻，最重要的是整理成內容充實又扎實的理論基礎。

常見初次撰寫論文者將所蒐集的研究變數定義列表呈現，包括作者、年代、定義。這種方式只是把所蒐集的定義有如編字典般一一呈現，並沒有詳加探討，這樣的定義就沒能發揮效果了。請記得論文第二章是在探討文獻，重點是在回顧相關文獻、消化文獻，然後整理成可以支持你所要撰寫論文的理論基礎。

# 三、研究變數的類型

探討研究變數的類型、型態、分類、構面、種類，是文獻探討很重要的一環。

探討研究變數的相關文獻時，通常都會回顧先前的學者針對此一變數所做的類型、型態、構面、種類等分類方法，以便進一步瞭解研究變數的內涵及其意義。儘管學者們所使用類型的名詞不盡相同，但是可以確定的是都在表達同一件事，也就是都在論述研究變數的類型或分類。探討研究變數的分類、類型，可以從中發現更豐富的內容，以及論文第三章所要引用的構面。這些分類或構面有助於我們對研究變數的進一步理解，也可以指引我們衡量研究變數的方向與方法。

探討變數類型、型態、分類與構面的要領，要把握三個原則：第一是忠於原著，第二是摘錄重點，第三是精準論述。忠於原著是指原作者所做的分類，或所列出的構面項目必須一一呈現，無論是否全數引用到你的論文之中，在文獻探討階段，這些分類項目都必須忠實呈現。摘錄重點是要做重點式討論，原作者的論述或許十分詳細、內容豐富、篇幅較長，而當你探討其文獻時，只須摘錄要點，做重點描述即可。精準論述是要掌握各分類項目所論述內容中最精華的部分，精準的論述其意義、重要性、應用、衡量等，為第三章所要引用的內容預先做好鋪路的工作。

例如：Schiffman and Kanuk（2007）將消費者的知覺風險區分為下列六種類型，這六種類型的意義如下：

## （一）功能風險（Functional Risk）

是指產品無法滿足預期功能所引起的風險，例如：新開發的PDA使用一個星期都不需要充電嗎？

## （二）身體風險（Physical Risk）

是指產品對自己及他人可能造成身體傷害的風險，例如：行動電話真的安全嗎？會釋放出有害人體的輻射線嗎？

## （三）財務風險（Financial Risk）

是指產品的價值與價格不相稱的風險，例如：新近開發且價格便宜的電漿電視螢幕，在未來六個月會很普及嗎？

## （四）社會風險（Social Risk）

是指選錯產品在社交場合可能造成窘境的風險，例如：我的同學們會嘲笑我剪了個學生頭嗎？

## （五）心理風險（Psychological Risk）

是指選錯產品對消費者自尊可能造成的風險，例如：當我邀請朋友來聽我所購買已有五年的音響音樂時，我會覺得很丟臉嗎？

## （六）時間風險（Time Risk）

　　是指花費時間尋找產品，若所選購的產品無法達到預期的功能，則可能是一種浪費的風險，例如：我還要再重新購買一次嗎？

　　例如：Kotler and Keller（2009）在討論產品類別時，從三個角度將產品予以分類：

## （一）從耐用性與有形性的角度言

　　產品可區分為(1)非耐久財：是指只能消費幾次的有形產品，例如：香皂、啤酒等；(2)耐久財：是指可以多次使用的有形產品，例如：電冰箱、機械工具、衣服等；(3)服務：具有無形性、不可分離性、易變性、易毀性的產品，例如：理髮、法律諮詢、器具修護等。

## （二）從消費品的角度言

　　產品可區分為(1)便利品：是指消費者經常購買、立即購買、不希望花費太多時間去尋找的產品；(2)選購品：是指消費者刻意比較適合性、品質、價格、式樣等特性的產品；(3)特殊品：具有獨特性或品牌辨識效果，消費者願意花費時間與精力做特殊購買的產品；(4)忽略品：是指消費者所不知道或不會想要購買的產品。

## （三）從工業用品的角度言

　　產品可區分為(1)原料與零組件：是指完全成為生產廠商所製造產品的一部分；(2)資本項目：是指可以長期使用，且有助於研發或管理製成品的產品；(3)附屬品與商業服務：是指短期使用，且有助於研發或管理製成品的產品與服務。

　　又如，Freiden（1984）指出廣告代言人可分為四種類型：

## （一）名人

　　是指公眾或知名人物，透過其高知名度或魅力，希望利用消費者的移情作用，吸引消費者的注意，進而喜愛名人所推薦的產品。

## （二）公司高階經理人

　　高階經理人因為企業規模及知名度，可以影響消費者的注意力。高階經理人也是公司的高階主管，需要對企業負責，也最瞭解企業，廠商希望藉助他們的代言，增加產品的可信度，也因而提高消費者的購買意願。

## （三）專家

是指個人職業、專業訓練或特殊經驗等因素，使其具有非常獨特的社會地位，可提供消費者各種評估意見。

## （四）典型的消費者

是指廣告內容以消費者見證的方式呈現，是一般大眾型的代言人。因為經常使用，讓人覺得自然純真、未經掩飾，令消費者相信其所代言的產品而願意購買。

Kaikati（1987）進一步將名人廣告代言人區分為四種類型，即真正的名人、相似的名人、企業執行長或創辦人、聯想的名人。

在探討研究變數的類型時，每一種類型或構面都需要詳加討論，以便深入瞭解各種類型的意義與內容，為接下來在論文第三章應用時打好基礎。因此，在探討研究變數的類型、分類或構面時，最重要的要領是每一種類型、型態、分類、種類、構面，都必須深入探討且明確釐清其意義。

# 四、研究變數的相關理論

研究變數的相關理論是文獻探討很重要的一部分，這些理論很可能作為你建構論文的理論基礎，因此這一部分的深入探討自然不可少。

例如：在回顧策略聯盟的相關文獻時，交易成本理論、資源基礎理論、資源依賴理論、策略行為理論、社會交換理論、網絡理論、價值鏈理論、組織學習理論、統合理論，都需要納入並做簡要討論。在探討激勵內容的相關文獻時，必須探討需要層級理論、二因子理論、三需理論。在回顧激勵的過程觀點時，期望理論、公平理論、目標設定理論的探討必不可或缺。同理，在回顧領導的權變理論時，需要探討LPC理論、路徑－目標理論。

探討研究變數的相關理論時，必須掌握的要領主要是精簡、扼要，因為理論本身的內容相當豐富，鉅細靡遺的介紹勢必會占用很多篇幅，此時，探討的重點應該擺在如何將相關理論應用在你的論文中。例如：每一種相關理論的定義、內容、應用、重要性、管理意涵及其影響力等，都需要做精簡、扼要的探討，並予以有系統的整理。

【實例】
「不同聯盟型態之下經濟誘因與信任之相對重要性研究——以臺灣清涼飲料產業為例」，有關交易成本理論文獻探討實例
（林隆儀、黃營杉、吳青松，2004）

　　……交易成本理論是從經濟觀點來解釋交易方式，旨在探討透過市場機能運作的市場自由交易，或是經由組織內部化進行組織間交易，在兩者之間做最經濟的抉擇。交易成本理論的前提是，公司會內部化自己有能力以較低成本經營的活動，而依賴他人有優勢活動的市場。當交易成本過高時，企業會將參與交易的成員融入到同一組織內，運用組織內部的溝通協調機制取代市場機能（Williamson, 1975）。簡言之，企業會選擇生產及交易成本最低的交易方式。

　　企業要獲得資源，確保競爭優勢，除了經由企業內部化及透過市場機能之外，策略聯盟也是重要選擇之一。Williamson（1991）認為內部化的各種長期供給或僱用契約屬於組織層級，價格機制下的市場買賣行為屬於市場因素，而策略聯盟則是介於兩者之間的一種混合體（Hybrid）。組織的內部化成本低於市場機制時，廠商會選擇自製方式；反之，內部化成本高於市場機制時，廠商會選擇外購方式。組織內部化無法如願取得所需要的一切資源，或內部化成本過高，尋求市場交易又受到市場不確定性、資訊不對稱與不完整、競爭對手的阻撓等限制，使得市場機能受到挑戰，或交易成本太高時，此時若選擇極端策略，採取自製方式，勢必會空留成本高昂之憾。同理，若採取外購方式，由於受到上述因素的影響，顯然也非明智抉擇。此時，透過策略聯盟的方式合縱連橫，互補不足，不但成為可能，而且是企業強化體質、維持競爭優勢的重要手段。混合統治結構的策略聯盟無須成立新的組織體，使聯盟作業迅速簡便，又不涉及組織間股權交換等複雜問題，使合作內容單純化，聯盟效率也因此為之提高。

　　依據交易成本理論的精神，企業會選擇生產及交易成本最低的交易方式，所以，降低成本、追求經濟利益便成為組織締結策略聯盟的首要考量因素。Harrigan（1985）、Porter and Fuller（1986）、Lin and Darling（1999）、Saffu and Mamman（2000）、吳青松（1990, 1996）的研究均認為，降低成本、分擔風險、避免重複投資、獲得規模經濟、進入新市場、加速創新，是策略聯盟重要的六項經濟誘因，其中更以降低成本與分擔風險最具重要性。

# 五、研究變數的特徵與重要性

　　探討研究變數的特徵與重要性，可幫助研究者對研究變數有更深入的理解，同時也可以使往後的論述與應用更順利。當我們在回顧文獻時，會發現有些作者把研究變數的特徵與重要性詳細列出，並且有深入的討論，讓我們可以方便引用。也有可能發現不一定每一篇文獻都有提到研究變數的特徵及其重要性，這也就是文獻要「看得多、讀得精」的道理。因此，在探討文獻時，必須特別留意他人對研究變數所提出的特徵，以及其重要性的相關論述。

　　撰寫研究變數的特徵與重要性時，最重要的要領是要將他人對研究變數特徵或重要性的描述，做簡要的歸類與整理，或以條列方式呈現，並附上簡潔的說明，好讓讀者可以迅速進入狀況、掌握重點。

---

### 【實例】
### 「服務品質、議題行銷及企業形象對購買意願之影響——顧客信任的干擾效果」，有關服務特徵之文獻探討實例
（林隆儀、胡瑋純，2009）

　　……Dickens（1996）的研究指出，服務具有四種特性。

### 1.無形性（Intangible）

　　即服務具有無形之特性。管理者、服務提供者及顧客，對於產品內容及評估方式有不同的標準與期待，顧客在接受服務之前無法感受服務品質之良莠，也無法清楚掌握成本及判斷服務之價值，所以為了招攬顧客，通常銀行業者會著重將「無形事物予以有形化」，具體陳述其品質優良之事實，讓顧客容易瞭解，進而容易體會。

### 2.不可分割性（Inseparability）

　　因為服務的產生與消費密不可分，通常是同時進行的，提供服務者和接受服務者之間的互動關係，都有可能影響服務的結果。也由於此一特性，顧客無法事前評估，因此可能造成服務與顧客之預期價值之間存在若干差異，而導致顧客滿意度降低。

### 3.變動性（Variability）

隨著服務提供者之不同，或提供服務的時間與環境不同，會使服務的效果不一致。當此現象明顯時，可能會發生所提供之服務與顧客的期望出現落差，造成顧客往後不願再使用同一產品或服務。為降低此落差，管理者可透過嚴格的人員甄選、確實的訓練，以及制定具體的衡量標準等，設法提升服務品質，並使服務業產品標準化。

### 4.易逝性（Perishable）

服務是無法儲存的，服務也無法事前製造，因此服務提供之事前規劃，必須充分掌握時機，才能使服務達到預期的效果。

---

## 【實例】
## 「創意＋特色　開啟農產品活路行銷之路」，有關農產品組織成員購買行為的特徵文獻探討實例
### （林隆儀，2010）

……農產品組織成員購買行為，具有下列特徵：

### 1.專業採購

購買數量龐大，通常都由專人負責專業採購。

### 2.多人參與採購決策

循著組織層級的採購權責，採購案通常都由多人參與決策。

### 3.直接向生產者採購

直接向生產者採購，取得第一手市場資訊，掌握貨源，降低成本。

### 4.以人員銷售為主

農產品帶有地方特性，比較少透過大眾媒體進行全國性推廣工作，因此都以人員銷售為主。

### 5.互惠採購

買賣雙方基於建立長期關係，通常都會進行互惠採購。

### 6.契約採購

為確保供應不至中斷，以及降低成本與風險的考量，通常都會簽訂採購合約。

### 7.契作採購

有些特殊農產品供給量少，又是廠商重要的加工原料，於是由政府提供輔導，協助廠商與農民簽訂契作合約，農民負責栽種，廠商保證收購，達到雙贏的境界。

---

### 【實例】
### 「廣告訴求、廣告代言人、廣告態度與購買意願的關係」，有關廣告訴求之重要性文獻探討實例
（林隆儀、張聖潔，**2009**）

……Zeithmal and Kirmani（1993）認為企業應以廣告訴求不同的屬性層級，來配合不同的產品形象，以創造廣告的最大效果。Meenaghan（1995）在論述產品形象的重要性時，指出公司在發展產品形象時，廣告扮演一個核心角色，因此，廣告與企業所要塑造的產品形象息息相關，使用一則有利的廣告，可以幫助企業塑造在消費者心目中所要建立的產品形象。

廣告訴求可以透過劇情表現或生活片段方式呈現，進而使消費者對廣告中的產品有所共鳴，認同廣告所推薦的產品，並產生投射作用（Fournier, 1998）。Golden and Johnson（1983）的研究發現，理性訴求廣告比感性訴求廣告更能引起消費者的喜愛，且購買意願也比較高，因為理性訴求包含較佳的產品資訊與實際內容。

【實例】
「老年經濟安全保障、理財知識與逆向抵押貸款意願之研究」，理財知
識之重要性文獻探討實例
（林隆儀、商懿勻，2015）

　　大多數家庭對於退休後生活的事前準備是覺得不足夠的（Lusardi & Mitchell,
2005），其主要原因在於理財知識的普遍不足。在面臨退休之際，大部分是沒有
存款且面臨重大財務困難（Lusardi & Mitchell, 2007）。由此可知，理財知識對
消費者的財務決策影響很大，他們辦理理財知識的研究調查對象，是針對51至56
歲財產累積幾乎已達頂點的受訪者，檢驗他們多項財務決策，包括房屋抵押貸
款、汽車貸款及信用卡、退休準備等基本金融知識，研究中指出對理財知識的忽
視，可能會帶來許多嚴重後果，包含不良借款行為。

　　Noctor, Stoney & Stradling（1992）、Lusardi & Mitchell（2007）的研究皆指
出瞭解理財知識為金融消費者理財規劃應具備的知識，包括如何規劃借款及退休
準備，其中：(1)借貸規劃：金融消費者因財務需求進行借款要善加規劃，需避
免不當的借款行為及膨脹自己的所得能力；(2)退休規劃：為避免年長退休欠缺
收入，退休規劃應在年輕時即需籌備，若退休後收入不足因應支出，年長者應善
用既有的財產取得收入因應退休生活。

　　理財知識對消費者金融服務的重要性在於，每位消費者每日都會面臨到基本
財務決定的制定，包含該如何花錢及省錢？如何規劃預算？到哪裡去投資？財務
的風險如何處理？需要舉債多少以支應開銷？要採取何種舉債方式等？這些決定
有些複雜，皆需要具備基本的理財知識（Widdowson & Hailwood, 2007）。而理
財知識對金融體系穩健與效率重要性，於Widdowson & Hailwood（2007）的研究
發現理財知識對金融體系穩健與效率的影響很明顯，影響方式有下列幾種：(1)
理財知識在一定的範圍內會協助家庭財務更加審慎，相對就能減少銀行等金融機
構的貸款風險；(2)理財知識的增長導致消費者更小心謹慎的過濾投資及金融商
品，因此促進金融機構創新回應消費者的需求，使金融體系效率提升；(3)理財
知識較先進的社會期待金融機構能加強市場紀律，尤其是對特定金融機構及其商
品的風險要嚴格審議。相對地，嚴格的市場紀律要求金融機構及高規格的金融服
務需審慎管理風險；(4)消息靈通的投資決策是基於進階理財知識，期望經由時
間導致更有利可圖的資源配置，以反應更挑剔的方式來平衡報酬與風險，如此有
助潛在的高成長率，可減低經濟週期性波動，以及為長期金融穩定的優勢。

# 六、研究變數的衡量方法

　　完成研究變數的特徵與重點的探討之後，必須接著探討研究變數衡量方法。論文第三章需要明確說明你所要採用的研究變數衡量方法，所以，文獻探討必須包括「變數衡量方法」這一項目。

　　衡量（Measurement）是指根據某些事先設定的規則，將有興趣之標的的某些特徵，加上數字或其他符號的標準化過程（林隆儀、黃榮吉、王俊人譯，2005）。衡量通常以數字表示，因為數學及統計分析只能以數字表現；此外，數字也能夠不需要經過任何翻譯，就可以同樣形式進行溝通，而且為人們所理解。為了要讓衡量過程成為標準化的作業過程，研究變數的衡量具有兩個特性。第一，被衡量的標的必須要有一對一的數字和特性的對應。第二，作業規則必須不因經過時間的演變而改變，而且衡量標的也都不會改變。

　　變數衡量和所使用的尺度密不可分。尺度（Scaling）是指根據標的所擁有的可衡量特性的數量，所創造出來的一個連續過程。尺度可分為名目尺度、順序或等級尺度、區間尺度、比例尺度等四種類型。研究上常使用的一個尺度規範，如性別的二分法尺度，例如：男性特徵的標的給予數字1，女性特徵的標的給予數字0。這個尺度符合衡量過程所要求，既是一對　，而且不會因時間或標的而改變。衡量和尺度是科學方法上的基本工具，被用在幾乎每一個研究上。

　　論文寫作上最常用的研究變數衡量尺度，有李克特尺度（Likert Scales）及語意差異尺度（Semantic-Differential Scales）。至於最常用的尺度範圍，以五點尺度與七點尺度居多。

　　探討研究變數衡量方法的要領，是要在研讀相關文獻後，找出作者在該篇文章中所使用的研究變數衡量方法，明確指出使用什麼尺度，以及所使用尺度的範圍。

【實例】
「廣告訴求、廣告代言人、廣告態度與購買意願的關係」，有關購買意
願的衡量方法文獻探討實例
（林隆儀、張聖潔，2009）

......Mackenzie et al.（1986）所設計的購買意願問卷，共分為購買傾向、試用傾向、購買意願及購買行為等四個項目。

### 1.購買傾向

用以量測受測者「是否願意多花時間取得實驗產品的其他相關資訊」，利用「很不同意」到「很同意」的五點尺度來衡量。

### 2.試用傾向

用以量測受測者「是否願意試用實驗產品」，利用「很不同意」到「很同意」的五點尺度來衡量。

### 3.購買意願

用以量測受測者「是否認為實驗產品值得購買」，利用「很不同意」到「很同意」的五點尺度來衡量。

### 4.購買行為

用以量測受測者「是否願意購買實驗產品」，利用「很不同意」到「很同意」的五點尺度來衡量。

Schiffman and Kanuk（2007）認為購買意願愈高，表示購買的機率愈大。而衡量購買意願的方式，例如：詢問消費者在下次購買時是否會選擇A產品？並提供「我絕對會買」、「我可能會買」、「我不確定會買」、「我會買」、「我可能不會買」......之選項。Shamdasani（2001）採用產生購買動作的可能性與推薦程度，做為衡量購買意願的標準，並以李克特七點尺度衡量。林隆儀、陳彥芳（2005）則針對大臺北地區3C連鎖家電做價格促銷、認知價值與商店形象對購買意願影響之研究中，「購買意願」之衡量，是參考Zeithaml（1988）與Dodds（1991）等學者所發展的量表，利用李克特五點尺度來衡量受測者的購買意願高低，每題尺度從非常不同意到非常同意，依次分別給予1分到5分，數字愈大，代表受測者的購買意願愈高。

**【實例】**

**「老年經濟安全保障、理財知識與逆向抵押貸款意願之研究」，逆向抵押貸款意願衡量方法文獻探討實例**

（林隆儀、商懿勻，2015）

　　逆向抵押貸款的推行，應視為政府重視及因應老年化社會之必要社會福利政策指標；王健安（2009）的研究在「社會福利分析」中：(1)以退休前薪資水準為「所得替代率」之基礎，當比率設定在比照先進國家的70%，且逆向抵押貸款是唯一退休後收入來源的假設下，反推回承作逆向抵押貸款之條件大致是「65歲長者終期壽命預估為85歲，在3%利率水準下，持有原始房價大約在1,000萬（貸五成）左右」。若以原始房價約500萬來看，月領之逆向抵押貸款加計其他公勞保退休金等，總計仍可達到經建會建議之理想替代率70%之目標。(2)以「逆向抵押貸款對長期照護保險之助益」來分析，其中逆向抵押貸款支應10%的醫療照顧費用並無問題，但是對於其他85%-90%屬生活照顧費用方面，不管是在「公部門」長期照護社會保險制度，或是在「私部門」保險公司現在所銷售的「長期看護險」，逆向抵押貸款只能作為提升老年長期照護品質的「補充品（Complement）」或「選項」之一；所得替代率及對長期照護保險之助益即為逆向抵押貸款衡量項目，評估尺度就是需達到所得替代率的七成以上才足以支應醫療照顧費用。

　　林左裕、楊博翔、徐偉棋（2009）在「逆向房屋抵押貸款在臺推行之可行性研究」研究中，設計的問卷調查內容認為申請逆向房屋抵押貸款的意願主要受下列因素影響：(1)教育程度：教育程度愈高，對申請逆向房屋抵押貸款的意願有顯著正向關係，評估尺度分六個等級來衡量；(2)購買保險：有購買理財型保險對有意願申請逆向房屋抵押貸款有顯著正向影響，評估尺度分為是或否兩個尺度來衡量；(3)資產持有：資產持有以股票、債券或基金為主者，可認為較具有金融商品投資經驗及風險負擔能力，對於申請逆向房屋抵押貸款有顯著正向影響，評估尺度分為是或否兩個尺度來衡量；(4)富裕程度：愈富裕愈無意願申請逆向房屋抵押貸款之可能，原因是退休後的生活準備可能很周全，評估尺度分五個等級來衡量；(5)傳承遺產：認為父母有傳承其名下房屋給後代的義務，則對於申請逆向房屋抵押貸款之意願有顯著負向影響，評估尺度分為必要或不必要來衡量；(6)是否分居：父母較傾向與子女分居，享受獨立生活空間，較有意願於年老之時申請逆向房屋抵押貸款，評估尺度分為是或否來衡量。

# 七、研究變數之間的關係

　　以上所介紹的是個別研究變數的探討內容與要領，無論論文中有幾個研究變數，都需要掌握以上的要領，並一一探討。

　　完成個別研究變數的文獻探討之後，接著要探討研究變數之間的關係，為論文第三章進行研究假說推論預先鋪路。此時若沒有探討研究變數之間的關係，等到寫論文第三章研究假說推論時，就會出現「巧婦難為無米之炊」的窘境，結果不是所論述的推論無法有力的支撐研究假說，就是根本沒有推論就憑個人主觀的臆測，武斷的直接提出研究假說，這種做法對寫作一篇完整的論文，會造成很大的傷害。

　　研究變數之間的關係，顧名思義是要探討兩個研究變數之間所可能存在的關係。讀者會發現前述回顧研究變數的定義、分類或類型、特徵與重要性、衡量方法等，都是針對個別研究變數所做的探討，沒有涉及研究變數之間的關係，而此時所要回顧的是兩個研究變數之間的關係。

　　研究變數之間的關係，有可能是正向的影響關係，或稱為正向的相關，例如：A對B有正向的影響；有可能是負向的影響關係，或稱為負向的相關，例如：A對B有負向的影響；也有可能是沒有關係，或稱為沒有顯著的相關。無論他人的研究發現兩個研究變數之間的關係是正向、負向、或沒有相關，都需要一一探討、忠實呈現。

　　探討研究變數之間關係的要領，是要根據觀念性架構圖上研究變數之間所連結的線條或箭頭，逐一回顧它們之間所存在的關係。

**【實例】**

**「The Influence of Corporate Image, Relationship Marketing, and Trust on Purchase Intention: The Moderating Effects of Word-of-Mouth」，有關企業形象與信任的關係文獻探討實例**

（Lin and Lu, 2010）

　　……Zeithaml（1988）強調評估顧客的未來意向，進而瞭解顧客與企業維持關係的潛在可能性之重要性，認為唯有顧客與企業建立起高度的信任，顧客與企業才能維持長久的關係。Smeltzer（1997）認為，供應商和購買者可以透過對彼此心理上的認同、形象和名聲的感覺，來影響雙方的信任程度。Doney and Cannon（1997）認為供應商組織名聲、規模會影響信任。供應商本身在其產業裡帶給他人的信譽，讓大家感覺到供應商是真誠、誠信、坦率的，並且關心其顧客，就會贏得顧客的信任。Selnes（1998）認為買方認同供應商的能力時，其信任度也會相對提高。Luo（2002）指出網站可以經由網站聲譽來建立消費者的信任。Mcknight and Chervany（2001）研究發現一個擁有較高聲譽的網路商店，將會使顧客產生較高的信任。

【實例】
**「The Influence of Corporate Image, Relationship Marketing, and Trust on Purchase Intention: The Moderating Effects of Word-of-Mouth」，有關關係行銷與信任之關係文獻探討實例**
（Lin and Lu, 2010）

……Morgan and Hunt（1994）認為信任與承諾是促使關係行銷成功的重要因素。Leuthesser et al.（1995）認為買賣雙方頻繁互動，會產生更多資訊處理，而減少雙方不確定的感受。廠商透過互動瞭解消費者並反映消費者之需求，進而可以提升消費者對廠商產生信心。Garbarino and Johnson（1999）認為關係行銷可以有效的增加顧客信任與承諾方面的知覺。Lin et al.（2003）在研究中發現對銀行業而言，想要和顧客建立長期的往來關係，財務性、社交性、結構性結合等三種關係行銷結合類型，對於信任和承諾有顯著的正向影響；關係行銷的實踐，可以增加顧客的信任程度。

【實例】
**「The impact of advertising appeals and advertising spokespersons on advertising attitudes and purchase intentions」，變數之間關係文獻探討實例**
（Long-Yi Lin, 2011）

The Impact of advertising appeal on advertising attitude

Advertising appeal refers to packaging products, services, organizations, or individuals in a variety of ways that clearly deliver a certain benefit, stimulation, identification, or reason to explain what consumers are thinking about and why they buy products (Kotler, 1991). Berkman and Gilson (1987) defined advertising appeal as an attempt at creativity that inspires consumers' motives for purchase and affects consumers' attitude towards a specific product or service. Schiffman and Kanuk (2007) defined advertising appeal as suppliers' application of a psychologically motivating power to arouse consumers' desire and action for buying while sending broadcasting signals to change receivers' concepts of the product. Hence, advertising appeal is applied to attract the consumers' attention, to change the consumers' concept of the product, and to affect them emotionally about a specific product or service (Belch and Belch, 1998; Schiffman and Kanuk, 2007).

To meet the varying demands of their target consumers, advertisers commonly use rational appeal and emotional appeal in their advertising in an attempt to influence consumer behavior (Chu, 1996). By rational advertising appeal, the product can be emphasized by its benefits, in which the consumers' self-benefit is the key proposition, and the function or benefit requested by consumers of the product or service is articulately presented in advertising. On the other hand, emotional advertising appeal places stress on meeting consumers' psychological, social, or symbolic requirements, where many purchase motives come from. Kotler (1991) defined rational appeal as rationally oriented purchase stimulated by directly giving explanations of a product's advantages. Rational appeal focuses on the benefits consumers may enjoy. In an advertisement, it emphasize that a product or service could achieve the function and benefits consumers desire. He defined emotional appeal as the stimulation of consumers' purchase intentions by arousing their positive or negative emotions. Positive emotional appeal covers humor, love, happiness, etc, while negative emotional appeal involves fear, a sense of guilt, and so on.

Attitude is an essential concept in psychology, but it is also widely applied in the social sciences and marketing. Fishbein and Ajzen (1975) defined attitude as a learning orientation based on which a state of constant like or dislike is generated towards a certain object. Kotler (1991) suggested that attitude refers to an individual's long-lasting perceived evaluation of like, dislike, emotional feelings, and action intention towards an object or idea. Schiffman and Kanuk (2007) stated that attitudes are a psychological tendency accrued from learning and a continual evaluation towards a subject. Lin (2008) defined advertising attitude as a continuously reactive orientation learned from a certain object. Such an orientation represents an individual's personal standards such as like and dislike, and right and wrong. The attitude held by consumers caused by advertising can be classified into two components: cognition and affection. Cognition and affection stand for thinking and feeling, respectively (Vakratsas and Ambler, 1999). Allport (1935) pointed out that the difference between the two components lies in that cognition stands for an individual evaluation towards external stimulation, while affection reflects an individual's internal feelings.

According to Belch and Belch (1998), advertising appeal is applied to attract consumers' attention. Advertising appeal aims at influencing consumers' attitude and emotions about a related product or service. It is classified into rational and emotional appeals (Chu, 1996; Belch and Belch, 1998), Schiffman and Kanuk (2007) indicated that advertising appeal may change consumers' attitude. By using broadcast messages to trigger consumers' inner momentum psychologically, consumers are likely to echo and recognize the advertising messages and further change their attitude towards the advertised product. Ray and Batra (1983) pointed out that emotional identification comes before rational identification during a cognitive process. Emotional messages are more vivid and thus rational appeal works better than emotional appeal in attracting consumers' attention. Aaker and Norris (1982) found that the advertising attitude created by rational appeal is better than that by emotional appeal. Rational appeal appears to provide information explicitly and directly related to a product, which attracts consumers' attention more easily and generates a better advertising attitude.

# 八、文獻評析

　　文獻探討的最後一個環節，就是要進行文獻評析。文獻評析顧名思義是要就以上所探討的相關文獻，做一番綜合評述與評論，進而提出自己的見解。一段精彩的文獻評析不但可以使讀者更清楚瞭解你所探討文獻的結果，同時也可以讓讀者瞭解你的看法與意見。

　　前面曾經提到文獻探討的要領之一是要回顧他人的文獻，必須做到務實探討、忠實呈現，因此，文獻探討階段不宜加入太多自己的意見。但是進入文獻評析階段，就是要提出自己的見解與意見，這些見解與意見也必須以建構論文的理論基礎為原則，不宜無限上綱，甚或離題太遠。

文獻評析就是要將所探討過的許多文獻做一番綜合評論，因此最重要的要領是要掌握「綜合評論」原則，儘量不要批判個別文獻。既然是綜合評論，就要發揮文獻評析的功夫，站在高處觀看，從整體的觀點下筆，從大方向來論述，將文獻探討結果做一個總結。從綜合評論中可以發現，所探討的文獻都在討論些什麼、有什麼特色、最新的研究發現、研究方向與方法的演進、有什麼沒有納入研究，以及該研究領域的未來發展等。這些資訊對你構思研究題目、思考研究動機、選擇研究變數、發展觀念性架構、研擬研究假說、建構研究方法、激發研究靈感，都有關鍵性的影響。

---

**【實例】**
**「企業自然環境管理研究之回顧與展望」，有關企業自然環境管理類型分類的評論**
（高明瑞、黃義俊、張乃仁、蔡依倫，**2008**）

……雖然分類的價值在於實務和教育目的，不過現有的模型不容易應用於組織真實的行為（Kolk and Mauser, 2002）。例如：Hass（1996）企圖操弄Hunt and Auster（1990）的模型，應用8家挪威食品加工和印刷產業之研究發現，雖然Hunt and Auster（1990）的構念是基於環保管理的分類，不過僅提供初淺的瞭解公司回應自然環境這個議題。Schaefer and Harvey（1998）嘗試以英國水和電力產業為研究對象實證研究方式，驗證Hunt and Auster（1990）、Roome（1992）的模型，研究發現這兩個模型與企業實務營運上的配適度不佳。

為了改進線性連續式模型的缺點，在1990年代後期發展出第二代環境管理的模型。例如：Winn and Angell（2000）關注於政策的承諾和執行的方法。Ghobadian et al.（1998）的模型是一種非線性的分類，包括內部和外部兩個面向。

---

# 九、結語

文獻探討是在尋求及建立論文的靈魂，沒有回顧文獻的論文，猶如沒有靈魂的軀體；文獻探討不足的論文，就好像失去某些靈魂的軀體，不只是大幅降低寫作論文的價值，甚至連登「論文之堂」都大有問題。

文獻探討的目的是在建構整篇論文的理論基礎，理論基礎愈深厚，研究的貢獻愈大；理論基礎愈扎實，論文的參考價值愈高；理論基礎投入愈多，寫作的收穫愈豐碩；引經據典的功夫愈務實，論文的可讀性愈高。

論文的結構中，回顧文獻所占的篇幅最多，研究者所花的時間也最可觀，絕對不是短時間內可以完成，也絕對不是趕工可以完成的。試想找到你所要的文獻需要時間，何況找到的文獻常常不是正好你想要的；閱讀文獻需要時間，摘錄文獻要點需要時間，推敲及評估文獻的可用性需要時間，整理文獻更需要時間。所以必須牢記「慢工出細活」的道理，及早準備、儘早開工，方為上策。

常看到許多初學者寫不出東西，苦無對策、毫無進展，究其原因就是文獻看得太少。沒有探討文獻，就沒有靈感；沒有靈感，就只好陷入停擺的狀態了。

# 第三章
# 研究方法

## 一、前言

　　研究方法（Research Methods）又稱為研究設計（Research Design），主要是在論述及交代整篇論文所使用的研究方法。研究方法是整個研究及論文寫作的核心，也是讓讀者瞭解研究進行方式的重要資訊。設計嚴謹、面面俱到的研究方法，不僅可吸引讀者的興趣，也可以提高論文的可讀性與貢獻價值，所以，研究者在設計研究方法時都非常審慎且力求嚴謹。

　　研究方法的設計必須圍繞著研究題目，呼應論文構思階段所思考的研究目標，並且根據文獻探討所獲得的相關資訊，作為設計研究方法的依據。簡言之，就是要將論文第二章文獻探討所獲得的資訊，運用到第三章來設計及交代研究所要進行的方法。

研究方法到底要寫些什麼、要如何寫、要交代到什麼程度、有沒有一定的原則可循，這是一個非常重要，也是非常務實的問題。一般研究方法的教科書雖然都有討論研究方法的詳細內容，但是都因為篇幅太廣泛、編排太分散，以致常常有見樹不見林的感覺，讓初學者難以窺其全貌，無法掌握其重點，不知該寫些什麼，當然也就不知該如何下筆了。每位指導教授對研究方法的偏好各不相同，對研究設計的要求各異其趣，因此研究方法該寫些什麼，缺乏一致的共識，甚至言人人殊、莫衷一是，也讓學生無所適從。

作者深深感覺到上述的問題與學生的困擾，於是一直在思索學術論文的寫作應該有一套簡易可行的方法，指引學生寫作要領，讓初學者融會貫通，而且有一個規範可循，幫助學生按部就班的完成論文寫作。

根據作者這幾年指導研究生的經驗，擔任校內外論文口試委員的心得，以及應邀擔任校內外學術期刊審稿委員的收穫，整理出一套簡潔、明確的研究方法架構，教導研究生按此架構設計研究方法及撰寫論文，不僅學生容易掌握方向，瞭解各章節該寫些什麼，也知道該怎麼寫，寫出來的論文也得到相當高的評價。

這一套架構的內容（論文第三章），包括構思觀念性架構、發展研究假說、交代研究變數的操作性定義與衡量方法、設計抽樣方法、執行問卷設計與前測、規劃資料蒐集方法、選擇資料分析方法等七個項目。本章將依序論述及介紹這七個項目，以及每一個項目的寫作要領。

# 二、觀念性架構

觀念性架構（Conceptual Framework）是指將整篇論文所要操作的研究變數及其構面，以及變數與變數之間的關係，設計成精簡、明確、容易連貫、容易理解的操作藍圖。觀念性架構的設計，通常都需要投入許多心思，花費不少時間，參考所探討的文獻，不斷思考與修正，向指導教授請益，再三思索與精煉，務必釐清所要研究的題目，說清楚要研究什麼，以及把研究變數之間的關係說清楚、講明白，具體呈現出來。

設計觀念性架構的目的是要指引論文寫作的方向與方法，有了這份觀念性架構，就可以避免迷失方向，防止不知所云的現象。所以研究者在撰寫論文之前，值得多花一些心思與時間來思考及設計觀念性架構。

　　論文構思階段所提出的觀念性架構初稿，經過文獻探討階段回顧相關文獻，深入瞭解每一個研究變數之理論的來龍去脈，熟知詳細內容及其分類、特徵、重要性、衡量方法之後，到第三章描述觀念性架構時，最重要的要領就是需要進一步論述每一個研究變數及其構面的參考來源，以及說明選擇這幾個研究變數及其構面的理由。

　　觀念性架構圖猶如建築師所設計的建築藍圖，藍圖的設計並非一朝一夕可以完成，而是需要建築師實地勘查現場環境，實施地質探測，然後苦心積慮的思考，和業者不斷的溝通，逐步設計與修正，最後才定案。建築藍圖一經定案，房子使用什麼建材、採用什麼工法及如何施工、施工進度的管控，以及完工後的房子長什麼模樣，幾乎都已經浮現了。定案後的建築藍圖，每一部分都有完整的細部設計，並附有施工說明，承接後續作業的營造廠就根據這一份藍圖執行建築施工的工作。同理，論文的觀念性架構一旦設計完成，要研究什麼、如何進行研究、研究可能獲得什麼結果，也已經大致底定。

　　觀念性架構需要具體指出所要操作的研究變數，每一個研究變數的構面，以及變數與變數之間的關係，通常都利用線條及箭頭來連接，表示其間的關係或影響關係。由此可知，觀念性架構中所呈現的研究變數、構面、線條、箭頭等，都有其特定的意義。有些論文會在觀念性架構圖的線條上，以$H_i$的方式標示研究假說的序號，使整個研究內容更清楚。圖3-1是「議題行銷的社會顯著性、活動持續度與執行保證對品牌權益的影響」觀念性架構實例，提供參考。

　　觀念性架構中所呈現的研究變數及其構面，都是參考論文第二章回顧相關文獻的結果而來。這一部分的撰寫要領有三：第一是觀念性架構的導出應有依據，必須引經據典、具體指出參考來源；第二是不納入研究的變數、構面，以及不相關的線條、箭頭不要出現在觀念性架構圖上；第三是研究變數及其構面的選用，不僅要有文獻的支持，而且還要說明選用這些構面的理由。例如：探討「知覺風險」的文獻時，Schiffman and Kanuk（2007）將知覺風險區分為功能風險、身體風險、財務風險、社會風險、心理風險、時間風險等六項，你所要研究的「知覺風險」不一定涵蓋這六個項目，因此不一定要照單全收；但是你的研究若只要引用其中四項，則需要說明為何把另兩項排除在外的理由。

　　論文的第三章第一節，通常都需要介紹或說明觀念性架構設計的來龍去脈，具體指出參考來源。無論是介紹或說明，都必須要有適當、適切的論述，然後才引出觀念性架構圖。不能沒有任何論述就只寫「本研究的觀念性架構如圖3-1所示」，接著便出現一幅觀念性架構圖。

---

**【實例】**

**「議題行銷的社會顯著性、活動持續度與執行保證對品牌權益的影響」，觀念性架構描述實例**

（林隆儀，**2010**）

……許多研究都發現個人與議題的關聯程度，會影響議題行銷的成功（Nichols, 1990; Webb, 1999）。公司是否僅藉由議題銷售產品或真誠關心議題，容易使消費者產生到底是議題行銷或議題圖利之疑慮（Barone, Miyazaki and Taylor, 2000）。本研究參考Cobb and Elder（1972）對社會顯著性之定義，在前測中選出受訪者關心程度最高與最低的議題類型，代表社會顯著性高、低的議題類型，同時參考Varadarajan and Menon（1988）對議題行銷活動時間長短的觀點，以及參考Barnes and Fitzgibbons（1991）對議題行銷活動之分類來定義活動持續度，並將持續度依活動是否具有效期，區分為高、低兩種類型。

至於執行保證，則參考Varadarajan and Menon（1988）與黃俊閎（1995）對議題行銷應予公開之論點，以議題行銷活動是否採行執行保證，區分為有、無執行保證兩種類型，以探討議題行銷中，企業的品牌是否可藉由選擇社會顯著性高的議題，對議題的長期承諾，以及提供公示公信的方式而獲得助益。參考上述文獻發展出本研究的觀念性架構，如圖3-1所示。

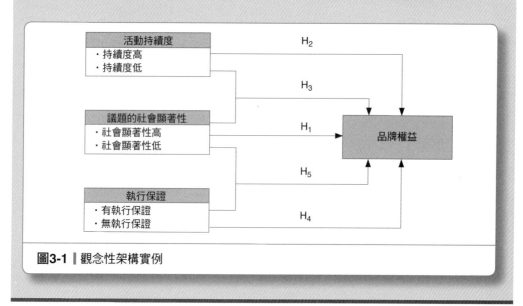

**圖3-1** 觀念性架構實例

【實例】
「**促銷方式對私有品牌產品知覺品質的影響——促銷情境與產品類別特徵的干擾效果**」，觀念性架構描述實例
（林隆儀，**2010**）

……本研究旨在探討及比較不同促銷方式對私有品牌產品知覺品質的影響，以及研究及比較不同促銷情境與不同產品類別特徵，在促銷方式對私有品牌產品知覺品質影響的干擾效果。促銷方式的種類很多，本研究參考Inman et al.（1997）及Mela et al.（1997）的分類方法，將促銷方式區分為價格導向的促銷方式與非價格導向的促銷方式，探討及比較不同促銷方式對私有品牌產品知覺品質的影響。因為折扣優待是最常見的消費者促銷方式，因此以折扣優待代表價格導向的促銷方式；附贈贈品也是現實生活中最常見的非價格方式之一，因此以附贈贈品代表非價格導向的促銷方式，做為本研究促銷方式的構面。

本研究參考Inmam et al.（1997）及李秉倫（2000）的研究，將促銷情境區分為限時促銷與限量促銷，探討及比較不同促銷情境在促銷方式對私有品牌產品知覺品質影響的干擾效果。

本研究參考Delvecchio（2001）所提出私有品牌產品類別特徵中的三個構面，即產品類別複雜度、產品類別品質差異、購買間隔時間，探討及比較這三種產品類別特徵在促銷方式對私有品牌產品知覺品質影響的干擾效果。本文未將產品類別公眾性及價位納入研究，主要是考量先前學者的研究發現產品類別公眾性對私有品牌知覺品質沒有干擾效果；一般認為私有品牌產品類別價位通常都比較低，而且先前學者的研究也發現產品類別價位對私有品牌知覺品質的影響不大（Delvecchio, 2001；林隆儀與曾彥嘉，2004）。

參考上述文獻及學者的論點，發展出本研究的觀念性架構如圖3-2所示。

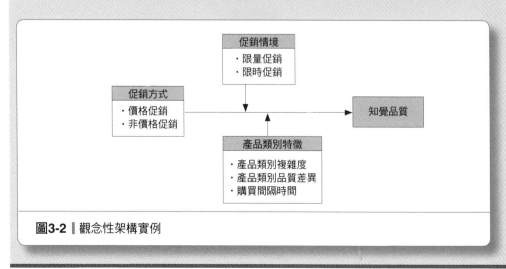

**圖3-2** ┃ 觀念性架構實例

【實例】

**「The Influence of Service Quality, Cause-related Marketing, Corporate Image on Purchase Intention: The Moderating Effects of Customer Trust」，觀念性架構描述實例。**
（Long-Yi Lin, 2011）

The main objectives of this study were to investigate the influence of service quality, the social significance of cause-related marketing and corporate image on purchase intention, and to examine the moderating effects of customer trust in the influence of trust on consumer purchase intention. Referring to Parasuraman et al. (1985), this study chose reliability, tangibility, responsiveness, assurance, and empathy as the dimensions for the measurement of service quality. For cause-related marketing, the idea proposed by Cobb and Elder (1983) was adopted; we classified the cause into high and low level of social significance for measurement. A company that possesses good corporate image will attract consumers' purchase intention (Fisk et al., 1993; Keller, 1993; Shapiro, 1982).

From the literature review, we found that few researchers had concentrated on the moderating effect of customer trust in the influence of corporate image on purchase intention. Customer trust was a key factor when consumers make the purchase decision in practice. Therefore, this paper chose customer trust as a moderating variable to explore the moderating effect of customer trust contributing to the effect of corporate image on purchase intention in the banking industry.

By referring to the above literature, the conceptual structure of this study was developed as shown in Figure 3-3.

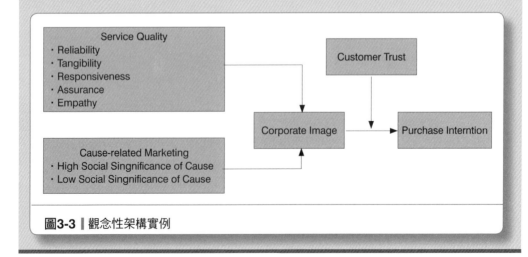

**圖3-3** ▍觀念性架構實例

# 三、研究假說與命題

命題（Proposition）和假說（Hypotheses）不同，但是卻有著密切的關係，研究者對這兩個用詞常常混淆不清。命題和假說是學術研究中非常重要的部分，有必要釐清。命題是指針對某一項觀念的描述，此一描述若以可觀察的現象為依據，則可以判斷其真假；而假說是除了將命題做有系統的說明之外，更進一步作為實證檢定的題材（Cooper and Schindler, 1998）。

簡言之，命題僅止於對某一項觀念做完整的描述後所推導出來的結論，並沒有進行實際驗證，通常都用在質化研究中所推演出來的結論；而假說則是將參照文獻探討所推導出來的結論，進一步進行實際驗證，證明假說是否獲得支持。量化研究就是在檢定研究假說是否獲得檢定數據的支持。

假說可分為描述性假說（Descriptive Hypotheses）與關係性假說（Relational Hypotheses）。前者旨在描述某一變數之現況，例如：形狀、大小、分配情形等事實；後者則是在說明兩個變數之間的關係。關係性假說又可以區分為相關關係（Correlational Relationship）與因果關係（Causal Relationship）。相關關係僅止於說明兩個研究變數一起變動的關係；因果關係則在描述一個研究變數（自變數）的變動，會影響另一個研究變數（依變數）。

無論是命題或是研究假說，都是經過嚴謹的推論過程推導出來的結果，研究假說是要進一步檢定所推論出來的結果是否獲得實證數據的支持。研究假說的發展，必須和研究目的及觀念性架構圖上所列出的研究變數及其構面相呼應。變數與變數之間關係的發展，稱為主假說（Main Hypotheses）；構面與構面之間關係的推論，稱為子假說（Sub-hypotheses）。簡言之，只要是出現在觀念性架構圖上的變數及其構面，都是你希望驗證的研究結果，因此都要一一發展研究假說。

撰寫命題或研究假說的第一個要領，是要引經據典，針對每一項研究假說逐一推論，並且引用足以支持你所建立研究假說的相關文獻。第二個要領是命題或假說的推論必須合乎邏輯，要務實的推論，而不宜只說「本研究認為……」。至於足以支持命題或研究假說的相關文獻，主要是來自論文第二章文獻探討「變數之間關係的相關研究」中所整理出來的文獻。第二章所鋪陳的文獻中，有關變數之間的相關研究結果，無論是正向相關、負向相關或不相關，也無論是正向影響關係、負向影響關係或沒有影響關係，都已經在第二章中一一探討。而且文獻相當豐富自不待言，但是此時要引用來支持命題或研究假說時，最重要的要領就是要引用對推論命題或研究假說有利的文獻。

---

**【實例】**
**「來源國形象與品牌知名度的組合效果對消費者購買意圖的影響——產品涉入的干擾效果」命題發展實例**
（林隆儀、陳俊碩，**2010**）

⋯⋯Lin and Chen（2006）指出品牌來源國形象對消費者購買意圖會有顯著的正向影響；Thakor and Katsanis（1997）的研究也發現產品來源國為消費者知覺品質的基礎；Han and Terpstra（1988）在探討混合產品或多國籍產品的結論中指出，來源國與製造國兩者對消費者購買意圖都有顯著的影響效果；Narasimhan et al.（2004）的研究證實，製造來源國與品牌來源國都會影響消費者對產品的評價；Lee et al.（2001）的研究發現，不同國家消費者的購買意圖與產品來源國的經濟發展呈現正相關，且對不同國家製造的汽車的購買意圖會有顯著的差異，其中對已開發國家所製造汽車的購買意圖，大於低度開發國家所製造的汽車；吳淑樺（2005）的研究發現，不同的製造來源國與品牌來源國對消費者的購買意圖會有顯著的影響，而製造來源國與品牌來源國也有顯著的交互作用；謝佳玲（2005）的研究也指出，品牌來源國形象愈高，搭配高形象製造來源國形象，會顯著提高消費者購買意願。

根據以上的文獻，可推論出本研究的研究命題1如下：

命題1：品牌來源國形象與產品製造國形象之組合，對消費者購買意圖會有
　　　　顯著的正向影響。

Keller（1993）指出品牌知名度在消費者決策過程中，扮演非常重要的角色。而在來源國相關的研究當中，品牌是重要的外顯線索之一（Saeed, 1994）。Hong and Wyer（1989）的研究指出，當消費者接觸到來源國線索與其他線索時，例如：價格或品牌，來源國效應在消費者的認知過程中，可由量輪效果與彙總建構效果兩方面來觀察。而不論是量輪效果或是彙總建構效果皆指出，國家形象會間接或直接影響到消費者的品牌態度，顯示國家形象與品牌態度之間彼此互相有影響。Hullard（1999）的研究以單純只給消費者一些品牌名稱，來測試品牌名稱與品牌來源國是否會影響消費者對產品的評價。結果發現儘管不提供消費者品牌來源國線索，其來源國效應依然是不容忽視的，由此可知，品牌來源國形象與品牌名稱在消費者做決策時，扮演很重要的角色。Wall et al.（1991）指出品牌

與來源國形象具有交互作用，來源國形象對產品評價的影響，比價格和品牌資訊更為重要；尤其是當品牌知名度較低時更為明顯。Ahmed and Astous（1993）指出在汽車這個產品類別，品牌與來源國形象具有交互作用。Thakor and Katsanis（1997）指出消費者對於產品品質的認知，容易受到來源國效應的影響；但是當產品屬於搜尋性或經驗性產品時，品牌形象能移轉消費者所受到的產品來源國效應之影響。Keller（1993）與Shocker et al.（1994）的研究皆指出，來源國形象可以增加品牌權益。Thorelli et al.（1989）研究來源國形象、保證和商店印象對產品評價相對重要性時，發現三者對消費者的知覺品質有顯著的三階交互影響，他們同時也發現保證和來源國形象兩者對知覺品質有二階交互作用。

根據以上的文獻，可推論出本研究的研究命題2～4如下：

命題2：品牌來源國形象與品牌知名度之組合，對消費者購買意圖會有顯著的正向影響。

命題3：產品製造國形象與品牌知名度之組合，對消費者購買意圖會有顯著的正向影響。

命題4：品牌來源國形象、產品製造國形象、品牌知名度之組合，對消費者購買意圖會有顯著的正向影響。

Ahmed and Astous（1995）的研究顯示，當產品的涉入程度高時，品牌來源國形象對消費者購買意圖的影響程度大於製造來源國形象。簡佑容（2007）的研究發現，來源國效果對購買意願之關係，會受到產品涉入之干擾效果而呈現顯著正向之關係。秦兆瑋（2002）的研究指出，在產品涉入程度高時，消費者在面對高製造來源國國家形象產品之資訊搜尋意願、產品評價與購買意圖上，皆高於中、低製造來源國國家形象產品。Lin and Chen（2006）指出在不同產品涉入之下，品牌來源國國家形象對消費者購買決策會有顯著的正向影響。Ahmed et al.（2004）與Zeithaml（1988）的研究皆指出，產品涉入程度不同，消費者受到來源國效果的影響也不同。廖淑靜（2006）發現在不同產品涉入程度下，品牌來源國形象對消費者知覺品質與購買意願的影響並不顯著，但製造來源國訊息對消費者在知覺品質與購買意願都有顯著的影響，且不見得因涉入程度的提升而使製造來源國減弱。

根據以上的文獻，可推論出本研究的研究命題5如下：

命題5：消費者的產品涉入對品牌來源國形象與產品製造國形象之組合，對消費者購買意圖影響會有正向干擾效果。

Hong and Wyer（1989）的研究指出，不論是量輪效果或是彙總建構效果，皆指出國家形象會間接或直接影響到消費者的品牌態度，顯示國家形象與品牌態度之間彼此互相有影響。Ahmed and Astous（1993）指出在汽車這個產品類別，品牌與來源國形象具有交互作用。Lin and Shang（2008）指出形象來源國與感性廣告訴求的組合，對產品態度有顯著的正向影響。吳文村（2001）指出當產品為高品牌知名度時，由於消費者對於該品牌知名度存在較高的熟悉度及接受度，雖然較差的製造來源國形象可以由高品牌知名度來彌補，進而對產品有較佳的評價。Shocker et al.（1994）的研究也發現，來源國形象可以增加公司的品牌權益。游文憲（2004）的研究則指出，在廣告訴求對廣告效果的影響過程中，品牌知名度與產品涉入有顯著的交互作用。Swindyard（1993）指出對於低涉入之產品或服務，容易受到廣告的影響，而進行衝動性購買；但對於高涉入的產品或服務，消費者在進行消費前，會花費較多時間搜尋相關資訊，選擇最適合的產品或服務，而來源國訊息與知名的品牌名稱，則可以提供給消費者對產品及服務的信心與保證。Petty et al.（1983）以推敲可能性模式發現在高產品涉入下，品牌態度與購買意圖之間的相關性，會顯著大於低產品涉入。

根據以上的文獻，可推論出本研究的研究命題6～8如下：

命題6：消費者的產品涉入對品牌來源國形象與品牌知名度之組合，對消費者購買意圖的影響會有正向干擾效果。

命題7：消費者的產品涉入對產品製造國形象與品牌知名度之組合，對消費者購買意圖的影響會有正向干擾效果。

命題8：消費者的產品涉入對品牌來源國形象、產品製造國形象、品牌知名度之組合，對消費者購買意圖的影響會有正向干擾效果。

---

### 【實例】

### 「議題行銷的社會顯著性、活動持續度與執行保證對品牌權益的影響」研究假說推論實例

（林隆儀，2010）

……議題對消費者的重要程度會影響消費者對議題的支持，因此，許多企業都樂於結合社會顯著性高的議題，以進行議題行銷活動的被接受度（Nichols, 1990）。Yechiam, Barron, Erev and Erez（2003）認為企業藉由對社會可接受的議題捐款或受歡迎的活動，可間接提高消費者的態度。Faircloth, Capella and Alford（2001）的研究發現，消費者對品牌的態度會影響該品牌的形象，而品牌形象則

會影響品牌權益。Varadarajan and Menon（1988）認為企業透過執行議題行銷可以提高公司形象、增進品牌知名度、提升品牌形象。由此可知，高社會顯著性的議題比低社會顯著性的議題，更容易激起消費者對活動喜愛的態度，並間接轉嫁到與活動結合的品牌上，使得與議題相結合的品牌在消費者心中獲得更高的評價，進而提升品牌權益。

參考上述文獻，可據以推論出本研究的研究假說1如下：

假說1：企業實行議題行銷時，選擇社會顯著性高的議題，對品牌權益的影
　　　響顯著高於社會顯著性低的議題。

Miller（2002）指出相較於短期關係，長期關係顯示企業對議題做了更多的承諾，更有助於企業建立顧客忠誠度。Polonsky and Speed（2001）認為當消費者認為公司實行議題行銷，是對議題進行圖利而非贊助時，消費者會改變他們對公司的評價。因此，企業就議題投注持續之關注，有助於消費者認同企業支持議題的行為，減少消費者認為企業是藉由議題圖利之疑慮，對結合活動之品牌產生更正面的態度，進而反映在品牌權益上。

參考上述文獻與論點，可據以推導出本研究的研究假說2如下：

假說2：企業實行議題行銷時，活動持續度高的計畫對品牌權益的影響，顯
　　　著高於活動持續度低的計畫。

社會顯著性低的議題，消費者視為較不具重要性，因而容易因為缺乏關注，而使品牌不容易在短期間內達到藉由議題提升品牌權益的目的。但是對議題付出長期承諾，應有助於藉由改善消費者認為企業是藉由議題圖利的疑慮，進而認為企業（品牌）參與活動是出於真正關懷議題的動機，因而改善消費者對企業（品牌）的評價。消費者視為重要的議題，容易取得消費者認為議題是值得幫助的認同，而使社會顯著性高的議題具有較高的議題擴展性（孫秀蕙，1997）。因此，社會顯著性高的議題，容易在短期間內即引起消費者的注意力，迅速將與議題結合的企業（品牌）善行，轉化為眾所周知的良好聲譽，取得消費者對企業（品牌）參與活動動機的信任，達到迅速提升品牌權益的目的。所以，品牌結合社會顯著性高的議題，雖然也長期間對議題抱持以持續性的關注，卻因為結合高社會顯著性議題的效果，而對品牌權益之助益有限。

參考上述文獻與論點，可據以推論出本研究的研究假說3如下：

假說3-1：企業實行議題行銷，選擇社會顯著性低的議題結合活動持續度高

　　　　　　　的計畫，對品牌權益的影響顯著高於結合活動持續度低的計畫。

假説3-2：企業實行議題行銷，選擇社會顯著性高的議題時，無論是結合活
　　　　　動持續度高的計畫或活動持續度低的計畫，對品牌權益的影響無
　　　　　顯著差異。

　　Barone, Miyazaki and Taylor（2000）認為當消費者認為參與議題行銷的公司，主要的動機是正面時，相較於消費者認為公司主要的動機是負面時，消費者更有可能青睞發起活動的企業（品牌）。消費者知覺到公司參與議題行銷活動動機的努力，會影響消費者對發起活動公司的態度（Barone, Miyazaki and Taylor, 2000）。Varadarajan and Menon（1988）指出，公開是議題行銷道德性非常重要的決定因素。黃俊閎（1995）的研究也發現，超過半數受訪者不相信企業承諾會將消費者消費金額的一定比例做為捐贈或贊助之用，而不致食言或短報捐助金額數目；受訪者對企業募款的管理、支應方式和公信力等，都抱持不信任的態度，他們的懷疑程度足以影響支持議題行銷的程度。因此，企業在參與議題行銷活動時，對提供執行保證有助於消除消費者的疑慮，而改用更正面的態度看待企業所參與的活動，此舉除了有助於消費者對參與活動之企業（品牌）的態度之外，也有助於提高品牌權益。

　　參考上述文獻，可據以推論出本研究的研究假説4如下：

假説4：企業實行議題行銷時，有執行保證的活動對品牌權益的影響，顯著
　　　　高於無執行保證的活動。

　　如同活動持續度在消費者知覺企業參與議題行銷所扮演的角色，當企業所選擇的議題之社會顯著性不足時，若能對募款過程所承諾之款項及其流向提出確切的保證，取得消費者的信賴，便可以改善消費者對企業實行議題行銷在募款過程中普遍所抱持的疑慮，如此一來，可以使消費者感受到企業參與活動的正面動機，改善消費者看待參與活動企業（品牌）的態度，對品牌形象有加分效果，進而提高品牌權益。消費者視為重要的議題，容易迅速將與議題結合的品牌善行轉化為眾所周知的良好聲譽，取得消費者對品牌參與活動動機的信任，達到迅速提升品牌權益的目的。因此，品牌結合社會顯著性高的議題，雖然也為表達公開誠信的態度而提供執行保證，卻因為結合高社會顯著性議題的效果，而對品牌權益之助益有限。因此，可據以推導出本研究的研究假説5如下：

假説5-1：企業實行議題行銷，選擇社會顯著性低的議題結合有執行保證的
　　　　　活動，對品牌權益的影響顯著高於無執行保證的活動。

假説5-2：企業實行議題行銷，選擇社會顯著性高的議題，無論結合有無執行保證的活動，對品牌權益的影響無顯著差異。

## 四、變數操作性定義與衡量

定義（Definition）者，對一事一物所做的正確解釋也。衡量（Measurement）則是根據某些預先設定的規則，將有興趣的某些特徵賦予數字或其他符號的標準化過程（林隆儀等譯，2005）。例如：男生用「1」表示，女生用「0」表示；對某一問題非常不同意給予「1」分，非常同意給予「7」分。無論是做研究或寫論文，都必須就所要操作的研究變數賦予明確的定義，同時要考慮其衡量方法。

定義可區分為觀念性定義（Conceptual Definition）、文義性定義（Semantic Definition）及操作性定義（Operational Definition）。觀念性定義是指利用其他觀念來描述某一觀念的定義，例如：「態度」的觀念性定義是指某人對某一刺激物所表現出來正面或負面的反應，此一定義顯然是借用「某一刺激物」與「某人的正面或負面反應」來界定「態度」的定義。文義性定義是指一般性定義、望文生義的定義、放諸四海皆準的定義，我們從字典上所查到的名詞定義，通常都屬於這種定義。操作性定義則是指研究者為了研究的需要，針對研究變數及其構面所賦予的特定定義。至於操作性定義是指描述一項活動的程序，這些活動是為了要以經驗方法證實某一觀念存在的程度；也就是將觀念性定義加以界定，使其可以進行實際衡量。由此可知，觀念性定義或文義性定義用在不同的地方或場合，不至於改變事物的定義；但是不同的研究者對同一個研究變數及其構面所做的操作性定義，則可能各異其趣。無論是做研究或寫論文，研究變數及其構面都必須做操作性定義，也就是要將定義做到操作化；定義予以操作化，才能進行下一步的衡量。

文義性定義和操作性定義表面上看似相同，實際運用在研究上卻有很大的差別。例如：凝聚力（Cohesiveness）的文義性定義是指人與人之間相互吸引之力，而其操作性定義則具體的指出成員對群體忠誠與承諾的程度。例如：Hofstede（1980）的研究指出，權力差距（Power Distance）的操作性定義是指，在對權威的服從關係上，所存在的一種社會不均衡與差距的程度。不確定性規避（Uncertainty Avoidance）是指，社會中的人們對於模糊不清的情境所要求避免的程度。又如「顧客滿意」的文義性定義是指「顧客購買公司產品或服務後，感到心滿意足」。此一定義所言「心滿意足」太過籠統，缺乏一個聚焦的標準，以致無法進行後續的衡量工作。然而「顧客滿意」的操作性定義則是指「顧客購買公司產品或服務後，感到心滿意足的程度」，此一定義很明確的指出是要衡量「顧客滿足的程度」，因此就可以進行後續的衡量工作。例如：設計幾題足以測出「顧客滿足的程度」的研究問項，採用李克特七點尺度衡量「非常不滿意」到「非常滿意」，分別給予1分到7分。

撰寫研究變數操作性定義的要領，必須引經據典，先引用幾則別人所做的定義，然後參考這些人的定義，精準的寫出你自己的操作性定義。論文第二章探討研究變數的相關文獻時，第一段通常都先界定研究變數的定義，而且探討許多學者從不同的觀點所提出不同的定義，所引用的這些定義可能只是文義性的定義，也可能是操作性定義。此時要引用別人的定義來支持你的操作性定義，最簡單的方法，就是引用那些最足以支持你的操作性定義的文獻。

---

**【實例】**
**「服務品質、品牌形象、顧客忠誠與顧客再購買意願的關係──以臺北市銀行產業的顧客為例」，有關「品牌形象」變數的操作性定義實例**
（林隆儀、周佩琦，**2010**）

……Aaker（1991）將品牌形象定義為消費者對品牌的想法、感受與需求；Keller（1993）將品牌形象定義為消費者記憶中對某個品牌的聯想，並反映對該品牌認知的概念。本研究參考Aaker（1991）與Keller（1993）的看法，將品牌形象定義為銀行基於顧客需求所賦予的品牌意義，以及對金融產品所認知品牌形象的程度。本研究進一步採用Park et al.（1986）的觀點，將消費者所認知到的品牌形象，區分為功能性形象（Functional Image）、象徵性形象（Symbolic Image）及經驗性形象（Experiential Image）等三種類型，並將功能性形象定義為銀行顧客購買該銀行金融產品所獲得實質利益的大小；將象徵性形象定義為銀行顧客購買該銀行金融產品及接受服務所獲得附帶利益的大小；將經驗性形象定義為銀行顧客購買該銀行金融產品及接受服務感覺到滿足的程度。

【實例】
「品牌策略與企業形象對消費者購買意願的影響 —— 涉入的干擾效果」，有關「購買意願」變數的操作性定義實例
（林隆儀、曾席璋，**2008**）

......Dodds et al.（1991）指出購買意願是代表消費者願意去購買該產品的可能性，消費者對該產品的知覺價值愈高，購買該產品的意願就愈強烈。Schiffman and Kanuk（2000）認為購買意願乃衡量消費者購買產品的可能性，購買意願愈高，即代表購買的機率愈大。本研究參考Dodds et al.（1991）及Schiffman and Kanuk（2000）的論點，將購買意願定義為消費者購買一項產品機率的高低，購買機率愈高，表示購買意願愈強烈。

【實例】
「廣告訴求、廣告代言人與廣告態度對購買意願之影響」，有關「廣告態度」變數的操作性定義實例
（林隆儀、張聖潔，**2009**）

......Gardner（1985）認為廣告態度意指訊息接受者對於整體廣告的意見。MacKenzie et al.（1986）將廣告態度定義為消費者對某特定廣告的喜愛程度。林建煌（2000）認為廣告態度是指對一個特定對象所學習到的持續性反應傾向，此一傾向代表著個人的偏好與厭惡、對錯等個人標準。本研究參考Gardner（1985）、MacKenzie et al.（1986）與林建煌（2000）的觀點，將廣告態度定義為消費者對某一整體廣告所形成的主觀知覺喜愛程度。

　　研究變數的衡量方法是研究過程中非常重要的一環。如前所述，研究變數予以操作化定義之後，才知道要衡量什麼；知道要衡量什麼之後，接著就要具體指出衡量方法。研究變數的衡量，涉及了衡量所使用的尺度與衡量方法。衡量尺度可區分為名目尺度（Nominal Scale）、順序尺度（Ordinal Scale）、區間尺度（Interval Scale）與比例尺度（Ratio Scale）。名目尺度只是將變數予以分類，例如：性別分為男性與女性，男性用「1」表示，女性用「0」表示。名目尺度唯一的特性是呈現個體，數字的任何比較都是沒

有意義的。比例尺度則有非常精確的特性，數字可用來執行加減乘除的運算。至於順序尺度、區間尺度則介於名目尺度與比例尺度之間，順序尺度可以表示變數的等級或排序，不能用來算術運算；區間尺度顧名思義是指每一相鄰等級的區間都相等，只能用來做算術的加減運算，而不能用來做算術的乘除運算。研究者所選用的衡量尺度類型，和後續適合使用的統計檢定方法，具有密切的關係。衡量尺度的特性及統計量與適合採用的統計檢定方法，如表3-1所示（林隆儀等譯，2005）。

**表3-1**
衡量尺度類型及其特性

| 衡量尺度的類型 | 態度尺度的類型 | 指派號碼的規則 | 典型的運用 | 統計量／統計檢定 |
|---|---|---|---|---|
| 名目尺度 | 二分法的「是」或「不是」尺度 | 標的是相同或不同 | 分類（依性別地理區域、社會地位） | 百分比、眾數／卡方 |
| 順序或等級順序 | 比較的、等級順序、項目化的種類、成對的比較 | 標的是大於或小於 | 等級（偏好、層級地位） | 百分位數、中位數、等級順序相關／Friedman、ANOVA |
| 區間尺度 | 李克特、索思通、史德培、相關性、語意差異 | 每一相鄰等級區間相等 | 指數、溫度尺度、態度衡量 | 平均值、標準差、積差相關／t檢定、ANOVA、迴歸、因數分析 |
| 比例尺度 | 有特殊指示的某些尺度 | 零是有意義的，所以絕對值的比較是可能的 | 銷售值、收入、生產的單位、成本、年齡 | 幾何及調和平均數、變異係數 |

資料來源：林隆儀等譯（2005），行銷研究，頁307。

撰寫研究變數衡量方法的要領，也必須引經據典，先引用幾則別人所做的衡量方法，然後參考這些人的方法，具體寫出你自己的衡量方法。所謂參考，不一定要完全依照他人的衡量方法，研究者可以視需要而加以修正，並說明從哪幾個方向觀察，採用什麼尺度衡量。例如：他人採用語意差異法衡量研究變數，你可以採用李克特尺度衡量之；他人採用李克特五點尺度，你可以改用李克特七點尺度；其餘類推。

【實例】

**「The Influence of Corporate Image, Relationship Marketing, and Trust on Purchase Intention: The Moderating Effects of Word-of-Mouth」，有關「關係行銷」變數衡量方法實例**
（**Lin and Lu, 2010**）

　　……Pressey and Mathews（2000）以(1)雙方高度信任，(2)雙方高度承諾，(3)關係時間長度，(4)雙方溝通管道暢通使資訊得以交流，(5)顧客利益第一，(6)雙方對品質的承諾，(7)誠心誠意保留顧客，採用七個關係行銷的指標，以李克特五點尺度衡量之。Lin et al.（2003）與Hsieh et al.（2005）在他們的研究中，將關係行銷結合類型分為財務、社交、結構性等三種類型，以李克特七點尺度衡量之。本研究參考Pressey and Mathews（2000）、Lin et al.（2003）與Hsieh et al.（2005）的方法，將關係行銷結合類型分為財務性、社交性、結構性等三種類型，並以李克特七點尺度衡量之，依受訪者對研究題項的認同程度，分別以1分到7分標示測量值，代表非常不可能、不可能、有點不可能、無意見、有點可能、可能與非常可能。

【實例】

**「品牌策略與企業形象對消費者購買意願的影響──涉入的干擾效果」，有關「購買意願」變數衡量方法實例**
（林隆儀、曾席瑝，**2008**）

　　……Schiffman and Kanuk（2007）指出衡量購買意願的方式如下，例如：詢問消費者在下次購買產品時，是否會選擇A品牌？並且提供(1)我絕對會買，(2)我可能會買，(3)我不確定會買，(4)我可能不會買，(5)我絕對不會買等五個選項，衡量受訪者的購買意願，並以李克特五點評量尺度來衡量。

　　Schiffman and Kanuk（2007）認為在行銷與消費者研究上，行為意願成分經常被視為消費者購買意願的用語，購買者的意願尺度被用來評估消費者購買某一產品或確定行為方式的可能性，並以李克特五點評量尺度來衡量。本研究參考Schiffman and Kanuk（2007）所提出衡量消費者購買產品可能性的方法，採用李克特七點尺度來衡量，依受訪者對研究題項的認同程度，分別以1分到7分標示測量值，代表非常不可能、不可能、有點不可能、無意見、有點可能、可能與非常可能。

# 五、抽樣方法與樣本數

　　許多研究受限於某些主客觀因素，無法進行普查；有些研究採用普查不僅有其困難度，高昂的普查成本更會使研究陷入不經濟的窘境，此時就需要採用抽樣方法。抽樣方法是研究過程中非常重要的工作，因此選擇某種抽樣方法的理由，必須在論文中做適當的說明。抽樣方法是要說明研究樣本如何取得、樣本數大小如何決定，以及樣本是否具有代表性。從抽樣方法說明中可以看出研究設計的嚴謹度，進而影響到論文的參考價值，所以研究者在此多下一些功夫是值得的。

　　如果研究母體（Population）中所有的成員都要列入訪問，而且也有可能納入研究，這種調查方式稱為普查（Census）或全數調查。如果研究母體的規模小，研究者不希望遺漏母體中任何一個成員，此時就適合進行普查。換句話說，普查就是全數訪問，因此也就沒有抽樣的問題。例如：臺灣區飲料公會的會員廠商只有117家，研究者希望將這117家廠商全數納入調查，這就是一種普查工作。如果所要研究的只是要觀察或調查母體中具有代表性的一部分成員，這種部分列舉的方法稱為抽樣（Sampling）。例如：從臺灣一千大製造業中抽選500家作為調查樣本，這就是抽樣方法的應用；又如常見媒體利用電話訪問做民調，訪問2,000人對某一議題的看法，也是抽樣方法的應用。

　　研究者如果決定要進行抽樣調查，接下來就必須把抽樣過程中的每一個步驟做詳實的說明，交代清楚。這些步驟包括確定研究母體、決定抽樣架構、處理母體與抽樣架構的差異、選擇抽樣方法、決定樣本大小、執行抽樣、蒐集受訪者資訊的方法、處理無反應偏差，以及產生提供決策用的資訊等，如圖3-4所示（林隆儀等譯，2005）。

　　確定研究母體就是要說明研究母體所涵蓋的範圍，例如：研究者所要調查的是臺灣食品GMP發展協會224家的會員廠商，則此224家廠商就是研究母體。抽樣過程中用來取得樣本的母體名錄或名單，稱為抽樣架構（Sampling Frame）。例如：取得臺灣食品獲得CAS認證的會員廠商共有297家，這297家認證廠商名錄就是一份抽樣架構，可據以抽取所需要的研究樣本。如果可以取得研究母體的成員名錄，作為抽樣的根據，那將是最好的選擇。如果訪問的對象是一般顧客或消費者，無法取得消費者名錄，所選用的抽樣方法就不一樣了。

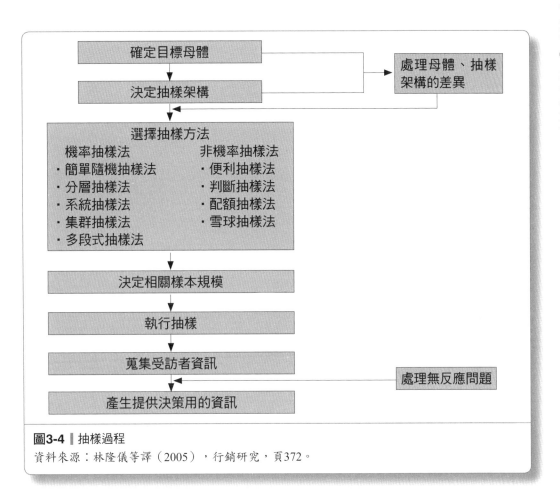

**圖3-4** ∥ 抽樣過程

資料來源：林隆儀等譯（2005），行銷研究，頁372。

　　當抽樣架構和母體定義不一致時，就會產生三個問題，研究者必須審慎處理。第一是子集合問題（Subset Problem），即抽樣架構的成員數比母體小。例如：某一產業公會有許多廠商尚未加入該公會，母體的某些因素不會出現在抽樣架構中，此時研究者就必須以抽樣架構重新定義母體，或從其他來源獲得母體資訊。第二是超集合問題（Superset Problem），即抽樣架構的成員數大於母體規模。例如：臺灣食品GMP發展協會採用生產線認證制度，有些會員廠商擁有多條生產線，抽樣架構顯然大於廠商家數，但卻包含了母體所有的因素，此時研究者就必須設計過濾問題來確認研究樣本。第三是交互作用問題（Intersection Problem），即母體的某些因素從樣本中被省略，以及樣本架構所包含的因素超過母體，此時研究者就必須重新定義母體。

　　由圖3-4可知，有許多抽樣方法可供研究者選擇，包括機率抽樣法（Probability Sampling）與非機率抽樣法（Non-Probability Sampling）。

前者包括簡單隨機抽樣法（Simple Random Sampling）、分層抽樣法（Stratified Sampling）、集群抽樣法（Cluster Sampling）、系統抽樣法（Systematic Sampling）、多段式抽樣法（Multistage Sampling）；後者包括判斷抽樣法（Judgmental Sampling）、滾雪球抽樣法（Snowball Sampling）、便利抽樣法（Convenience Sampling）、配額抽樣法（Quota Sampling）。

研究者必須充分瞭解各種抽樣方法的意義、原理，以及實際應用的方法。便利抽樣法是一般研究應用之最普遍的抽樣方法，但是研究者常常將便利抽樣與隨機抽樣混淆不清。隨機抽樣法是指母體中每一個成員，以及每一個可能的樣本，被選到的機率都相同且已知的一種抽樣方法。例如：在實驗設計研究場合中，八種實驗情境分配給八組實驗小組，可以採用隨機抽樣方法決定分配結果。而便利抽樣法，顧名思義是基於研究者方便取得研究樣本一種權宜之計的抽樣方法。例如：在街頭攔截訪問過路行人、在商店門口訪問購物的消費者、在校園訪問學生對某一議題的意見等，都是便利抽樣法的應用，而不是隨機抽樣，兩者不可混為一談。

樣本大小攸關樣本的代表性，也是評估研究品質的一個重要指標。若所選擇的抽樣方法適當，抽樣過程也正確無誤，接下來便必須考量樣本數大小。樣本數太少，恐失去其代表性，因而降低研究的參考價值；樣本數太多，則抽樣成本提高，形成浪費，並非明智的選擇。由此可知，樣本數大小，過與不及，均非所宜。

在母體知識已知的情況之下，決定所要抽取的樣本數大小較為簡單，可以根據統計學推論母體平均數的原理，利用樣本統計量估計母體平均數，求得所需的樣本數。樣本統計量抽樣分配的平均數及標準差，以及母體平均數與抽樣母體的標準差有密切相關，其公式為$\sigma_x = \sigma / \sqrt{n}$，其中$\sigma_x$為平均數的標準誤，$\sigma$為母體標準差，n為樣本數。求解此一公式，所得到的n值，即為所需要抽取的樣本數（黃俊英，1999）。

研究進行中，研究母體的知識通常都所知有限，甚至一無所知，此時就無法使用上述公式求得所需的樣本數了。此時可根據Roscoe（1975）所提出的四項原則中的兩項作為參考標準，分別是(1)適合做研究的樣本數目，以30至500個樣本數較為恰當；(2)在進行多變量分析時，樣本數至少要大於研究中變數的數倍以上，並且以10倍或以上為最佳。

根據簡單抽樣法的抽樣原則，樣本數大小的估計方法如下（黃俊英，1999）：

$$n \geq \left[\frac{Z\frac{\alpha}{2} \times \sqrt{P \times (1-P)}}{E}\right]^2 = \left[\frac{1.96 \times \sqrt{0.5} \times (1-0.5)}{0.05}\right]^2$$

$$n \geq 384.16 \cong 385$$

其中n表示應抽取的樣本數；E表示可容忍的誤差；Z(α/2)=1.96為標準常態隨機變數的臨界值；P為樣本比率；α為顯著水準。其中若對P值一無所知，可以採取較保守的態度，設定為0.5，使得n值為最大。若設定α為0.05，求得有效樣本數至少為385。根據上述之原則，求出適當的樣本數約為385（黃俊英，1999；顏月珠，1996）。也就是說，在缺乏母體知識的情況下，抽取的樣本數必須達到385以上才具有代表性。

蒐集受訪者資訊的方法，又稱為研究工作的現場作業管理，是指如何進行實地訪問或調查、如何發出問卷、採用什麼方法及如何催收問卷、如何收回問卷等作業細節，都需要一一交代。這些細節將在本章第七節詳細討論。

---

**【實例】**
**「服務品質、品牌形象、顧客忠誠與顧客再購買意願的關係——以臺北市銀行產業的顧客為例」，有關抽樣方法及決定樣本數實例**
（林隆儀、周佩琦，**2010**）

……本研究以臺北市銀行產業財富管理部門往來顧客為研究的目標對象，以向我國15家金融控股公司旗下的銀行購買金融產品的顧客為研究母體，15家金融控股公司在臺北市區的銀行分行共有536家。本研究為顧及樣本代表性，選擇向各金融控股公司旗下銀行業務量前三大分行購買金融產品的顧客為抽樣對象，每家分行按業務量比率分配樣本數，據以抽取所需樣本。

本研究樣本大小的決定，依據 Roscoe（1975）所提出的四項原則中的兩項為參考標準，以及參考黃俊英（1999）與顏月珠（1996）所建議簡單隨機抽樣的樣本大小之估計方法，在樣本比率未知時，採取保守態度，將樣本比率設定為0.5，使樣本數達到最大，在顯著水準為0.05之下，適當的樣本數為385。

本研究參照上述之條件及建議，以及依照各金融控股公司旗下前三大銀行業務量比率，同時為提高研究的有效性與樣本代表性，決定抽取470份樣本，各分行的樣本數分配如表3-2所示。

**表3-2**
抽樣樣本分配表

| 機構名稱 | 分行數 | 前三大分行 | 百分比% | 樣本數 |
|---|---|---|---|---|
| 臺灣金融控股公司 | 65 | 天母、龍山、大安 | 12.12 | 60 |
| 第一金融控股公司 | 54 | 中山、忠孝東路、營業部 | 10.07 | 50 |
| 華南金融控股公司 | 52 | 民生、士林、信維 | 9.70 | 45 |
| 富邦金融控股公司 | 77 | 安和、北投、天母 | 14.36 | 70 |
| 國泰金融控股公司 | 58 | 營業部、南京東路、復興 | 10.82 | 50 |
| 兆豐金融控股公司 | 30 | 石牌、臺大、大同 | 5.59 | 25 |
| 新光金融控股公司 | 33 | 營業部、南京東路、莊敬 | 6.15 | 30 |
| 元大金融控股公司 | 15 | 營業部、臺北、南京東路 | 2.79 | 10 |
| 永豐金融控股公司 | 48 | 松德、敦北、敦南 | 8.95 | 45 |
| 玉山金融控股公司 | 29 | 城東、南京東路、敦南 | 5.41 | 25 |
| 臺新金融控股公司 | 20 | 營業部、敦南、建橋 | 3.73 | 15 |
| 日盛金融控股公司 | 13 | 營業部、南京東路、松江 | 2.42 | 10 |
| 中華開發金融控股公司 | 1 | 總行 | 0.18 | 0 |
| 國票金融控股公司 | 0 | 無銀行分行 | 0 | 0 |
| 中國信託金融控股公司 | 41 | 天母、城中、永吉 | 7.46 | 35 |
| 合計 | | | 100 | 470 |

---

**【實例】**

**「促銷方式對私有品牌產品知覺品質的影響──促銷情境與產品類別特徵的干擾效果」，研究對象、抽樣方法與樣本數實例**

（林隆儀，2010）

## 1.研究對象

　　家樂福量販店在臺灣共有47家賣場，大臺北地區有16家，佔34%，是量販店在臺灣地區賣場密度最高者，具有代表性，因此選定臺北縣市地區之家樂福賣場為研究地區。

　　本研究的樣本取自到家樂福量販店購買其私有品牌產品的消費者，從家數密度最高的臺北縣市16家家樂福量販店賣場，事先將每一家量販店予以編號，採用隨機抽樣方式抽取6家賣場，結果抽選到中和、板橋、三重、桂林、大直、天母等六家賣場，因此以到這六家賣場購買其私有品牌產品的消費者為研究對象。

## 2.抽樣方法

本研究正式問卷的樣本是在家樂福量販店購買其私有品牌產品的消費者，採用便利抽樣方法進行調查訪問。為確保樣本及資料來源的正確性，本研究採用人員訪問法蒐集初級資料，由受過專業訓練的訪問人員至各受訪之量販店結帳出口處進行調查。

本研究參考黃俊英（1999）及顏月珠（1991）的建議，以簡單隨機抽樣的比率推估式$n \geq Z^2 \cdot p(1 - p)/e^2$，在容忍誤差$e = 0.05$，信賴係數$1 - \alpha = 0.95$的前提下，求出樣本要具有代表性所需要抽選的樣本數$n \geq 384$，亦即最少需要有效樣本384位，本研究決定發出400份問卷。這400份問卷按佔地坪數比例分配至六家賣場，其中家樂福中和店2,600坪、板橋店1,700坪、三重店2,900坪、桂林店1,500坪、大直店3,600坪、天母店1,300坪，問卷按比例分配，中和店訪問75份、板橋店50份、三重店85份、桂林店45份、大直店105份、天母店40份。

無反應偏差（Nonresponse Bias）又稱為無反應誤差（Nonresponse Error），是屬於非抽樣誤差中的一種非觀察誤差。無反應偏差是指無法從母體所選定的部分單位，以及所設定的樣本獲得足夠的資訊，因而所產生的誤差（林隆儀，2000）。也就是在計算樣本統計量時，所應包括之受訪者的資訊，卻沒有包括在內，被選中為樣本的受訪者，因為某種原因而被排除在外，當無反應者的特徵和研究變數有某種程度的關係時，這種排除所產生的偏差（Wilcox, 1977）。

抽樣調查告一段落後，需要檢視樣本回收情形。檢視回收的問卷和無反應的問卷，確定沒有無反應偏差的問題存在，以提高調查的嚴謹度。處理無反應偏差的方法有三：(1)改進研究設計，以降低無反應的數量；(2)反覆聯繫多次，催收問卷，以降低無反應率；(3)估計無反應偏差。

【實例】
「Drivers for the Participation of Small and Medium-Sized Suppliers in Green Supply Chain Initiatives」無反應偏差處理實例
（Lee, 2008）

……Lee（2008）在研究中小企業的供應廠商參與綠色供應鏈的動機時，採用比較及檢定早期回應者與晚期回應者的意見，以電話催收問卷前後時間點為基準，將回應者區分為兩個群體，並從調查問卷中隨機抽選七個題項，針對這兩個群體的受訪者進行t檢定（$n_1 = 53$，$n_2 = 76$），檢定結果顯示所檢視的七個題項間沒有統計顯著性，因此可以確定沒有無反應偏差。

【實例】
「Green Consumption or Sustainable Lifestyles? Identifying the Sustainable Consumer」無反應偏差處理實例
（Gilg, Barr and Ford, 2005）

……Gilg, Barr and Ford（2005）在研究英國Devon地區的綠色消費與持久生活型態時，為了提高都市與鄉村的樣本代表性，以當地電話號碼簿做為抽樣架構，採用隨機抽樣法選取受訪的家戶；若遇到無反應者或有家戶不願意接受訪問時，則選擇該戶的鄰居做為訪問對象，利用這種方法處理無反應偏差的問題。

　　抽樣方法有很多種，研究者可根據研究設計的需要，選擇適合的抽樣方法。其中最重要的要領是所選用的方法必須務實可行，可以抽選到所需要的樣本，所決定的樣本數必須具有代表性，並且以具體數據呈現，而且要講清楚、說明白。

## 六、問卷設計

　　問卷（Questionnaire）又稱為量表，是蒐集受訪者資訊及衡量受訪者對某一議題之態度的重要工具，也是論文結構中很重要的一個要項。問卷設計之良窳，攸關研究的成效，所以研究者都花很多心思在問卷設計上。問卷設計有時也是研究的主要貢獻，有些研究的目的就是在發展問卷。例如：Oplatka and Hemsley-Brown（2007）在研究學校文化的市場導向時，目的就是要發展研究量表，他們從顧客導向、競爭導向、功能協調等三個方向，發展出34個題項的問卷。又如心理學家致力於發展人格測驗量表、性向測驗量表、成就測驗量表等，他們的研究目的就是在發展測驗量表。然而，大多數人的研究都是屬於應用導向，而非致力於發展問卷，所以都是參考他人所發展出來的問卷，加以修改後作為蒐集資訊的工具，進而達到研究的目的。

初次寫論文的學生常常誤認為研究就是在設計問卷，因此一開始就信誓旦旦的著手設計問卷，後來才發現白費功夫、毫無助益，因為這種沒有邏輯、毫無根據、不知道要衡量什麼的問卷，根本無法使用。問卷設計有其理論基礎、有其邏輯原理，必須按照研究程序逐步進行，要達到什麼目的，根據研究變數的操作性定義，知道要蒐集什麼資料、要衡量什麼，然後再來設計所需要的問卷，這樣的問卷才是研究者所需要的問卷。

問卷設計可根據填答方式，區分為兩種形式：一是將訪問的問題設計成封閉式問題（Closed-response Questions），二是將問題設計成開放式問題（Open-response Questions）。封閉式問題或稱結構式問題（Structured Questions），是要請求受訪者從研究者所列出的幾個可能答案中，勾選一個最適合的答案，通常都用在量化研究場合。開放式問題或稱非結構式問題（Unstructured Questions），是研究者只提出問題，而沒有提示可能的答案，讓受訪者自由回答他（她）的想法或意見，通常都用在質化研究的場合。

問卷設計的第一個要領就是根據研究目的與邏輯，參照研究變數的操作性定義，參考他人所設計的問卷，並適當、審慎的加以修改，然後發展出適合用來蒐集初級資料的問卷。第二個要領就是要註明問卷設計的參考來源，一則顯示引經據典、二則表現出重視研究倫理。第三個要領就是每一題項只問一個問題，讓受訪者可以清楚、明白的瞭解問卷在問些什麼，也知道該如何填答。例如：「我所往來的銀行所提供的金融資訊值得信賴」，讓受訪者可以很清楚的瞭解是在問金融資訊值得信賴。又如，「我所往來的銀行所提供的金融資訊與服務值得信賴」，到底是在問金融資訊值得信賴，或是在問所提供的服務值得信賴，不得而知，受訪者自然也就無法正確填答了。第四個要領就是衡量一個變數或構面不宜只用一個單一題目，須使用複數題目才能提高量表的效度。例如：在詢問顧客滿意的程度時，不宜只用一題「我對貴銀行所提供的服務感到很滿意」。第五個要領是設計封閉式問卷供受訪者勾選，尤其是進行量化研究時採用封閉式問卷，不但可以使受訪者容易填答，也有助於回收問卷的處理。第六個要領就是所使用的題目也不宜無限增加，適當的題目數不但符合經濟與效率原則，也可以避免徒增問卷篇幅，如此才能提高受訪者填答的意願。第七個要領是問卷版面的設計，最先出現的是訪問函，接著按照研究變數的順序安排各研究變數的問項，最後才出現受訪者基本資料。第八個要領是問項題目的編排，簡單易答的題目排在前面，以提高受訪者的填答意願。

---

**【實例】**
**「The Relationship of Consumer Personality Trait, Brand Personality and Brand   Loyalty: An Empirical Study of Toys and Video Games Buyers」，問卷設計方法實例**
（**Long-Yi Lin，2010**）

According to the objectives of this study and research variables, as well as different dimensions in the conceptual structure, the questionnaire was organized into four parts: personality traits, brand personality, brand loyalty and the respondent's basic information. In terms of personality traits, this study uses the Big Five Model scale: extroversion, agreeableness, conscientiousness, neuroticism and openness, developed by McCrae et al. (1986), together with the questionnaire designed by Chow (2004). Regarding brand personality, Aaker et al. (2001) divided Japanese brand personality into five dimensions: excitement, competence, peacefulness, sincerity and sophistication. This study uses the Japanese brand personality scale proposed by Aaker et al. (2001) and refers to the questionnaire designed by Aaker et al. (2001) to design the questionnaire of personality trails.

For brand loyalty, this study refers to the two major dimensions of brand loyalty proposed by Chaudhuri and Holbrook (2001) and the questionnaires designed by Chaudhuri and Holbrook (2001), Parasuraman et al. (1996) and Aaker (1996) to measure consumers' brand loyalty toward toy and video game brands, respectively, in terms of affective loyalty and action loyalty. As for respondents' basic information, the respondents are requested to fill in their gender, age, education level, occupation, income and marital status in the questionnaire.

The pre-test of the questionnaire targeted the consumers browsing for or purchasing toys or video games at Taipei City Mall of Taipei Main Station, in order to make sure that the reliability of respective scales would all be in compliance with the research design. A total of 40 samples of the pre-test questionnaire were distributed and 35 validity samples were collected. The pre-test result showed that the Cronbach's α value of the respective variables were all above 0.5 which demonstrated that the questionnaire used in this study meets a qualified level of reliability.

　　研究的目的如果不是要發展問卷，通常都會參考他人的量表，適當加以修改，以達到研究的目的。因為他人所發展的量表通常都會檢視其信度與效度，有信度又有效度的量表，才是符合研究要求的量表。這就是研究者在設計問卷時，如果是參考他人的問卷加以修改而成者，需要註明問卷設計參考來源的原因。

　　人們在日常溝通及意見表達中，常常會有語意上的問題，亦即不同的人對相同的用字或語詞，可能代表不同的意義，以致有不同的解讀。為了避免這種現象，研究問卷設計完成後，必須進行前測（Pre-test），或稱為試訪，也就是將所設計的問卷初稿進行小樣本測試，確認問卷中的用詞及意義是否正確傳達研究的本意，測試受訪者填答時是否充分瞭解問卷題項的意義，對問卷題項是否有不同的認知，填答問卷是否有困難，然後再根據前測的結果，將問卷做必要的調整與修正。經過這一道檢視程序，更能突顯問卷設計的嚴謹度。前測的另一個重要目的，就是要檢視問卷的信度與效度。

　　信度（Reliability）與效度（Validity）是判定問卷設計良窳的兩個重要指標。信度是指衡量結果的正確性或精確性，通常用來檢視衡量結果的一致性或穩定性。例如：測量張三的身高，上個月測量結果是175公分，這個月測量也是175公分，醫生親自測量是175公分，護士小姐測量也是175公分，此時即可宣稱所使用的這一把尺（量表）具有信度。又如研究者想要衡量顧客的品牌忠誠度，在同一期間A君和B君測量的結果相同或很接近，表示這份量表具有高度一致性，符合信度的要求。

　　通常都以Cronbach's α值作為信度的判定值。根據Guielford（1965）所提出的Cronbach's α係數判定準則，α值愈大，表示研究變數／構面內各問項間的相關性愈高，亦即一致性愈高。當α值大於0.7時，表示該量表具有高信度；當α值介於0.3～0.7時，表示該量表的信度可以被接受；當α值小於0.3時，表示該量表僅有低信度，僅有低信度的量表就不值得採用了。Cronbach's $\alpha$值有一個很重要的特性，當所使用的問項題目增加時，或訪問的樣本數增加時，$\alpha$值會隨之提高。簡言之，正式訪問結果採用大樣本所計算出來的Cronbach's $\alpha$值，會略高於前測小規模訪問所計算出來的結果。

效度是指量表衡量的結果，可以真正測量到研究者所要衡量之事物特性的程度。例如：預防新流感（H1N1）流行，各機關、學校都忙著測量人們的體溫，所使用的體溫計（量表）若可以正確測量到人們的真正體溫，則可以宣稱此一體溫計具有效度。又如研究者想要衡量消費者的購買意願，每次衡量的結果都可以測量到消費者真正的購買意願，則稱此一量表符合效度的要求。

效度可區分為內容效度（Content Validity）、效標關聯效度（Criterion Validity）、構念效度（Construct Validity）等三類。(1)內容效度或稱表面效度（Face Validity），是指衡量結果可以足夠涵蓋研究變數的程度。(2)效標關聯效度或稱準則效度，又可以分為預測效度（Predictive Validity）和同時效度（Concurrent Validity），前者是指問卷可以預測或估計所要研究的事物或行為，後者是指可以根據所觀察到的現象予以正確的分類。(3)構念效度是指問卷實際衡量的是什麼。

由此可知，效度有多種類型，研究者必須確實理解各種效度的意義與特性，撰寫論文時必須根據所要衡量的變數特性與目的，選擇適當的效度，而且不應該只選用一種效度；更不宜只寫「本研究所使用的問卷是根據文獻探討，以及參考他人使用過的量表加以修正而來，所以應該具有內容效度」，最好是同時採用兩種以上的效度。

效度和信度的意義雖然不同，但是卻有密切的關係。信度對效度來說是必要條件，但不是充分條件。研究上所要求的是作為衡量工具的量表，必須是既有效度又有信度，這樣的量表才能精準的測量到研究變數的真正特質，而且所測得的結果具有穩定的一致性。

例如：打靶或射箭時，射中目標的正確性所衡量的是效度，沒有射中標靶當然是無效（沒有效度）；射擊的精準度所衡量的是信度，雖然射中標靶，但著彈點分散四處，形成有效度但沒有信度的結果；若每一次都射中標靶的紅心，則形成既有效度又有信度的局面，這是最理想的狀況。請參閱圖3-5的解析。

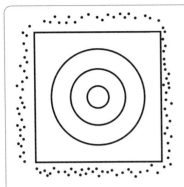

1. 散彈槍射擊：
   無效度，無信度

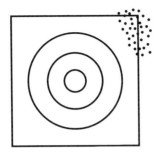

2. 散彈槍射擊：
   無效度，有信度
   但是無濟於事

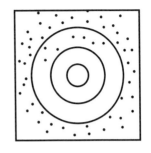

3. 散彈槍射擊：
   有效度，無信度

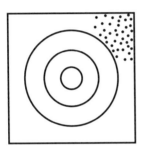

4. 來福槍射擊：
   有效度，有信度
   但非所期望

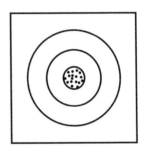

5. 來福槍射擊：
   既有效度，又有信度
   符合期望

**圖3-5** ▎效度與信度的解析

# 七、資料蒐集方法

　　資料蒐集方法又稱為研究的現場作業管理，主要是在說明問卷調查過程的細節，包括選擇研究對象及樣本的理由，以及如何發出調查問卷、在何處進行訪問、何時進行調查、如何收回問卷、如何催收問卷、如何處理無反應偏差等一連串的作業管理問題。無論是採用郵寄問卷訪問法，或人員指導的問卷訪問法，或問卷留置調查法，或電話訪問法，都需要說明資料蒐集方法。說明資料蒐集方法，是要將調查過程透明化，增加研究的嚴謹度，提高研究的可信度及研究結果的參考價值。

例如：採用郵寄問卷調查法時，需要說明調查期間、如何寄出調查問卷、郵寄對象、有無附上回郵信封、有無附上訪問小禮物、寄出幾份問卷、如何催收問卷、催收問卷幾次、問卷回收情況，以及填答不完整的問卷如何處理等，都需要有所交代。

如果是採用人員指導的問卷訪問法，在大賣場訪問前來購物的顧客，則需要說明為何選擇這一家賣場。早上、下午、晚上等不同時段的顧客可能有不同的特徵，對某一議題（問項）可能也有不同的看法，因此，進行調查訪問時必須兼顧不同的訪問時段，以提高研究樣本及分析結果的代表性。問卷如果是由多人協助調查時，除了上述作業管理外，還必須說明如何訓練協助調查的訪問人員。

初次做研究的人常常把資料蒐集工作看得過度樂觀，認為發出問卷後幾天內就可以順利完成回收問卷，這種樂觀的期待往往換來一場空。訪問或調查進行中，常常會遇到一些難以掌控的情況。例如：郵寄問卷訪問中，受訪者沒有收到問卷，或是問卷雖然有收到，但是卻遺失了，或是暫時沒有空填答，不然就是不想填答，或是寄回的問卷被遺失了，狀況百出、不一而足。又如街頭或商店攔截訪問法中，被拒絕的機率很高，匆匆忙忙接受訪問所填答的問卷常欠缺完整性，甚至有填答不實的情況。再如透過他人協助調查時，受託人積極的程度不一，用心的認知程度也不相同，這些都足以使訪問及調查的時間拉長。研究者需要充分瞭解這些可能的狀況，預留足夠的時間進行資料蒐集與催收問卷。

---

### 【實例】
**「服務品質、議題行銷及企業形象對購買意願之影響——顧客信任的干擾效果」，有關資料蒐集方法實例**

（林隆儀、胡瑋純，**2009**）

……在資料蒐集與問卷發放部分，預計於本研究的標的銀行之營業據點門口10公尺內，發放問卷給剛購買金融產品或接受過服務的顧客。由於銀行的營業時間為早上9點至下午3點30分，為求精準起見，本研究將調查時間平均分成早（早上9點至中午12點前）、午（中午12點後至下午3點30分）兩時段發放問卷，採用的方法為人員指導的問卷訪問法（Personal Administered Questionaries）以蒐集初級資料，由受過嚴謹訓練的訪問人員親自發放問卷與回收問卷。因為採用此方法可以在受訪者填寫問卷有疑問時，有人員指導填寫問卷，不但可以在短時間回收問卷，當受訪者有疑問時亦可當面立即獲得澄清，有助於提高問卷的回收率與正確率。

---

**【實例】**
「**The Influence of Corporate Image, Relationship Marketing, and Trust on Purchase Intention: The Moderating Effects of Word-of-Mouth**」，有關資料蒐集方法實例
（**Lin and Lu, 2010**）

⋯⋯本研究的訪問對象是針對18歲以上國內網路旅行社的消費者，資料蒐集採用網路問卷調查法。由於在衡量消費者的網路行為時，受測者在網路環境中作答，問卷的可靠度較高。本研究將網路問卷刊登於旅遊相關之網路論壇、電子布告欄（BBS）、社群討論區，告知相關問卷資訊以進行問卷調查和資料蒐集。由於無法掌握研究母體數量，本研究在網路問卷調查的起訖時間為民國九十八年三月二日至四月二日為期一個月蒐集問卷，預定蒐集有效問卷400份。

---

# 八、資料分析方法

　　論文寫作過程中所使用的資料分析方法，也是研究設計很重要的一部分。資料分析的方法很多，每一個人或每一篇論文所使用的資料分析方法都各不相同，為了提高論文的可讀性、理解性與可信度，研究者有必要把論文中所使用的資料分析方法做清楚的交代。

　　交代資料分析方法的必要性在於：(1)引導研究者取得其他地方所無法獲得的資訊及洞察力；(2)協助研究者避免做出錯誤的判斷及結論；(3)提供一種有助於解釋與瞭解由他人所做的分析基礎；(4)提供我們對資料分析技術的瞭解，並對研究目的及研究設計產生建設性的影響（林隆儀等譯，2005）。

　　資料分析方法選擇正確、適當，可使研究結果的解釋更清晰、更生動、更有說服力，使論文更具有可讀性、更有參考價值。資料分析方法若選擇不當或應用錯誤，可能會毀壞了設計完美的研究設計，造成功虧一簣的遺

憾，研究者不可不慎。

　　詳實說明資料分析方法，顯然是在為論文第四章所要進行的資料分析工作指引方向。實務應用上都把第四章所用到的資料分析方法，先在此做重點式的說明，例如：敘述性統計分析方法、信度分析、效度分析、相關分析，以及用來檢定研究假說的方法。

　　資料分析有多種方法可供選擇，而每個人所熟悉的方法及興趣也各異其趣，所以此部分的寫作要領就是要選對方法，選擇最熟悉的方法，並且選擇最有助於達成目標的方法。

---

### 【實例】
### 「服務品質、議題行銷及企業形象對購買意願之影響——顧客信任的干擾效果」，有關資料分析方法實例
（林隆儀、胡瑋純，2009）

　　……根據本研究之研究目的以及所推論之研究假說，本研究將採用以下的統計方法進行資料分析：

#### 1.敘述性統計分析

　　本研究將以18歲以上受訪者之基本背景資料，運用百分比統計量，藉以瞭解樣本之特性，以及樣本於各構面間的分布狀況。

#### 2.信度分析

　　內部一致性是指量表中衡量內容的一致性程度，亦即一般人所稱的信度分析。本研究採用Conbanch's $\alpha$係數來檢定各研究變數其衡量問項的信度，以確認問卷的內部一致性，在本研究中主要運用以確認量表的可靠程度。

　　本研究依據Guielford（1965）提出之Conbanch's $\alpha$係數的信度準則，$\alpha$係數愈大，顯示構面中各問項間的相關性愈大，亦即內部一致性愈高。當$\alpha$大於0.70即代表高信度，若介於0.70與0.35間的信度為尚可，而如小於0.35則表示信度低。

#### 3.效度分析

　　效度是指衡量工具能夠測出研究者所欲測量事物特性的程度，效度愈高，表示量測的結果愈能顯現所欲衡量對象的真正特徵。本研究採用內容效度與建構效度做為衡量問卷效度的工具，以驗證本研究之問項在內容效度上與適切性上，具有一定的效度。

### 4.相關分析

　　相關性是討論兩變數相關的方向與關係的程度。本研究以Pearson相關分析確認各構面間的關聯性，分析服務品質、議題行銷之議題顯著性、企業形象、購買意願與顧客信任等各構面之間的關係。

### 5.迴歸分析三個前提假設

　　(1)變異數齊一性之檢定：各常態母體變異數皆相等，運用Levene Test來檢定變異數是否相等。(2)常態性之檢定：每個因子水準所對立之機率分配，皆服從常態分配，運用各變數之殘差值標準化殘差次數分配圖與標準化殘差P-P圖，進行驗證是否為常態性。(3)獨立性之檢定：所有樣本都是隨機抽取且彼此獨立，運用迴歸式D-W值來檢定所有樣本是否具有獨立性。

### 6.迴歸分析

　　迴歸分析是將所要研究的變數區分為依變數與自變數，並根據相關理論建立依變數為自變數的函數，然後利用所獲得的樣本資料去估計模型中之參數的方法。本研究將利用迴歸分析來檢定各項研究假說。

# 九、結語

　　論文第三章是在說明研究設計的來龍去脈，是整篇論文的核心，也是呈現研究設計之嚴謹度的關鍵資訊。初學者尚未進入情況，往往無法體會研究設計的重要性，不瞭解研究設計應該包括哪些要項，每一個要項該寫些什麼內容，更不知道每一個要項的寫作要領。本章提出研究設計的七大要項及其要領以供參考，只要順著這七大要項，按部就班的進行，掌握寫作要領，用心撰寫，通常都可以完整且明確的描述整個研究方法。

　　觀念性架構的呈現必須說明研究變數及其構面的參考來源。命題與研究假說的出現必須引經據典、詳實推論。研究變數與構面的定義必須予以操作化、明確化。抽樣方法及樣本數大小需要有清楚的交代。問卷設計需要說明參考來源，設計完成的問卷必須進行前測，確認量表的信度。選擇資料蒐集方法需要說明理由，並且詳實描述取得資料的方法。資料分析需要說明所使用的各種統計分析方法。

# 第四章
## 資料分析

## 一、前言

　　問卷調查所回收的問卷，須一一經過檢查，剔除填答不全、填答錯誤、極端傾向，以及答案無法辨識等無效問卷之後，接著就要進行資料處理工作。資料處理就是根據論文第三章所描述的資料分析方法，逐項進行資料處理與統計分析。由於電腦科技發達，無須假手人工計算，資料處理工作利用電腦配合適當的統計軟體處理之，可以迅速獲得所需要的處理與分析結果。由此可知，資料分析是要把問卷調查所蒐集到的初級資料進行有系統的處理，目的是要將處理結果進一步分析、解釋與解讀。

　　資料分析與解釋在研究過程中扮演非常重要的角色，前段研究設計無論規劃得多完美，也無論調查工作進行得多順利，如果資料處理不當、分析失真、解讀錯誤，將會導致整個研究工作不知所云，甚至造成功虧一簣、前功盡棄的後果。研究者在進行資料分析時，除了要有耐心與恆心之外，還需要熟悉資料處理的各種要領與技巧。

　　整體而言，資料分析的要領在於將資料處理結果所獲得的資訊，充分且適當的揭露，並做正確的解釋與解讀，進而從中發現有意義、有價值的訊息。資料分析包括正確列表、比較分析、說明細節、利用佐證數據判定研究結果等。

# 二、樣本特性描述

　　論文第四章通常都是從描述樣本特性開始，這一部分屬於敘述統計分析的範疇，主要是在說明問卷發出及回收狀況，呼應論文第三章所提出的抽樣樣本數及資料蒐集方法，以及描述回收的問卷中，個人（廠商）基本資料統計分布情形，讓閱讀者對樣本結構有一個初步的認識。

　　樣本特性描述通常都以列表方式呈現，再輔之以文字做重點式說明。一方面有文字描述，可收簡明、扼要之效；一方面有數字佐證，可以傳達具體、可信的資訊，達到務實呈現樣本輪廓的目的。利用文字描述樣本特性的要領，是要將表列樣本資料所顯現比較特殊的數據提出來做重點式說明即可，而無須將樣本統計數據從頭到尾一一再解釋一遍，因為詳細資料都已經詳列在表中，「特性描述」就是在做畫龍點睛的工作，不要落入畫蛇添足的圈套。

　　統計資料的整理與列表呈現也是一種很重要、很實用的技巧，研究者需要深諳其中的奧妙，良好的資料整理與列表，便可讓人一目了然。電腦處理結果的資料可能包括許多初始資料，這些初始資料不一定都是研究者所要的資料，因此需要研究者發揮審慎取捨的功夫、去蕪存菁。電腦所列印出來的表格也可能不是研究者所要呈現的表格，此時更有賴研究者善用解讀資料的創意，做最適當、最充分、最完美的呈現。

【實例】
「服務品質、議題行銷及企業形象對購買意願之影響——顧客信任的干擾效果」，有關樣本基本資料描述實例
（林隆儀、胡瑋純，2009）

    ……本研究樣本蒐集期間為民國九十八年三月到九十八年四月中旬，以大臺北地區玉山銀行經紀本部、雙和分行、新莊分行、松江分行、仁愛分行、土城分行、臺大分行、士林分行、南京東路分行、城中分行共十家分行之顧客為抽樣對象，共計發出450份問卷，扣除資料不全及過度集中的無效問卷31份，收回有效問卷共419份，有效回收率為93%。分行名稱、發出問卷數與收回有效問卷數整理如表4-1所示。

**表4-1** ▌
分行名稱與收回有效問卷數

| 分行名稱 | 發出問卷數 | 收回有效問卷數 |
|---|---|---|
| 經紀本部 | 45 | 43 |
| 雙和分行 | 45 | 41 |
| 新莊分行 | 45 | 43 |
| 松江分行 | 45 | 42 |
| 仁愛分行 | 45 | 40 |
| 土城分行 | 45 | 44 |
| 臺大分行 | 45 | 42 |
| 士林分行 | 45 | 43 |
| 南京東路分行 | 45 | 42 |
| 城中分行 | 45 | 39 |
| 合計 | 450 | 419 |

    本研究樣本結構資料整理如表4-2所示。有效樣本受訪者性別顯示男性顧客（53.5%）比例高於女性顧客（46.5%）。受訪者年齡主要集中於19～30歲（54.9%），其次為31～40歲（18.6%）。受訪者的婚姻狀況為已婚者（65.4%）的比例大於未婚者（34.6%）。受訪者之職業以服務業（17.7%）、金融保險業（14.3%）為最多。受訪者之教育程度集中在專科或大學程度為最多（58.7%），其次為研究所以上（23.9%）及高中職（12.2%）。受訪者同

時在三家以上銀行開戶者的比例最多（74%），同時在兩家銀行開戶者次之（23.2%），只在一家銀行開戶者比例最少（2.9%）。受訪者平均月所得集中於20,000元以下者最多（25.8%），其次為30,001～40,000元（22%）。受訪者使用銀行的頻率大多集中在每月3～5次（38.2%）。

**表4-2**
樣本結構

| 項目 | 基本資料 | 有效問卷 | 百分比（％） |
|------|----------|----------|--------------|
| 性別 | 男 | 224 | 53.5 |
| | 女 | 195 | 46.5 |
| | 小計 | 419 | 100.0 |
| 年齡 | 19～30歲 | 230 | 54.9 |
| | 31～40歲 | 78 | 18.6 |
| | 41～50歲 | 53 | 12.6 |
| | 51～60歲 | 54 | 12.9 |
| | 61歲以上 | 4 | 1.0 |
| | 小計 | 419 | 100.0 |
| 婚姻狀況 | 未婚 | 145 | 34.6 |
| | 已婚 | 274 | 65.4 |
| | 小計 | 419 | 100.0 |
| 職業 | 電子資訊業 | 52 | 12.4 |
| | 金融保險業 | 60 | 14.3 |
| | 農林漁牧礦 | 7 | 1.7 |
| | 家管 | 34 | 8.1 |
| | 製造業 | 42 | 10.0 |
| | 服務業 | 74 | 17.7 |
| | 軍公教 | 31 | 7.4 |
| | 自由業 | 33 | 7.9 |
| | 學生 | 48 | 11.5 |
| | 其他 | 38 | 9.1 |
| | 小計 | 419 | 100.0 |
| 教育程度 | 國（初）中以下 | 22 | 5.3 |
| | 高中（職） | 51 | 12.2 |
| | 專科或大學 | 246 | 58.7 |
| | 研究所（含）以上 | 100 | 23.9 |
| | 小計 | 419 | 100.0 |

**表4-2**
樣本結構（續）

| 項目 | 基本資料 | 有效問卷 | 百分比（%） |
|---|---|---|---|
| 在幾家銀行開戶 | 一家 | 12 | 2.9 |
| | 兩家 | 97 | 23.2 |
| | 三家（含）以上 | 310 | 74.0 |
| | 小計 | 419 | 100.0 |
| 平均月所得 | 20,000元（含）以下 | 108 | 25.8 |
| | 20,001～30,000元 | 80 | 19.1 |
| | 30,001～40,000元 | 92 | 22.0 |
| | 40,001～50,000元 | 65 | 15.5 |
| | 50,001～60,000元 | 31 | 7.4 |
| | 60,001元以上 | 43 | 10.3 |
| | 小計 | 419 | 100.0 |
| 使用銀行服務的頻率（每月） | 2次及以下 | 107 | 25.5 |
| | 3～5次 | 160 | 38.2 |
| | 6～8次 | 65 | 15.5 |
| | 8～11次 | 39 | 9.3 |
| | 12次以上 | 48 | 11.5 |
| | 小計 | 419 | 100.0 |

# 三、信度與效度分析

　　論文第三章進行前測時，曾利用小樣本檢測量表的信度。第四章回收問卷後，需要針對回收問卷再次檢視量表的信度。信度的意義、重要性、分析要領與判定準則和第三章所述相同，為節省篇幅，不再贅述。

【實例】
「服務品質、議題行銷及企業形象對購買意願之影響——顧客信任的干擾效果」，有關正式問卷之信度分析實例
（林隆儀、胡瑋純，2009）

⋯⋯本研究正式問卷之信度檢測結果，整理如表4-3所示，其中服務品質之Cronbach's α值為0.951，議題顯著性之Cronbach's α值為0.917，企業形象之Cronbach's α值為0.949，購買意願之Cronbach's α值為0.782，顧客信任之Cronbach's α值為0.938。由此可知，各變數的Cronbach's α值皆大於0.8，顯示本研究各變數內部一致性相當良好，表示本研究所使用的量表具有高信度。

表4-3
正式問卷之信度分析

| 變數 | 構面 | 題號 | Cronbach's α 值 | |
|---|---|---|---|---|
| | | | 構面 | 變數 |
| 服務品質 | 可靠性 | 12～14 | 0.844 | |
| | 實體性 | 9～11 | 0.846 | |
| | 反應性 | 15～17 | 0.881 | 0.951 |
| | 保證性 | 18～20 | 0.832 | |
| | 關懷性 | 21～23 | 0.858 | |
| 議題顯著性 | 議題顯著性高 | 1～4 | 0.842 | 0.917 |
| | 議題顯著性低 | 5～8 | 0.906 | |
| 企業形象 | | 24～35 | | 0.949 |
| 購買意願 | | 36～38 | | 0.782 |
| 顧客信任 | | 39～42 | | 0.938 |

論文第三章曾討論量表的各種效度，並建議檢視量表效度時，視研究需要選擇合適的效度，而且不宜只選用一種效度，尤其不宜只採用內容效度，才能提高論文的可讀性與可信度。

【實例】
「服務品質、議題行銷及企業形象對購買意願之影響——顧客信任的干擾效果」，有關量表效度分析實例
（林隆儀、胡瑋純，2009）

……本研究採用內容效度（Content Validity）與建構效度（Construct Validity）來檢視問卷的效度。內容效度主要反映測量工具本身內容範圍廣度的適切程度。本研究之問卷題項內容係參考國內外學者所提出並已多次使用之研究量表，並經相關文獻的探討，加以適當修改而成，因此具有相當之理論基礎。且在問卷設計的過程中，經過多次修訂及前測後才定稿，因此，本研究所使用之問卷內容應具有相當之內容效度。

建構效度係指測量工具能測得一個抽象概念或特質的程度。本研究量表的建構效度判斷標準採用因素特徵值（Eigenvalue）須大於1，且以最大變異數（Varimax）法做直交轉軸後，因素負荷量絕對值大於0.5（邱皓政，2006）。本研究因素分析與效度分析結果，整理如表4-4所示。由表4-4的數據顯示，各題項的因素負荷量皆大於0.5，各構面的因素特徵值皆在1以上，解釋變異量也皆大於43%以上，顯示本研究問卷除具備內容效度外，同時亦可宣稱具有良好的建構效度。

**表4-4**
因素分析與效度分析

| 變數 | 構面 | 題號 | 因素負荷量 | 因素特徵值 | 解釋變異量(%) |
|------|------|------|------------|------------|----------------|
| 服務品質 | 可靠性 | 12 | 0.745 | 1.66 | 55.333 |
| | | 13 | 0.740 | | |
| | | 14 | 0.747 | | |
| | 實體性 | 9 | 0.689 | 1.51 | 50.333 |
| | | 10 | 0.709 | | |
| | | 11 | 0.727 | | |
| | 反應性 | 15 | 0.737 | 1.47 | 0.490 |
| | | 16 | 0.698 | | |
| | | 17 | 0.666 | | |
| | | 18 | 0.645 | | |
| | 保證性 | 19 | 0.699 | 1.31 | 43.666 |
| | | 20 | 0.638 | | |
| | 關懷性 | 21 | 0.766 | 1.09 | 54.500 |
| | | 22 | 0.710 | | |

**表4-4**
因素分析與效度分析（續）

| 變數 | 構面 | 題號 | 因素負荷量 | 因素特徵值 | 解釋變異量(%) |
|------|------|------|-----------|-----------|-------------|
| 議題行銷 | 顯著性高 | 1 | 0.734 | 2.55 | 63.750 |
| | | 2 | 0.853 | | |
| | | 3 | 0.789 | | |
| | 顯著性低 | 4 | 0.815 | 2.94 | 73.500 |
| | | 5 | 0.828 | | |
| | | 6 | 0.882 | | |
| | | 7 | 0.851 | | |
| | | 8 | 0.865 | | |
| 企業形象 | | 23 | 0.655 | 6.77 | 56.417 |
| | | 24 | 0.524 | | |
| | | 25 | 0.742 | | |
| | | 26 | 0.813 | | |
| | | 27 | 0.755 | | |
| | | 28 | 0.838 | | |
| | | 29 | 0.822 | | |
| | | 30 | 0.825 | | |
| | | 31 | 0.815 | | |
| | | 32 | 0.819 | | |
| | | 33 | 0.716 | | |
| | | 34 | 0.612 | | |
| 購買意願 | | 35 | 0.592 | 1.82 | 60.667 |
| | | 36 | 0.839 | | |
| | | 37 | 0.875 | | |
| 顧客信任 | | 38 | 0.853 | 3.07 | 76.750 |
| | | 39 | 0.854 | | |
| | | 40 | 0.898 | | |
| | | 41 | 0.898 | | |

# 四、相關分析

相關係數（Coefficient of Correlation）是在檢定兩個變數線性相關的統計技術，其數值為一標準化分數，相關係數的特性為介於 + 1與−1之間，不受變數特性的影響。相關數值愈接近 + 1時，表示變數關聯性屬於正向相

關；反之，則屬於負向相關。當數值等於 + 1時，稱為完全正相關。絕對值介於0.70～0.99之間為高度相關，0.40～0.69之間為中度相關，0.10～0.39之間為低度相關，0.10以下為微弱或無相關（邱皓政，2006）。

相關分析結果的呈現要領有三：第一，當研究變數單純時，只呈現研究變數之間的相關關係，此時所列出的相關分析表比較簡潔。第二，當研究變數包含有數個構面時，需要呈現各研究變數及其構面之間的相關關係，此時所列出的相關分析表比較詳細。第三，相關分析表內的係數數字必須標示顯著水準符號，並在表下方註明符號的意義。

---

### 【實例】
## 「服務品質、議題行銷及企業形象對購買意願之影響──顧客信任的干擾效果」，有關研究變數相關分析實例
（林隆儀、胡瑋純，**2009**）

⋯⋯本研究以Pearson積差相關分析來確認各變數與構面的關聯性，構面之間的Pearson相關程度整理如表4-5所示。由表中數據可知，相關程度最高是企業形象與顧客信任兩構面（相關係數為0.783），其次為服務品質與企業形象兩構面（相關係數為0.713），最低的是服務品質與購買意願兩構面（相關係數為0.514）。從相關係數矩陣可知，兩兩構面間皆為顯著正相關，顯示自變數間的相關無負面之影響。

**表4-5**
研究變數的Pearson相關分析

| 變數 | 1 | 2 | 3 | 4 | 5 |
|---|---|---|---|---|---|
| 服務品質（1） | 1.00 | | | | |
| 議題顯著性（2） | 0.526*** | 1.00 | | | |
| 企業形象（3） | 0.713*** | 0.486*** | 1.00 | | |
| 購買意願（4） | 0.514*** | 0.378*** | 0.632*** | 1.00 | |
| 顧客信任（5） | 0.688*** | 0.460*** | 0.783*** | 0.631*** | 1.00 |

註：＊：$p<0.1$；＊＊：$p<0.05$；＊＊＊：$p<0.01$

【實例】
「學校行銷策略、學校形象對家長選校決策的影響——知覺風險的干擾效果」，有關研究變數相關分析實例
（林隆儀、李明真，2010）

……本研究變數及其構面的相關分析結果，整理如表4-6所示。

**表4-6**
Pearson 積差相關分析表

| | 產品 | 訂價 | 通路 | 推廣 | 校長 | 教師 | 學生 | 學校 | 社區 | 財務 | 社會 | 時間 | 家長選校決策 |
|---|---|---|---|---|---|---|---|---|---|---|---|---|---|
| 產品 | 1 | | | | | | | | | | | | |
| 訂價 | 0.189** | 1 | | | | | | | | | | | |
| 通路 | 0.479** | 0.251** | 1 | | | | | | | | | | |
| 推廣 | 0.331** | 0.348** | 0.431** | 1 | | | | | | | | | |
| 校長 | 0.490** | 0.167** | 0.390** | 0.316** | 1 | | | | | | | | |
| 教師 | 0.570** | 0.140** | 0.355** | 0.241** | 0.638** | 1 | | | | | | | |
| 學生 | 0.518** | 0.230** | 0.437** | 0.491** | 0.627** | 0.689** | 1 | | | | | | |
| 學校 | 0.519** | 0.204** | 0.446** | 0.385** | 0.677** | 0.751** | 0.748** | 1 | | | | | |
| 社區 | 0.438** | 0.249** | 0.462** | 0.431** | 0.560** | 0.562** | 0.667** | 0.740** | 1 | | | | |
| 財務 | 0.160** | 0.256** | 0.304** | 0.236** | 0.159** | 0.192** | 0.257** | 0.212** | 0.248** | 1 | | | |
| 社會 | 0.042 | 0.305** | 0.183** | 0.347** | 0.048 | 0.050 | 0.147** | 0.103** | 0.148** | 0.526** | 1 | | |
| 時間 | 0.084* | 0.219** | 0.262** | 0.230** | 0.079** | 0.069 | 0.146** | 0.131** | 0.199** | 0.594** | 0.670** | 1 | |
| 家長選校決策 | 0.257** | 0.288** | 0.475** | 0.327** | 0.252** | 0.267** | 0.371** | 0.318** | 0.352** | 0.319** | 0.280** | 0.325** | 1 |

註：**在顯著水準為0.01時（雙尾），相關顯著。

# 五、變數殘差分析

　　檢定統計量的前提假設會影響統計方法的選擇。例如：兩樣本t檢定的前提假設為：(1)兩樣本皆為獨立；(2)每一群樣本的母體中，所研究的特徵值呈現常態分配；(3)兩母體的變異數相等（林隆儀等譯，2005）。又如迴歸模式的前提假設為：(1)殘差項呈現常態分配；(2)殘差項的平均值等於

0；(3)殘差項的變異數為常數，且獨立於X；(4)殘差項之間為相互獨立，即觀察值獨立抽出；(5)自變數X的值固定（林隆儀等譯，2005；陳景堂，2004）。

　　兩樣本t檢定及迴歸分析，學生比較熟悉，這兩種方法被選用來檢定研究假說的機會也比較高，因此介紹這兩種檢定方法的前提假設。

---

**【實例】**
**「服務品質、議題行銷及企業形象對購買意願之影響──顧客信任的干擾效果」，有關變數殘差分析實例**
（林隆儀、胡瑋純，**2009**）

---

　　……本研究將採用迴歸分析檢定各項研究假說，在進行迴歸分析前，先採用「殘差分析」來檢定三項假設條件。首先使用SPSS與Excel統計軟體，得知各變數之預測值與殘差值，之後再利用預測值與殘差值得出標準化殘差P-P圖，以驗證變數殘差的常態性；接著利用杜賓－瓦特森統計值（Durbin-Watson Statistic，D-W值），確認資料是否符合獨立性的基本假設以驗證獨立性，最後以殘差值與預測值的散佈圖驗證齊一性。

**常態性檢定**
　　本研究的標準化變數殘差次數分配圖如圖4-1所示，標準化變數殘差P-P圖如圖4-2所示。由圖4-1及圖4-2的圖形可知，變數殘差的機率分配近似常態分配，也就是每一誤差變數均具有常態分配。

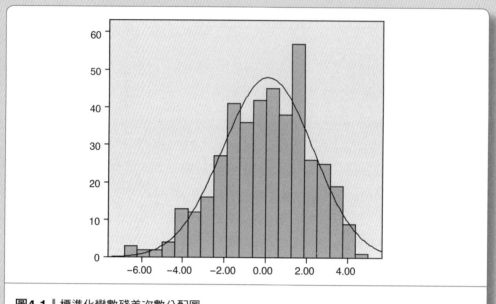

**圖4-1** ▎ 標準化變數殘差次數分配圖

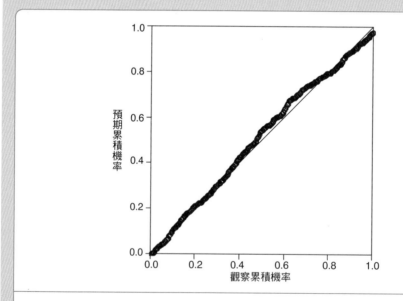

**圖4-2** ▎ 標準化變數殘差P-P圖

### 獨立性檢定

　　樣本獨立性是指樣本是隨機抽選而得，且彼此間互相獨立，亦即觀察值必須是彼此獨立（黃俊英，2000）。本研究針對各迴歸模型杜賓－瓦特森統計值，確認資料是否符合獨立性的基本假設。邱皓政（2006）指出所計算的杜賓－瓦特森統計值若介於1.5～2.5之間，即表示誤差項之間無自我相關存在。本研究變數殘差之獨立性檢定結果整理如表4-7所示，由表中數據可知，本研究各模式之D-W值皆介於1.5～2.5之間，顯示殘差項之間無自我相關存在，故本研究樣本資料符合獨立性的基本假設。

**表4-7**
迴歸模式之D-W值

| 模式 | D-W值 | F值 |
|------|-------|-----|
| 模式一 | 1.927 | 188.032*** |
| 模式二 | 1.986 | 771.019*** |
| 模式三 | 1.968 | 66.293*** |
| 模式四 | 2.081 | 276.72 *** |
| 模式五 | 2.063 | 157.977*** |

註：*：$p < 0.1$；**：$p < 0.05$；***：$p < 0.01$

### 齊一性檢定

　　本研究變數殘差值與預測值的散佈圖如圖4-3所示，由圖上之散佈情形可知，其對應點皆散佈於正、負10之間，其結果呈現一帶狀分布之圖樣，且例外值（Outlier）所占比例非常小，表示誤差分配之變異數相等的假設是可以接受的，即符合齊一性的假設。

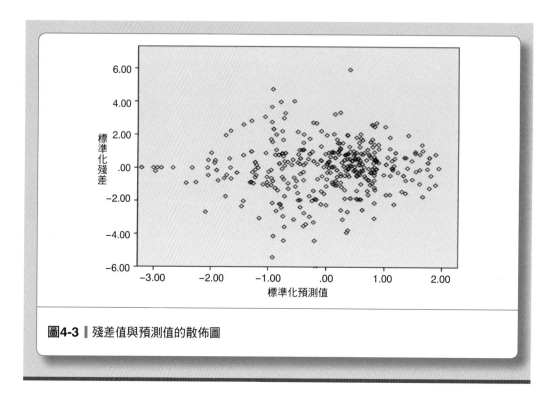

**圖4-3** ▍殘差值與預測值的散佈圖

# 六、假說檢定

　　檢定研究假說是整個研究工作的重頭戲，目的是要利用科學的統計方法檢定論文第三章所發展出來的各項研究假說，檢定這些研究假說是否獲得支持。既然檢定是要證明研究假說是否獲得支持，檢定過程中必須提出具體數據佐證，作為科學判定的基準。

　　檢定研究假說的要領，首先是要選擇正確的統計方法。第三章討論衡量尺度的類型及其特性時，曾介紹各種衡量尺度的特性及適合的統計檢定方法，讀者可以參閱並選擇正確的統計方法。其次是順著所發展出來的研究假說逐一檢定、逐一判定，並做明確的結論。第三是檢定過程必須列表並指出佐證數據，作為判定依據。第四是所有假說檢定完成後，整理出檢定結果彙總表，作為檢定的結論。第五是研究假說檢定結果需要進行討論，討論研究假說獲得支持與未獲得支持的主要原因。

　　每一個人選用的統計方法可能各不相同，每一篇論文所採用的統計檢定方法也可能各異其趣，本節介紹最常被使用的四種假說檢定方法，即變異數分析法（ANOVA）、迴歸分析法（Regression Analysis）、階層迴歸分析法或稱層級迴歸分析法（Stepwise Regression Analysis）、線性結構方程式法（LISREL），以供參考。至於討論將在下一節介紹。

**【實例】變異數分析法**
**「議題行銷之社會顯著性、活動持續度及執行保證對品牌權益的影響」，研究假說檢定實例**
（林隆儀，2010）

### 1.議題的社會顯著性對品牌權益的影響

議題的社會顯著性對品牌權益的影響，經過敘述性統計分析結果，社會顯著性高的平均數為80.98，標準差為1.13；社會顯著性低的平均數為79.88，標準差為1.09。經採用平均數差t檢定檢視結果，兩組平均數差具有統計顯著性，即議題的社會顯著性高、低，對品牌權益的影響有顯著差異。

議題的社會顯著性對品牌權益的影響，經採用變異數分析檢定結果，整理如表4-8所示。由表中的數據可知，$F = 20.39$，$p = 0.000 < 0.01$，具有統計顯著性，表示社會顯著性高的議題，對品牌權益的影響顯著高於社會顯著性低的議題，因此假說1獲得支持。

**表4-8**
議題的社會顯著性對品牌權益影響的變異數分析

|  | 平方和 | 自由度 | 平均平方和 | F檢定 | p值 |
|---|---|---|---|---|---|
| 組間 | 3794.12 | 1 | 3794.112 | 20.39 | 0.000*** |
| 組內 | 55644.77 | 299 | 186.103 |  |  |
| 總和 | 59438.89 | 300 |  |  |  |

註：***為p值 < 0.01，**為p值 < 0.05，*為p值 < 0.1

### 2.活動持續度對品牌權益的影響

議題行銷活動的持續度對品牌權益的影響，經過敘述性統計分析結果，活動持續度高的平均數為79.66，標準差為1.08；活動持續度低的平均數為75.28，標準差為1.18。經採用平均數差t檢定分析結果，兩組平均數差具有統計顯著性，即活動持續度高、低，對品牌權益的影響有顯著差異。

議題行銷活動的持續度對品牌權益的影響，經採用變異數分析結果，整理如

表4-9所示。由表中數據可知，F = 7.43，p = 0.007 < 0.01，具有統計顯著性，表示企業實行議題行銷時，活動持續度高的計畫對品牌權益的影響，顯著高於活動持續度低的計畫，因此假說2獲得支持。

**表4-9**

議題行銷的活動持續度對品牌權益影響的變異數分析

|  | 平方和 | 自由度 | 平均平方和 | F檢定 | p值 |
|---|---|---|---|---|---|
| 組間 | 1440.47 | 1 | 1440.47 | 7.43 | 0.007*** |
| 組內 | 57998.42 | 299 | 193.98 |  |  |
| 總和 | 59438.89 | 300 |  |  |  |

註：***為p值 < 0.01，**為p值 < 0.05，*為p值 < 0.1

### 3.社會顯著性與活動持續度的組合對品牌權益的影響

議題的社會顯著性與活動持續度組合的敘述性統計分析結果，顯著性低、活動持續度高的平均數76.89，標準差為1.44；顯著性低、活動持續度低的平均數為70.82，標準差為1.57；顯著性高、活動持續度高的平均數為82.43，標準差為1.57；顯著性高、活動持續度低的平均數為79.57，標準差為1.63。經分別採用平均數差t檢定分析結果，兩組平均數差具有統計顯著性，即社會顯著性高、低與活動持續度高、低的組合，對品牌權益的影響有顯著差異。

議題的社會顯著性與活動持續度組合，對品牌權益影響的變異數分析檢定結果，整理如表4-10所示。由表中數據可知，社會顯著性低與活動持續度高組合的F = 8.15，p = 0.005<0.01，具有統計顯著性，表示廠商選擇社會顯著性低的議題搭配持續度高的活動，對品牌權益的影響顯著大於搭配持續度低的活動，因此假說3-1獲得支持。

社會顯著性高與活動持續度低組合的F = 1.59，p = 0.209>0.10，不具有統計顯著性，表示廠商選擇社會顯著性高的議題搭配持續度高的活動，對品牌權益的影響不見得大於搭配持續度低的活動，所以假說3-2未獲得支持。

**表4-10**
社會顯著性與活動持續度組合對品牌權益影響的變異數分析

|  |  | 平方和 | 自由度 | 平均平方和 | F檢定 | p值 |
|---|---|---|---|---|---|---|
| 社會顯著性低 | 組間 | 1371.96 | 1 | 1371.96 | 8.15 | 0.005*** |
|  | 組內 | 24737.86 | 147 | 168.29 |  |  |
|  | 總和 | 26109.82 | 148 |  |  |  |
| 社會顯著性高 | 組間 | 309.74 | 1 | 309.74 | 1.59 | 0.209 |
|  | 組內 | 29225.20 | 150 | 194.84 |  |  |
|  | 總和 | 29534.94 | 151 |  |  |  |

註：***為p值＜0.01，**為p值＜0.05，*為p值＜0.1

### 4.議題行銷執行保證對品牌權益的影響

　　議題行銷執行保證對品牌權益影響的敘述統計分析結果，有執行保證的平均數為78.47，標準差為1.21；無執行保證的平均數為76.47，標準差為1.08。經採用平均數差t檢定分析結果，兩組平均數差具有統計顯著性，即議題行銷有無執行保證，對品牌權益的影響有顯著差異。

　　議題行銷執行保證對品牌權益影響的變異數分析結果，整理如表4-11所示。由表中數據可知，F = 1.52，p = 0.219>0.10，不具有統計顯著性，表示廠商實行議題行銷時，有無執行保證，對品牌權益的影響沒有顯著的差異，因此假說4未獲得支持。

**表4-11**
議題行銷執行保證對品牌權益影響的變異數分析

|  | 平方和 | 自由度 | 平均平方和 | F檢定 | p值 |
|---|---|---|---|---|---|
| 組間 | 299.93 | 1 | 299.93 | 1.52 | 0.219 |
| 組內 | 59138.95 | 299 | 197.79 |  |  |
| 總和 | 59438.88 | 300 |  |  |  |

註：***為p值＜0.01，**為p值＜0.05，*為p值＜0.1

### 5.社會顯著性與執行保證組合對品牌權益的影響

　　議題的社會顯著性與執行保證組合的敘述性統計分析結果，顯著性高、有執行保證的平均數75.08，標準差為1.59；顯著性高、無執行保證的平均數為72.69，標準差為1.48；顯著性低、有執行保證的平均數為81.76，標準差為1.75；顯著性低、無執行保證的平均數為80.20，標準差為1.44。經分別採用平均數差t檢定分析結果，兩組平均數差具有統計顯著性，即社會顯著性高、低與有、無提供執行保證，對品牌權益的影響有顯著差異。

　　社會顯著性與執行保證組合對品牌權益影響的變異數分析結果，整理如表4-12所示。由表中數據可知，社會顯著性高與執行保證組合的F = 1.21，p = 0.274>0.10，不具有統計顯著性，表示廠商選擇社會顯著性高的議題搭配有執行保證，對品牌權益的影響不見得大於搭配無執行保證，因此假說5-1未獲得支持。

　　社會顯著性低與執行保證組合的F = 0.48，p = 0.492>0.10，不具有統計顯著性，表示廠商選擇社會顯著性低的議題搭配有執行保證，對品牌權益的影響不見得大於搭配無執行保證，所以假說5-2未獲得支持。

**表4-12**

社會顯著性與執行保證組合對品牌權益影響的變異數分析

| | | 平方和 | 自由度 | 平均平方和 | F檢定 | p值 |
|---|---|---|---|---|---|---|
| 社會顯著性高 | 組間 | 212.37 | 1 | 212.37 | 1.21 | 0.274 |
| | 組內 | 25897.46 | 147 | 176.17 | | |
| | 總和 | 26109.83 | 148 | | | |
| 社會顯著性低 | 組間 | 93.16 | 1 | 93.16 | 0.48 | 0.492 |
| | 組內 | 29441.78 | 150 | 196.28 | | |
| | 總和 | 29534.94 | 151 | | | |

註：***為p值＜0.01，**為p值＜0.05，*為p值＜0.1

**【實例】迴歸分析法**

**「服務品質、議題行銷及企業形象對購買意願之影響」，研究假說檢定實例**

（林隆儀、胡瑋純，2009）

　　……服務品質各構面對企業形象之影響的迴歸分析結果，整理如表4-13所示。由表4-13的分析結果顯示，$\bar{R}^2$ = 0.691，F = 188.032，p = 0.000<0.01，具有統

計顯著性，模型可解釋69.1%的變異量，模型具有解釋能力；同時D-W = 1.927，顯示在1%的顯著水準下，殘差項之間無自我相關存在。共線性統計量的VIF值介於2.334～3.863之間，VIF值皆小於10，符合迴歸分析無共線性需求（Kennedy, 1992），可看出共線性不明顯，因此不會影響本研究中有關統計數據的精確性與結果解釋。

服務品質的可靠性對企業形象影響之β係數為0.388，t = 7.839，p = 0.000<0.01，具有統計顯著性，表示服務品質的可靠性對企業形象具有顯著的正向影響，所以假說1-1獲得強烈支持。服務品質的實體性對企業形象影響之β係數為0.117，t = 2.809，p = 0.005<0.01，具有統計顯著性，表示服務品質的實體性對企業形象具有顯著的正向影響，所以假說1-2獲得支持。服務品質的反應性對企業形象影響之β係數為0.125，t = 2.339，p = 0.020<0.05，具有統計顯著性，表示服務品質的反應性對企業形象具有顯著的正向影響，所以假說1-3獲得支持。服務品質的保證性對企業形象影響之β係數為0.122，t = 2.472，p = 0.014<0.05，具有統計顯著性，表示服務品質的保證性對企業形象具有顯著的正向影響，因此假說1-4獲得支持。服務品質的關懷性對企業形象影響之β係數為0.211，t = 4.349，p = 0.000<0.01，具有統計顯著性，表示服務品質的關懷性對企業形象具有顯著的正向影響，所以假說1-5獲得強烈支持。

由以上檢定結果可知，假說1-1、假說1-2、假說1-3、假說1-4、假說1-5均獲得支持，因此假說1獲得支持。

**表4-13**
服務品質各構面對企業形象影響之迴歸分析

| 模式一應變數 | 自變數（服務品質） | β值 | t值 | p值 | VIF值 |
|---|---|---|---|---|---|
| | 可靠性 | 0.388 | 7.839 | 0.000*** | 3.312 |
| | 實體性 | 0.117 | 2.809 | 0.005*** | 2.334 |
| 企業形象 | 反應性 | 0.125 | 2.339 | 0.020** | 3.863 |
| | 保證性 | 0.122 | 2.472 | 0.014** | 3.320 |
| | 關懷性 | 0.211 | 4.349 | 0.000*** | 3.185 |

$R^2 = 0.695$；$\overline{R}^2 = 0.691$；$D - W = 1.927$；$N = 419$；$F = 188.032$；$p = 0.000***$

註：* : $p < 0.1$；** : $p < 0.05$；*** : $p < 0.01$

【實例】階層迴歸分析法
「服務品質、品牌形象、顧客忠誠與顧客購買意願的關係——以臺北市銀行產業的顧客為例」，研究假說檢定實例
（林隆儀、周佩琦，2010）

### 1.顧客忠誠在服務品質對再購買意願影響的中介效果

Baron and Kenny（1986）指出檢驗中介效果主要有三個步驟：(1)自變數對中介變數影響的迴歸分析，但不包括依變數；(2)中介變數對依變數影響的迴歸分析；(3)自變數與中介變數同時對依變數影響的迴歸分析。

若自變數影響中介變數，且中介變數影響依變數，則符合以下的情況：(1)自變數必定會影響中介變數；(2)自變數也必定會影響依變數；(3)中介變數必定會影響依變數；(4)自變數對依變數的影響在上述步驟(3)的情況會小於步驟(2)的情況。此外，在中介變數被控制的情況下，若自變數對依變數影響程度為0，則具有完全中介效果（Full Mediation）；若自變數對依變數的影響小於步驟(2)的情況，但仍具有統計顯著性，則稱為具有部分中介效果（Partial Mediation）。

本研究顧客忠誠在服務品質對顧客再購買意願影響的中介效果，採用階層迴歸分析，將兩組自變數——服務品質與顧客忠誠及品牌形象與顧客忠誠依序投入模型中，以顧客再購買意願做為依變數，觀察加入控制中介變數（顧客忠誠）前後，對結果變數（顧客再購買意願）的影響力（β值）及解釋能力（$\triangle R^2$）的變化，檢定結果整理如表4-14所示。比較模型2與模型4，可以發現

表4-14

顧客忠誠在服務品質對顧客再購買意願影響的中介效果分析

| | 依變數 | | | |
|---|---|---|---|---|
| | 顧客忠誠 | 顧客再購意願 | 顧客再購意願 | 顧客再購意願 |
| | 各模型β係數 | 各模型β係數 | 各模型β係數 | 各模型β係數 |
| 自變數 | 模型 1 | 模型 2 | 模型 3 | 模型 4 |
| 服務品質 | 0.713** | 0.660** | | 0.311** |
| 顧客忠誠 | | | 0.672** | 0.489** |
| $R^2$ | 0.418 | 0.370 | 0.466 | 0.513 |
| $\triangle R^2$ | | | | 0.143 |
| F值 | 307.851** | 252.040** | 374.195** | 226.136** |

註：* 為 p 值 < 0.1，** 為 p 值 < 0.05，*** 為 p 值 < 0.01

模型2服務品質對顧客再購買意願有顯著的影響（β = 0.660，p<0.05）。在模型4加入顧客忠誠後，服務品質對顧客再購買意願仍然有顯著的影響（β = 0.311，p<0.05），但β值由0.660降為0.311，顯示顧客忠誠在服務品質對顧客再購買意願的影響之間具有部分中介效果，因此研究假說獲得支持。

## 2.顧客忠誠在品牌形象對再購買意願影響的中介效果

顧客忠誠在品牌形象對再購買意願影響的中介效果，經採用層級迴歸檢定結果整理如表4-15所示。比較模型2與模型4，可以發現模型2品牌形象對顧客再購買意願有顯著的影響（β = 0.659，p<0.05）。在模型4加入顧客忠誠後，品牌形象對顧客再購買意願仍然有顯著的影響（β = 0.373，p<0.05），但β值由0.659降為0.373，顯示顧客忠誠在品牌形象對顧客再購買意願的影響之間具有部分中介效果，因此研究假說獲得支持。

**表4-15**
顧客忠誠在品牌形象對顧客再購買意願影響的中介效果分析

| 自變數 | 依變數 | | | |
|---|---|---|---|---|
| | 顧客忠誠 | 顧客再購意願 | 顧客再購意願 | 顧客再購意願 |
| | 各模型β係數 | 各模型β係數 | 各模型β係數 | 各模型β係數 |
| | 模型1 | 模型2 | 模型3 | 模型4 |
| 品牌形象 | 0.676** | 0.659** | | 0.373** |
| 顧客忠誠 | | | 0.672** | 0.424** |
| $R^2$ | 0.448 | 0.442 | 0.466 | 0.544 |
| $\triangle R^2$ | | | | 0.102 |
| F值 | 347.884** | 339.057** | 374.195** | 255.191** |

註：* 為 p 值 < 0.1，** 為 p 值 < 0.05，*** 為 p 值 < 0.01

## 1.研究假說1之檢定

本研究之觀念性架構如圖4-4所示，LISREL模型架構如圖4-5及表4-16所示。本文模型以LISREL最大概似估計法估計結果，模型路徑圖如圖4-6所示。

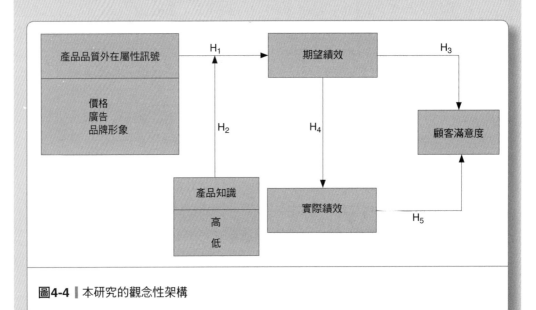

**圖4-4** ┃ 本研究的觀念性架構

在產品品質外在屬性訊號上，本研究預期價格、廣告與品牌形象對期望績效的影響係數為正值，且達到統計顯著性。由圖4-6可以發現，價格訊號對期望績效影響符號為負值（$\gamma_{11} = -0.019$），但未達統計顯著性；而廣告與品牌形象對期望績效影響符號皆為正值（$\gamma_{21} = 0.105$，$\gamma_{31} = 0.327$），並且都達到統計顯著性。由此可知，消費者應該會首先考量以品牌形象與廣告訊號做為筆記型電腦品質的訊號。此一訊息透露出當消費者所認知該筆記型電腦廠商的廣告量愈多，以及該廠商的品牌形象愈好時，對該筆記型電腦的期望品質會較高。所以，經由上述數據驗證結果顯示，研究假說1獲得部分支持，即價格會影響消費者對產品期望績效的假說未獲得支持，而廣告與品牌形象會影響消費者對產品期望績效的假說均獲得支持。

### 2.研究假說2之檢定

研究假說2是要驗證消費者產品知識的高低，影響產品品質外在屬性訊號對產品期望績效的干擾效果，乃參考林若慧（1988）、蘇明芳（1999）認為LISREL模式中存在著干擾變數的處理方法，分別處理高產品知識群與低產品知識群的LISREL模型。

本研究從問卷中的產品知識的五個題項，由受訪者勾選自己所擁有產品知識的自信程度，每題分數最高分為7分，最低分為1分，將每一位受訪者依五題平均分數之高低，由低到高排序，測量受訪者的主觀產品知識。另參考Bettman and Park（1980）指出消費者有中度產品知識群存在的觀點，故以整體消費者產品知識平均分數4.47為基準，將平均分數在5分以上者歸為高產品知識群，平均分數在4分以下者歸為低產品知識群，以確保能確實區分出高產品知識的消費者與低產品知識的消費者。最後以變異數分析檢定這兩群的F值為476.63（p<0.05），結果顯示高產品知識群與低產品知識群，確實呈現統計顯著性。高產品知識群與低產品知識群的LISREL的模型，如圖4-7所示。

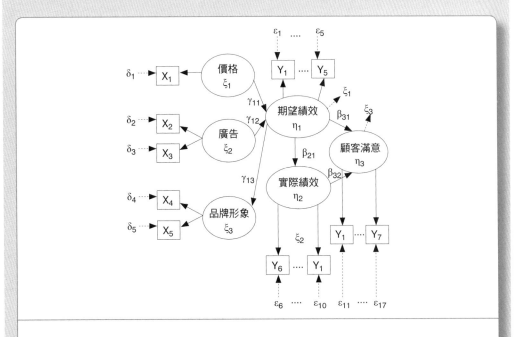

**圖4-5** ┃LISREL模型架構圖

　　至於低產品知識群對產品品質外在屬性訊號對產品期望績效認知之干擾效果，本研究發現除了價格訊號為負值，且未達統計顯著性（$\gamma_{11} = -0.052$）之外，廣告訊號與品牌形象均會顯著且正向的影響期望績效（$\gamma_{21} = 0.164$，$\gamma_{31} = 0.309$）。而在高產品知識群對產品品質外在屬性訊號對產品期望績效認知之干擾效果中，本研究發現除了價格不會顯著的影響實際績效（$\gamma_{11} = 0.027$）之外，廣告與品牌形象對實際績效的影響均呈統計顯著性，而且是正向影響效果（$\gamma_{21} = 0.156$，$\gamma_{31} = 0.273$）。根據上述數據驗證結果顯示，本研究假說2獲得部分支持，也就是子假說2-1未獲得支持，子假說2-2與2-3均獲得支持。

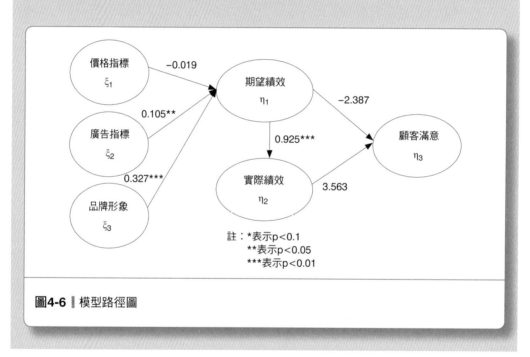

**圖4-6** ▎模型路徑圖

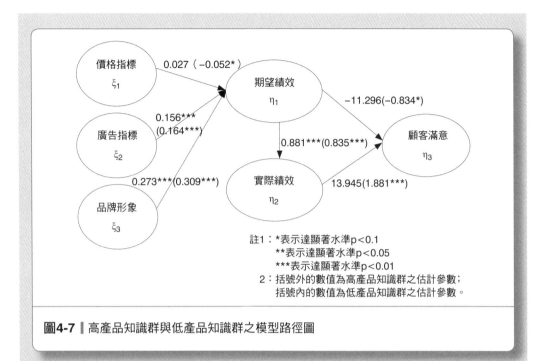

**圖4-7** ｜ 高產品知識群與低產品知識群之模型路徑圖

### 3.研究假說3、4、5之檢定

　　本研究在內生隱藏變數的探討中，分別探討消費者對產品的期望績效、實際績效與顧客滿意三者之間的關係。由表4-18的數據可知，在直接效果方面，本研究發現期望績效對實際績效之影響效果為正數（$\beta_{21} = 0.925$），且有高度統計顯著性，與理論預期相吻合，顯示期望績效愈高，會正向影響實際績效。其次，期望績效對顧客滿意的影響為負數（$\beta_{31} = -2.387$），不過並未達到統計顯著性，雖然$\beta_{31}$估計值頗大，不過由於此參數的標準誤頗大，達2.652（$t = -2.387/2.652 = -0.9$），模式內的每一個參數值是否都達到顯著水準，也是檢測模式內在品質的一項重要訊號。由於本模式的參數共有$\lambda^x_{31}$、$\beta_{31}$、$\beta_{32}$與$\gamma_{11}$四個估計參數未達統計顯著水準，故本模式內在品質似乎不盡理想。另外，本研究也發現實際績效對顧客滿意的影響為正向，不過並未達到統計顯著性（$\beta_{32} = 3.563$，$t = 3.563/2.80 = 1.272$）。由上述的驗證可知，就直接影響效果而言，研究假說3與研究假說5未獲得支持，而研究假說4則獲得強烈支持。

　　在隱藏變數（$\xi$與$\eta$）之間接效果與總效果（總效果＝直接效果＋間接效果）的驗證方面，首先以表4-17彙總外生隱藏變數對內生變數之間接效果。由表4-17可知廣告與品牌形象對期望績效影響的總效果為最大（分別為0.105與0.327），且達到統計顯著水準，表示做為產品品質外在屬性訊號的功能很強。同時，由於廣告與品牌形象對期望績效、實際績效（0.097與0.302）與顧客滿意（0.095與0.297）之總效果均為正，且達到統計顯著水準。由此可知，消費者對該廠牌的廣告量與品牌形象的認知評價愈高，會正向的提升期望績效與實際績效，進而提高顧客滿意程度。在各項效果影響的程度而言，品牌形象都大於廣告與價格訊號。

其次，以表4-18說明內生隱藏變數之間的間接效果與總效果。由表4-18的數據可知，期望績效對實際績效與顧客滿意之總效果均為正數，且達到統計顯著水準（0.925與0.907），此一數據除了再次證實研究假說4獲得支持之外，亦證實期望績效透過實際績效影響顧客滿意的間接效果。而實際績效對顧客滿意之總效果為正數（3.563，t = 1.272），不過並未達到統計顯著水準，期望績效對顧客滿意程度的總效果為最大（0.907，t = 5.533），此一結果透露一個事實，即實際績效與期望績效不具單獨影響效果，兩者必須相輔相成，才足以影響顧客滿意，因為顧客滿意通常是以實際績效與期望績效比較的結果來評價的。此一結果與Churchill and Suprenant（1985）、林陽助（1996）、李佳璋（1997）的研究發現並不一致，這幾位學者認為，在耐久財中（收音機與汽車），實際績效為影響顧客滿意度的最重要因素。此外，期望之表現透過實際績效的間接影響，最後對顧客滿意的總效果為0.907（t = 5.533），其影響力甚至比實際績效對顧客滿意之總效果（3.563，t = 1.272）還來得大，此結果與李佳璋（1997）的研究結果相吻合。

**表4-16**

潛在變數與觀察變數

| 潛在變數 | |
| --- | --- |
| 自變數 | 依變數 |
| $\xi_1$：價格 | $\eta_1$：期望績效 |
| $\xi_2$：廣告 | $\eta_2$：實際績效 |
| $\xi_3$：品牌形象 | $\eta_3$：顧客滿意 |

| 觀察變數 | | |
| --- | --- | --- |
| 自變數 | 依變數 | |
| $X_1$：購買該筆記型電腦時的價位 | $Y_1$：期望績效廣告可信度 | $Y_2$：期望績效經銷商表現 |
| | $Y_3$：期望績效產品品質與功能表現 | $Y_4$：期望績效外型表現 |
| $X_2$：消費者受廣告宣傳的影響程度 | | $Y_6$：實際績效廣告可信度 |
| | $Y_5$：期望績效售後服務 | $Y_8$：實際績效產品品質與功能表現 |
| | $Y_7$：實際績效經銷商表現 | |

**表4-16**
潛在變數與觀察變數（續）

| | 潛在變數 | |
|---|---|---|
| 自變數 | 依變數 | |
| $X_3$：消費者所認知的 廣告量 | $Y_9$：實際績效外型表現 | $Y_{10}$：實際績效售後服務 |
| $X_4$：消費者所認知筆 記型電腦廠牌的 優點 | $Y_{11}$：顧客滿意的廣告可信 度 | $Y_{12}$：顧客滿意的經銷商表現 |
| $X_5$：消費者所認知該 廠牌與其他廠牌 之差異 | $Y_{13}$：顧客滿意的售後服務 $Y_{15}$：顧客滿意的外型表現 | $Y_{14}$：顧客滿意的產品品質與功能 表現 $Y_{16}$：就整體品質而言，價格的合 理性 $Y_{17}$：就價格而言，整體品質的合 理性 |

**表4-17**
ξ 對η的直接效果、間接效果與總效果

| | 效果 | 價格（$\xi_1$） | 廣告（$\xi_2$） | 品牌形象（$\xi_3$） |
|---|---|---|---|---|
| | 直接 | −0.019(−0.610) | 0.105(2.007) | 0.327(4.701) |
| 期望績效$\eta_1$ | 間接 | 0.000 | 0.000 | 0.000 |
| | 總效果 | −0.019(−0.610) | 0.105(2.007) | 0.327(4.701) |
| | 直接 | 0.000 | 0.000 | 0.000 |
| 實際績效$\eta_2$ | 間接 | −0.018(−0.609) | 0.097(2.003) | 0.302(4.648) |
| | 總效果 | −0.018(−0.609) | 0.097(2.003) | 0.302(4.648) |
| | 直接 | 0.000 | 0.000 | 0.000 |
| 顧客滿意$\eta_3$ | 間接 | −0.017(−0.601) | 0.095(2.018) | 0.297(4.839) |
| | 總效果 | −0.017(−0.601) | 0.095(2.018) | 0.297(4.839) |

註：括號內的數值為t值

**表4-18**
η對η的直接效果、間接效果與總效果

| | 效果 | 期望績效（$\eta_1$） | 實際績效（$\eta_2$） | 顧客滿意（$\eta_3$） |
|---|---|---|---|---|
| | 直接 | 0.000 | 0.000 | 0.000 |
| 期望績效（$\eta_1$） | 間接 | 0.000 | 0.000 | 0.000 |
| | 總效果 | 0.000 | 0.000 | 0.000 |
| | 直接 | 0.925(5.252) | 0.000 | 0.000 |
| 實際績效（$\eta_2$） | 間接 | 0.000 | 0.000 | 0.000 |
| | 總效果 | 0.925(5.252) | 0.000 | 0.000 |

表4-18 |
η對η的直接效果、間接效果與總效果（續）

| | 效果 | 期望績效（$\eta_1$） | 實際績效（$\eta_2$） | 顧客滿意（$\eta_3$） |
|---|---|---|---|---|
| | 直接 | −2.387(−0.900) | 3.653(1.272) | 0.000 |
| 顧客滿意（$\eta_3$） | 間接 | 3.249(1.226) | 0.000 | 0.000 |
| | 總效果 | 0.907(5.533) | 3.653(1.272) | 0.000 |

註：括號內的數值為t值

---

## 【實例】
## 「老年經濟安全保障、理財知識與逆向抵押貸款意願之研究」，假說檢定方法實例
### （林隆儀、商懿勻，2015）

　　本研究所蒐集的資料採用階層迴歸分析，其檢定結果整理如表4-19所示。

### 1. 老年經濟安全保障對逆向抵押貸款借款意願的影響

　　由表4-19中模式一的檢定結果可知，其對逆向抵押貸款意願的解釋能力為45.0%（$R^2 = 0.450$；$\Delta R^2 = 0.450$；$F = 66.119$），判定模型合適性的$p < 0.01$，具有統計顯著性。共線性統計量的VIF值皆小於10，符合迴歸分析無共線性需求（Kennedy, 1992），可知共線性不明顯，並不會影響本研究中有關統計數據的精確性與結果解釋。

　　其中基本生活需求之β係數為0.112，$t = 2.868$，$p < 0.05$，具有統計顯著性，表示基本生活需求對逆向抵押貸款借款意願有顯著的正向影響，故假說1-1獲得支持；經濟安全需求的β係數為0.088，$t = 2.220$，$p < 0.1$，具有統計顯著性，顯示經濟安全需求對逆向抵押貸款借款意願有顯著的正向影響，假說1-2亦獲得支持。

**表4-19**

階層迴歸分析（依變數：逆向抵押貸款借款意願）

| 自變數 | 模式1 | 模式2 | 模式3 | VIFs |
|---|---|---|---|---|
| 主效果 | | | | |
| 基本生活需求 | 0.112**(2.868) | 0.124***(3.212) | 0.133***(3.427) | 1.228 |
| 經濟安全需求 | 0.088*(2.220) | 0.074*(1.891) | 0.070*(1.790) | 1.239 |
| 借貸規劃 | 0.076*(2.059) | 0.080*(2.231) | 0.097*(2.649) | 1.094 |
| 退休規劃 | 0.098*(2.623) | 0.153***(4.123) | 0.152***(4.113) | 1.123 |
| 涉入 | 0.601***(15.802) | 0.569***(15.304) | 0.577***(15.514) | 1.137 |
| 雙因子交互作用 | | | | |
| 基本生活×借貸規劃 | | 0.106*(2.612) | 0.101*(2.494) | 1.336 |
| 基本生活×退休規劃 | | 0.068*(1.825) | 0.070*(1.880) | 1.137 |
| 經濟安全×借貸規劃 | | 0.073*(1.849) | 0.075*(1.908) | 1.261 |
| 經濟安全×退休規劃 | | 0.071*(1.911) | 0.078*(2.097) | 1.132 |
| 基本生活×涉入 | | 0.122**(3.174) | 0.123***(3.202) | 1.209 |
| 經濟安全×涉入 | | 0.098*(2.577) | 0.121**(3.082) | 1.263 |
| 借貸規劃×涉入 | | 0.098*(2.550) | 0.107*(2.778) | 1.208 |
| 退休規劃×涉入 | | 0.065*(1.767) | 0.067*(1.816) | 1.105 |
| 三因子交互作用 | | | | |
| 經濟×理財×涉入 | | | 0.084*(2.170) | 1.238 |
| F | 66.119*** | 32.101*** | 30.424*** | |
| ΔF | 66.119*** | 6.411*** | 4.711*** | |
| $R^2$ | 0.450 | 0.513 | 0.519 | |
| Adjusted $R^2$ | 0.443 | 0.497 | 0.502 | |
| $\Delta R^2$ | 0.450 | 0.063 | 0.006 | |

註：*為 p 值 < 0.10，**為 p 值 < 0.05，***為 p值 < 0.01

### 2. 理財知識對逆向抵押貸款借款意願的影響

　　同表4-19模式一的檢定結果顯示，借貸規劃的β值為0.076，t = 2.059，p < 0.1，具有統計顯著性，顯示借貸規劃對逆向抵押貸款意願有顯著的正向影響；退休規劃的β值0.098，t = 2.623，p < 0.1，具有統計顯著性，表示退休規劃對逆

向抵押貸款借款意願有顯著的正向影響。因此，假說2-1、假說2-2獲得支持。

### 3. 老年經濟安全保障與理財知識的交互作用對逆向抵押貸款借款意願的影響

本研究進一步檢定老年經濟安全保障與理財知識對逆向抵押貸款借款意願的交互作用，首先將所有變數進行中心化（Centering）後，再進行分析以避免共線性的問題產生（Aiken & West, 1991）。由表中數據可如，模式二可解釋逆向抵押貸款借款意願51.3%的變異量（$R^2 = 0.513$；$\Delta R^2 = 0.063$；$F = 32.101$；$p < 0.01$）。VIF值皆小於10，符合無共線性需求（Kennedy, 1992）。

依據表4-19模式二之分析結果顯示，基本生活需求與借貸規劃的交互作用的$\beta$值0.106，$t = 2.612$，$p < 0.1$；基本生活需求與退休規劃的交互作用之$\beta$值為0.068，$t = 1.825$，$p < 0.1$；經濟安全需求與借貸規劃的交互作用的$\beta$值為0.073，$t = 1.849$，$p < 0.1$；經濟安全需求與退休規劃的交互作用的$\beta$值為0.071，$t = 1.911$，$p < 0.1$。根據結果得知，老年經濟安全保障與理財知識的交互作用對逆向抵押貸款借款意願有顯著的正向影響。故研究假說3獲得支持。

### 4. 涉入在老年經濟安全保障對逆向抵押貸款借款意願影響的干擾效果

探討涉入程度在老年經濟安全保障對逆向抵押貸款借款意願干擾效果分析，其檢定結果如模式二所示，基本生活需求與涉入干擾的$\beta$值為0.122，$t = 3.174$，$p < 0.05$；經濟安全需求與涉入干擾的$\beta$值為0.098，$t = 2.577$，$p < 0.1$。根據結果得知，基本生活需求和經濟安全需求在涉入的干擾下對逆向抵押貸款借款意願有顯著的正向影響，研究假說4-1、假說4-2獲得支持。

### 5. 涉入在理財知識對逆向抵押貸款借款意願影響的干擾效果

將涉入在理財知識對逆向抵押貸款借款意願的干擾效果進行迴歸分析，其檢定結果如模式二所示，涉入程度在借貸規劃對逆向抵押貸款借款意願的干擾效果之$\beta$值0.098，$t = 2.550$，$p < 0.1$；退休規劃對逆向抵押貸款借款意願的影響，涉入的干擾效果之$\beta$值為0.065，$t = 1.767$，$p = 0.1$。根據結果得知，涉入在理財知識對逆向抵押貸款借款意願的影響有顯著的正向干擾效果，研究假說5-1、假說5-2亦獲得支持。

### 6. 涉入在老年經濟安全保障與理財知識的交互作用對逆向抵押貸款借款意願影響的干擾效果

在探究涉入程度在老年經濟安全保障與理財知識的交互作用對逆向抵押貸

款借款意願的干擾效果時，首先將所有變數進行中心化後，再進行分析以避免共線性的問題產生（Aiken & West, 1991）。由表4-19中數據可知，模式三整體可解釋逆向抵押貸款借款意願51.9%的變異量（$R^2 = 0.519$；$\Delta R^2 = 0.006$；$F = 30.424$），判定模型合適性的$p < 0.01$，具有統計顯著性，VIF值小於10，符合無共線性需求，並不會影響研究中統計數據的精確性與結果解釋（Kennedy, 1992）。

如模式三所示，涉入程度在經濟安全保障與理財知識的交互作用對逆向抵押貸款意願的影響中，其干擾β值為0.084，$t = 2.170$，$p < 0.1$。根據結果得知，涉入在老年經濟安全保障與理財知識的交互作用對逆向抵押貸款借款意願影響的正向干擾效果。研究假說6亦獲得支持。

# 七、討論

完成研究假說檢定之後，需要進行討論，將檢定過程中所發現的現象或結論做一番討論。討論的要領之一是，獲得支持的研究假說需要做摘要式討論，沒有獲得支持的研究假說則需要做深入討論，明確指出研究假說未獲得支持的主要原因，讓讀者有更深一層的瞭解。

討論的第二個要領是，除了審視檢定過程中的細節與數據之外，可以回過頭來檢視相關分析所獲得的數據，通常都可以為研究假說未獲得支持找到可能的原因。例如：研究假說檢定結果雖然具有統計顯著性，但是正負符號卻相反，因此判定未獲得支持，此時再回過頭檢視相關分析，發現兩個變數之間呈現負相關，如此一來，研究假說未能獲得支持的原因就更明朗了。

> **【實例】**
> **「議題行銷之社會顯著性、活動持續度與執行保證對品牌權益的影響」，檢定結果討論實例**
> （林隆儀，2010）

……假說1檢定結果顯示，企業參與議題行銷活動，選擇社會顯著性高的議題比選擇社會顯著性低的議題，對企業品牌權益有較佳的增強效果。有些研究討論到參與議題行銷時，大多與企業或產品特性相配適為出發點（顏龍蒂，1999；江雨潔，2002）。諸如味全公司選擇環保概念的「救地球」議題，TVBS選擇關懷偏遠地區「兒童教育」議題，Nike運動鞋選擇體育類活動，不勝枚舉。品牌形象包含品牌聯想的強度，因此符合品牌形象的活動誠然無害於品牌權益。然而消費者通常都喜歡選用評價較高品牌的產品，但是對與品牌相配適的活動往往抱著低度關心。企業在建立品牌權益或轉換品牌形象時，結合目標消費者所關心的活動，更有助於吸引較多消費者的注意，進而改善品牌形象。因此透過結合議題行銷活動的品牌，在選擇活動議題時，應思索目標消費者是否關心公司所選擇搭配的議題，或是應尋求目標消費者所關心的議題。畢竟議題行銷是結合產品銷售與消費者對議題之興趣與贊助的一種活動，選對議題更有助於運用議題行銷提高品牌權益。

假說2檢定結果顯示，企業實行議題行銷時，採行持續度較高的活動對企業品牌權益具有較佳的增強效果。議題行銷對許多品牌而言已是行之有年的活動，其中有許多品牌以類似認養議題的方式，長期參與活動而獲得消費者的信任，這些企業視議題行銷為贊助議題的好機會，容易被認為參與活動是出自於真正關心議題，而有助於品牌權益之增進。尤其是議題行銷活動的特質結合銷售及募款活動時，容易使消費者認為企業參與活動是經由議題圖利或懷疑其贊助議題，而形成負面評價。但經由企業對議題長期參與之宣示與行動，不但可消除消費者之疑慮，另一方面也可將消費者對議題之關心轉化為對參與活動品牌之喜愛，進而對於其品牌權益有所助益。

假說3-1與假說3-2的檢定結果顯示，企業實行議題行銷時，選擇社會顯著性低的議題，搭配持續度高的活動，對企業的品牌權益具有較佳的增進效果；企業實行議題行銷，選擇社會顯著性高的議題時，活動持續度高、低對其品牌權益的影響沒有顯著差異。此一結果反映出消費者在企業結合社會顯著性高的議題時，因為認同此議題應獲得贊助，所以容易信任參與活動的品牌，將贊助議題之喜愛轉嫁於對參與活動品牌之評價，因而在企業長期參與的宣示下，不容易在短時間內消除消費者對議題的懷疑，對品牌權益的增進也就幫助不大了。但選擇社會顯著性低的議題時，因消費者並不視此議題應獲得積極參與，或不支持對議題的贊助，因而不容易信任參與活動的品牌；但藉由長期參與活動之宣示，表達企業的真誠態度，因而影響消費者對其品牌之評價，則有助於增進品牌權益。

假說4檢定結果顯示，企業實行議題行銷時，有無執行保證對其品牌權益的影響沒有顯著的差異。這也許是消費者對一般活動委託專業人士進行監督，或公布相關活動重要訊息的方式，不認為具有公信力，使得消費者對企業是否實踐其主張，仍然抱持懷疑的態度。若企業能發展出更具公開化的方式，或由更具公信力之團體監督活動之進行，例如：活動之初便將產品銷售收入交付信託，或許可以消除消費者的疑慮。也有可能是消費者實際上並不認為提供活動監督在議題行銷活動中扮演重要角色，意即在改善消費者的疑慮，使消費者信賴企業參與活動動機方面，消費者也許更注重企業對議題的持續關注，而不認為提供對活動的公信力就能表達企業真誠關心議題。此時，消費者也許不會將企業在活動中所表達的公信力轉化為對品牌的良好評價，畢竟當消費者感覺到企業執行議題行銷的目的是在促銷產品時，縱使消費者相信企業所提供具有公信力的訊息，以及對活動之監督，仍難以消除消費者對企業藉由議題圖利之疑慮，以致令企業無法因此有所作為而達到改善消費者對其品牌權益之評價。

假說5-1與假說5-2的檢定結果顯示，企業實行議題行銷，選擇社會顯著性高的議題時，有無執行保證之活動，對品牌權益的影響沒有顯著的差異。企業實行議題行銷，選擇社會顯著性低的議題，搭配有無執行保證之活動，對品牌權益的影響也沒有顯著的差異。此結論顯示，不論企業選擇社會顯著性高或低的議題，有無執行保證，皆不影響消費者對品牌權益之評價。如同假說4檢定結果，本研究發現執行保證很難使消費者對品牌權益產生正面的評價，即使結合社會顯著性有所差異的議題亦同。

---

**【實例】**
**「消費遠視症者之反自我控制問題研究」，檢定結果綜合討論實例**
（商懿勻，2021）

本研究假設消費者先天皆具有消費決策遠視症，即消費者為符合社會規範的期望與道德束縛，壓抑內在對於放縱性決策的渴望與需求，產生放縱性避免的決策行為，以預防負面情緒的產生。共設計一系列四組購買實驗情境，用以幫助消費遠視者掙脫反自我控制的影響。主要目的為幫助消費遠視症者掙脫反自我控制的影響，鼓勵消費遠視症者勇於放縱自我，以避免長期而言損害自身的幸福感，甚至產生後悔的情緒。本研究於購物方案決策前／後不同時間點，藉由（正面／負面）情緒帳戶與（正性／負性）訊息框架的干擾組合，探討不同操弄機制對於放縱性避免影響效果優劣。將各實驗研究結果整理如表4-20所示。

論文寫作要領

**表4-20**
放縱性避免影響效果比較表

| | 情境 | 干擾因素 | 放縱性避免 | 平均 | 減緩效果 | 平均 | 減緩效果排名 |
|---|---|---|---|---|---|---|---|
| 實驗一 | A | 負面情緒 | 62.82% | 60.63% | 6.74% | 8.93% | 8 |
| | B | 正面情緒 | 58.44% | | 11.12% | | 6 |
| 實驗二 | C | 負性訊息框架 | 45.88% | 37.11% | 23.68% | 32.46% | 4 |
| | D | 正性訊息框架 | 28.33% | | 41.23% | | 1 |
| 實驗三 | E | 負面情緒 + 正性訊息框架 | 40.90% | | 29.46% | | 2 |
| | F | 負面情緒 + 負性訊息框架 | 59.26% | 49.19% | 10.30% | 20.57% | 7 |
| | G | 正面情緒 + 正性訊息框架 | 44.45% | | 25.11% | | 3 |
| | H | 正面情緒 + 負性訊息框架 | 52.17% | | 17.39% | | 5 |
| | | 總平均 | 48.93% | | 20.63% | | |

說明：影響效果為與對照組的69.56%放縱性避免程度相較之結果

　　由表4-20可知，無論於消費者購物前或後，施行任何干擾都能順利減緩反自我控制效果，平均可提升20.63%，成功幫助原先偏好實利性決策導向的消費遠視症者掙脫反自我控制的問題。其中在消費者心中已有既定決策方案雛型時（平均：32.46%），再施於增強物的刺激，其減緩效果較消費者未有既定方案時（平均：8.93%）高出近3.6倍之多，可能的原因為當消費者內心已有既定的決策方案時，表示決策者在做出決策方案前，勢必歷經一定程度的產品資訊蒐集與涉入，已具有相當程度的產品知識且確實具有購物慾望，但礙於消費遠視症者獨特的決策特質，最後可能會因為反自我控制的約束力，屈就於現實、責任、價值觀，和社會輿論的道德壓力，迫使自己選擇最適當的決策品項或方案，並非內心所喜好或渴望的夢幻逸品。因此，在消費者已有既定決策方式時（決策後），再適時施行訊息框架效應，來逆轉消費遠視症者的購物屬性偏好是最佳的時機點。其中又以正性訊息框架，最能幫助消費遠視症者洗滌從事放縱性決策的罪惡感，並獲得決策合理化與正當性，具有自我增強的效果（Strahilevitz and Myers, 1998），成功達到減緩消費遠視症者反自我控制問題的影響，這是所有干擾機制中效果最佳的型式。

若是消費者在尚未做出實際的購買決策前，就先行操弄情緒帳戶的影響力，誘發前事實思考影響購買決策，亦可降低放縱性避免，提升放縱性決策偏好，但無論是正面情緒帳戶或負面情緒帳戶其效果有限。其中若是於購買決策前進行負面情緒帳戶干擾，會使得消費遠視症者因消費金錢來自非正當性來源，而產生罪惡、自責、羞愧感等負面情緒的連結，決策者為平衡情緒矛盾感，並且又要符合社會大眾所期待的規範標準，反而會更加傾向實利性的決策方案，以修補負面情緒減輕罪惡與自責感（O'Curry and Strahilevitz, 2001）。此心理運作都是反自我控制所帶來的影響，因消費遠視症者為避免後悔與內疚情緒，進而產生過度遠視和自負的決策思維，使最初的購買決策方案會偏向實利性導向產生放縱性避免的情況，倘若能於消費遠視症者有初步的購買想法後，再實施正性訊息框架干擾，便可提供消費遠視症從事放縱性行為決策的正當性理由，安撫消費遠視症者因為負面情緒帳戶誘發的罪惡與自責感，產生淨化效果，得以順利幫助消費遠視症者掙脫反自我控制的影響。因此，廠商應當避免讓消費者在尚未購物前，對於消費購物金產生負面情緒的感受，應誘導消費者對於金錢產生正面情緒的思考，幫助消費遠視症者洗滌內心的罪惡感，並提升採購的意願。若是消費者於一開始就對金錢來源已有根深蒂固的負面感受，亦可在其建構最終購買決策方案前，及時執行正性訊息框架機制的二次干擾，亦可達到一定程度的減緩效果。其中雙種干擾又以負面情緒帳戶（決策前）和正性訊息框架（決策後）的干擾組合，最具影響效力。

# 八、結語

資料分析是要把研究過程中所蒐集的資料（Data），利用各種統計方法，轉換為具有特定意義與參考價值的資訊（Information），也是使研究結果充分表現出科學精神的一面。一則讓研究者得以更有技巧的呈現研究成果，將研究成果做更有意義的解讀與更有價值的貢獻；再則可以讓閱讀者更

容易掌握重點，更有助於吸取及應用研究的精華。尤其是企業經理人日常工作繁忙，通常都希望從他人的研究結論中吸取具有實務參考價值的資訊，所以，資料分析除了分析及呈現研究結果之重要資訊外，還扮演解讀及應用等臨門一腳的角色。

資料分析結果除了以文字描述之外，適當的以圖、表呈現，往往可發揮畫龍點睛的效果。資料分析結果輔之以圖、表的呈現，除了可以發揮佐證的功能之外，還具有讓讀者一目了然的功效。尤其是高階主管日理萬機，通常都希望迅速掌握重點、快速進入情況，此時以圖、表呈現最能發揮功效。畫圖與列表也是一種重要的技巧，研究者在專精於研究之外，也需要熟悉畫圖和列表的技巧。

資料分析的過程相當冗長，研究者需要按部就班、耐心的逐步分析、一一驗證，把檢定所獲得的資訊與結果，做最真實、最生動的呈現。利用簡明的圖、表來說明複雜的概念，利用具體的數據增強溝通與說服效果，甚至利用圖、表的呈現技巧協助思考與邏輯，都是使論文更加活潑生動的方法。資料分析的每一個細節都很重要，描述及交代愈詳細，讀者愈容易瞭解；佐證數據列舉愈具體，愈能突顯文章的可信度及參考價值。

# 第五章
# 結論與建議

## 一、前言

　　研究資料經過統計分析及假說檢定之後，接著就要具體提出研究結論與建議。論文第五章「結論與建議」，通常必須包括研究結論、管理意涵、研究限制、研究建議等四部分。研究結論（Conclusion）旨在將前述各章節所做的論述、分析、研究假說檢定結果，以及研究發現做一個總結，並做最後的論斷。管理意涵（Management Implication）是要指出研究所獲得的結論及發現，在管理上、理論上或實務應用上，具有什麼特殊的意義與貢獻。研究限制（Limitation）是在說明研究設計及研究計畫執行過程中所受的限制。研究建議（Suggestion）則是要根據研究所獲得的結論，提出有意義的建議。

# 二、研究結論

　　結論者，結束上文的論述，並做最後的論斷也。論文撰寫進行到第五章，表示研究工作已經完成一大半，並且進入收尾階段。研究結論主要是要把第四章資料分析結果，最具精華、最重要的研究發現一一呈現出來，讓讀者可以一目了然的掌握本研究的重要發現，以及本篇論文的具體結論。

　　研究結論看似簡單，但是只要翻閱已經完成的論文，就會發現研究結論內容的呈現手法各異其趣、寫法參差不齊、編排方式不一，顯然是沒有掌握研究結論的寫作要領。

　　撰寫研究結論有幾個要領，只要掌握這幾個要領，就可以把研究所獲得的結論做有系統且有意義的呈現。撰寫研究結論的第一個要領是檢視研究命題推論結果，以及研究假說檢定結果，將推論及檢定結果以條列方式具體寫出來；如果有必要，僅做簡單扼要的說明即可，無須長篇大論。檢視研究命題是質化研究的重頭戲，檢定研究假說則是實證研究最重要的目的，發展研究命題的目的是在提出合乎科學與邏輯的命題，以發展模型為目的的研究更需要具體提出研究模型。因此，在研究結論中，必須優先檢視研究命題發展、假說檢定、模型發展等結果，並做具體的呈現。

　　第二個要領是以研究發現為基礎，確實、忠實、務實、踏實的寫出研究所獲得的結論，與研究發現沒有直接關係的資訊則不宜出現在研究結論中。研究結論是要將整個研究做一個總結，既然是「結論」與「總結」，就必須直截了當的提出研究結論，不宜拖泥帶水，更不宜納入風馬牛不相關的資訊。

　　第三個要領是以文字方式呈現，無須再重複列表，因為第四章已經將研究命題發展結果及研究假說檢定結果列表呈現。研究結論的呈現必須做到直接、簡潔、扼要，做最佳的呈現，讓讀者容易閱讀、容易理解。

**【實例】**

**「來源國形象與品牌知名度的組合效果對消費者購買意圖的影響——產品涉入的干擾效果」研究結論實例**

（林隆儀、陳俊碩，2010）

……本研究經命題發展結果，獲得下列重要結論：

1. 品牌來源國形象與製造國形象之組合，對消費者購買意圖會有顯著的正向影響。

2. 品牌來源國形象與品牌知名度之組合，對消費者購買意圖會有顯著的正向影響。

3. 產品製造國形象與品牌知名度之組合，對消費者購買意圖會有顯著的正向影響。

4. 品牌來源國形象、產品製造國形象、品牌知名度之組合，對消費者購買意圖會有顯著的正向影響。

5. 消費者的產品涉入，在品牌來源國形象與產品製造國形象之組合，對消費者購買意圖的影響會有正向干擾效果。

6. 消費者的產品涉入，在品牌來源國形象與品牌知名度之組合，對消費者購買意圖的影響會有正向干擾效果。

7. 消費者的產品涉入，在產品製造國形象與品牌知名度之組合，對消費者購買意圖的影響會有正向干擾效果。

8. 消費者的產品涉入，在品牌來源國形象、產品製造國形象、品牌知名度之組合，對消費者購買意圖的影響會有正向干擾效果。

**【實例】**

**「議題行銷的社會顯著性、活動持續度與執行保證對品牌權益的影響」研究結論實例**

（林隆儀，2010）

……本研究經實證結果，獲得下列重要結論：

1. 企業選擇社會顯著性高的議題，對品牌權益的影響顯著高於社會顯著性低的議題。

2. 議題行銷活動持續度高，對品牌權益的影響顯著高於持續度低的活動。

3.企業選擇社會顯著性高的議題結合持續度高、低的活動，對品牌權益的影響沒有顯著的差異；企業選擇社會顯著性低的議題結合持續度高的活動，對品牌權益的影響顯著高於結合持續度低的活動。

4.議題行銷有無執行保證，對品牌權益的影響沒有顯著的差異。

5.企業選擇社會顯著性高或低的議題，無論是結合有無執行保證的計畫，對品牌權益的影響都沒有顯著的差異。

---

## 【實例】
## 「寬頻網路關係行銷結合類型、服務品質、關係品質與轉換成本對顧客忠誠之影響」研究結論實例
### （林隆儀、徐稚軒、陳俊碩，2009）

……本研究經實證結果，獲得下列重要結論：

### 1.關係行銷結合類型對關係品質有顯著正向影響

根據研究結果發現，關係行銷結合類型對關係品質有顯著的正向影響。雖然三種關係行銷結合類型對關係品質的影響程度順序，與研究假說的推論並沒有完全相符，但是仍舊以結構性結合為最高，代表結構性結合是提升顧客對廠商的信任與承諾最有效的策略。

### 2.關係行銷結合類型對轉換成本有顯著的正向影響

根據研究結果發現，關係行銷結合類型對轉換成本有顯著的正向影響。雖然三種關係行銷結合類型對轉換成本的損失績效成本之影響程度，與研究假說的推論並不完全一致，但三種關係行銷結合類型對轉換成本都有顯著的正向影響，表示關係行銷結合類型可以有效提升顧客的轉換成本。

### 3.服務品質對關係品質有顯著的正向影響

根據研究結果發現，服務品質對關係品質有顯著的正向影響，表示企業服務品質的好壞，可以決定顧客是否願意信任該企業及對該企業的承諾。雖然目前所有企業都強調服務品質，服務品質確實可以有效提升顧客與企業之間的關係品質。

### 4.服務品質對轉換成本有顯著的正向影響

　　根據研究結果發現，除可靠性外，服務品質的其餘構面，對轉換成本皆有顯著的正向影響。因此，當消費者欲轉換供應商而考量到轉換成本時，企業的服務品質好壞，會成為消費者衡量轉換成本的一項重要因素。而當消費者感受到愈優良的服務品質，其知覺到的轉換成本也愈高。

### 5.關係品質對顧客忠誠有顯著的正向影響

　　根據研究結果發現，關係品質對顧客忠誠有顯著的正向影響，表示當顧客對企業的信任與承諾程度愈高，愈願意持續對該企業表現忠誠行為。

### 6.轉換成本對顧客忠誠有顯著的正向影響

　　根據研究結果發現，轉換成本中的沉沒成本對顧客的態度忠誠、轉換成本中的損失績效成本與沉沒成本對顧客的行為忠誠，皆有顯著的正向影響。因此對顧客而言，轉換成本的存在可以使顧客在轉換供應商時，因為受到轉換成本的限制而持續與該企業保持交易關係。

# 三、管理意涵

　　管理意涵（Management Implication）或稱理論意涵（Theory Implication），是指研究發現在管理上或理論上所具有的特殊意義，這些意義之所以「特殊」，就是因為研究發現有其獨特之處，和其他意義有著明顯的差異，也是研究的主要貢獻之所在，值得提出來和讀者分享。研究過程中無論是研究設計或調查工作之執行，研究者都力求嚴謹與完美、全力以赴，因此，所獲得的研究結論通常也都具有獨特的意涵。研究結論既然具有獨特的意涵，就有必要、也值得將這些意涵做完整的呈現，以彰顯研究的貢獻與參考價值。

　　管理意涵到底要寫些什麼？如何寫？要寫到什麼程度？這是初學者最感困擾的課題之一。很多論文在結論中都沒有寫出「管理意涵」，因而留下遺珠之憾，殊屬可惜；有些論文雖然安排有「管理意涵」這個標題，但是所寫的內容和「管理意涵」相去太遠，殊屬不妥。為什麼會出現這種現象呢？問題就出在「管理意涵」確實不容易寫，而且不知如何下手，所以需要有人指點迷津、需要有人道破其中的盲點。

常見的現象是研究者把管理意涵、研究建議、研究限制混淆不清，或是將這三個項目的內容寫得很相似，甚至寫得一模一樣。其實意涵是意涵、建議是建議、限制是限制，絕對是不一樣的，不可混為一談。研究者需要頭腦清晰、冷靜思考，用心檢視你所寫管理意涵的內容，就不難發現所寫的內容是否適當。如果發現管理意涵的內容和研究建議相似，或和研究限制雷同，就表示一定有問題，這時候的問題通常都出現在管理意涵。

管理意涵的撰寫需要從多方面思考，前後呼應、用心評估、務實撰寫，才能夠寫出具有參考價值的管理意涵。管理意涵撰寫有下列幾個要領，第一個要領是拉高層次，站的高、看的遠，從管理或策略的角度思考研究發現的貢獻與價值。第二個要領是以研究發現為主軸，從中找出獨特的見解與意義。第三個要領是回過頭來對照論文第二章所探討的相關文獻，找出研究發現和文獻的異同，尤其是相異之處，引申出獨特的意義。第四個要領是務實的論述，完整呈現研究的貢獻與價值。

---

## 【實例】
### 「不同聯盟型態之下經濟誘因與信任之相對重要性研究──以臺灣清涼飲料產業為例」管理意涵實例
（林隆儀、黃營杉、吳青松，2004）

……本研究的結論與發現，具有下列三項管理意涵：

### 1.外包式策略聯盟型態有脈絡可循

外包式策略聯盟型態因過去缺乏相關研究，以致研究者無從得知其內涵與型態。本研究從價值活動的觀點，探討外包式策略聯盟的內涵，發現有五種聯盟型態。此一發現使外包式策略聯盟型態從此有脈絡可循，不僅可填補理論之部分空隙，在實務運用上也有一明確的型態可供參考。

### 2.豐富策略聯盟觀念與理論建構

以往學者探討策略聯盟，都是從單一理論著手。本研究參照Candace and Wiersema（1999）的觀點，提出一個兼具交易成本理論與社會交換理論的架構，同時融入交易成本理論與社會交換理論，有助於釐清策略聯盟觀念與彌補單一理論解釋之不足。同時引用兩個理論的觀點所形成的觀念架構，使策略聯盟觀念獲得嶄新的詮釋，一改以往單一理論解釋上的偏頗與不足之憾，不僅使策略聯盟理論結構更趨完整與合理，也因而豐富了策略聯盟觀念與理論的建構。

### 3.以經濟誘因抗衡信任風險

策略聯盟所涵蓋的價值活動項目愈多，愈偏向社會交換關係，因此也愈重視聯盟夥伴的信任。但是本研究的研究子假說4-3、4-4、5-3及5-4，經統計檢定結果卻未獲得支持。究其原因是價值活動項目愈多的策略聯盟，愈重視聯盟夥伴的信任；也因為過分重視聯盟夥伴的信任，而帶有信任的風險。風險沒有獨立性，聯盟安排太過單純時，廠商會尋求抗衡風險的方法。管理者在做決策時不能忘記，策略聯盟的基本目標是要以低成本、低風險的方法，透過聯盟機制的運作，追求最大的經濟利益，不能因為過分重視聯盟夥伴的信任，而犧牲聯盟的基本目標，此時最佳的決策，就是以經濟誘因抗衡信任風險。

此外，此一發現尚具有一重大的理論涵義。因為此一訊息正透露出經濟誘因乃是策略聯盟的基本目標，廠商締結策略聯盟無非是要追求經濟利益，因此沒有經濟誘因，策略聯盟即無存在的價值可言。

### 【實例】
## 「Consumer Perceptions of Price, Quality, and Value: A Means-End Model and Synthesis of Evidence」管理意涵實例
### （Zeithaml, 1988）

……本研究的結論，具有下列五項管理意涵：

### 1.縮小品質知覺的落差

雖然經理人愈來愈瞭解品質的重要性，但是許多經理人仍然繼續以公司的觀點來界定及衡量品質。縮小客觀與知覺品質之間的落差，需要從消費者的觀點看待品質。本研究所發現的線索非常重要，行銷經理必須深入瞭解消費者如何根據技術、客觀線索形成品質的印象。公司也可以從本研究的發現中，瞭解消費者所期望的品質構面而獲益。

### 2.辨識內在與外在屬性信號

行銷經理最優先的工作，是要發覺消費者用來辨識品質的許多內在與外在線索，此一過程包括審視消費者購買及使用產品的情境因素。不同產品類別的品質

是否有很大差異？品質是否不易評估？消費者購買之前，是否擁有足夠的產品內在屬性資訊？或是直到第一次購買之後，才根據簡單的外在線索評估品質？競爭者提供哪些線索？從消費者觀點瞭解品質信號的重要性，進而傳達這些信號，通常都會使消費者對品質知覺更清楚。

### 3.承認品質知覺的動態性

消費者的品質知覺會隨著時間的推移、附加的資訊、產品類別競爭加劇，以及不斷變化的期望而有所改變。品質的動態性指出行銷經理必須長期追蹤消費者的品質知覺，然後根據這些改變，研擬產品與推廣策略。因為產品與知覺的改變，行銷經理可以教導消費者評估品質的方法，廣告、產品包裝上所提供的資訊，以及產品本身可以看得見的相關線索，都可以用來激起消費者對品質知覺的期望。

### 4.瞭解消費者如何解讀貨幣及非貨幣價格

本研究所提出的模型，可以縮小實際與知覺價格的差距，這一點在瞭解消費者如何解讀產品價格方面，至為重要。例如：時間與精力等非貨幣成本，都需要一一瞭解。許多消費者，尤其是人口眾多的職業婦女，認為時間是一種非常重要的商品。融入產品中有助於減少時間、精力，以及搜尋成本的任何因素，都可以降低知覺的損失，因而提高知覺的價值。

### 5.認識提高附加價值的多重方法

本研究所提出的模型，指出提高產品與服務之附加價值的許多種策略。提高知覺價值的每一種策略，都附有提高價值知覺的方法。降低貨幣與非貨幣成本、減少知覺的損失、增加顯著的內在屬性、激起較高層級的相關知覺，以及使用外在線索提高價值，都是公司可用來影響消費者價值知覺的可行策略。行銷經理需要根據顧客所定義的價值，為特定產品或市場區隔選擇合適的策略。根據顧客價值標準與知覺所制定的策略，比根據公司的標準所制定的策略，可更有效率的使用資源，更能迎合顧客的期望。

---

### 【實例】
### 「議題行銷的社會顯著性、活動持續度與執行保證對品牌權益的影響」管理意涵實例

（林隆儀，2010）

……本研究的結論與發現，具有下列兩項管理意涵：

#### 1.議題選擇決策的策略焦點

以顧客為基礎的品牌權益，具有三項要素：差異化效果、品牌知識，與消費者對行銷的反應（Keller, 1993）。當企業運用議題行銷提高品牌權益時，選擇與企業既有品牌形象相配適的議題，可強化消費者心中對於品牌聯想的節點。以目標消費者所關心的議題為出發點，是強化消費者心中節點最好的方法，也是發掘及建立消費者心中正面新節點的有效途徑。當企業運用議題行銷增強品牌權益時，目的如果是在強化既有品牌形象，理應符合與企業相配適的議題。如果企業運用此類活動的目的，是為了增進消費者心中正面節點時，例如：改善或轉換品牌形象，則以目標消費者所關心之議題為基礎，有助於企業達成此一目的，同時也有助於擴大企業決策範圍與產生創意。

選擇與企業既有品牌形象相配適的議題，可能發生的盲點在於，與企業既有品牌形象相配適的議題，或許並非消費者所關心的議題。例如：消費者可能對Nike運動鞋具有高度評價，喜歡穿Nike運動鞋，但卻不一定關心籃球運動。因此，議題選擇若能符合目標消費者之期待，將更有助於激起消費者對產品之需求，進而提高活動成功的機會，有助於運用品牌發揮議題行銷的效果，值得企業做議題選擇決策之參考。

#### 2.建構長期優勢的重要基礎

議題行銷的基本特質，是結合銷售產品與贊助議題，一舉兩得；但也容易使消費者認為廠商假借議題之名而行圖利之實的疑慮，尤其是當消費者感覺到企業參與此類活動的商業行為太濃厚時，更會產生負面的評價。因此，如何消除消費者對活動之疑慮，是議題行銷活動非常重要的一環。本研究發現長期承諾有助於激起消費者對參與活動的廠商或品牌產生正面的評價，因為短期的議題行銷活動往往被企業定位為促銷活動，消費者也將短期的議題行銷活動視為商業行為濃厚的一種交易，容易使消費者對參與活動的廠商或品牌產生不良的評價，所以，企業在實行議題行銷的目的，若是為了增進品牌權益，就必須有長期支持所選擇議

題的決心。

本研究發現社會顯著性高的議題，無論是搭配持續度高或低的活動，對品牌權益之影響，並沒有顯著差異；社會顯著性低的議題，搭配持續度高的活動，比搭配持續度低的活動，更有助於提高消費者對品牌權益的正面評價。也就是說，長期性的議題行銷活動，有助於強化社會顯著性低的議題，激起消費者對品牌權益的評價。根據本研究此一發現，企業對議題行銷活動若抱持特殊理念或其他考慮因素，而選擇社會顯著性低的議題時，將活動做長期性的規劃或長期性的承諾，是提高消費者對品牌評價的重要手段。

對於關心社會顯著性低之議題的非營利組織而言，說服企業長期支持其經營議題，也可以達到既有助於企業又有利於議題的雙贏局面。企業不能因為結合社會顯著性高的議題，就認為無須對議題付出長期的關懷，因為短期的議題行銷往往被企業定位為促銷活動，若企業皆以短期性贊助議題搭配銷售活動，消費者便會因為看穿企業的技倆或對企業產生誤解，而改變對品牌的評價。

---

### 【實例】
### 「老年經濟安全保障、理財知識與逆向抵押貸款意願之研究」，管理意涵實例
### （林隆儀、商懿勻，2015）

### 1. 探討老年經濟生活與理財知識符合社會之需求

因應高齡社會的到來，國人健康狀況與平均壽命的延長，長者自身的理財知識與資源配置能力將成為晚年生活品質與資金來源的最佳保障（Piggot, Sherris & Mitchell, 2006）。老年經濟安全保障即在強調對年長者基本生活、經濟安全的保障；理財知識中的借貸、退休規劃，對年長者退休後的經濟狀況至為重要（Noctor, Stoney & Stradling, 1992; Lusardi & Mitchell, 2007），然而逆向抵押貸款提供其自主性的現金流量使用，自定給付金額的穩定性，用以維持長者尊嚴並保持老年生活經濟的穩定與自主性（Wang, Valdez & Piggott, 2009; Ahlstrom, Tumlinson & Lambrew, 2004; Reed & Gibler, 2003）。涉入程度是指對重要事務，會花較多時間考慮並蒐集較多相關的資訊，對現今社會上經濟狀況弱勢的年長者而言，在思考如何解決日常生活費用時，其實就是老年經濟安全保障與理財知識在涉入干擾的情況下，形成對逆向抵押貸款需求的影響。

### 2. 逆向抵押貸款可為年長者增加收入來源，保障退休生活品質

逆向抵押貸款的實施可使老年經濟安全保障的措施更完整；此論點與本研究探討老年經濟安全保障影響逆向抵押貸款借款意願的模式相符。逆向抵押貸款是將住房與養老結合的一種特殊金融工具，因應全球人口老化現象攀升，逆向抵押貸款改變國人既定財產（不動產）傳承的思維，推廣「以房養老」理念，提升長者資源配置的活用性，開拓新的金融營運範疇，成為長者退休後的生活品質與資金來源的保障，緩解養老資源不足的難題，調整家庭養老負擔，化解老齡化危機的重要工具（Piggot, Sherris & Mitchell, 2006）。

### 3. 提供逆向抵押貸款推廣策略的參考

逆向抵押貸款將房屋和養老保障緊密地結合在一起，對年長又相對貧弱的長者提供一種全新概念的養老的途徑，因其具有強烈的公共福利色彩，得以強化社會保障功能，使得逆向抵押貸款不單只是簡單的融資行為，更能表現出全新的福利資助政策。

推廣逆向抵押貸款，可為長者建構更具規劃性的老年經濟安全保障，以彌補現行國民退休金之替代率不足的缺憾，使逆向抵押貸款成為長者老年退休金準備的重要融資工具之一（Wang, Valdez & Piggott, 2009; Fratantoni, 1999），同時可提升房產資源的優化配置，提前變現多重運用，使家庭財富最大化，提升晚年經濟生活品質與生活資金需求的多樣性（Ong, 2008; Rowlingson, 2006）。其中逆向抵押貸款強調「以房養老」的理念，可鼓勵中青年者努力賺錢購屋，作日後養老之用，亦能刺激國內房屋市場之交易，達到雙贏的局面。

## 四、實務意涵

實務意涵（Practical Implication）又稱為應用價值（Application Value），是指研究發現在實務應用上所具有的特殊意義、參考價值與貢獻。經過嚴謹的設計與務實執行的實證研究，所獲得的研究結論，在實務應用上應該也會有獨到的見解與特殊的貢獻價值，此時就是讓研究者抒發獨特意義與實務應用價值的最佳時刻。

實務意涵撰寫要領，和管理意涵的寫作要領相似，所不同的是偏重在管

理的實務面，主要是提供給實證的產業或組織參考。研究者可以從四個角度思考實務意涵的寫作要領：第一是從高階管理者的立場思考，你希望從研究發現中得到什麼啟示，以便將重要的研究發現應用在你的公司決策上。第二是從部屬的立場思考，你希望提供什麼有價值的資訊給高階主管，幫助高階主管做有效率又有效能的決策。第三是站在組織中平行溝通的立場思考，你的研究發現可以提供什麼有價值的訊息給平行單位參考，例如：行銷研究單位將研究結論提供給行銷單位、廣告單位或研究發展單位參考。第四是從需求單位的立場思考，你希望研究發現如何用來改善工作，例如：營業單位希望行銷研究單位提供因應市場競爭，以及消費習慣改變的狀況。

---

## 【實例】
## 「不同聯盟型態之下經濟誘因與信任之相對重要性研究——以臺灣清涼飲料產業為例」實務意涵實例
### （林隆儀、黃營杉、吳青松，2004）

……本研究的結論與發現，具有下列三項實務意涵：

### 1.生產活動聯盟重視經濟誘因

本研究所提出的研究假說1與研究假說2，經統計檢定結果，均獲得強烈的支持，證實生產活動策略聯盟以追求經濟利益為主。此一涵義至少傳達了三個重要的訊息，即廠商在做(1)快速推出新產品，搶占市場先機；(2)追求大量生產的規模經濟，獲得成本優勢；(3)避免冒然推出新產品所導致的錯誤投資風險等決策上，策略聯盟是一絕佳的選擇。

### 2.配銷活動聯盟重視夥伴的信任

本研究的研究假說3，經統計檢定結果，四組子假說都獲得強烈的支持，顯示涉及配銷活動的策略聯盟，特別重視聯盟夥伴的信任。此一涵義顯示涉及廣告與銷售活動的策略聯盟，因為聯盟活動作業標準化程度低、不確定因素多且程度高，產品銷售成敗掌握在聯盟夥伴手上，因此管理者在做策略聯盟決策時，特別重視聯盟夥伴的信任。

### 3.消除同業相忌的心理障礙

臺灣清涼飲料產業的策略聯盟以現有同業廠商之間的合作為主，約占75%。此一現象正應驗了Hamel et al.（1989）所言，隨著競爭局勢的升高，公司都學會和其他組織合作，甚至和競爭者建立策略聯盟關係，以便成為競爭中的贏家，因為策略聯盟可使公司迅速自外界獲得某些專長與優勢。和同業的競爭者合作，既然是提高競爭力的絕佳途徑，無論是選擇哪一種型態的聯盟，管理者在做策略聯盟決策時，都需要有聯盟的素養與策略的胸襟，消除過去同業相忌的心理障礙，從攜手合作共創綜效的新觀點看待策略聯盟，才能營造雙贏的局面。

---

## 【實例】
## 「表演品質、服務品質、顧客滿意與顧客忠誠的關係之研究」實務意涵實例
### （林隆儀、許廷偉，2006）

……本研究的結論，具有下列兩項實務意涵：

### 1.行銷決策的意涵

本研究從人口統計資料分析結果發現，觀賞表演藝術的群眾，集中在單身、女性、年輕、大學程度、月收入不高、學生等特質，與陳亞萍（2000）的研究發現相吻合，和Valentin（2005）的研究發現女性在藝術和文化產品的消費比男性更多的結論相一致，但年齡（45～54歲）與職業（高水準）卻有顯著的差異。由此可知，表演藝術的發展可能因國情的不同，在人口統計的分布方面亦略有差異。此一訊息透露表演藝術行銷的成功，和顧客的共同特徵息息相關。區隔目標市場，才能獲得較高的顧客滿意與顧客忠誠。

### 2.服務品質比表演品質對顧客滿意更具有影響力

根據本研究驗證結果顯示，對顧客滿意的影響效果中，從前述表2及表3（作者按：由於篇幅有限，本書將原文中的表2及表3予以省略）的數據可知，表演品質的$\beta$為0.560，服務品質$\beta$為0.681；再從前揭圖1（作者按：由於篇幅有限，本書將原文中的圖1予以省略）的路徑分析可知，表演品質的影響力為0.164，服務品質的影響力為0.225，此一訊息意謂著劇場所提供的硬體設備，表演環境的氣氛及服務，對顧客滿意比演出團體的表演品質更具有影響力。表示觀眾在整個表演活動過程中，除了在意表演者的優美演出或節目適切的安排外，舉凡劇場的地點、交通、設備、觀賞前購票、觀賞中與表演結束後所接觸到的服務人員，都與劇場的服務品質有關，對顧客滿意的影響程度也比較深，因此，服務品質對顧客滿意的影響力，勝過表演品質對顧客滿意的影響力。

【實例】

「學校行銷策略與學校形象對家長選校決策的影響——知覺風險的干擾效果」實務意涵實例

（林隆儀、李明真，2010）

……本研究的結論，具有下列三項實務意涵：

**1.因應社會潮流脈動，調整學校經營策略**

學校面對愈來愈競爭的社會，必須隨時思考學校經營的理念與方向，調整學校經營的策略。本研究發現家長在選校決策上，在學校行銷策略中以通路行銷策略取代過去的產品行銷策略，亦即家長認為學校所在的便利性，比學校的教育品質來得重要。學校必須要有能力去察覺學生家長的需求正隨著時代潮流在改變的事實，務實的調整學校經營策略。

**2.降低知覺風險在家長選校決策的干擾**

知覺風險強調的是個人主觀的感受，若家長知覺到的風險程度超過了可接受的範圍，家長便會採取行動來降低風險。本研究發現家長在選校決策上，會受到知覺風險的干擾，尤其受到財務及時間風險的影響最顯著。學校可透過學校行銷策略的運作及良好的學校形象，來減低家長主觀上認知會發生損失的可能性，亦即增加家長對於選校結果有利的確定性感覺。

**3.學生是推廣學校行銷、學校形象的活廣告**

現在的青少年問題多，尤其國中生正值叛逆期，更令人覺得難於管教，多數家長亦為此深感困擾。本研究發現目前在家長選校考量中，學生素質形象取代過去教師專業的形象。此一訊息透露當前在推廣學校行銷及建立學校形象上，不再以教師為主體，學生素質才是家長最關心的變數，學生才是推廣學校行銷、學校形象的活廣告。

# 五、研究限制

任何一位研究者都很用心地做研究，研究結果也都獲得重要的發現與具體的結論。但是研究過程中難免都會受到某些因素的影響，尤其是研究者無

法控制的外來因素限制，以致形成研究結果有不夠完美的現象，這種不夠完美的現象，稱為研究限制。研究過程受到哪些限制？為何受到這些限制？這些限制的影響有多大？如何處理這些限制？這一連串的問題，只有研究者最清楚。

為什麼要交代研究限制，有幾個理由值得研究者思考。第一個理由是基於研究倫理的考量，研究者必須誠實、務實的把研究過程中所受的限制交代清楚。第二個理由是基於參考價值的考量，讓讀者可以理解研究所受到的限制，進而判斷研究的參考價值。第三個理由是基於謙虛為懷的考量，交代研究過程中所受到的限制，讓讀者感受到你的研究風格與風度，更有助於突顯研究結論的參考價值。第四個理由是基於善意揭示的考量，研究者主動揭示論文的限制與缺失，讓後續研究者免於重蹈覆轍，進而寫出更完整、更完美的論文。

有些論文沒有交代研究限制，無形中使論文欠缺一項重要要件，因而留下不完美的遺憾。有些論文雖然有寫出研究限制，但是所寫的內容不屬於研究限制的範圍，不僅留下牛頭不對馬嘴的現象，也使論文留下更大的缺陷。

常看到論文的研究限制中出現因為缺乏知識、預算不足、時間不夠、身心俱疲、體力不支等原因，以致造成研究不夠完美的後果。其實這些原因都和研究限制的意義無關，當然也就不是研究限制的好體裁了。

撰寫研究限制的要領，可以從幾個方向思考。最重要的是研究設計及研究工作執行過程中受到外來因素的影響，例如：研究變數與構面選擇不夠完整、研究設計或實驗設計的缺失、抽樣方法的不完美、抽樣執行的誤差、樣本取得的限制、樣本數的限制、統計分析方法的限制等，從這些方向務實的思考，才不會陷入研究限制的迷惘中。

有些論文把研究限制和建議結合在一起，但是大多數的論文都把研究限制和建議分開來寫。若要寫在完整的論文中，以分開來寫比較清楚，也比較恰當；如果是要發表在期刊的文章，因為有可能受限於篇幅，可以將研究限制和建議結合在一起。

---

**【實例】**
**「不同聯盟型態之下經濟誘因與信任之相對重要性研究——以臺灣清涼飲料產業為例」研究限制實例**
（林隆儀、黃營杉、吳青松，2004）

……本文的研究限制有四，即(1)變數項目的限制：經濟誘因與信任的因素很多，隨著研究目的之不同，每個人所選擇的因素也各不相同。本研究參考多位學者的看法，選擇四個變數雖是一種權宜之計，觀其解釋的變異量也都達到可接受的水準。又研究變數的萃取雖儘量做到謹慎與嚴謹，但是只選取四個研究變數，難免存在遺珠之憾。(2)外部效度的限制：本研究以臺灣清涼飲料產業為研究對象，實證結果雖然有重要的研究發現，但是此一結論畢竟只侷限於此一產業，研究結果無法一般化。如欲將研究結論推論到其他產業，必須再經過實證證實，以提高研究的外部效度。(3)衡量量表的限制：臺灣清涼飲料產業的策略聯盟，因過去缺乏相關研究，因此缺乏適當的衡量量表可供參考。本文參考以往學者用於相關研究議題的衡量量表，再加以適當修改，以及透過試訪做必要的修正，以達到一般量表所要求的信度與效度。有關量表的發展，通常必須經過相當嚴謹的理論推理與反覆驗證，因此，本研究所發展的衡量量表尚有改善的空間。(4)配銷協定型、產品線延伸型、品牌授權型等三組，屬於小樣本檢定，雖符合常態性假設，但難免有檢定效率較低的情況；尤其是品牌授權型策略聯盟僅蒐集到四個樣本，樣本數少，恐會影響統計檢定結果與推論。

此外，本研究的觀念性架構中，企業價值活動子系統與經濟誘因、信任之間，應存在一定的關係；又經濟誘因與信任之間，勢必也存在互動關係，然而這些關係都不是本研究所要探討的範圍，因此均未加以研究。

---

### 【實例】
### 「議題行銷的社會顯著性、活動持續度與執行保證對品牌權益的影響」研究限制實例
（林隆儀，2010）

……本研究所使用的方法與研究設計，雖盡力做到理性與嚴謹，實證結果也獲得重要而有價值的發現，但是在執行過程中難免受到一些限制，以致使研究有不夠完美的感覺。本研究在研究過程中受到以下的限制，根據這些研究限制提出對後續研究的建議。

#### 1.外部效度的限制

本研究僅以報業中的《蘋果日報》為研究對象，所獲得的結論恐無法擴充、延伸到相同產業的其他品牌或不同產業的品牌。建議後續研究可增加其他公司或其他產業的品牌，進行廣泛之探討。

### 2.樣本對象的限制

本研究之實驗樣本係以北部地區大學生為研究對象，同時也忽略人口統計變數的影響，恐無法完整反映整體消費者的行為。建議後續研究可擴大抽樣範圍，並納入人口統計變數，做更深入的研究。

### 3.問卷設計的限制

本研究在平面廣告設計上雖力求真實，但實際上仍僅止於虛擬的情境，無法完全確保受訪者對廣告內容的接受度。建議後續研究可以採用真實的情境，提高受訪者對廣告的接受度。

### 4.研究範圍的限制

本研究僅以交易為基礎的議題行銷活動為研究標的，但議題行銷的範圍相當廣泛，僅以其中一類做研究，恐無法涵蓋所有議題行銷。建議後續研究可針對其他類型的議題行銷，進行分析與比較。

### 5.變數類型的限制

活動持續度的型態並非僅有高、低兩種類型，本研究僅將活動持續度簡化為高、低兩種，恐有不夠周延的缺失。建議後續研究可加入或改變其他類型的持續度，做深入的探討與比較。

# 六、對業者的建議

從事管理實務的業者，平時專注於企業經營及管理實務工作，無暇兼顧該產業有系統的學術研究，但是又迫切需要有專業研究資訊作為經營決策的參考依據，此時就有賴外界專業研究的支援。此一現象正好為產學合作，共創雙贏，提供一個絕佳的交流平臺。實證研究結果的重要發現，往往可提供給業者很高的參考價值，所以，論文章節都安排有「對業者的建議」這個章節，讓研究者有機會對業者提出客觀而寶貴的建議。

術業有專攻，產學不易兼備。學術研究與企業經營分屬於不同的專業領域，要做到兩者兼備，往往有其主觀與客觀的限制。學術研究的重要發現，可貴之處在於後續的參考與應用價值，尤其是實務應用價值。所以，除了前述的實務意涵之外，進一步針對相關業者提出具體、務實、客觀、可行的建議方案，更能突顯論文的應用價值。再從業者的角度言，研究者在進行研究時，業者或許也曾經協助填寫問卷，對研究工作也有些許貢獻，也企盼能分享研究結果。

對業者的建議也有幾項撰寫要領，第一、誠懇、忠實的提出可行的建議方案，以第三者的立場，客觀地提出善意的建議。第二、所提出的建議必須具體、務實、可行，讓業者可以從中獲益。第三、所提出的建議必須以研究發現為基礎，不宜天馬行空，讓業者摸不著邊際。第四、以條列方式呈現，輔之以簡潔的說明，清楚的提出建議。

## 【實例】
## 「議題行銷的社會顯著性、活動持續度與執行保證對品牌權益的影響」對業者的建議實例
### （林隆儀，2010）

……根據本研究的發現及其管理意涵，提出下列建議供管理者參考：

### 1.選擇社會顯著性高的議題

企業在選擇議題及搭配相關行銷活動、增進品牌權益時，選擇社會顯著性高的議題，對增進品牌權益有較好的效果。若企業運用議題行銷的目的是要改善或轉換品牌形象，則考慮社會顯著性高的議題，將更有助於企業達成預定目的。

### 2.要有超越長期承諾的決心

企業在推行議題行銷活動以增進品牌權益時，考慮長期性計畫，做長期性承諾，對增進品牌權益有較好的效果。企業基於特殊理念或其他因素而必須結合社會顯著性較低的議題時，更應將長期的活動視為增進品牌權益的重要方法。

**【實例】**

**「行動商務應用對公司經營績效的影響──市場導向的干擾效果」對業者的建議實例**

（林隆儀、方業溥，2006）

　　……根據本研究的發現，提出下列建議供業者參考：

## 1.建立有效的情報蒐集系統

　　流通相關產業的公司對於管理者或行銷主管而言，每日業務同仁在外拜訪客戶的各種資訊，包含顧客對公司的意見、競爭者的策略行動，以及對公司產品的各種意見，可做為研擬行銷活動、產品定價策略，以及顧客關係維繫等決策的依據。過去憑藉紙本作業模式，既不科學，效率又差；透過行動商務的應用，可有效蒐集和分享市場情報，進而迅速做出正確的回應。建議有意導入行動商務的企業，可建立有效的情報蒐集系統，優先從市場情報蒐集與應用切入。

## 2.導入行動商務系統

　　流通相關產業作業繁複，且需耗費大量人工成本，企業耗費鉅資引進後臺作業管理系統之後，卻只能提供在辦公室作業的同仁使用；一旦離開辦公室之後，即無法適時取得足夠的資訊，以致延緩、甚至延誤業務的推展。對企業而言，在第一線面對客戶的業務人員或服務人員，無論是查詢庫存或產品價格，都需要適當的工具以提高其作業品質與速度。導入行動商務系統，利用行動商務的優點，可有效提升服務品質，加速服務的進行。

## 3.提供顧客應用行動商務

　　顧客是企業賴以維生的來源，提高顧客滿意度，贏得顧客的青睞，業績自然蒸蒸日上。本研究證實企業提供顧客應用行動商務，對公司經營績效有正向且顯著的影響效果。流通相關產業的公司藉由提供顧客應用行動商務，除了有助於提高公司經營績效之外，也可以從提供顧客應用行動商務中，再次蒐集顧客的相關資料，可謂一舉兩得也。

# 七、後續研究的建議

　　基於研究倫理的精神，論文的最後一節都需要提出對後續研究的建議，指引對類似題目有興趣的後續研究者一個善意的研究方向。研究設計及執行的來龍去脈、研究發現的重要意涵、研究限制與研究的缺失等，只有研究者才能瞭若指掌，也只有研究者可以提出中肯的建議。

　　後續研究的建議若能做到中肯、務實，往往具有高度的啟發與參考價值。有些後續研究的建議是為自己的後續研究預留空間，對類似題目有興趣的研究者，也可以從後續研究的建議中找到研究的題材與靈感。

　　後續研究建議的撰寫要領有四：第一，可以參照研究限制所言，誠懇地提出彌補缺失的建議。第二，建議案必須務實可行，以縮短後續研究者摸索的時間。第三，不宜漫無邊際的出題目，以免後續研究者摸不著頭緒。第四，任何建議都必須以剛完成的研究為基礎。

---

**【實例】**

**「不同聯盟型態之下經濟誘因與信任之相對重要性研究——以臺灣清涼飲料產業為例」後續研究建議實例**

（林隆儀、黃營杉、吳青松，2004）

　　……後續研究的建議方面，本文提出下列研究方向供參考：

1. 納入更多研究變數，從宏觀的角度探討策略聯盟的相關議題。
2. 擴大研究對象產業，一方面可將研究結論一般化，一方面可比較不同產業的廠商在既定策略聯盟型態之下選擇聯盟夥伴時，所考量的決策因素是否有所不同，以及其相對重要性是否有差異。
3. 以廠商為分析單位，可歸納出比較一般化的結果，提高研究的外部效度。
4. 衡量量表的改進，更謹慎而嚴謹的發展一份完整的衡量量表，可做為後續研究的一項建議。
5. 增加研究樣本的蒐集，以提高研究的參考價值。

**【實例】**
**「行動商務應用對公司經營績效的影響——市場導向的干擾效果」後續研究建議實例**

（林隆儀、方業溥，**2006**）

......本研究提出下列建議，供後續研究者參考：

**1.納入更多研究變數**

公司經營績效的評量有許多構面，本研究僅以作業時程、市場占有率、交易成本、顧客滿意度四個構面做為衡量指標。後續研究者可納入更多與行動商務績效有關的指標衡量之。

**2.擴大研究對象**

本研究以流通相關企業為對象，未來研究者可擴大研究範圍，選取其他業態做為研究的對象。又本研究受訪對象為公司資訊或行銷部門主管，後續研究者可考慮將其他部門與不同功能職位的員工納入研究對象。

**3.增加樣本的蒐集**

本研究的研究對象限定臺灣地區流通業，只蒐集到81個有效樣本，樣本數少，可能產生推論上的偏誤。建議後續研究者擴大研究對象後，可擴大蒐集研究樣本，以提高研究的參考價值。

# 八、發表論文

寫完後續研究建議，論文並非就此完成，接下來還有論文發表的挑戰。經過精心設計及嚴謹執行的研究計畫，一定已獲得豐碩的研究成果。這些豐碩的成果若未能加以應用，常常會留下遺珠之憾，論文若就此告停，未免太可惜。基於「獨樂樂，不如眾樂樂」的精神，這些研究成果應該公開發表，和更多人分享，做更有意義的貢獻，方為上策。博士班學生畢業之前，必須在國內、國外學術期刊發表論文，或參加在國外舉辦的國際學術研討會。各學校都已經有此規範，所以，博士生修業期間就必須在國內外學術期刊發表論文。最近幾年很多學校也都建立鼓勵碩士班學生及提升研究風氣的機制，鼓勵學生畢業之前必須參加研討會並發表論文，或投稿到國外學術期刊並取得收件函，才能申請畢業考試。所以，完成論文寫作之後，還必須準備發表論文。

準備發表的論文，必須按照學術研討會或期刊的要求與規範，將原始論文寫成發表的文稿，而且必須掌握「麻雀雖小，五臟俱全」的原則與要領，將原始論文濃縮、精簡成適合發表的文章。無論是研討會所發表的文章，或是學術期刊所刊登的文章，由於受到文章定位及篇幅的限制，只能接受符合規範範圍及格式的文章。文章內容包括題目、作者姓名及職稱、摘要、本文、參考文獻等要項，文長通常都以A4紙張20頁左右為原則。文章內容愈短，寫作的困難度愈高；要把一本原始論文濃縮成20頁左右的文章，確實是一大挑戰。

參加研討會的文稿通常比較精簡，期刊所刊登的文章或許可以略微長一些，但是也有部分期刊嚴格限制文章字數，例如：*Journal of Research in Marketing and Entrepreneurship*要求文長限制在3,000～4,000字之間，*European Journal of Marketing*要求字數不得超過8,500字。有些期刊要求摘要不得超過500字，有些期刊將摘要字數限制在300字以內。有些期刊嚴格要求論文摘要的寫法，例如：聞名全球、擁有將近200種學術期刊的英國Emerald出版公司，旗下的期刊一律要求採用該公司的「結構式摘要」（Structured Abstract）書寫。所謂結構式摘要，包括嚴格要求必須具體寫出研究目的、研究設計／方法論／研究方法、研究發現、原創性／價值等項目。若屬於應用性研究，必須另行提供研究限制與意涵、實務意涵；摘要字數以250字為限，關鍵詞則以六個為限，同時還必須提供文章屬性的分類，例如：實證性文章、重要觀點文章、技術性文章、觀念性文章、個案研究式文章、文獻回顧式文章、一般評論性文章等。

發表論文大致可分為兩種方式，第一是參加研討會，並在研討會上以口頭或海報揭示方式發表論文；第二是投稿到學術期刊，以刊登文章方式發表論文。研討會又可分為在國內舉辦的研討會，以及在國外舉辦的研討會；學術期刊也可分為國外學術期刊，以及國內學術期刊。國外學術期刊有些被收錄在某些索引之資料庫，根據期刊之影響係數（Impact Factor）等指標而有不同的等級分類，例如：SCI、SSCI、AHCI、EI等。國內期刊也有被收錄在某些索引之資料庫者，例如：TSCI、TSSCI、ECONLIT、EI等。研究者可以依照學校的要求，或根據自己的需要，選擇適合的發表方式、選擇合適的研討會及期刊發表論文。

　　參加研討會通常都需要研究者親自出席參加並發表論文。參加研討會的機會很多，很多學校及研究機構都在舉辦研討會。任何研討會都有其獨特的要求與規範，例如：研討會主題、投稿方式、文稿格式、文稿長短、截稿時間、審稿機制等。研究者必須瞭解這些要求與規範，文稿才能順利被接受，並受邀參加研討會。

　　做簡報、報告論文也是一門學問，研究者必須熟練簡報要領與技巧。學生完成論文計畫書（前三章）後，需要接受論文計畫書考試；整篇論文完成後，必須接受畢業考試，這兩次考試都必須以口頭報告方式報告論文的精華。口頭報告時間有一定的限制，通常是以20～30分鐘為原則。參加研討會需要在會上發表論文，研討會時間通常安排得很緊湊，每一篇論文發表時間都有一定的限制，通常每一篇論文只有15～20分鐘的時間可供作者發表，國際研討會每一篇論文發表時間更嚴格限制在15分鐘。研究者發表之前必須做好充分的準備、審慎規劃，做重點式的報告，在可供使用時間的限制之下，做最精準、最精彩的報告。準備工作包括投影片的製作、簡報技巧的熟練、報告流程的順暢、文章重點的掌握、口齒清晰、清楚表達等，都必須事先演練再演練，因為有很多人對你的研究有興趣，很多人想要聆聽你的研究成果。

　　學術期刊對研究主題、投稿方式、文稿格式、文稿長短、審稿機制等，也都有自己的要求與規範。國外學術期刊投稿方式有三種：第一種是線上投稿，有些期刊要求透過其文稿處理中心的線上系統投稿，研究者必須先上其網站完成註冊手續，然後按照投稿系統的規範與指示，一步一步完成投稿，例如：*Journal of Consumer Research*、*European Journal of Marketing*就是採用這種投稿方式。第二種是E-mail投稿，研究者依照期刊的規範與要求，將文稿及其必要資料直接E-mail給期刊主編，例如：*Tourism Review*、*The Journal of Advertising*、*Asia Pacific Journal of Marketing and Logistics*，就是採用這種投稿方式。第三種是紙本投稿，研究者依照期刊的要求，將紙本文稿直接郵寄給期刊主編，例如：*Journal of Consumer Marketing*、*Journal of Product & Brand Management*，都是採用這種方式投稿。國內期刊大多採用E-mail及紙本郵寄方式投稿。完成投稿程序後，期刊主編會進行初審，初審結果若符合期刊要求的主題及要件，才會進入實質審查（匿名審稿）。此時，編輯委員會通常會發給一份收件函，通知文稿已經收到並給予一個審稿編號，以方便後續聯絡，然後正式將文稿送審。

　　審稿作業採用匿名審稿方式，文稿送給誰審查一律予以保密，僅由編輯委員會專人負責和作者聯絡，所以作者不會知道誰在審稿，審稿者也無從得知作者是何許人也。通過學術期刊審稿程序而被接受的文稿，期刊編輯委員會會發給一份接受刊登函，從接受刊登到實際刊登，通常會有一段時間上的落差；也就是說，被接受的文稿可能要經過一段時日才會刊登在期刊上。學生只要接到此一接受刊登函，即可申請畢業考試；研究者收到此一接受刊登函，即可進行後續工作。

撰寫報告及上臺報告有一個很重要的要領，要掌握BRONS法則，也就是必須做到簡潔有力（Brevity）、和主題相關聯（Relevancy）、公正客觀（Objectivity）、清晰明白（Non-ambiguity）、具體呈現（Specificity）。

無論是參加學術研討會或投稿到學術期刊，都必須留意研討會與期刊的要求和規範，尤其是論文寫作格式，每一個研討會或每一個期刊的要求皆各不相同，符合其要求才有被接受的機會。本書第六章將接著討論論文寫作的格式。

# 九、結語

論文寫作是一段漫長的歷程，需要按部就班、務實累積，才會有成果。論文寫作只有方法與要領，沒有捷徑可循，也沒有速成班，絕對不是短期間內可以完成的工作，也絕對不是急就章式的做法可以竟全功的事。從第一章緒論到第五章結論與建議，每一章都需要精心規劃、嚴謹設計、務實執行，做最精彩的呈現；必須確實瞭解每一節的意義與功能，掌握寫作要領、用心投入，做最細膩的論述。

根據本人這幾年指導研究生的經驗與心得，發現要寫一篇好的論文，唯一的祕訣就是儘早開始，持之以恆。有些學生深諳其中道理，胸有成竹，考取研究所之後就開始在思索所要撰寫的論文題目，同時積極洽請指導教授指導。有些學生一進入研究所認識老師之後，就開始展開論文寫作的布局，包括構思題目、洽請指導教授、開始進行Meeting。由於儘早開始、積極行動，遵照指導教授的引導，掌握正確方法與要領，即可在緊湊的兩年碩士班生涯中，輕鬆愉快的完成論文寫作。

# 第六章
# 個案研究實例

　　研究方法可區分為兩大類別：量化研究與質化研究。量化研究主張以群體的足夠樣本數作為研究對象的基礎，目的在於檢視研究變數之間的關係，細數及衡量事物的數量化特性。質化研究主張以個體或少數樣本為研究對象，探索及描述事物的自然特質，不採用數量方法，目的在詮釋事物的特定現象。這兩種研究方法名稱與性質雖然有明顯的差別，但是研究的精神與基本原理、使用的方法與程序，卻有很多異曲同工之處，都可以達到所期望的研究目的。

　　本書第一、二版以介紹量化研究方法為主，透過大樣本資料，利用科學統計方法檢視研究變數之間的關係。近年來質化研究備受重視，尤其是有些學術領域的論文主張採用個案研究方法，以致許多人對質化研究產生濃厚興趣，很想瞭解質化研究或個案研究的特質、實施方法與要領。

　　為滿足讀者及學生的需求，正值本書第三版修訂之際，特別增加一章個案研究實例，以實例呈現方式，介紹個案研究方法的意義、特性、程序、優點與缺點、實施方法與要領，回饋讀者的期待。

# 二、質化研究與個案研究

　　質化研究方法（Qualitative Research Methods）或稱為質性研究方法、定性研究方法，顧名思義是以非數量性的方法，詮釋及描述研究標的之特性，歸納針對個體所做的研究發現，並將其推論到一般化的一種研究方法。近年來質化研究方法備受重視，廣泛被應用在各種領域的研究中，但是學校在教導研究方法時，卻很少有系統的介紹質化研究方法與個案研究方法，以致讓初學者常常「只知其一，不知其二」，不知如何下手。

　　質化研究方法和量化研究方法（Quantitative Research Methods）的方法論雖然各異其趣，但是基本的研究設計、研究程序、資料蒐集方法、問卷設計、研究發現的管理意涵、研究限制、後續研究建議，並沒有太大差別。甚至在某些領域，例如：有關社會科學、行為科學、教育議題、應用心理學、社區發展、企業經營領域的研究，反而可以獲得更深入的理解與啟發。

　　一般而言，就研究設計的構思，所需投入的時間與分析方法角度言，質化研究需要有更高瞻遠矚的策略思維、更周詳完整的研究設計、更高超的研究能力，因此研究過程比量化研究所需要的思考時程更冗長，而且無法利用電腦程式執行資料分析（Berg, 1995）。質化研究方法通常以文字描述事物現象與特徵為主，無法像量化研究方法採用具體數據，檢定及證明研究變數之間的關係。儘管如此，質化研究方法在社會科學領域締造了觀念上與理論上的貢獻，功不可沒（Bogden, 1972）。

　　質化研究方法與量化研究方法有許多不同的地方，也有許多相同之處，兩種研究方法的比較詳如表6-1所示。

**表6-1**
質化研究方法與量化研究方法之比較

| 比較項目 | 質化研究方法 | 量化研究方法 |
|---|---|---|
| 1.研究精神 | 科學精神 | 科學精神 |
| 2.研究核心 | 個體 | 群體 |
| 3.特性 | 非數量化、事實詮釋 | 數量化、驗證變數之間關係 |
| 4.目的 | 用文字描述事物、現象的特質 | 細數及衡量研究變數的數量 |
| 5.樣本數 | 個體或有限樣本 | 足夠大量的樣本 |
| 6.問卷設計 | 開放式問卷、非結構化問卷 | 封閉式問卷、結構化問卷 |
| 7.資料蒐集方法 | 深度訪問法為主 | 問卷訪問法為主 |
| 8.資料分析方法 | 比對、推論、歸納法 | 各種統計方法、演繹法 |
| 9.電腦化程度 | 無法用電腦進行資料分析 | 可以用電腦進行資料分析 |
| 10.對研究者的要求 | 邏輯推論能力 | 統計檢定能力 |

# 三、個案研究的意義與研究程序

　　Platt（1992）將「個案研究」定義為，設計研究方案必須遵循的一種邏輯準則，只有當所要研究的問題與環境互相適應時才會使用的方法，而不是無論什麼環境下都可以硬套上去的一種教條式研究方法。由此定義可知，個案研究方法有其侷限性與適用性，並非放諸四海皆可行的方法，通常只適用於特定研究問題與環境相配適的場合，不見得適用於研究者想怎麼做就怎麼做的一種研究方法。

　　個案研究（Case Study）為質化研究方法的一個重要支流，通常是指針對單一個案或少數幾個個案進行科學研究的一種方法。質言之，個案研究是針對某些少數案例或個案，進行深入、詳盡的研究，對個案各種因素的相互關係有一完整的瞭解，進而推論出某些命題（Proposition）。

　　個案研究的目的在於根據研究發現，提出解決個案所遭遇的問題，這一點和其他研究方法的目的並沒有太大差別。只是個案研究所要解決的是個案所遭遇的問題，期望歸納出研究結論，推論應用於其他一般化場合。簡言之，個案研究聚焦於特殊事件，相對完整的呈現其風貌來達成理解現象、命題一般化、理論建構與知識創新（瞿海源等人，2015）。根據此一精神，個案研究在選擇研究對象時就顯得非常重要。一般而言，研究者必須選擇具有代表性的個案進行研究才有意義，這樣所獲得的研究發現也才有價值與貢獻可言。

個案研究可以根據不同面向，區分為三種類別：內部性個案研究、工具性個案研究、集體性個案研究（Stake, 2000）。

1. 內部性個案研究：旨在彰顯個案本身的獨特性，因為個案太多了，必須審慎篩選，才不會掉入功虧一簣的泥沼中。無論是從什麼角度言，並非所有個案都值得去研究，要研究的個案必須具有獨特性才值得進行研究。

2. 工具性個案研究：個案除了具備獨特性之外，還要具有代表性，否則個案之多有如過江之鯽，沒有代表性的個案，不值得研究者花費寶貴時間去探索，即使進行探索也是毫無意義，更不用說會有什麼研究價值。

3. 集體性個案研究：個案研究以單一個案或少數個案為研究對象，集體性個案顧名思義是以少數幾個個案為研究對象，可以就這些個案研究結果進行比較，做更有意義的邏輯推論。

個案研究方法之所以受到重視，主要是根據小樣本的研究發現，可幫助人們對廣大社會現象的理解，研究過程中可以避開複雜的統計方法，使研究在知難行易原則下，相對容易進行。此外，個案研究具有五大功能或用途：(1)可用以解釋人們現實生活中，各種因素所存在的關聯性；(2)可以描述某一刺激因素及其所處現實生活的場景；(3)採用描述的形式，有系統述說及評估活動的主題；(4)因果關係不夠明顯或其關聯複雜多變時，可以進一步深入探索；(5)可以進行事後分析與評估（楊雪倫校訂，2009）。

個案研究的研究程序或步驟，和其他研究方法相類似，請參閱本書第一章第6頁論文寫作程序圖（圖1-1）。謹將個案研究程序簡述如下：

1. 研究構思：構思研究題目、動機、目的。
2. 文獻探討：探討相關文獻。
3. 研究命題：推論研究命題。
4. 研究設計：整體研究設計。
5. 資料蒐集：初級資料與次級資料蒐集方法。
6. 資料分析：資料分析與比對。
7. 研究發現：推論出研究發現。

8. 研究結論：提出研究報告。

9. 管理意涵：提出研究發現在管理與應用上的意涵。

10. 研究建議：提出研究建議與研究所受到的限制。

# 四、個案研究的設計與實施要領

　　個案研究看似簡單，實則不然。事前的研究設計扮演關鍵性角色，初學者或功力不高的研究者，常誤以為只要選擇一個個案，約定訪問對象，進行訪問並蒐集相關資料，整理資料然後提出報告，大功即可告成。殊不知這樣的報告常淪為走馬看花式的參訪報告，頂多只能算是粗淺的「訪問報告」，距離學術殿堂所要求的「學術論文」非常遙遠。

　　第一次接觸論文寫作的人，尤其是還沒有進入職場工作的MBA學生，常常認為只要找一家熟識的公司，訪問該公司相關人員，蒐集公司經營資料，就可以寫出一篇論文。即使擁有豐富職場經驗的在職學生，也常常會選擇以自己服務的產業或公司做為研究個案，或選擇自己負責的業務做為論文寫作的題材，認為對自己的公司或業務瞭若指掌，以個案研究方法寫成論文，應該可以收到事半功倍效果。然而每當和指導教授Meeting，報告研究構想時，常面臨無法回答教授質疑寫作可行性與適合性的窘境，以致難免會有嚐盡「被打回票」的感覺，此時才恍然大悟，原來自己想像中的個案研究方法，和學術論文所要求的個案研究方法，有一段很長的差距。

　　個案研究常被認為設計不夠嚴謹，欠缺科學研究方法的支撐，推論過程及研究結果的一般化程度，不夠具體，不夠精準，因而留給研究者與讀者有很大的自我解釋空間，無法和量化研究方法相提並論。加上研究者見解與功力參差不齊，引用的方法各異其趣，不是出現見樹不見林現象，就是令人摸不著邊際，以致留下不夠完美的批評。其實個案研究方法之所以自成一格，在研究方法中佔有舉足輕重的地位，自有一套適合應用的科學方法，只是學校教學偏重量化研究方法的傳授，甚少涉及教導質化的個案研究方法。

　　個案研究屬於質化研究的領域，「質化」無法用數量證明變數之間的關係，只能利用文字描述事物的本質。不同研究者對同一件事物的解讀常常各異其趣，以致會出現言人人殊現象，本質上就帶有相當程度的困難度。個案研究的設計要領可以整理如下：

1. 界定研究問題：從7W4H著手，也就是須思考要研究什麼（What）？為何要研究此一題目（Why）？何時進行研究（When）？在何處進行研究（Where）？由誰執行研究（Who）？研究對象是誰（分析單元），研究發現要提供給誰（Whom）？採用哪一種方法蒐集資料及分析資料（Which）？如何進行研究（How）？需要花費多長研究期間（How Long）？預計投入多少資源與預算（How Much）？如何評估研究成效（How to Measure）？

2. 推論研究命題：根據文獻探討及個案資訊的蛛絲馬跡，參照上述Why與How，引經據典的比對、推論研究命題。

3. 確定分析單元：分析單元可能是個別企業、個人或案例，只有釐清分析單元，而後才能精準的蒐集到所需要的資料。

4. 資料連結命題：推論命題的要領，除了必須做到引經據典之外，還必須符合邏輯關係的連結，這樣的推論才有意義。

5. 解釋研究發現：研究發現的解釋必須「有所本」，也就是要根據所蒐集到的資料，客觀分析、平實解釋，不宜信口開河，或無限上綱的做過度解釋。

　　完成嚴謹的研究設計後，必須再三檢視，再次確認個案的每一個細節。若確信研究方案可以據以實施，而且可以達成研究目的，即可按計畫步驟實施。實施過程中必須掌握下列要領，才不致偏離方向：

1. 確認要研究什麼（What）？
2. 次級資料有哪些？分散在哪裡（Where）？
3. 要蒐集哪些初級資料？然後據以設計問卷。
4. 採用什麼方法（Which）蒐集初級資料？
5. 如何進行資料分析（How）？
6. 如何推論出研究發現或結論？

　　個案研究方法通常都採用開放式問卷，作為蒐集初級資料的工具。個案研究的問卷題目或許沒有像量化研究的問卷題目那麼多，但是問卷設計要領中，最重要的是根據所要蒐集的資料，設計能夠蒐集到所要資料的問卷題目。質言之，要蒐集什麼資料，就要設計什麼問卷題目。設計對的問卷，才能蒐集到所需要的資料，如此才不會功虧一簣。

　　進行深度訪問，逐一發問，讓受訪者暢所欲言，並留意受訪者的臉部表情、說話語氣與肢體動作，瞭解受訪者的語意與意圖。訪問過程中必須專注聆聽受訪者的談話內容，並且記錄重點，事後可以補充發問，也可以輔之以電話訪問，確認談話細節與內容。訪問過程中若需要錄音或錄影，必須事先徵得受訪者同意，並尊重受訪者的智慧財產權。個案研究訪問要領可以整理如下（Berg, 1995）：

1. 融洽氣氛展開訪問：珍惜訪問對象慨允的訪問機會，除了充分準備之外，記得尊重訪問對象，營造現場融洽的氣氛，才能順利進行訪問工作。

2. 務必牢記訪問目的：受訪者通常都是忙碌的重要人士，時間非常寶貴，訪問過程中，必須牢記研究目的及訪問題目，不宜偏離題目，而淪為聊天的場合。

3. 輕鬆愉快進行訪問：訪問就是要來「挖寶」，訪問者必須心存感激，只有訪問者及受訪者都保持輕鬆愉快的心情進行訪問，才能夠挖到「真正的寶」。

4. 傾聽受訪者的談話：訪問過程中，除了必要的發問之外，必須用心傾聽受訪者的談話，留意受訪者的臉部表情及肢體語言，確實聽懂談話的真正意義。

5. 面帶微笑表示興趣：訪問者除了用心傾聽之外，還要保持面帶微笑，頻頻點頭示意，一方面表示尊重，一方面表示對受訪者的談話內容深感興趣。

6. 選擇合適訪問地點：訪問地點以尊重受訪者的方便為原則，通常會選擇在受訪者的公司，方便翻閱相關資料，受訪者若希望在其他地點，則悉聽尊便。

7. 尊重受訪者的意見：訪問者必須抱著前來請益的心情，尊重受訪者的談話內容，讓他（她）暢所欲言，翔實記下受訪者的談話內容要點與意見。

8. 不要滿足於簡單回答：訪問過程中隨時留意對方提供資料的完整性，遇有不瞭解的地方，或認為有進一步請益的地方，可以禮貌的請求詳加說明。

9. 演練、演練、再演練：訪問題目雖然經過嚴謹設計，為求圓滿而有效蒐集到所需資料，最好安排自我演練，只有演練、演練再演練，才能圓滿達成任務。

10.態度誠懇，感激受訪者：受訪者通常是忙碌的重要人士，慨允撥冗接受訪問，已經是非常難得的事，全程訪問過程必須態度誠懇，心存感激受訪者。

# 五、個案研究的優點與缺點

任何研究方法都有其優點，也免不了潛藏有其缺點。個案研究方法最大的優點在於研究對象少，研究人員操作相對容易，而且可以做深入研究，獲得有價值的研究發現。其餘優點可以整理如下：

1. 研究對象侷限於單一或少數個案，可以做到單點直入的深度研究。
2. 問卷設計相對簡單，訪問時間比較簡短。
3. 研究規模縮小，所需研究時程相對縮短。
4. 研究者可以自己執行訪問，無需藉助他人協助訪問，可以減少偏差。
5. 推論是從整個情境或實體個案中獲得，可提高研究結果的可靠性。
6. 針對真實事件或情境所做的描述，使研究發現「有所本」。
7. 研究者和受訪者直接訪談，可獲得第一手可靠、珍貴資料。

個案研究方法執行容易，而且具有許多優點，適合探索某些研究現象或議題，有時甚至是唯一可行的研究方法。然而，研究者必須瞭解及承認，研究者的功力若不是很高強，會嚴重影響研究結果；此外具有代表性的個案常常「一案難求」，而且很多場合不見得適合採用個案研究方法。從實務應用角度言，個案研究方法受到下列的批評與缺點（楊雪倫校訂，2009）：

1. 研究設計不像量化研究方法那麼嚴謹，可靠度略有不足。
2. 無法提供科學歸納的基礎。
3. 思考研究方法論時，需要花費很多心思。
4. 需要投入大量時間做資料分析與比對。
5. 研究結論的呈現淪為冗長繁瑣的文件。
6. 僅針對個案進行研究，可能造成不夠客觀的結果。
7. 關鍵受訪者不容易找，約定訪問時間也不容易。
8. 受訪者所提供的資料可能不夠完整或無法提供。

9. 樣本數少，推論的一般化能力可能會受到限制。

10. 研究者的經驗、認知與能力，可能影響研究結果。

# 六、個案研究實例

　　個案研究方法的原理和其他研究方法並沒有太大的差別，只是個案研究更重視特定事務的實務應用。探討個案研究方法除了介紹原理之外，最好的方式就是輔之以實例解說，述說研究過程中每一個步驟的要領。

　　本章接下來將採用作者在《產業管理學報》所發表的個案研究實例，「臺灣中小型家族企業生產技術發展之研究：自販機製造業金雨公司之個案研究」，逐一說明個案研究進行程序及其要領。

## （一）研究動機與目的

　　研究題目：臺灣中小型家族企業生產技術發展之研究：自販機製造業金雨公司之個案研究（林隆儀，2000）。

　　自動化一直是政府施政的重點政策，當時經濟部將自動化列為策略性工業，積極輔導產業升級，鼓勵廠商研發以自動化取代傳統作業方式，提高效率，提升競爭力。自動化不限於生產作業，而是擴及商業、服務業及其他各行各業，其中自動販賣被看好將是未來最有發展潛力的產業之一。

　　自動販賣機簡稱自販機，起源於美國卻在日本被發揚光大，我國很多廠商積極引進，到處都可以看到廠商所擺設的自動販賣機，販賣各種各樣的產品。自販機產業屬於新興產業，由於市場規模不夠大，投資成本卻非常龐大，廠商投資意願低落，以致我國市場上所見的自販機90%以上都來自日本。此一新興產業潛力雄厚，在乏人問津投資之際，我國有一家廠商金雨企業正值經營轉型，憑著自己的板金與電子技術，毅然投入自動販賣機生產業務，成為我國唯一一家生產自動販賣機的廠商。

　　這家屬於家族企業的金雨公司，經營者獨具慧眼，力行企業轉型，趁著大規模家電廠商尚在觀望之際，積極展開策略布局，勇敢投入生產，憑著低成本優勢及就近服務的便利性，不但快速進入市場，而且經營有成，躍升為股票上市公司，產品外銷到日本及其他國際市場。中小型家族企業能夠成功扮演新興產業開路先鋒角色，金雨公司這個個案殊屬難得、機不可失，乃選定此一非常獨特、具有代表性、有意義的個案作為研究的對象。

　　中小型企業規模小、人才少、資源短缺、發展緩慢，而且大多數屬於家族企業，由此可知家族企業和中小型企業關係非常密切。中小型家族企業大多由技術起家，家族成員的技術專長往往成為創業、轉型、升級與發展的基礎。自販機技術門檻高，受到內需市場規模有限的影響，金雨公司自行研發倍感艱辛，這些都突顯當時的產業經營問題。

自販機被應用的非常普遍，但是針對此一新興產業做有系統研究的卻有如鳳毛麟角，此乃本文研究此一題目的動機。基於此本文的研究目的有四：包括(1)探討家族特質對中小型家族企業特質的影響；(2)中小型家族企業生產技術的內涵及其主要來源；(3)中小型家族企業生產技術升級的主要途徑；(4)中小型家族企業生產技術發展過程中所遭遇的問題，然後根據研究發現提出命題。

## （二）探討相關文獻

確定研究題目後，接著開始探討相關文獻，作為建構本研究的理論基礎。文獻探討包括相關文獻與次級資料，相關文獻分散在各個領域，需要研究者根據本書第二章所介紹的文獻探討要領，詳細探討相關文獻並做有系統整理。

本研究所探討的文獻包括下列各要點，為節省篇幅，文獻探討細節予以省略：

1. 中小型企業與家族企業的定義與關係。
2. 家族企業的類型與特質。
3. 生產技術的定義與內涵。
4. 生產技術的主要來源。
5. 生產技術升級的途徑。
6. 生產技術發展所遭遇到的問題。

## （三）研究設計

研究設計旨在說明研究所要採用的具體方法，本文的研究設計包括下列各項：(1)導出觀念性架構；(2)說明選取研究對象的理由；(3)交代資料蒐集與分析方法。

本研究根據相關文獻，探討各研究變數之間的關係，包括中小型企業、家族企業、生產技術，以及根據本文的研究動機與目的，推導出觀念性架構，如圖6-1所示。

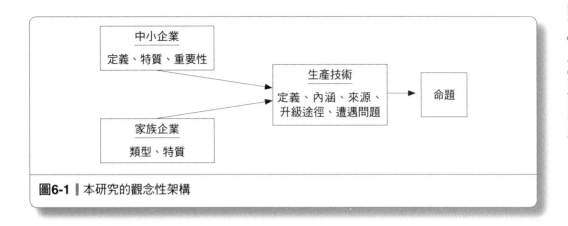

**圖6-1 ┃ 本研究的觀念性架構**

　　觀念性架構是以圖像方式呈現研究所涉及的變數及其構面，以及研究變數之間的關係，並以箭頭表示，一方面指引研究者正確的研究方向，一方面讓閱讀者一目了然研究規劃與內容。推導觀念性架構最重要的要領，在於要「有所本」，也就是要引經據典、有文獻支持、符合科學的邏輯精神，這樣的觀念性架構鏗鏘有力、精實有物，可以提高研究的清晰度與研究價值。

　　觀念性架構有如論文的靈魂或中心思想，沒有推導出觀念性架構的論文，猶如沒有靈魂的軀體，常會陷入不知所云的深淵，自貶研究價值。常見許多學術論文，不是沒有提出觀念性架構，就是沒有任何推論就直接寫「本研究的觀念性架構如下」，唐突的出現一張架構圖，會讓讀者有不知來龍去脈的感覺。

　　交代研究對象的要領，旨在具體指出所選取的研究對象，並說明選取的理由，讓讀者瞭解研究的價值。本研究選擇臺灣自販機製造業中，第一家（也是唯一的一家公司）投入生產，規模最大、最具代表性、產品種類最多，市場占有率高達95%的金雨公司為個案研究對象。

　　資料蒐集與分析方法旨在交代採用什麼方法蒐集與分析資料，讓讀者可以理解研究的可信度。資料蒐集與分析方法不限於只採用一種方法，研究者可以根據實際需要，同時採用多種方法，但是必須交代清楚。本研究定位為探索性研究，因此採用質化研究中的個案研究方法，以面對面深度訪問法蒐集初級資料，事前將訪問大綱傳送給受訪者，方便有所準備。訪問對象包括一起創業的董事長和總經理兩兄弟。訪問後再輔之以電話訪問，確認部分細節，提高資料的正確性與可信度。

　　資料分析方法是將訪問所獲得的初級資料，和文獻探討所整理的資料互相比對、印證，作為本研究發展命題的基礎。

## （四）個案描述

個案描述旨在扼要描述所選擇研究的個案，有系統地呈現個案公司的創業經過、經營現況與績效、所遭遇的問題，以及未來展望，為節省篇幅，個案描述細節予以省略。

本研究的個案描述包括下列各要點：

1. 自販機產業概況與特性。
2. 金雨公司創立及發展經過。
3. 家族特質與企業特質。
4. 生產技術的內涵及其來源。
5. 生產技術升級的途徑與技術發展所遭遇的問題。

## （五）命題發展

誠如本書第三章所討論，命題僅止於針對某一項觀念做完整描述所推導出來的結論，並沒有進行實際驗證與檢定。命題發展是本研究的重頭戲，其要領在於將文獻探討及訪問所獲得的資訊互相比對，以找出研究變數的對應關係，然後逐一推導出研究命題。

家族特質對企業特質的影響，企業特質和文獻探討所獲得家族企業一般特質的對應關係，如圖6-2所示。

金雨公司八項企業特質，主要受到五項家族特質的影響，八項企業特質和家族企業十二項特質中的十項特質相互呼應。可知金雨公司的企業特質深受家族特質的影響，而其企業特質和我國家族企業一般特質相一致。利用因果關係類比法可以做如下的推論：顧氏家族特質明顯的影響金雨企業的特質，而金雨企業特質和家族企業一般特質相近似，所以推論家族特質會影響家族企業的一般特質。因此，可發展出下列命題：

**命題1：家族特質會影響中小型家族企業的特質。**

金雨公司創業時以金屬加工為其技術切入點，雖然歷經金屬加工、OEM、自製自販機等三個階段，仍然以金屬加工為其核心技術，再以此核心技術為中心，逐漸發展其他技術。受到家族背景和特質的影響，形成創業的根基除了金屬加工技術，別無其他選擇的局面，和一般中小型企業技術廣

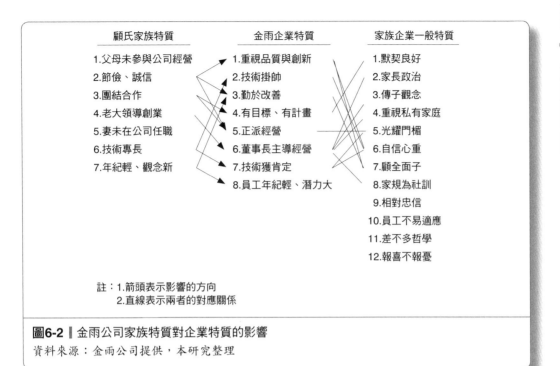

**圖6-2**┃金雨公司家族特質對企業特質的影響

資料來源：金雨公司提供，本研究整理

---

義的內涵相比較，顯得具體而狹義，主要偏重在產品發展、製程改善、品質
改良等方面，這些實用的金屬加工技術受到家族特質的影響，後來發展成為
公司的核心技術，因此可發展出下列命題：

　　**命題2：家族特質會影響中小型家族企業的技術選擇。**

　　**命題3：創業者的專長技術往往成為中小型家族企業的核心技術。**

　　金雨公司生產技術主要來源，和一般中小型企業技術來源比較，如圖
6-3所示。由此可知，金雨公司生產技術取得的管道和一般中小型企業並沒
有太大的差異。

　　金雨公司以金屬加工技術進入自販機製造業，由於對技術的重視與執
著，以原有單項技術為基礎，發展關聯性技術，結合成實用性與自主性更
高的群組技術，使技術發展更上一層樓。自販機八項（機構（板金）、電
子、通信、模具、網印、冷凍冷藏、自動控制、可靠度）技術中，有五項
（板金、電子、通信、網印、可靠度）是自行研發迎合市場需求的新技
術。因此，可發展出下列命題：

　　**命題4：創業者專長技術的成就，會激發中小型家族企業自行研發的興
　　　　　　趣與信心。**

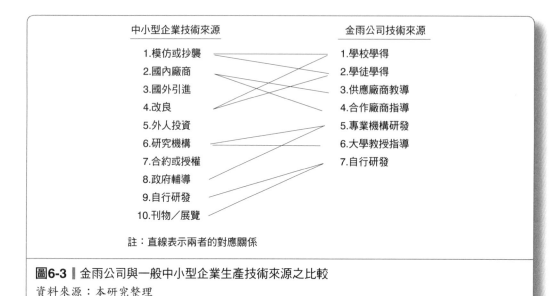

**圖6-3** ▎金雨公司與一般中小型企業生產技術來源之比較
資料來源：本研究整理

金雨公司和一般中小型企業技術升級的途徑，如圖6-4所示。金雨公司生產技術升級的八項途徑中，有五項和取得技術的管道相同；也就是說，技術升級的途徑和取得技術的途徑大同小異。據此可發展出下列命題：

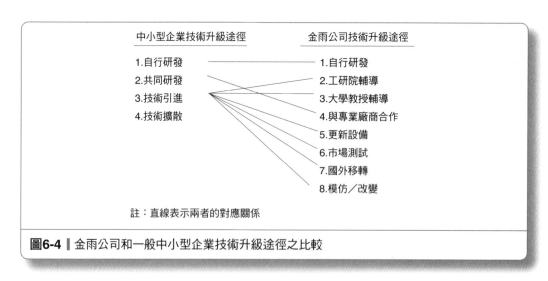

**圖6-4** ▎金雨公司和一般中小型企業技術升級途徑之比較

**命題5：中小型家族企業取得技術的管道往往是技術升級的重要途徑。**
金雨公司生產技術來源的管道及技術升級的途徑中，有一部分超越既有的技術領域，非短期所能學得，於是求助於政府專業機構，例如：委託經濟部工業技術研究院進行電子自動控制技術研究，聘請大學教授指導冷凍冷藏技術，彌補原有技術之不足。因此，可發展出下列命題：

命題6：中小型家族企業遭遇技術瓶頸時，往往求助於政府專業機構。

金雨公司技術發展所遭遇的問題，集中於人才、技術知識、管理能力、資訊、訓練等五項，和一般中小型企業比較，如圖6-5所示。

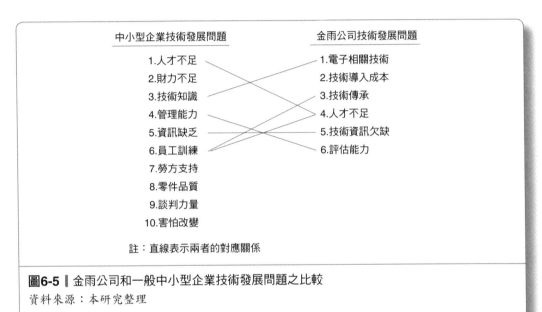

**圖6-5｜**金雨公司和一般中小型企業技術發展問題之比較
資料來源：本研究整理

電子相關技術不足，這是金雨公司技術發展過程中最大的瓶頸。此外，人員管理、合作對象的評估等均屬於管理技術領域，也是公司成長歷程中所遭遇的問題，這些都不是創業者的專長領域。據此可發展出下列命題：

命題7：創業者專長技術以外的技術領域，往往成為中小型家族企業技術發展的瓶頸。

## （六）研究結論

中小型家族企業兼具中小型企業的一般特質，以及家族企業的獨特特性，經營規模雖小，但家數眾多、彈性大、適應力強。中小型家族企業大多數靠技術起家，生產技術良窳足以左右經營績效。創業者既是企業所有權人，也是經營者，因此家族成員的特徵深深影響企業特質。

　　中小型家族企業生產技術來源，包括(1)學校學得；(2)創業前以學徒身分學得；(3)供應廠商教導；(4)合作廠商指導；(5)委託專業研究機構研發；(6)聘請大學教授指導；(7)自行研發。

　　中小型家族企業生產技術發展遭遇到的問題，包括(1)專長領域以外的技術能力不足；(2)技術導入成本高昂；(3)技術水準之維持與傳承不易；(4)缺乏人才；(5)資訊不足；(6)評估合作對象不易。

　　本研究利用個案資料比對法，根據文獻探討及訪問所蒐集到的資料，發展出上述七項命題。為節省篇幅，七項命題不再重複列出。

## （七）管理意涵

　　管理意涵旨在指出，研究發現在管理上所具有的特殊意義與貢獻，這是學術論文中很重要的部分，但卻常常被忽略。管理意涵寫作要領，請參閱本書第五章。本文根據研究發現所推論的七項命題，在管理上具有下列四項意涵。

### 1.開啟我國自販機產業研究先鋒

　　我國廠商引進自販機已經有很長一段時間，販賣的產品種類非常廣泛，其中以飲料自販機最為普遍。由於受到擺設地點的限制，雖然沒有像日本那樣普及，但是能見度也相當高，提供給消費者一個方便購買的通路，功不可沒。自販機擺設廠商很多，整個產業獨缺有系統的研究，本文以個案研究方式，選擇我國唯一一家自販機生產廠商進行研究，開啟自販機產業研究先鋒，具有拋磚引玉效果，對產業發展盡一點棉薄。

### 2.家族企業轉型的最佳典範

　　家族企業的共同特徵，不外乎資源有限、勢單力薄、轉型不易、生命力脆弱、競爭力相對薄弱。本文研究的個案公司，眼見為日本通信集團代工的訂單愈來愈少，亟需轉型，於是在「窮則變、變則通」的理念下，洞悉大規模家電廠商卻步的大好商機，毅然投入自販機生產行列，不但轉型成功，而且大放異彩。本文的研究過程與發現，見證了家族企業成功轉型的最佳典範。

### 3.技術領域擴大成競爭優勢

　　技術起家的家族企業，難脫既有專長技術的窠臼，又受到規模小、人才奇缺等限制，擴大技術領域談何容易。本文研究發現，創業時兩兄弟專長分別為板金與電子，自知擴大技術領域與技術層次升級將是家族最大挑戰。雖然如此，仍不畏艱難，積極尋求擴大技術領域與技術升級，從多種管道著手，包括求助於政府專業機構、向供應廠商請益、聘請專家指導，皇天不負苦心人，不但深化原有技術，並達到技術升級目標，更可貴的是因此建立了獨特的競爭優勢。

### 4.填補自販機產業研究文獻

我國自販機應用範圍相當廣泛，整個產業卻沒有人做有系統的研究，以致參考文獻非常有限。本文率先以公司為研究對象，以個案研究方式進行探索性研究，獲得許多極具參考價值的資訊，同時發展出七大命題，這些發現與結論可以填補參考文獻的部分空間，方便後續研究者參考、查閱。

## （八）建議與研究限制

本文根據研究發現，提出六項建議供金雨公司參考：(1)擴大延攬人才，加速企業發展；(2)建立嚴密管理制度，鞏固企業根基；(3)善用家族豐沛人脈資源，邁向企業家族；(4)記取「創業維艱，守成不易」的古訓；(5)致力於投幣機的研發，落實技術生根；(6)放眼國際市場，拓展產品外銷業務。

本研究進行過程受到下列限制：(1)僅以一家個案公司做探索性研究，會影響研究結果一般化程度；(2)雖然採用人員訪問法，輔之以電話訪問，但可能因受訪者個人的認知與主觀判斷，而影響研究結果的客觀性；(3)採用質化研究法，可能因研究者個人主觀的認知，而造成推論上的偏誤。

本研究提出兩項後續研究建議，提供給有興趣做後續研究者參考：(1)訪問同業其他公司，取得更多樣本，以及更完整資料，對整個產業做更深入研究，並進行實證分析；(2)研究機器製造業，探討和自販機製造業相近的機器製造業生產技術發展的相關問題，互相比較。

# 七、結語

個案研究法屬於質化研究方法的領域，本來就受到許多的限制，以致困難度相當高，包括有價值的個案難求、邀約受訪者不容易、研究者欠缺過人的研究功力。研究者必須熟悉訪問技術細節，訪問過程中必須專心傾聽受訪者的談話，觀察受訪者的談話語氣及肢體語言與其意義，才能蒐集到有意義、有價值的資料。資料分析過程中必須審慎、客觀的比對，再三推敲，才能推論出有意義的命題，獲得有價值的結論。

　　本文以作者所做過的個案研究為實例，比較質化研究方法與量化研究方法之異同，介紹個案研究的意義與研究程序，說明個案研究的設計與實施要領，分析個案研究的優點與缺點，呈現個案研究實例供參考，期能具有拋磚引玉效果。

# 第七章
# 論文寫作格式

## 一、前言

　　為了便於溝通、交流、互相學習，論文寫作需要有一定的格式，國內外皆然。格式是指一種式樣或標準。論文寫作格式是指論文寫作的標準式樣、規範或規定，寫作者或研究者必須遵照此一標準式樣、規範或規定撰寫。哪一章節該寫些什麼，哪一部分該怎麼寫，都有一個標準規範可循，不只可指引寫作的要領，同時也可以指引閱讀的方法。論文寫作格式提供寫作者和閱讀者一個說同樣語言的平臺，雙方透過此一平臺得以互相瞭解、互相溝通、互相學習，進而達到互相交流的目的。

　　論文可以依照其用途及呈現的方式，分為原始論文、研討會論文、比賽論文、期刊論文等四種類型。

1. 原始論文是指研究者按照研究程序所完成的完整論文，通常都是厚厚的一本，少者有七、八十頁，多者達一百多頁；至於論文格式，則各學校的規範不盡相同。

2. 研討會論文是指研究者將原始論文濃縮、改寫，參加研討會所發表的論文，研討會流程通常都安排得很緊湊，可供研究者發表的時間有一定的限制，除了文章篇幅不宜太長之外，文章格式也有一定的規範。

3. 比賽論文是指研究者將原始論文改寫後，參加比賽所發表的論文。許多單位為鼓勵學術創作、提高研究風氣，舉辦有論文比賽，主辦單位對參賽的論文格式有一定的要求。

4. 期刊論文是指研究者將原始論文濃縮、改寫後投稿到學術期刊，經接受後刊登在學術期刊上的文章。學術期刊每一期只刊登幾篇文章，篇幅有限，故文稿不宜太長。至於其寫作格式，也各有不同的規定。

　　論文格式一般要求不外乎規範下列項目，例如：

1. 題目：中英文題目的字體及大小。
2. 作者資訊：姓名、服務單位、職稱及E-mail帳號。
3. 摘要：內容結構、字數及關鍵詞。
4. 章節與標題：編排位置、字型及字體大小。
5. 引用文獻：引用文獻的寫法、年代的標示方法。
6. 圖表的標示方法、註解的寫法、英文專有名詞大小寫的寫法、參考文獻作者姓名的寫法、問卷及次要資料編排方法、頁碼的標示方法等。

　　論文格式寫作必須掌握「怎麼規定、就怎麼寫」的要領，仔細閱讀學校、研討會、比賽主辦單位，以及期刊所規定的論文格式，確實按照所規定的格式書寫。

　　本章將介紹及討論原始論文、研討會論文、比賽論文、期刊論文所要求的一般格式。

# 二、原始論文格式

　　每一所學校及研究所都訂定有論文寫作格式與規範，學生必須遵照學校的規範撰寫，如此一來，學生所撰寫的論文就可以做到統一格式、同一標準的境界。

　　原始論文的格式規範通常從封面、題目、章節、內文、註解、圖表、參考文獻、字體大小、標點符號等，鉅細靡遺的一一規範。

　　論文架構可以區分為篇首、本文、附錄等三大部分，這三大部分的撰寫內容及格式都有一定規範。

## （一）篇首

　　篇首是在揭示論文本文之前的相關資訊，包括下列各項目：

1. 論文封面：包括學校名稱、系所名稱、學位種類、指導教授姓名、論文題目、研究生姓名、論文完成日期等。論文封面必須同時以中英文書寫。以往的論文都以平裝裝訂為主，近年來許多學校採用精裝封面。

2. 空白頁：封面與標題頁之間留一空白頁。

3. 標題頁：標題頁所揭示的內容和封面相同。

4. 學位論文授權書：作者是否同意將論文著作財產權授予行政院國家科學委員會科學技術資料中心、國家圖書館及作者畢業學校圖書館，在不限地域、時間與次數，以微縮、光碟或數位化等各種方式重製後散布發行或上載網路。學位論文授權書需要由指導教授及研究生簽名。

5. 準學位推薦函：學生完成學校所規定之修業課程及論文寫作訓練，符合學校學位考試申請資格，由指導教授向學位資格審查小組推薦其論文初稿，參加學位資格考試及論文口試。推薦函需要由指導教授簽名。

6. 簽名頁：包括研究生姓名、論文中英文題目，論文口試委員會主任委員、委員，以及系主任／所長的簽名。

7. 致謝：研究生所撰寫的致謝詞。

8. 中文摘要頁：論文的中文摘要，包括關鍵詞。

9. 英文摘要頁：論文的英文摘要，包括關鍵詞。

10. 目錄頁：整篇論文的目錄，包括參考文獻及附錄（問卷）。目錄頁的頁碼以羅馬數字編排順序，所標示內容的頁碼必須和內文相一致。

11. 圖目錄頁：整篇論文中所出現的圖形，編成圖目錄頁，所標示內容的頁碼必須和內文相一致。

12.表目錄頁：整篇論文中所出現的表格，編成表目錄頁，所標示內容的頁碼必須和內文相一致。

## （二）本文

本文是論文的主體，通常包括下列章節：

### 第壹章　緒論

第一節：研究背景與問題

第二節：研究動機

第三節：研究目的

### 第貳章　文獻探討

每一節探討一個研究變數，完成個別變數之文獻探討後，接著探討變數間關係的相關研究，最後一節為文獻評析。

### 第參章　研究方法

第一節：觀念性架構

第二節：研究假說

第三節：變數操作性定義與衡量

第四節：抽樣方法與樣本數

第五節：問卷設計與前測

第六節：資料蒐集方法

第七節：資料分析方法

### 第肆章　資料分析

第一節：樣本特性分析

第二節：信度與效度分析

第三節：相關分析

第四節：變數殘差分析

第五節：假說檢定

第六節：討論

### 第伍章　結論與建議

第一節：研究結論

第二節：管理意涵，包括理論意涵與實務意涵

第三節：研究限制

第四節：研究建議，包括對業者的建議與對後續研究的建議

### 參考文獻

論文中所引用的文獻必須一一列在參考文獻中，以供查考。參考文獻排列方法，中文在前、英文在後。中文文獻按照作者姓氏筆畫順序排列，英文文獻按照作者姓氏字母順序排列。年代置於作者名字之後或置於頁碼之前，英文文獻第二位、第三位作者名字的寫法、期刊名稱、書籍名稱是否加上引號或採用斜體字等細節，必須按照學校的規範書寫。

## （三）附錄

蒐集資料所使用的問卷、實驗設計所使用的圖片和照片、訪問廠商名錄，以及其他未置於論文本文的參考資料，可以安排在附錄中。

論文寫作格式雖然有一定的規範，但是各學校及各研究所所定的規範與要求不盡相同，謹摘錄國立臺北大學企業管理學系碩士論文製作格式供參考。

# 國立臺北大學企業管理學系碩士論文製作格式

## 一、畢業論文規格

裝訂後大小以A4尺寸：長29.7公分，寬21公分，請加打封背，內封面且內容頁皆須插入學校飛鳶浮水印，硬皮的外封面則為系徽。

## 二、紙張厚度

封面及封底採用一百五十磅封面紙。內頁採用八十磅之白色模造紙印刷。

## 三、封面、封背顏色

依學年度由系上統一規定。（98學年度為灰色鑽石卡紙）

## 四、撰寫之語文

以中文、英文橫式撰寫。

## 五、字體大小

內文中文應以細明體或標楷體14號字撰寫，且字體應前後統一使用，格式為單行間距（要將「格式」→「段落」中的□文件格式被設定時，自動調整右側縮排、□文件格式被設定時，貼齊格線，將此二選項選為「空白」），中文段落要選取「左右對齊」。

內文英文應以Times New Roman 14號字撰寫，1.5倍行高（要將「格式」→「段落」中的□文件格式被設定時，自動調整右側縮排、□文件格式被設定時，貼齊格線，將此二選項選為「空白」）。章名稱應用標楷體18號字撰寫，節名則用標楷體16號字撰寫。

## 六、論文裝訂次序（本項目的附錄從略）

1. 封面和封面內頁：請參考【附錄一】。
2. 畢業論文通過證明書（口試委員簽名頁）：於論文口試通過後由考試委員共同簽名，並送交所辦經所長簽名，請參考【附錄二】。
3. 博碩士論文電子檔案上網授權書：請參考【附錄三】。
4. 謝詞（誌謝）：謝詞一頁並無硬性規定，此頁係供撰寫者感謝與論文有關之師友、親人與機構，請參考【附錄四】。
5. 中文論文提要：提要內容以說明研究目的、研究方法、資料來源、重要結論等為主，本提要請以14號字標楷體，單行間距，由左而右橫式繕打，以一頁完成為原則，依研究目的、文獻、研究方法、研究內容及結果、關鍵字，約500～1000字，請參考【附錄五】。
6. 英文論文提要（ABSTRACT）：Times New Roman 12 word type, single spaced throughout, must not exceed 500 words, approximately 1.5 pages. 請參考【附錄六】。
7. 目錄：「目錄」字樣置於距上緣3公分正中央處。先列謝詞、摘要、圖次、表次，再列各章節。各章節名稱須與文內所用名稱完全相同，最後列參考文獻。如有附錄，則列於參考文獻之後，請參考【附錄七】。（皆以標楷字體MS-Word功能自動產生）
8. 圖次、表次：皆為14號標楷字體，「目錄」之後依次為「圖次」與「表次」（與「目錄」相同位置），用以列示各表之表次及表頭（如「表一：各國人口與經濟成長率」）。表次列於圖次之後，格式相同，僅列二層為限，請參考【附錄八】。
9. 表次：請參考【附錄九】。
10. 本文：請參考【附錄十～十三】。
11. 參考文獻（中文、英文）：請參考【附錄十四】。
12. 附錄：如文內使用許多特殊「符號」或「縮寫字」，可在此列示之。

13.著作權聲明書：請參考【附錄十五】。

14.簡歷：請參考【附錄十六】。

15.封背：請參考【附錄十七】。

## 七、論文編排格式

❖版面配置

1.中文左右對齊四邊之空白，偶數頁右側約留3公分空白，左側約留2公分；右側留較多空白乃作為裝訂之用。奇數頁右側約留2公分空白，左側約留3公分；左側留較多空白乃作為裝訂之用。紙張上留3公分空白，下留白為2公分。而可供正文或說明圖表使用之範圍為長22.7公分，寬16公分的長方框。請參考【附錄十、附錄十一】。

❖編頁與標點符號

1.除了封面及封底外，論文中的每一頁均須編製頁首且字體為標楷體10號字，偶數頁首為「章次名」，奇數頁首為「論文名　頁碼」（章名與頁碼中間為兩格半形空白）。

2.章起首頁必在奇數頁，且不須插入頁首（儘管頁碼不須印出，但仍須計算）。

3.中式數字「三、四、五、……」，或「Ⅰ、Ⅱ、Ⅲ、Ⅳ、Ⅴ、Ⅵ、……」用於本文之前，其中包括謝辭頁、目錄、圖次、表次等，其位置編於距下緣1.5公分之中央處。

4.中文之標點符號皆為全形，包括『，』、『「　」』、『；』、『：』、『。』、『、』、『！』、『／』、『——』（兩格長度）、『＿＿』（底線）、『等等』、『？』及『』。注意中文並無"···"，應改為『...』（三點）。另外，英文中之連字元號"-"（hyphen），在中文中最好不用。

5.英文標點符號皆為半形且後面須空一格半形空格。（例外：句點後須空二格半形空格；左括弧前面須空一格，左括弧後面不空；冒號前不空格。）

6.文獻引用之標點符號，除中文文獻部分，其他標點符號以半形為主，且須注意標點符號後須有半形空格。

❖章節、段落位置

1.各章之名稱應置於奇數頁上方正中央處，距上緣3公分。各節之名稱應與上下隔一行，並置中排列。

2.中文內文應靠左對齊並左右切齊，每一段開頭空全形空白，即2字元。請參考【附錄十二】。

❖章節編排之次序

1.以中文數字為主，例如：第一章、第二章；第一節、第二節等。

2.論文篇幅較長，須在章節之上以「篇」標之者，宜用中文大寫標楷體20號粗體字示之，例如：第壹篇、第貳篇等。

3.第一節之下，若再有細分段落者，以阿拉伯數字標示之，其層次如下：（一）、1.、(1)、a、(a)皆為漸次內縮一個中文字（全形空白）且凸排。

❖段落

1.本文內各段之起首，應自左空全形兩格寫起，章節之下再分小段者亦同。

2.章節段落內，有敘述而須列舉項目時，依次使用壹、一、（一）、1.、(1)、a、(a)等表示之。

❖註

1.『註』主要是用來指出與論文相關性低，但重要的題外話，或說明不想強調的論點，或作數學證明，以及其他有害正文連貫性但具參考價值的解說。注意：勿將重要之論點置於註中。

2.『註』之使用，須在正文中，中文稿將以『註』帶頭的阿拉伯連續編號用括弧（）嵌在相關文句後，例如：（註2）。英文稿則用阿拉伯數字順序標明在右上角，例如：A number of reason for the imposition of trade barrier have been advocated by protectionists.[3]

3.『註』之編號可全文連貫，但最好是每章自成單元。『註』本身逐一註於相關正文同頁之下端。

4.行文中如引用他人著作而須提示文獻時，應直接將作者括在行文適當地方且與文獻參考相同，中文在前、英文在後（依標點符號位置，注意標點符號的全半形；以中文方式標示標點符號，且須成雙成對）。例如：（Shujaa, 1992）、（陳明終，1994；Shujaa, 1992）、（陳明終，1994；何慧儀，2000；Shujaa, 1992）。

❖圖表

1.每一圖（表）的結構包括：圖（表）說、內容及表（圖）尾，且圖（表）內文字為8～12彈性字體，以清晰完整為原則。

　(1)表標題應包含表次、標題（或與單位），且置於內容之上方且靠左對齊。表尾則包含資料來源且置於表內容之下方靠左。

　(2)圖標題應包含圖次、圖名且置於圖之置中下方。請參考【附錄十三】。

2.各圖表應緊跟於正文中提到該圖表之後，且應安置在同一頁之內或次頁。

3.須進行比較的圖表，應以上下對照方式呈報。

4.各圖形內容縱座標本身與橫座標本身的單位要一致，且不論縱座標或橫座標，標題要明確。

5.正文中圖表之編號以分章為之標號。如第一章內之圖表可自表1-1、表1-2；或圖1-1、圖1-2開始；不可為表1-1-1或圖2-2-1。

6.表與圖分開編號，並分別包括於表次及圖次內。請參考【附錄八、九】。

❖附錄部分

1.附錄（包括附表）置於『參考文獻』之後，以容納過長的數學證明、原始資料、問卷、詳細統計結果。

2.附錄一律以附錄一、附錄二做區分。

3.各附錄應有標題及簡單說明。附錄編號及標題應包括在『目錄』中。附表最好能分門別類包括在不同附錄下，但亦可獨立編號，連同標題包括在『表次』中。

❖參考文獻

1.參考文獻置於全文之後，英文以APA撰寫格式為原則，中文則以知名期刊為格式參考撰寫；列舉文內所有引用之參考書目及論文。（凡表格內有提到的作者或文獻，最後都應附在參考文獻的部分。）

2.中英文之參考文獻應分開撰寫，應先列中文、後列英文文獻；外文之書名採*斜體*格式，中文之書名採<u>下標線</u>格式。無須標號且每筆參考文獻在第二行以後須向右內縮（凸排一字元）。請參考【附錄十四】。

(1)中文文獻格式

　　a.引用書籍則以：作者（西元年代），版別，<u>書名</u>，出版地點，出版商。

　　如引用翻譯書籍：原作者中文譯名（譯本出版西元年代），版別，<u>書名</u>（譯者譯），出版地點，出版商（原著出版年：####年）。

　　b.引用學報或期刊類：作者（西元年代），「文章名稱」，XX學報，X卷X期：頁xx-xx。

　　c.引用雜誌：作者（西元年代），「文章名稱」，雜誌名稱，X期：xx-xx頁。

　　d.引用報紙：報紙名稱（西元年代），「文章名稱」，X月X日，X版版名。

　　e.論文格式為：作者（西元年代），論文名稱，XX大學XX研究所未出版之博士（碩士）論文。

　　f.引用網路：網站名稱（西元年代），<u>http://www.xxx.xxx.xx/</u>，搜尋日期：xxxx年x月x日。

(2)英文文獻格式

　　a.如引用外文書籍：以Author, A. A. (1993). Book title (2nd ed.). Location: Publisher.

　　b.如引用外文期刊：須包含Author, A. A., Author, B. B. & Author, C. C. (1999). Title of article. *Title of Periodical, xx*(xx), xxx-xxx.

　　c.如引用外文雜誌：須包含Author, A. A. & Author, B. B. (2000, November 10). Article title. *Magazine Title, xxx*, xx-xx.

　　d.未出版之外文論文：Author, A. A. (1986). Dissertation title. Unpublished doctoral dissertation, University Name, Place.

　　e.引用網路：Author's Full name (Year). Title of the Article, Retrieved month day, year, from http://Web address.

3.文獻之排列應以作者為序，中文以作者姓氏之筆劃由少而多，同姓者則比較名字；英文依作者姓氏（last name）字母為序。

(1)同作者多篇論文應以出版時間先後為序；如同一年有兩篇，則按出版月分先後排列，並於出版時間後冠(a)、(b)，以便文中引用。如加以編號，則中英文應連貫成一體系。

(2)中文作者為兩人以上時，以頓點表之；如中文作者為六人以上時，在最後的作者之後加上「等人」。英文作者為兩人以上時，以逗點表之；若英文作者為六人以上時，在最後英文作者後加上et al.表示。

4.撰寫人之簡歷，應置於最後一頁（不編頁次），註明姓名、出生地（省、縣或市）、出生年月日、大專（含以上）學歷、經歷（如有）及學術著作（如有）。

# 三、研討會論文格式

學術研討會是提供校際、國際學術交流的一個絕佳平臺，為了使參加發表的論文容易閱讀與理解，主辦單位都訂有一定的格式規範。參加研討會者需要按照主辦單位所規定的格式書寫，並遵照大會安排的方式與議程，出席及發表論文。

由International Business Academics Consortium及Academy of Taiwan Information System Research 共同舉辦的International Conference on Business and Information（BAI），每年七月都在不同的國家（城市）舉辦國際學術研討會，有來自世界各地的學者、教授、學生參與盛會，每年發表的論文都在500篇以上。BAI研討會每年一月分報名，二月分審稿，三月初通知審稿結果，三月底完成註冊，七月上旬舉辦研討會。謹摘錄BAI國際學術研討會論文格式範例供參考。

## FINAL SUBMISSION FORMAT INSTRUCTIONS FOR PROCEEDINGS OF BUSINESS AND INFORMATION: PLEASE READ CAREFULLY

*Chih-Chien Wang,*

*Graduate Institute of Information Management, National Taipei University,*

*69, Sec 2, Jian-Kuo N. Rd, Taipei City 10433, Taiwan ROC*

*wangson@mail.ntpu.edu.tw*

**ABSTRACT**

The final version of your papers or abstracts for the Proceedings of Business and Information (ISSN 1729-9322) should be submitted electronically.

Manuscripts must be prepared using Microsoft Word. If you have complex tables, diagrams, or symbols in the paper, please send a hardcopy to us for proofreading purposes. The paper size should be A4 (i.e. 21.0 centimeters [8.27 inches] by 29.69 centimeters [11.69 inches]) and the margins should be set to Word's default: top and bottom 2.54 centimeters (1.00 inches), right and left 3.17 centimeters (1.25 inches). Papers that deviate from these instructions may not be published. Please ensure that pages are numbered. DO NOT use headers or footers. Be sure to spell check the manuscript. Editors do not assume any responsibility for spelling and typographical errors. After formatting, upload your paper to the conference website http://atisr.org/conference before March 31, 2010.

Keyword: BAI2010, Final Submission, Format

## TITLE

Type the title in bold type, all caps, single-spaced, and centered across the top of the first page, in 14 point Times New Roman, as illustrated above.

## AUTHORS

The author(s), affiliation(s), mailing address(es), and e-mail address(es) should be single spaced and centered on the line below the title, in 12 point italicized Times New Roman, as illustrated above. One line space should be used to separate author(s) from the paper title. Please do not use titles such as Dr., Professor, etc.

## HEADINGS

Headings should be in bold type, in 12 point Times New Roman. First-level headings should be centered and set in caps, as illustrated above. Second-level headings should be flush left with initial caps. Do not use headings other than these two types. At least one line space should separate headings from the preceding text.

## ABSTRACT AND BODY

Introduce the paper with an abstract of approximately 100-200 words, in 12 point Times New Roman. Begin with the centered heading ABSTRACT. All body paragraphs should begin flush left (no paragraph indent) and right justified.

Single-space the body of the paper. Use 12 point Times New Roman throughout. Figures and tables should be placed as close as possible to where they are cited. First-level headings state the table or figure number. All tables and images should be embedded into the file and sized appropriately. All photographs should be sampled at 300 dpi (dots per inch). Keep in mind that web graphics are typically sampled at 72 dpi. Photographs must be properly sized and positioned in the body of the paper.

## LENGTH REQUIREMENTS

Papers submitted to the Proceedings of Business and Information (in CD-ROM) should not exceed 30 pages. There will be a charge of US $35.00 for all additional pages. For author who chooses to submitted abstract only rather than full paper, one page is allowed.

## CITATION

The Proceedings of Business and Information follows the reference format of Academy of Management Journal. This format is available at the AMJ's website http://aom.pace.edu/amjnew/style_guide.html. The use of footnotes is discouraged.

## APPENDIX

The appendix should immediately follow the body of the paper and precede the references.

## REFERENCES

Fang, W. & Wang, C. C. *College students' perceptions of computer network retailing and non-store retailing in Taiwan*, Paper Presented at 28th Conference of Western Decision Science Institute, Nevada: Reno.

Wang, C. C. & Fang, W. 1999. Is computer network retailing trustworthy? A survey of college students' perception in Taiwan. *Pan Pacific Management Review*, 3 (1), 95-104.

Wang, C. C. & Lee, H. Y. 2003. *E-mail rumors and forwarding behavior.* Paper presented at the International Conference of Pacific Rim Management, Washington: Seattle.

# 四、比賽論文格式

　　為鼓勵學術創作、提高學術研究風氣、增進論文寫作水準,許多單位每年都舉辦論文比賽。例如:經濟部中小企業處所舉辦的「中小企業論文比賽」、104人力銀行所舉辦的「全國碩博士論文比賽」、臺灣電子商務學會所舉辦的「崇越論文大賞」。比賽主辦單位定有論文格式規範,參賽者必須按照規定的格式書寫。謹摘錄「崇越論文大賞」論文格式範例供參考。

## 2010 TOPCO崇越論文大賞

論文題目:

### 消費者線上轉售行為與購買意願之研究:心理帳戶觀點之應用

報名編號:　　　　A0011

# TOPCO崇越論文大賞論文格式說明

## 摘要

本文將說明TOPCO崇越論文大賞完稿排版格式，參加本論文大賞的論文，煩請務必依照本論文格式進行編排，不符規定者，主辦單位得斟酌情形，不予審查。

關鍵字：論文大賞、論文格式

## 壹、來稿格式規範

來稿請用A4大小電腦用紙打字完成，由左而右橫向排列，並註明頁碼於置中處。版面邊界上留3cm、下留2cm，左、右各留3cm，採單欄的編排格式。文章段落格式的設定包括：行高設為多行1.25行，與前後段距離均為0.5列，並請取消「文字格線被設定時，貼齊格線」的勾選。

來稿請包括封面頁、摘要、正文（含圖、表與照片）、參考文獻及附錄（若有需要）。其他格式設定包括下列幾個部分：

### 一、封面

請使用崇越論文大賞專用論文封面。為維持匿名審查的嚴謹性，封面僅能註明報名編號與論文題目，封面中不得出現作者與指導教授之姓名；封面標題字型中文採標楷體、英文採Times New Roman字體，24級，粗體字。

### 二、摘要

請包括研究問題與目的、研究方法、研究發現、研究意涵（若適用的話）及實務意涵（若適用的話），文長不超過200字，關鍵詞以六個為限；摘要內容字型中文採標楷體、英文採Times New Roman字體，12級，段落左右對齊，縮排指定第一行2字元。

### 三、內文標題

論文內文標題字型中文採標楷體、英文採Times New Roman字體，粗體字，級數自行決定。標題凡中文撰寫者，段落標號方式如下：

```
                    壹、導論
一、研究設計
  （一）設計量表
        1.可信度
      (1)…
            a.…
              (a)…
```

### 四、內文

　　中文字體請採用標楷體，英文字體請採用Times New Roman，內文文字級數應為12級。段落左右對齊，縮排指定第一行2字元，英文字體第一行不縮排。文稿中不得使用註釋。

## 貳、圖表與照片

　　文章中之圖、表與照片宜簡明清晰、斟酌數量，並注意將圖、表與照片適當編排於文中第一次引述該圖、表內容之後的適當頁面，表格並應注意勿被切分成兩頁各半。此外，有關其他的格式，說明如下：

### 一、圖與照片

　　圖的名稱置於圖下方，照片的名稱置於照片下方，對圖與照片內容的簡要說明，置於圖與照片下方。圖與照片之標號，一律以阿拉伯數字表示。字型中文採新細明體、英文採Times New Roman字體，段落置中，與後段距離設為一列。圖內之字體大小可依實際需要設定，但整體應以清晰可讀為基本原則，如圖7-1所示。

**圖7-1** ▎臺灣電子商務學會會徽

二、表

表的名稱置於表的上方，對表內容的簡要說明，置於表下方。表之標號，一律以阿拉伯數字表示。字型中文採新細明體，英文採Times New Roman字體，段落置中，與前段距離設為1列。表內之字體大小可依實際需要設定，但整體應以清晰可讀為基本原則，如表7-1所示。

**表7-1**
TOPCO崇越論文大賞預計時程表

| 日　期 | 進　度 |
|---|---|
| 2010/05/01-06/14 | 接受報名 |
| 2010/07/05 | 完成初審 |
| 2010/07/15 | 通知口試 |
| 2010/07/24 | 決　賽 |
| 2010/07/31 | 頒獎典禮 |

## 參、參考文獻格式

一、內文中引述參考文獻的寫法

內文中如果有參考文獻部分，以下列方式（舉例）表示：

（一）若所引註的文獻僅有一位作者時，可寫成：

範例：1.蕭銘慶（1994）曾提到……

2.這個問題先前曾被討論過（Fox, 1994）。

（二）若所引註的文獻有兩位作者時，可寫成：

範例：1.吳學燕、范紹強（2006）曾提到……

2.這個問題先前曾被討論過（Adams and Browns, 1997）。

（三）若所引註的文獻有五位以上作者時，可寫成：

範例：1.李紀珠等（1997）曾提到……

2.這個問題先前曾被討論過（Adams et al., 1997）。

（四）許多作者文獻並列時，可寫成：

範例：1.吳學燕（1993）、吳萬益、林清河（2000）、高新建等

（1995）曾提到……

2.這個問題先前曾被討論過（Ostroff, 1993; Klein and Kozlowsk, 2000; Coombs et al., 1995）。

## 二、文後參考文獻寫法

中文文獻列於前、英文列於後，按姓氏筆劃排列或字母順序排列，文獻不用加序號。中、英文參考文獻之年分一律使用西元歷年。文獻格式舉例說明如下：

### （一）書籍

範例：1.黃俊英，1989。企業與社會，臺北：管拓文化事業及企管顧問股份有限公司。

2.Casson, M., 1979. *Alternatives to the Multinational Enterprise*, London: Macmillan.

### （二）期刊

範例：1.張玉山、吳浚郁，1993。利益分配機制的特性與作法，中山管理評論，第一卷第一期，115-152。

2.Capizzi, M. T. and Ferguson, R., 2005. Loyalty Trends for the Twenty-First Century, *Journal of Consumer Marketing* , 22 (2), 72-80.

### （三）編輯書之章節

範例：1.林清山，1978。實驗設計的基本原則，收錄於社會及行為科學研究法，上冊，楊國樞等（編），臺北：東華書局，87-130。

2.Bessley, M. and Wilson, P., 1984. Public policy and small firms in Britain, in Levicki, C. (Ed.), *Small Business Theory and Policy*, London: Croom Helm, 111-126.

### （四）博、碩士論文

範例：1.賴文彬，1982。製造業生產過程成本與效率之分析，中山大學企業管理研究所碩士論文。

2.Smith, H., 1979. *A multidimensional approach to individual differences in empathy*, Unpublished doctoral dissertation, University of Texas, Austin, U.S.A.

（五）學術研討會論文

範例：1.胡國強、吳欽杉，1988。企業推廣教育學員參與程度及成效評估之分析，中華民國管理教育研討會論文集，46-50。

2.Calaf, J. E., 1995. *Value-Added Network in Contract Manufacturing Annual International Conference Proceedings*, American Production & Inventory Control Society, Virginia.

（六）討論稿

範例：1.陳月霞，1992。臺灣共同基金之投資期限及風險係數，討論稿，國立中山大學管理學院。

2.Duncan G., 1971. Multiple decision-making structures in adapting to environmental uncertainty, Working Paper, Northwestern University Graduate School of Management.

（七）報紙

範例：1.李政霖，1990。轉換公司債應瞄準法人機構遞招，中國時報，七月二十五日，十一版。

2.New drug appears to sharply cut risks of death from heart failure (1993, July 15), *The Washington Post*, A12.

（八）網站

範例：1.彭淑珍，2005。淺談網路書店，中原大學張靜愚紀念圖書館館刊，七月十五日，第一百一十八期，取自：http://web.lib.pu.edu.tw

2.Neuman, B. C., 1995. Security, payment, and privacy for network commerce, *IEEE Journal on Selected Areas in Communications*, 13(8), 1523-1531, available http://www.research.att.com

# 五、期刊論文格式

　　每一份學術期刊各有其特色，各有其知名度，也各有其學術地位。學術地位愈高的期刊，論文格式的規範愈嚴謹。有些期刊甚至規定未符合其規範的文稿將不送審，所以，投稿時必須確實遵照規定的格式書寫。

　　期刊論文格式不外乎規範論文題目、作者姓名及職稱、摘要、本文各章節、註解標示方法、資料呈現及製表方法、參考文獻的寫法。謹摘錄輔仁管理評論論文格式及Journal of European Marketing論文格式供參考。

## 輔仁管理評論稿約格式說明書範例

### 一、段落標明方式及字體

（一）以中文撰寫者

　　1.題目：粗體22pt，置中。

　　2.作者姓名：細明體14pt，粗體，置中。

　　3.摘要標題：中黑體12pt，靠左。

　　　摘要內容：細明體9pt。

　　4.關鍵字：標楷體9pt。

　　5.內文：新細明體11pt，分段落，左右對齊。

　　6.行距：最小行高18pt。

　　7.段落標明方式如下：

　　　　　　　壹、導論

一、研究設計

　　（一）設計量表

　　　　1.可信度

　　　　(1)

　　　　　　a.......

　　　　　(a).......

第一層標題：中黑體17pt，粗體，置中。

第二層標題：中黑體16pt，粗體，左右對齊。

第三層標題：中黑體13pt，粗體，左右對齊。

第四層標題：細明體11pt，粗體，左右對齊。

（二）以英文撰寫者

　　1.題目：Arial字型18pt，粗體，置中。每字的第一個字母為大寫，其餘小寫，置中。

　　2.作者姓名：Arial字型13pt，粗體，置中。

　　3.英文摘要（標題）

　　　(1)英文摘要：Times New Roman字型11pt，粗體，靠左。

　　　(2)摘要內容：Times New Roman字型7pt，粗體，左右對齊。

　　4.關鍵字：Arial字型8pt，靠左。

　　5.內文：Times New Roman字型11pt，分段落，左右對齊。

　　6.行距：最小行高18pt。

　　7.段落標明方式如下：

INTRODUCTION

1. Research Design

1.1 Instrument（置左）

第一層標題：Arial字型17pt，粗體，置中。

第二層標題：全真中黑體16pt，粗體，左右對齊。

二、註釋

　　（一）以中文撰寫者，附註於頁底。如下例：

假說 II：出現超常報酬的期間與出現成交量殘差為正值的期間無關。[2]

---

[2] 在Crouch（1970）及（1980）的實證研究發現，資訊不對稱期間的交易量異常大時，成交量殘差與報酬率殘差值將成正值，此現象為Crouch（1970）及Morse（1980）的實證研究所發現。

　　（二）以英文撰寫者，附註於頁底。如下例：

...However, it is easy to see that from the model setting, mathematically, when both inequalities in (13) hold strictly, it merely means that an investor is not allowed to hold an asset long and short simultaneously.[7]

---

[7] Stulz (1981, pp.927) states that "From first order conditions, it follows that both inequalities can hold strictly only if the investor does not hold that asset,...

### 三、文獻引用

【例1】近年來有關這方面的探討逐漸受到重視，尤其在有關組織行為與人事管理研究領域中「組織承諾」（Organization Commitment），是常被學者們提及的重要概念之一（Steers, 1977；Mowday, et al., 1982；O'Reilly & Chatman, 1986；黃國隆，1986）。

【例2】Olson(1977). Suggested that people are more likely to use price to infer product quality when judging an expensive product.

### 四、圖、表之處理

1.圖、表置正文內。

2.表的名稱置於表上方（表頭），圖的名稱置於圖下方（圖尾），並以國字區分不同之圖、表。

3.對圖、表內容（如表中之符號）作簡要說明時，請置於圖、表下方。

4.中文：置中，內容細明體9pt，標題標楷體11pt。

5.英文：置中，內容Arial字型9pt，標題Times New Roman字型11pt。

### 五、參考文獻

文獻部分請將中文（細明體9pt，左右對齊）列於前，英文（Times New Roman字型9pt，左右對齊）列於後，按姓氏筆劃或字母順序排列。

1.*書籍*

【例1】徐立忠，「老人問題與對策」，臺北：桂冠圖書公司，1985年。

【例2】Rokeach, M., "The Nature of Human Values", New York: Free Press, 1973.

【例3】Siegel J. J., "Stocks for the Long Run", 2$^{nd}$ ed., New York: McGraw-Hill, 1998.

2.*期刊*

【例1】方世榮、江淑娟、方世杰，「夥伴關係整合模型的實證研究—以中小企業為對象」，管理學報，第19卷，第4期，2002年8月，頁615-645。

【例2】Shleifer, A., "Do Demand Curves for Stocks Slope Down?", *Journal of finance*, July 1986, pp. 579-590.

【例3】Rousseau, D. M., Sitkin, S. B., & C. Camerer, "Not so Different After All: A Cross-Discipline View of Trust", Academy of Management Review, Vol. 23(3), 1998, pp. 393-404.

3.*編輯書*

【例1】林清山，「實驗設計基本原則」，收錄於社會及行為科學研究法，上冊，楊國樞等（編），臺北：東華書局，1978年，頁87-130。

【例2】Cohen, P. R. and Feigenbaum, E. A., *The Handbook of Artificial Intelligence*, Vol.3, Pitman, 1982.

4.*博、碩士論文*

【例1】賴文彬，「製造業生產過程成本與效率之分析」，中山大學企業管理研究所碩士論文，1982年。

【例2】Doren, D. Stock Dividends, "Stock Splits and Future Earnings: Accounting Relevance and Equity Market Response", Ph. D. dissertation, University of Pittsburgh, 1985.

5.*學術研討會論文*

【例1】黃英忠，「從前程發展的理念探討中老年人力的運用」，中老年人力運用與企業發展研討會，高雄：國立中山大學管理學院主辦，1990年6月30日，頁117-125。

【例2】胡國強，吳欽杉，「企業推廣教育學員參與程度及成效評估之分析」，中華民國管理教育研討論文集，1988年10月4日，頁45-50。

【例3】Hsu, George J. Y., "A New Algorithm of Multiobjective Programming Integrating the Constraint and NISE Methods", paper presented at the 8th International Conference on Multiple Criteria Decision Making. Manchester, England, August 1988, pp. 29-30.

【例4】Lin, T. and Liou, K., "A Comparative Analysis of the Skill Requirement of MIS Personnel", *Proceedings of the Fifth*

*International Conference on Comparative Management*. Kaohsiung, National Sun Yat-sen University, 1992, pp. 331-337.

6. *討論稿（Working Paper, Manuscript）*
【例1】陳月霞，「臺灣共同基金之投資期限及風險係數」，討論稿，國立中山大學管理學院，1992年，no.C9201。
【例2】Lin, N. P. and Krajewski L., "A Model for Master Production Scheduling in Uncertain Environments", Working paper, National Taiwan University, 1990.

7. *英文中譯書*
【例1】盧淵源譯，杉本辰夫著，「事業、營業、服務品質產制」，中興管理顧問公司，1986年。

8. *網頁*
【例1】王順民，「限播預借現金廣告的社會行銷意涵」，國政評論，2003年，http://www.npf.org.tw/publication/ss/092/ss-c-092-011.htm。
【例2】林惠君，「臺新銀行點燃現金卡新戰火」，新新聞，週報850期，http://www.new7.com.tw/weekly/old/850-085.html。

9. *其他：無作者或缺一作者*
【例1】──，「動腦323輯」，臺北：動腦雜誌，2003年。
【例2】──, H. B. Gregersen and M. E. Mendenhall, "Toward a Theoretical Framework of Repatriation Adjustment", *Journal of International Business*, Vol. 23(4), 1992, pp. 737-760.

# Journal of European Marketing論文格式範例

## Manuscript requirements

1. Normally manuscripts should not exceed 8,500 words, **inclusive of references, tables and appendices.**

2. A **title** of not more than eight words should be provided.

3. A brief **autobiographical note** should be supplied including:
   - Full name
   - Affiliation
   - E-mail address
   - Full international contact details
   - Brief professional biography

   **NB** This information should be provided on a separate sheet and authors should not be identified anywhere else in the article.

4. Authors must supply a **structured abstract** set out under 4-7 sub-headings (see our "**How to... write an abstract**" guide for practical help and guidance):
   - Purpose (mandatory)
   - Design/methodology/approach (mandatory)
   - Findings (mandatory)
   - Research limitations/implications (if applicable)
   - Practical implications (if applicable)
   - Social implications (if applicable)
   - Originality/value (mandatory)

   Maximum is 250 words in total.

5. Please provide up to six **keywords** which encapsulate the principal topics of the paper.

6. Categorize your paper under one of these **classifications:**

- ◦ Research paper
- ◦ Viewpoint
- ◦ Technical paper
- ◦ Conceptual paper
- ◦ Case study
- ◦ Literature review
- ◦ General review

7. **Headings** must be short, with a clear indication of the distinction between the hierarchy of headings. The preferred format is for headings to be presented in bold format, with consecutive numbering.

8. **Notes** or **Endnotes** should be used only if absolutely necessary and must be identified in the text by consecutive numbers, enclosed in square brackets and listed at the end of the article.

9. Each **Figure** and **Plate** should be supplied separately (i.e. not within the article itself). All **Figures** (charts, diagrams and line drawings) and **Plates** (photographic images) should be of clear quality, in black and white and numbered consecutively with arabic numerals.

Figures created in **MS Word, MS PowerPoint, MS Excel, Illustrator** and **Freehand** should be saved in their native formats. Electronic figures created in other applications should be copied from the origination software and pasted into a blank MS Word document or saved and imported into a MS Word document by choosing "Insert" from the menu bar, "Picture" from the drop-down menu and selecting "From File..." to select the graphic to be imported.

For figures which cannot be supplied in MS Word, acceptable standard image formats are: **.pdf, .ai, .wmf** and. **eps.** If you are unable to supply graphics in these formats then please ensure they are **.tif, .jpeg (.jpg)**, or **.bmp** at a resolution of at least 300dpi and at least 10cm wide.

To prepare screenshots, simultaneously press the "Alt" and "Print screen" keys on the keyboard, open a blank Microsoft Word document and simultaneously press "Ctrl" and "V" to paste the image. (Capture all the contents/windows on the computer screen to paste into MS Word, by simultaneously pressing "Ctrl" and "Print screen".)

Photographic images (**Plates**) should be saved as **.tif** or **.jpeg (.jpg)** files at a resolution of at least 300dpi and at least 10cm wide. Digital camera settings should be set at the highest possible resolution/quality.

In the text of the paper the preferred position of all tables, figures and plates should be indicated by typing on a separate line the words "Take in Figure (No.)" or "Take in Plate (No.)".

10. **Tables** should be typed and included as part of the manuscript. They should not be submitted as graphic elements. Supply succinct and clear captions for all tables, figures and plates. Ensure that any superscripts or asterisks are shown next to the relevant items and have corresponding explanations displayed as footnotes to the table, figure or plate.

11. **References** to other publications must be in Harvard style and carefully checked for completeness, accuracy and consistency. This is very important in an electronic environment because it enables your readers to exploit the Reference Linking facility on the database and link back to the works you have cited through CrossRef.

You should cite publications in the text: (Adams, 2006) using the first named author name or (Adams and Brown, 2006) citing both names of two, or (Adams et al., 2006), when there are three or more authors. At the end of the paper a reference list in alphabetical order should be supplied:

○ *For books*: Surname, Initials (year), *Title of Book*, Publisher, Place of publication.

e.g. Harrow, R. (2005), *No Place to Hide*, Simon & Schuster, New York, NY.

○ *For book chapters*: Surname, Initials (year), "Chapter title", Editor's Surname, Initials (Ed.), *Title of Book*, Publisher, Place of publication, pages.

e.g. Calabrese, F. A. (2005), "The early pathways: theory to practice - a continuum", in Stankosky, M. (Ed.), *Creating the Discipline of Knowledge Management*, Elsevier, New York, NY, pp. 15-20.

○ *For journals*: Surname, Initials (year), "Title of article", *Journal Name*, volume, number, pages.

e.g. Capizzi, M. T. and Ferguson, R. (2005), "Loyalty trends for the twenty-first century", *Journal of Consumer Marketing*, Vol. 22 No. 2, pp.

72-80.

- *For published conference proceedings*: Surname, Initials (year of publication), "Title of paper", in Surname, Initials (Ed.), *Title of published proceeding which may include place and date(s) held*, Publisher, Place of publication, Page numbers.

  eg Jakkilinki, R., Georgievski, M. and Sharda, N. (2007), "Connecting destinations with an ontology-based e-tourism planner", in *Information and communication technologies in tourism 2007 proceedings of the international conference in Ljubljana, Slovenia, 2007*, Springer-Verlag, Vienna, pp. 12-32.

- *For unpublished conference proceedings*: Surname, Initials (year), "Title of paper", paper presented at Name of Conference, date of conference, place of conference, available at: URL if freely available on the internet (accessed date).

  e.g. Aumueller, D. (2005), "Semantic authoring and retrieval within a wiki", paper presented at the European Semantic Web Conference (ESWC), 29 May-1 June, Heraklion, Crete, available at: http://dbs.uni-leipzig.de/file/aumueller05wiksar.pdf (accessed 20 February 2007).

- *For working papers*: Surname, Initials (year), "Title of article", working paper [number if available], Institution or organization, Place of organization, date.

  e.g. Moizer, P. (2003), "How published academic research can inform policy decisions: the case of mandatory rotation of audit appointments", working paper, Leeds University Business School, University of Leeds, Leeds, 28 March.

- *For encyclopedia entries (with no author or editor): Title of Encyclopedia* (year) "Title of entry", volume, edition, *Title of Encyclopedia*, Publisher, Place of publication, pages.

  e.g. *Encyclopaedia Britannica* (1926) "Psychology of culture contact", Vol. 1, 13th ed., Encyclopaedia Britannica, London and New York, NY, pp. 765-71.

  (For authored entries please refer to book chapter guidelines above.)

- *For newspaper articles (authored)*: Surname, Initials (year), "Article title",

*Newspaper*, date, pages.

e.g. Smith, A. (2008), "Money for old rope", *Daily News*, 21 January, pp. 1, 3-4.

◦ *For newspaper articles (non-authored): Newspaper* (year), "Article title", date, pages.

e.g. *Daily News* (2008), "Small change", 2 February, p. 7.

◦ *For electronic sources*: if available online the full URL should be supplied at the end of the reference, as well as a date that the resource was accessed.

e.g. Castle, B. (2005), "Introduction to web services for remote portlets", available at: http://www-128.ibm.com/developerworks/library/ws-wsrp/ (accessed 12 November 2007).

Standalone URLs, i.e. without an author or date, should be included either within parentheses within the main text, or preferably set as a note (roman numeral within square brackets within text followed by the full URL address at the end of the paper).

# 六、其他注意事項

　　論文寫作除了上述要領、技巧、格式之外，還有許多細節需要同時注意，才能使論文作最完美的呈現。

## （一）杜絕錯別字

　　現在的學生寫報告、做論文，都以電腦打字書寫。然而電腦打出的字偶爾會出現錯別字，研究者在完成論文寫作後必須仔細閱讀幾遍，精心核對，杜絕錯別字，避免留下不完美的遺憾。閱讀及核對時，可以請家人協助，或和同學交換閱讀，一方面交換寫作心得，一方面互相幫忙訂正錯別字。

## （二）避免用詞語病

　　一篇內容豐富的論文，篇幅都有一定的長度，研究者在寫作過程中偶爾會出現詞不達意的現象，甚至出現用詞上的語病。寫作過程中應避免這種現象，論文定稿之前必須反覆閱讀，以避免詞不達意及用詞上的語病。

### （三）引用外文文獻，要使用中文寫出其意義

論文中引用外文文獻時，要把所引用的內容以中文寫出來，不宜照本宣科的直接寫出外文。以中文書寫的論文必須以中文書寫為主，引用外文的文獻必須也用中文寫出。

### （四）圖、表的引出及標示要領

論文中常常採用圖、表幫助研究者解釋，以及增進閱讀者的理解。表的標題置於表格上方，圖的標題置於圖的下方。每當圖、表出現之前，需要有一句引導語引出該圖、表。例如：變數相關分析表出現之前，需要有一句「研究變數相關分析結果整理如表3所示」的引出語，好讓文章的閱讀有連貫及順暢的感覺。圖、表若是引用他人的文獻，還需要在圖、表下方註明「資料來源」，並且精準的標示該圖、表在原始文獻上的頁碼。圖、表若是研究者自行繪製者，只須標示標題即可，無須在圖、表下方註明「本研究整理」等字樣。

### （五）避免使用誇大之詞

研究者在論文寫作過程中必須表現出謙虛為懷的態度，不宜因為想要突顯個人的才華而採用誇大之詞。謙虛為懷不但可以表現出研究者的寫作風格，同時也可以提高論文被欣賞的機會。

### （六）善用附錄的功能

論文寫作原則之一是不宜出現不相關的資料，所以附錄中除了前測問卷及正式訪問問卷之外，研究者常常會遇到某些資料納入論文本文可能不是很適當，但是棄之又覺得可惜的情況。此時可以考慮善用附錄的功能，把這些圖形、圖片、照片、表格等佐證的參考資料，以及其他如受訪廠商名錄等，納入附錄中。

### （七）納入口試委員的指導意見

論文寫作過程中會有兩次考試機會，一次是論文計畫書考試，一次是論文的畢業考試，這兩次考試的考試委員都會提供改進論文的寶貴意見。考試委員所提供的指導意見相當珍貴，研究者必須虛心接受，審慎納入論文之中，使整篇論文更完整、更有可讀性、更具有參考價值。

### （八）掌握「信、達、雅」原則

研究工作和論文寫作都是一種非常專業的工作，無論是在研究階段或寫

作階段，研究者都必須確實掌握「信、達、雅」原則，務實的進行研究與寫作，忠實的呈現及寫出研究成果，以優雅流暢的文筆撰寫論文。

# 七、結語

　　格式猶如論文的滋潤劑，內容精彩的論文若沒有使用正確的格式書寫，就好像缺少了滋潤，也就難和良好論文結緣了。論文寫作有一定程序，各學校及研究所的書寫方式有一定規範，但是校際及發表的論文格式細節至今還沒有統一的規定，以致研究者完成論文寫作之後，準備發表論文時，需要針對研討會、比賽主辦單位，以及期刊的要求，再費一番功夫整理成符合規定的格式。

　　論文格式只要按照規定的格式書寫就對了。然而按照規定格式書寫看似簡單，細節卻相當複雜，尤其是整篇論文要面面俱到，精準的按照規定格式書寫，需要研究者細心、用心的詳讀論文格式規範，冷靜、耐心的書寫，要寫出符合規定格式的論文，也就不是很困難的事了。

# 第八章
## 附錄

# 附錄一、問卷

【關係行銷結合類型、服務品質與關係品質、轉換成本對顧客忠誠之影響——以臺灣北部地區寬頻網路消費者為例】問卷。

敬愛的小姐／先生，您好：

　　這是一份純學術性的問卷，主要目的在瞭解您對於「寬頻網路服務提供者」的一些感受與看法。本問卷採不記名方式作答，您所填寫的資料僅供學術研究與整體分析之用，絕不做其他用途，請安心做答。因本問卷發放數量有限，所以您寶貴的意見對本研究的結果相當重要，故請仔細閱讀後再作答。最後，感謝您寶貴的意見及協助。

　　敬祝

身體健康　萬事如意

真理大學管理科學研究所

指導教授：林隆儀 博士

研 究 生：徐稚軒 敬上

聯絡電話：0919905333

## 第一部分

　　以下是衡量您對目前所使用的寬頻網路服務提供者實行關係結合的同意程度。請依照您心目中的想法在下列各項問題中勾選適當的答案，每個問題均為單選題。

| | 非常不同意 | 不同意 | 稍微不同意 | 沒意見 | 稍微同意 | 同意 | 非常同意 |
|---|---|---|---|---|---|---|---|
| 1.申請寬頻服務後，我可以得到免費贈品或折扣等優惠。 | □ | □ | □ | □ | □ | □ | □ |
| 2.當我使用時間愈久，該業者提供我較高的續約折扣。 | □ | □ | □ | □ | □ | □ | □ |
| 3.該業者有提供折扣以吸引消費者申請寬頻網路服務。 | □ | □ | □ | □ | □ | □ | □ |
| 4.在特定節日會收到該業者的卡片或禮物。 | □ | □ | □ | □ | □ | □ | □ |
| 5.該業者會試圖與顧客保持聯絡。 | □ | □ | □ | □ | □ | □ | □ |
| 6.該業者設有討論或聯誼性的社群。 | □ | □ | □ | □ | □ | □ | □ |
| 7.該業者會提供與產品或服務相關的知識。 | □ | □ | □ | □ | □ | □ | □ |

8.該業者有提供完善的售後服務。 □ □ □ □ □ □ □

9.該業者會對於產品有清楚詳細的介紹。 □ □ □ □ □ □ □

10.該業者有提供附加服務,如:線上掃毒、線上 □ □ □ □ □ □ □
硬碟、E-mail空間。

11.該業者可以針對不同的顧客需求提供多種連線 □ □ □ □ □ □ □
頻寬。

## 第二部分

　　以下是衡量您對目前所使用的寬頻網路服務提供者服務品質的同意程度。請依照您心目中的想法在下列各項問題中勾選適當的答案,每個問題均為單選題。

|  | 非常不同意 | 不同意 | 稍微不同意 | 沒意見 | 稍微同意 | 同意 | 非常同意 |
|---|---|---|---|---|---|---|---|
| 1.該業者擁有現代化設備服務顧客,使連線品質良好。 | □ | □ | □ | □ | □ | □ | □ |
| 2.該業者提供顧客完整易懂的寬頻上網服務功能之相關操作說明。 | □ | □ | □ | □ | □ | □ | □ |
| 3.該業者的員工衣著整齊。 | □ | □ | □ | □ | □ | □ | □ |
| 4.該業者能履行對顧客承諾的服務。 | □ | □ | □ | □ | □ | □ | □ |
| 5.顧客遭遇問題時,服務人員能為顧客著想並提供協助。 | □ | □ | □ | □ | □ | □ | □ |
| 6.該業者擁有良好的公司信譽,取得顧客之信任。 | □ | □ | □ | □ | □ | □ | □ |
| 7.該業者的障礙查修迅速確實。 | □ | □ | □ | □ | □ | □ | □ |
| 8.服務人員對於顧客有關上網服務的諮詢,能立即給予滿意答覆。 | □ | □ | □ | □ | □ | □ | □ |
| 9.該業者的服務人員樂於幫助顧客。 | □ | □ | □ | □ | □ | □ | □ |
| 10.該業者的服務人員不會因為忙碌而沒有回應顧客。 | □ | □ | □ | □ | □ | □ | □ |
| 11.該業者承諾顧客之服務均能確實達成。 | □ | □ | □ | □ | □ | □ | □ |

12.該業者的服務人員之服務態度親切有禮。 ☐ ☐ ☐ ☐ ☐ ☐ ☐

13.該業者的服務人員有足夠的專業知識，並獲得 ☐ ☐ ☐ ☐ ☐ ☐ ☐
　顧客信任。

14.該業者的服務人員瞭解顧客的需求。 ☐ ☐ ☐ ☐ ☐ ☐ ☐

15.該業者願意配合顧客時間進行服務，如：裝機 ☐ ☐ ☐ ☐ ☐ ☐ ☐
　或維修服務。

16.該業者能以顧客利益為導向。 ☐ ☐ ☐ ☐ ☐ ☐ ☐

## 第三部分

　　以下是衡量您對目前所使用的寬頻網路服務提供者關係品質的同意程度。請依照您心目中的想法在下列各項問題中勾選適當的答案，每個問題均為單選題。

| | 非常不同意 | 不同意 | 稍微不同意 | 沒意見 | 稍微同意 | 同意 | 非常同意 |
|---|---|---|---|---|---|---|---|
| 1.該業者是可信任的。 | ☐ | ☐ | ☐ | ☐ | ☐ | ☐ | ☐ |
| 2.與該業者交易是很安全的。 | ☐ | ☐ | ☐ | ☐ | ☐ | ☐ | ☐ |
| 3.該業者是負責任的。 | ☐ | ☐ | ☐ | ☐ | ☐ | ☐ | ☐ |
| 4.即使可以，我也不想選擇使用其他網路服務提供業者。 | ☐ | ☐ | ☐ | ☐ | ☐ | ☐ | ☐ |
| 5.我願意長期地使用這家寬頻網路服務提供業者的服務。 | ☐ | ☐ | ☐ | ☐ | ☐ | ☐ | ☐ |
| 6.該業者值得我與他保持關係。 | ☐ | ☐ | ☐ | ☐ | ☐ | ☐ | ☐ |

## 第四部分

　　以下是衡量您對目前所使用的寬頻網路服務提供者轉換成本的同意程度。請依照您心目中的想法在下列各項問題中勾選適當的答案，每個問題均為單選題。

| | 非常不同意 | 不同意 | 稍微不同意 | 沒意見 | 稍微同意 | 同意 | 非常同意 |
|---|---|---|---|---|---|---|---|
| 1.我的寬頻網路服務提供業者提供我一些其他業者所沒有的待遇。 | □ | □ | □ | □ | □ | □ | □ |
| 2.失去該業者的優惠是很可惜的。 | □ | □ | □ | □ | □ | □ | □ |
| 3.假如轉換到其他寬頻網路服務業者，我會損失許多目前累積的優惠方案。 | □ | □ | □ | □ | □ | □ | □ |
| 4.我已經投入許多時間精力在這項產品。 | □ | □ | □ | □ | □ | □ | □ |
| 5.我很在意在此寬頻網路提供業者所做過的消費。 | □ | □ | □ | □ | □ | □ | □ |
| 6.我對於該業者已經做過許多投資。 | □ | □ | □ | □ | □ | □ | □ |

## 第五部分

　　以下是衡量您對目前所使用的寬頻網路服務提供者顧客忠誠的同意程度。請依照您心目中的想法在下列各項問題中勾選適當的答案，每個問題均為單選題。

| | 非常不同意 | 不同意 | 稍微不同意 | 沒意見 | 稍微同意 | 同意 | 非常同意 |
|---|---|---|---|---|---|---|---|
| 1.當其他寬頻網路業者有優惠促銷時，我仍願意持續使用現在的寬頻服務業者。 | □ | □ | □ | □ | □ | □ | □ |
| 2.我認為我是該業者的忠誠顧客。 | □ | □ | □ | □ | □ | □ | □ |
| 3.當我再次需要寬頻網路服務時，我會選擇現在的寬頻網路服務業者。 | □ | □ | □ | □ | □ | □ | □ |
| 4.我願意主動推薦我現在所使用的寬頻網路業者給我的親朋好友。 | □ | □ | □ | □ | □ | □ | □ |
| 5.我願意購買該寬頻網路業者的其他相關服務。 | □ | □ | □ | □ | □ | □ | □ |

## 第六部分

個人基本資料：

1.性別　□男　□女

2.年齡　□20歲以下　□21～30歲　□31～40歲　□41～50歲
　　　　□51歲以上

3.職業　□電子資訊業　□金融保險業　□自由業　□一般服務業
　　　　□魚林農牧礦　□軍公教　□學生　□其他_____

4.月所得　□19,999元以下　□20,000元～29,999元
　　　　　□30,000元～39,999元　□40,000元～49,999元
　　　　　□50,000元～59,999元　□60,000元～69,999元
　　　　　□70,000元以上

5.您是哪一家寬頻網路業者的用戶？
　　□Hinet　□Seednet　□速博　□臺灣固網　□東森（亞太）
　　□Sonet　□其他_____

6.婚姻狀況　□未婚　□已婚

# 附錄二、論文寫作心得

## 信、達、雅精神之追求

臺北大學博士班研究生　陳俊碩

　　論文寫作對許多研究生、甚至是博士生來說，都是極富挑戰的一個課題。筆者也曾在論文寫作的茫茫大海中迷失過方向，但何其有幸，能獲恩師林隆儀教授的指點，以其「信、達、雅」的論文寫作精神，走出了曾經迷失的方向，也發現了自己的一片天。

　　正當某日埋首於博士班的課業時，突接獲恩師林隆儀教授的來電，電話中希望筆者能撰寫一篇有關論文寫作要領的心得文章，放在老師的大作中。但一想到自己在論文的撰寫上還差老師太多，本想婉拒老師的好意，但老師說這本書的撰寫是希望能提供所有對論文撰寫有疑惑的人士一點幫助時，猛然想起唸研究所甫準備撰寫碩士論文的那時，那種焦慮不安、充滿疑惑的心情，頓時感同身受。筆者深知自己在論文撰寫上還有待努力，但總希望能貢獻一己之力，藉此機會提供自己的一些心得，希冀能對所有對論文撰寫有疑惑的人士有所幫助。

　　在接下這個重責大任之後，筆者開始蒐集一些相關資料，從中發現了當初在撰寫碩士論文時的準備資料，拿起來的第一個感覺就是「好厚啊！」。沒錯，撰寫論文的第一個體認，就是必須要有充足的時間來做資料蒐集與撰寫的工作，一般從開始著手到完成大約需要花一年至一年半左右的時間來投入。論文撰寫是個繁雜的工作，在撰寫之前必須花費時間蒐集與閱讀大量的參考資料和文章，才能從中發現是否在某些議題上還有所遺漏而須補強之處，抑或是有趣且有價值而別人尚未發現之處，兩者都是訂定論文題目的好方向。

　　在修習博士班課程時曾聽老師說：學術猶如一座礦山，許多人都在努力的挖，期待能從中挖出一些有價值的東西。然而，當挖的人愈來愈多，或是某個地區已經挖得差不多時，想要再挖出些有價值的金礦可能已經不容易，但也許還能挖到些許銅礦，端看論文撰寫者本身對於這篇文章的定位。因此，在撰寫論文之前，透過大量的閱讀來挖掘題目的方向是絕對必要的。

　　筆者碩士論文的題目與架構，也是在經過百般波折下才正式確定。從當初找出的資料中發現，光是訂定題目與架構，就與指導教授討論了十多張A4紙才確定，耗費時間大約就有三至四個月；但一旦題目與架構確定了，第一個難關也算是克服了。

　　在此要提醒的是，論文題目的訂定有幾個原則：第一是要適合研究，在研究者能力與範圍許可的條件下，找尋適合研究的題目。第二是題目要能清楚地指出要研究的是什麼，讓讀者能一看到題目就知道本篇論文是在研究什麼。第三是題目必須與研究架構相呼應，而不是兩者各不相同。最後一點則是研究題目不宜太大，這跟文章長短的道理一樣，並不是愈長的論文就愈有學問，只要有價值，短短的題目也可以讓讀者激賞。

　　筆者在就讀研究所期間，因為所上每週都固定有學術文章的研討課程，因而就此發現了自己的研究興趣，並藉此研讀了許多相關的國內、外學術文章。再加上當時發生了所謂的泰瑞公司以新電視機殼搭配舊映像管當新電視賣的時事事件，筆者因此更加確認了自己對來源國國家形象的研究興趣。

　　在確認了題目之後，就可以開始著手規劃論文的寫作計畫。一般商管類的論文會包括七個部分，包含有第一章緒論、第二章文獻探討、第三章研究設計、第四章資料分析、第五章結論與建議，以及參考文獻、附錄等。在規劃論文的寫作計畫時，筆者強烈建議最好是搭配題目與架構做一完整的規劃，有點像是企業為達成目標所做的策略規劃書一樣，這個計畫等於是告訴指導教授與論文撰寫者，關於這篇論文在寫作時間的規劃上是如何、在研究的執行上是如何、遇到任何問題與困難時可能的解決方法有哪些等資訊。這樣在撰寫論文的過程中，撰寫者才不至於遇到一點小問題就亂了陣腳，而且還能更有信心地寫出一篇好的論文。當然，更重要的是，這個計畫必須與指導教授深入溝通並且獲得其肯定才行。

　　計畫書完成後，就可以開始進入論文研究的主體，也就是第一章緒論。第一章是很重要的一章，是整篇論文研究精神的所在，包含四個大項：研究背景、研究問題、研究動機與研究目的。第一章算是論文撰寫者與讀者之間溝通的橋梁，必須描述背景、點出問題、說明動機，並寫出目的。論文撰寫者在決定題目時，必定有研究當時的時空背景，撰寫者必須清楚的描述出來，讓讀者能清楚知道並融入研究當時的情境。在說明情境後，撰寫者是因為什麼樣的問題而想做此一研究，也必須點出來，讓讀者能夠瞭解此一論文研究能解決什麼樣的問題。之後是研究動機，研究動機簡單的說就是「Why study？」，亦即撰寫者為何要做此一研究，也必須清楚說明。最後則是研究目的，也就是「What to study？」，撰寫者做此一研究目的為何，也在此一併交代清楚。

　　第一章緒論完成後，算是完成論文研究的骨架，撐起了研究的主幹，接下來就開始要補上肌肉與神經，好讓論文研究能夠自在活動。接下來是第二章文獻探討，在第一章說明了研究的方向與目的後，撰寫者必須用一些理論來支持，告訴讀者何以撰寫者會有如此的觀點與疑惑，此時在撰寫論文之前所蒐集的資料，就可以派上用場了。以下有幾個重點可以當作參考：

　　第一是文獻必須經過消化再加以整理。這裡有許多初試者常常會犯的錯，以為文獻探討就只是把別人的文獻拿來抄一抄即可。其實不然，撰寫者在先前準備工作時已閱讀過相當多的資料，必須是加以消化而「內化」成自己可用的東西，而不是拿別人的文獻隨便抄一抄。

　　第二是要去探討跟論文相關的文獻，而不要探討一堆跟論文研究無關的文獻，應該切入研究所要探討的主題。

　　第三是各研究變數均應詳加探討。論文研究中所提及與欲研究的變數，在第二章都必須詳加探討，好讓讀者能對所有變數有所瞭解。

　　第四是各研究變數之間的關係亦應加以討論。論文研究所研究的是一個整體性的關係，因此變數與變數間的關係也必須討論，其中很重要的是邏輯的推演，A變數為何會與B變數有關，撰寫者都必須依邏輯細心推演，撰寫者的功力也可在此看出一二。

　　第五是變數的定義宜引用較權威的文獻。在說明變數的定義時，宜引用那個研究領域翹楚的定義，例如：談論到核心競爭力（Core Competence），就可以考慮引用Prahalad and Hamel（1990）所提出的定義，這樣對論文研究來說會比較有說服力。

　　第六是引用原始的文獻並忠實地呈現。現在論文常被人詬病的地方即在此，許多論文研究只是隨便看了另外一篇論文的文獻，即將其抄在自己的論文中，而沒有回頭去檢查原始文章作者的說法，導致別人翻譯也許有錯，自己也就跟著錯。

　　第七是所引用的文獻與註解應註明來源。因為是學術論文，資料來源的可靠度就相形重要，因此所引用的文獻與註解都應清楚標示來源，才不會讓讀者感覺有造假之嫌。

　　最後是文獻的整理應成為研究的理論基礎。文獻不只是在說明而已，撰寫者理應將此一部分當成是自身研究的理論基石。

　　完成了骨架的建立並補上肌肉之後，就要開始說明如何讓此論文研究自在的活動，論文撰寫者要採用何種方法讓它自在的活動。接下來也就是第三章研究設計的部分，商管類論文此部分一般包括有觀念性架構、研究假說、變數定義與衡量、抽樣設計、問卷設計、資料蒐集方法與資料分析方法等。以下幾點必須注意：

第一是觀念性架構的導出應有依據。這裡可以從第二章的資料借來用，告訴讀者何以撰寫者會有如此的想法而導出此一架構。

第二是研究假說應與研究目的、觀念性架構相呼應。跟先前提醒的一樣，不要一個說的是A，而另一個說的是B，這樣會讓讀者搞不清楚本篇論文研究的方向。

第三是假說或命題應有合理並合乎邏輯的推論。這裡常常有撰寫者會直接寫成「本篇研究的假說如下……」，然後就劈里啪啦把整篇論文研究的假說或命題全部傾洩而出，這會讓讀者有一種消化不良的感覺。應該在每一個假說或命題之前都有一段合理的推論，才能說服讀者接受這樣子的一個假說或命題。

第四是變數應予以操作化的定義，這麼做是為了讓讀者能夠瞭解論文撰寫者是如何衡量所探究的變數。此處操作性定義不宜再寫得如觀念性定義一般文謅謅，而是應該寫得清楚明瞭。

第五是變數的定義與衡量應引經據典，這樣讀者才比較能信服，且較能符合內容效度的要求。

第六是說明所選擇研究對象、研究方法與工具的理由。

第七是說明抽樣方法與樣本代表性。這裡關係到實證結果的可靠程度，論文撰寫者應審慎選擇並執行。

第八是問卷設計、參考來源、資料蒐集與分析方法應明確交代。這裡一樣關係到信度與效度的問題，論文撰寫者應審慎選擇並執行。

最後是問卷設計完成應施予前測。新問卷的完成，通常是將之前許多不同部分的問卷拿來修改及使用。結合起來使用也許會有論文撰寫者沒有發現到的問題，施予前測便可以提早發現問題，並做即時的修正，以避免正式發放問卷後才發現問題的窘境。

論文撰寫者提出了方法希望能讓論文自在活動，接下來就要檢測此方法是否真的可行，或是根本動不起來。第四章資料分析就是要做此一工作，一般包括有樣本基本資料分析、信度與效度分析、變數的相關分析、假說檢定與討論等部分。以下提出幾個重點分享：

第一是分析所得到的資訊應充分且適當的揭露，不要有暗藏不利資料與造假之事。

　　第二是應做信度與效度的檢驗。因為將之前許多不同部分的問卷拿來修改及使用，結合起來也許會有不合宜的情況，因此藉由信度與效度的檢驗，可以看出問卷是否能衡量到論文撰寫者真正想衡量的，且是否能精準的衡量。

　　第三是假說檢定的實證結果應有具體的數據來佐證。利用統計方法所呈現的數字來說話，而不是由論文撰寫者自己說。

　　第四是假說檢定結果之描述，應與實證數據一致，如此相互呼應，才能取信於讀者。

　　第五是假說檢定結果不論是獲得支持或未獲支持都應解釋，尤其是未獲支持的假說要有充分的討論。假說獲得支持，當然令人高興，代表論文撰寫者所抱持的觀點沒有被推翻；但假設未獲支持也許才應真正高興，因為很有可能論文撰寫者發現了有別於以往的東西。許多論文撰寫者在假設未獲支持時顯得憂心忡忡，其實大可不必，要做的事只要充分討論並探究原因，何以自己所推論的假說在這麼多理論的支持下卻未獲支持，其中必定有其原因。當然其中的原因可能有很多，涉及的層面也可能很廣，論文撰寫者必須謹慎且小心地提出看法，也許此一發現對產業與學術界助益會很大。

　　論文撰寫者提出了方法也做了測試，最後當然是要做一總結與建議，讓後人瞭解以後哪條路可行、哪條路是不可行的（哪個方法可以讓論文動起來，哪個方法論文根本不會動）。第五章是結論與建議，一般包括有研究結論、管理意涵（包括理論意涵與實務意涵）、研究限制、研究建議（包括對廠商的建議與對後續研究的建議）等部分。如上，筆者在此也提出一些拙見供大家參考：

　　第一是研究發現應具體的描述。在經過這麼冗長的撰寫與實證過程之後，將研究發現做一統整與描述，讓讀者能清楚的瞭解到本篇研究到底發現到了什麼。

　　第二是指出研究發現的管理意涵與理論意涵。這是論文研究很重要的部分，不僅能夠提供後續學術界做參考，還能讓廠商能夠依此在行銷策略上做修正，達成雙贏之局面，這是論文研究最大的貢獻之處。最後是研究限制與後續研究方法應交代。一般的論文研究不宜太大，同時也不可能太大。商管論文採用的是社會科學的方法，不可能如自然科學般以實驗室方法做研究，去假設在其他條件不變的情況下會有何變化。社會科學的實驗室就是整個世界，其範圍太過廣泛了，因此社會科學所做的研究一定會有其限制，因此論文撰寫者必須清楚交代，才不會搬石頭砸到自己的腳。另外，也應給予有興趣的讀者後續還可以繼續研究的方向，一同為此一領域努力付出。

至於參考文獻與附錄，則是提供給有興趣的讀者做參考，因此最基本的要求就是要正確。時下許多論文研究的內容都可能是從其他論文直接抄來，導致如果前人沒仔細查證，後人也會落入同樣的錯誤之中。例如：行銷大師Kotler的名字就常常被改名，也有許多大師的期刊文章其出版年代也常被提前或延後了好幾年。因此，論文撰寫者必須秉持著小心求證的精神，將參考文獻的每一筆資料都仔細檢查，不要一下是名字寫錯、一下是期刊的刊數漏寫或寫錯，這樣很有可能會讓讀者也犯錯。至於附錄，論文撰寫者可以把設計的問卷或是採用實驗設計時所設計的文宣附上，讓有興趣的後續研究者能加以參考。

總結來說，上述的內容其實就是「信、達、雅」論文寫作精神的完整呈現。所謂的「信」，就是在做研究與撰寫論文時，必須秉持著最高的學術倫理與道德標準，這樣做出來的研究才能讓讀者「信服」。而「達」的精神，則是在撰寫研究論文時，必須秉持著初衷（也就是第一章的研究動機與目的）去執行，讓論文能夠「辭達」原本的目的，這也是第一章如此重要的原因。第一章算是論文撰寫者與讀者之間溝通的橋梁，藉由第一章來告訴讀者，這一篇研究到底是在做什麼、為何而做。千萬不要原本設定目的為A，卻做到B去了。最後「雅」的精神，簡言之就是「言簡意賅」。一般人寫論文都有一個錯誤觀念，那就是文章寫得愈長，好像就愈有學問。試想，一本厚達百頁卻不知所云的書，與一本雖然只有短短幾十頁內容卻精彩萬分的書，讀者會比較想看哪一本？只要用最精準的文字來呈現出研究的精神即可，不需要寫出一大堆無用的文字。

仔細咀嚼上面的內容，聰明的讀者就可以發現，「信、達、雅」精神是環環相扣的，是整合在一起的整體，而非單一個體，也缺一不可。在論文寫作中若是少了其中任何一個精神，就會讓人感覺好像少了些什麼，也因此無法稱為一篇好的論文研究。

筆者深知自己在論文撰寫上還有待努力，其功力也還差恩師太多，因此很感念恩師能在百忙之中撰寫了一本如此實用的大作，相信對所有讀者來說，必定能在撰寫論文研究時感到百般受用。更感謝恩師能給筆者一個獻醜的機會，讓筆者能對論文撰寫這塊領域貢獻自己一點微薄的力量。

在撰寫本篇心得文章的同時，正好又有一篇與恩師合作的文章受到國立聯合大學學報的正式接受刊登。一路走來，點滴在心頭，感謝恩師林隆儀教授的指點與傾囊相授，相信所有的讀者在仔細研讀過此書後，必定也能在論文撰寫上大放異彩，並走出自己的一條路。

# 與論文的第一次接觸

真理大學管理科學所研究生　　李明真

　　在大學畢業十七年後，再重新拾起書本唸研究所。雖然大學本科系是商學系畢業，但畢業後就一直在教育界服務，對唸管理科學研究所是既期待又怕受傷害。期待的是能跳脫教育體系的思考模式，讓自己學習成長；怕的是待在國中學校教書太久，自己對外界變化變得遲鈍而應付不來。其實在找林老師當指導老師之前，這樣的心情就一直不斷地浮現，明知道跟林老師一起學習，收穫一定豐碩，但又怕達不到老師的要求，會陷自己於進退兩難的局面。最後靜下心來想想，唸研究所不就是想挑戰自我、提升自己，怎可入寶山卻空手而回呢？

　　老師從研一上就一直耳提面命，要儘早開工，逐步著手寫論文。在老師的督促下，兩年完成碩士論文變得輕鬆與容易。當然過程的辛苦與困難，也曾讓自己動過換指導老師的念頭，不過都在林老師認真的付出與指導下，感動自己要努力面對與克服，當老師的都如此認真投入，當學生的我更沒有理由不跟進，於是在研二放寒假之前，我完成了我的碩士論文。

　　在找研究議題上，我選擇與目前服務學校所面臨學生人數逐年減少的議題來探討。但因在國中教書年資已超過十年，一開始與林老師討論論文題目時，常會以自己的經驗影響到論文的寫作。老師總是不厭其煩地告誡我，研究是要以過去學者發表的論述為基礎，將原始構想轉換為可以研究的題目，所以第二章文獻探討內容要豐富且要有依據；也就是說，研究方向必須經過引經據典，而非自己憑空想像而來，這點很重要。

　　第三章觀念性架構是關係到整篇論文的價值性，所以老師以他過去指導論文的經驗，指導我從觀念性架構著手，接著提出初步的研究假說，以減少摸索的時間。一旦確立研究主題，回過頭來，開始蒐集國內外文獻來支撐整篇論文的架構。蒐集完整的文獻資料才是論文寫作的開始，我想只要是林老師指導過的學生，在第二章文獻探討想必和我一樣吃盡苦頭，尤其除了每一個變數都要清楚交代其定義、構面、功能或重要性外，變數如何衡量，以及變數與變數之間的關係也要清楚說明。老師如此強調第二章文獻的重要，就知道他對論文要求是如何的嚴謹了。

　　老師強調以第二章文獻探討作為第一章及第三章論述的根基，自然會有資料及靈感的呈現，於是整理完第二章後才開始著手寫第一章，從第二章文獻探討中找出第一章最關鍵的研究動機。研究動機是引發研究是否有其必要性與價值性的動能，所以，研究動機寫得好，便可增添研究結果的參考性。再來針對研究背景與問題也必須清楚點明，以補強研究議題的可探討性。在說明完研究背景與問題及研究動機之後，研究目的就呼之欲出了。

在寫第三章研究方法時，老師會要求觀念性架構及研究假設必須和第二章所探討的文獻相呼應，藉由文獻的融會貫通，作為觀念性架構及研究假設的引言。接著在變數操作性定義與衡量部分，除了引述學者的定義外，還要為自己所要研究的變數及構面下操作性定義，並說明使用何種工具來衡量。第三章前三節部分，對第一次從事論文寫作的人而言，是不容易理解的；而這樣的寫法是林老師的獨門祕方，因此凡是老師指導過的學生，寫到這裡想必都和我一樣，會在此停留一陣子，經老師再三指點才能走出這道關卡。進入到第四節探討抽樣方法時，記得務必要掌握抽取樣本的精神，亦即在抽樣的過程中，每一個環節都要清楚交代如何蒐集到樣本資料，以及樣本數的決定及其代表性。最後在問卷題目的設計上，根據變數及構面的操作性定義，參考學者已設計過的問卷內容並加以修改，是最穩健的方法。但如果能再經過一道專家效度的檢視，除了可提高問卷內容的信效度外，這樣的問卷設計更容易受到外界的肯定，對整體的研究具有加分效果。切記不要自行設計問卷，以避免問卷本身不具有信效度外，可能還會導致外界對研究結果的質疑。

而後將樣本資料蒐集完成後，進入第四章資料分析。剛開始不解老師為何要使用敘述統計分析、信效度分析、Pearson積差相關分析、殘差分析及多元迴歸分析等統計方法來分析資料，當自己邊寫邊跑資料時，才慢慢體會到老師採用這些方法的用意，其實是有學問的！

敘述統計分析可以說明樣本資料的分布情形，信效度分析在檢驗問卷設計是否得宜，Pearson積差相關分析在分析變數之間的關聯性，跑完敘述統計、信效度、Pearson 積差相關等分析，確定樣本資料是有意義的之後，使用迴歸分析來分析並檢定研究假設及呈現資料所代表的意涵。採用迴歸分析的理由在此分析已包含t檢定、變異數分析及相關分析，簡化使用統計方法的複雜性，並完整呈現資料所表示的意涵。且因迴歸分析是屬有母數統計，其資料必須來自常態分配，因此在進行迴歸分析之前，必須利用殘差分析來驗證使用迴歸分析的合理性。

完成第四章資料分析後，第五章結論與建議攸關了這篇論文的成敗，尤其管理意涵更讓我陷入苦思，幸好有老師在一旁指點，告訴我管理意涵其實就是論文研究的貢獻，於是我便從研究動機及結論的方向去思考，在老師的帶領下，一步一步地抓住了管理意涵的寫作要領。在指出論文的研究限制上，不諱言的將研究執行過程中遇到的限制與偏差，很誠實地寫出與面對。對後續研究建議的部分，也針對論文研究上的不足做出說明。寫到此，自己很清楚地將論文研究的貢獻與不足，藉由文筆完整地呈現。不過最讓我佩服的是經過老師的修改與詮釋，將第五章每一小節收尾部分都收得漂亮，才更得以突顯在學術上的價值與貢獻。而這時除了一切辛苦瞬間化為喜悅之外，更難以置信自己竟能寫出這樣的論文作品。

回首過去一年寫論文的日子，常常會因遇到瓶頸而苦惱，卻也因老師的一句鼓勵或讚許的話而開心不已，論文就在苦惱與讚許的話語中，不斷地重複上演下完成。很感謝也很慶幸在林老師的帶領下，走完這一趟學術研究之旅。當完成論文的那一刻，心靈的洗滌達到了最高峰，同時身心靈也達到前所未有的舒暢，這種感覺說來既神奇又奇妙，我想這應是選對指導老師所得到的福報吧！

記得剛來唸研究所時，若有人問我最感謝誰，我一定回答自己。但這一年來跟著老師學習，慢慢地發現最應感謝的是林老師，再來才是自己。因老師在論文寫作要求的嚴謹，讓我從不懂論文到懂得如何寫論文，從不懂研究到瞭解研究的技巧，扎實地奠定寫作論文的根基，也為日後唸博士學位打下良好的基礎。

# 按部就班，循序漸進，寫出一篇好論文

臺北大學企業管理學系博士　商懿勻

在碩博士養成的學術研究教育中，學術論文撰寫是每位研究生必經的一條天堂路，學術論文不單是取得學歷資格的基本門票，更是培育研究生邏輯思考、歸納分析與解決問題最好的訓練，藉此培養學術研究的能力與實力，亦是成為一名獨立研究者所必經之路。因此，對於學術論文的基本結構、脈絡與內容有更清楚的認識與瞭解，建立起基本的概念與認知，方能在寫作的過程中事半功倍，完成一篇高質量又具有研究價值的學術論文，鍛鍊自己成為一名獨立思考的研究者。

## 一、萬事起頭難，我該如何開始？

幾乎所有的研究生，特別是初次踏入學術領域的碩士生，對於如何選定論文題目，總是感到相當迷茫與無助。縱使在大學期間已經有過撰寫專題報告的相關經驗，仍然抓不到要點，不知所云，乃因學術論文屬於個人單獨完成的研究範疇，與團體報告的氛圍相當不同。學術論文主要的目的是訓練研究生有發現問題、找到方法、解決問題的能力，針對研究問題的推演，做出連貫性的思考與論述。因此，針對論文題目的找尋，可從以下幾個方向思考：

### （一）先構思你想做哪一種類型（領域）的研究。

最常聽到學生哀嚎著「這個題目有人做過了」、「這個主題已經很舊了」、「我不知道自己想要做什麼，想做的別人都做過了」。我認為在確定考取碩博士班時，就可以先利用入學前的第一個暑假，將系上同領域老師與學長姐們的學術著作快速瀏覽，針對有興趣的研究議題，進一步藉由「關鍵字」搜尋，透過學校圖書館典藏系統找到近五年內，公開發表在SSCI（Social Science Citation Index）或SCI（Science Citation Index）所收錄的國際期刊，站在巨人的肩膀上，快速且有效的掌握，該領域或議題目前的研究趨勢與走向。如此一來，不只可以快速地與系上學長姐們有共同的研究話題討論，藉由閱讀近五年的相關學術期刊，發現該研究領域的指標性學者們，嘗試著去瞭解近三年內該領域指標性學者們的研究走向與趨勢，發掘研究議題與現實狀態間的Gap，藉此找到專屬與您且真正感興趣的研究。然而，在找尋感興趣的研究題目與議題的過程中，其實也就是在為論文第貳章的文獻探討預做準備，藉由探索過去三至五年內的相關期刊文章，找到您的 Core Paper。

對碩士生而言，論文寫作的目的是在培養碩士生能具備獨立研究的能力，對於論文的創新度與貢獻性並不像博士生要求那麼高。因此，對於碩士生而言，並不用擔心自己的題目不夠新穎或執著於學術貢獻度的展現，此階段的論文寫作主要是能夠學習獨自發現問題，並透過正確地資料蒐集、整理與分析，將自己獨立思考及解決的研究問題，藉由學術論文的形式表達呈現，這樣的論文就相當具有價值與其存在的意義。

**（二）找出真正感興趣的議題，聚焦研究議題的深度而非廣度。**

論文寫作過程是一個非常好的訓練自我邏輯思維、組織能力與表達能力的訓練，讓抽象的問題具體化，清楚且有邏輯的系統性呈現，無論將來是否繼續朝向學術領域發展都能有所收穫。因此，論文最好是要找到真正感興趣，甚至覺得有趣的研究議題，而不是哪一個題目最好寫？最簡單？因為只有找到一個真正感興趣的研究議題，才能點燃內心對於學術研究的熱情，就算之後遇到評委們的質疑或其他困難，都澆不息您的研究衝勁與求知慾。在找尋論文題目的過程中，要不停的問自己：為什麼？為什麼會對這個議題有興趣呢？別人可能都已經做過相關研究了，為什麼還值得花上一年半以上的時間去探索？過去相關研究普遍忽略的是什麼？我要做的部分與其他研究不同之處在哪？該如何補足目前的缺漏？我比別人多想到的問題點又是什麼？此研究問題的重要性與價值是什麼？以上問題如果都能清楚並流暢的回應與說明，那恭喜您已經找到適合且屬於自己的論文題目了。

要記住，所撰寫的任何一篇無論是學位論文或期刊論文，都必須掌握一個要點「專注且單一」，每一篇論文都是在建立一個論點、驗證一個問題或一個觀點的過程。謹記這個重要觀念，聚焦於您的論點，專注於產生研究問題的背景與因素，精確、具體且單一的針對論點，用心去著墨與探索，您的論文將會更加嚴謹與專業。

## 二、我要如何下筆，認識學術論文的格式。

大多數學生都花太多時間在找尋所謂的「真正感興趣的研究題目與問題」，主要原因在於很多時候都只是「想」與「看」而已，真的有花時間深入去瞭解的人少之又少，碩博士生真正修業的時間其實非常緊湊，如何在有限的時間內做出最有效率的回饋，亦是每位研究生都必須學習的時間管理課題，學術論文並不像一般文章可自行撰寫想要表達的形式內容。學術論文有其既定的章法、格式與邏輯順序，不同領域之間會有些許不同，以商管領域的學術論文而言，主要章節架構可以區分為五大部分，分別為：第壹章：緒論；第貳章：文獻探討；第參章：研究方法；第肆章：實證分析；第伍章：結論與建議；以及參考文獻與附錄（問卷）。

其中第壹章：緒論。主要敘明研究動機、目的與範圍。掌握的要點在於先行描述目前的「研究背景」後，再清楚地說明「研究動機」，也就是確切地說明研究此一題目的原由。許多論文常常將研究動機與研究目的混淆，「研究目的」主要論述的其實是此研究所要達成的目標，或希望透過該研究能夠瞭解或補足的研究缺口。

第貳章：文獻探討。各研究變數之相關文獻回顧，此章節內容相對豐富，論述主要理論引經據典之餘，最好能以近五年內SSCI或SCI所收錄的國際期刊為主，以利後續做為第參章研究假說推導的文獻引用依據；主要針對不同學者所提出的變數定義、特性、模型，分類與構面，進行整理回顧，瞭解其重要性與應用價值，最後再針對各變數之間的關係探討結論。有些論文則會增加一節文獻評析或說明產業概況。

第參章：研究方法。將觀念性架構，以圖示化的呈現，幫助讀者可以更加快速且有效的掌握研究內容，提升易讀性。根據第貳章文獻回顧推導出研究假說，建立觀念性定義、操作性定義及衡量方法。內容都必須言之有物，有所依據且合乎邏輯性，有幾分證據就說幾分話，最忌諱出現「我覺得」、「我感覺」、「我認為」等字詞，因為學術論文是一種連貫性的思考，針對研究議題反覆正反面地推演與論述過程，內容必須要有所根據且講究研究結果與數據的佐證。最忌諱長篇大論毫無重點，學術論文要避免贅詞的產生，對於每一個文字與標點符號都要錙銖必較，並且避免模糊的字詞與定義。

第肆章：資料分析。主要針對樣本特性列表呈現、重點說明；研究變數信度、效度，個別是否達到標準；逐一檢定假說且明確的判定檢定結果，並進行討論，其中未獲得支持的研究假說更是必須特別提出說明討論，很多時候未獲得支持的假說，反倒是本篇論文最大的發現與賣點，是最有價值與研究發現的地方，所以當研究數據檢定結果呈現出「未顯著」時，千萬不要感到氣餒或想要美化而修改數據，這時候更該好好地探索背後的意涵，或許會有意想不到的收穫與研究價值產生。

第伍章：結論與建議。具體地指出研究結論與發現，條列式說明研究結果的主要意涵，細分為理論意涵與實務意涵兩部分。說明研究設計及執行過程中所受的限制，並針對後續研究提供未來研究方向建議，在此可試著拉高我們的視野，以一個管理領導者的角度，對相關產業提出具體且可行的建議事項，提升外部效度的應用價值。

### 三、重視學術倫理，絕不抄襲或剽竊，追求真善美的境界。

現在越來越多學校將學術研究倫理教育課程納入畢業條件之一，強化研究生對於學術論文原創性的尊重與引用，提升學術倫理涵養與研究品質。謹記不要輕率地將他人多年辛苦研究的心血，簡單地透過複製貼上就想移花接木，變成自己的東西。要記得在論文中所引用到的理念、文字，甚至圖表都要清楚地標示引用出處與來源。避免竄改與捏造的研究行為，重視愛惜自己的學術聲譽，不要違背學術倫理道德。

過去我也曾是個徬徨無助的菜鳥碩士生，很幸運地，從碩士班開始就跟著恩師林隆儀教授學習，一路到博士班畢業都是林老師親自指導，啟發我對於學術研究的興趣與熱情，諸多學術研究的基本功，都是林老師一步步帶領著我，紮穩馬步而奠定的基礎，直到現在即使在研究過程中遭遇困難與瓶頸也都能迎刃而解，其中林老師對於學術研究的執著與堅持，更是讓我欽佩也一直是我學習的楷模與典範。

畢業後我更將林老師的《論文寫作要領》視為經典之作收藏，並推薦給很多學弟妹以及業界再回到學校進修碩博士的朋友們，這真的是所有學術研究生必備的論文寫作工具書，也希望目前正在研讀本書的您，可以更佳掌握學術論文的寫作要領，順利完成論文寫作。

# 附錄三、發表論文範本

1. The influence of the country-of-origin image, product knowledge and product involvement on consumer purchase decisions: an empirical study of insurance and catering services in Taiwan

2. A study on the influence of purchase intentions on repurchase decisions: the moderating effects of reference groups and perceived risks

3. 寬頻網路關係行銷結合類型、服務品質、關係品質與轉換成本對顧客忠誠之影響

4. 老人經濟安全保障、理財知識與逆向抵押貸款意願之研究

發表論文範本

# Journal of Consumer Marketing

# The influence of the country-of-origin image, product knowledge and product involvement on consumer purchase decisions: an empirical study of insurance and catering services in Taiwan

**Long-Yi Lin**
*Graduate School of Management Sciences, Aletheia University, Taipei, Taiwan*
**Chun-Shuo Chen**
*Graduate School of Management Sciences, Aletheia University, Taipei, Taiwan*

Emerald

Journal of Consumer Marketing, Vol. 23 No. 5, 2006,
© Emerald Group Publishing Limited, 0736-3761

論文寫作要領

# Journal of Consumer Marketing

ISSN 0736-3761
©2006 Emerald Group Publishing Limited

**Editor**
**Richard C. Leventhal, PhD**
Arvada, Colorado, USA

**Book Reviews Editor**
**Geoff Lantos**
Stonehill College, North Easton, MA, USA

**Software Reviews and Internet Editor**
**Dennis Pitta**
University of Baltimore, USA

**Misplaced Marketing Editor**
**Herbert Jack Rotfeld**
Auburn University, AL, USA

**Case Section Editor**
**Rick Ferguson**
The COLLOQUY Group, USA

**Managing Editor**
**Richard Whitfield**

The *Journal of Consumer Marketing* is written by practitioners, consultants and marketing academics and is edited for marketers who desire to develop further insight into how people behave as consumers worldwide.

Each paper submitted to this journal is subject to a double-blind reviewing process.

Awarded in recognition of Emerald's production department's adherence to quality systems and processes when preparing scholarly journals for print

Certificate number .........

**This journal is also available online at:**
**Journal information**
www.emeraldinsight.com/jcm.htm
**Table of contents**
www.emeraldinsight.com/0736-3761.htm

**Emerald Group Publishing Limited**
60/62 Toller Lane, Bradford
BD8 9BY, United Kingdom
Tel +44 (0) 1274 777700
Fax +44 (0) 1274 785200
E-mail information@emeraldinsight.com

INVESTOR IN PEOPLE

**Regional offices:**

**For North America**
Emerald, 875 Massachusetts Avenue, 7th Floor,
Cambridge, MA 02139, USA
Tel Toll free +1 888 622 0075; Fax +1 617 354 6875
E-mail america@emeraldinsight.com

**For Japan**
Emerald, 3-22-7 Oowada, Ichikawa-shi, Chiba, 272-0025, Japan
Tel +81 47 393 7322; Fax +81 47 393 7323
E-mail japan@emeraldinsight.com

**For Asia Pacific**
Emerald, 7-2, 7th Floor, Menara KLH, Bandar Puchong Jaya, 47100 Puchong, Selangor, Malaysia
Tel +60 3 8076 6009; Fax +60 3 8076 6007
E-mail asiapacific@emeraldinsight.com

**For China**
Emerald, 12th Floor, Beijing Modern Palace Building No. 20, Dongsanhuan Nanlu, Chaoyang District, Beijing 100022, China
Tel +86 (0) 10 6776 2231; Fax +86 (0) 10 6779 9806
E-mail china@emeraldinsight.com

**Customer helpdesk:**
Tel +44 (0) 1274 785278; Fax +44 (0) 1274 785204;
E-mail support@emeraldinsight.com
Web www.emeraldinsight.com/customercharter

**Orders, subscription and missing claims enquiries:**
E-mail subscriptions@emeraldinsight.com
Tel +44 (0) 1274 777700; Fax +44 (0) 1274 785200

Missing issue claims will be fulfilled if claimed within four months of date of despatch. Maximum of one claim per issue.

**Reprints service:**
Tel +44 (0) 1274 785135
E-mail reprints@emeraldinsight.com
Web www.emeraldinsight.com/reprints

**Permissions service:**
Tel +44 (0) 1274 785139
E-mail permissions@emeraldinsight.com
Web www.emeraldinsight.com/permissions

**Emerald is a trading name of Emerald Group Publishing Limited**

**Printed by** Printhaus Group Ltd, Scirocco Close, Moulton Park, Northampton NN3 6HE

**Indexed and abstracted in**
Academic Research
Autographics
Business & Industry
Business Source
Cabell's Directory of Publishing Opportunities in Management and Marketing
Collectanea Corporate
Current Citations Express
Emerald Reviews (formerly Anbar)
EP Collection
e-psyche

Expanded Academic Index
Galileo
General Reference Center
Innovative
ISI Alerting Services
ISI Current Contents Connect/ Business Collection
Manning & Napier
MasterFILE
OCLC
Scandinavia
Scopus
Telebase

發表論文範本

# The influence of the country-of-origin image, product knowledge and product involvement on consumer purchase decisions: an empirical study of insurance and catering services in Taiwan

*Long-Yi Lin and Chun-Shuo Chen*
Graduate School of Management Sciences, Aletheia University, Taipei, Taiwan

## Abstract

**Purpose** – The main purpose of this study is to explore the influence of the country-of-origin image, product knowledge and product involvement on consumer purchase decision.

**Design/methodology/approach** – Taiwan, China and the USA were the three countries selected for research into the country-of-origin, insurance and catering services. Structured questionnaires and convenience sampling were used. Samples were collected from consumers in the Taipei area. A total of 400 questionnaires were distributed with convenience sampling method, and 369 effective samples were collected, the effective rate being 92.25 percent. Stepwise regression analysis was adapted to test hypothesis.

**Findings** – The main findings were listed as follows: the country-of-origin image, product knowledge and product involvement all have a significantly positive effect on consumer purchase decision; the country-of-origin image has a significantly positive effect on consumer purchase decisions under different product involvement; and product knowledge has significantly positive effect on consumer purchase decisions under different product involvement.

**Research limitations/implications** – Limitations of the study are: it is unable to infer to national consumers and to other service areas and the explanatory power of some empirical models is relative low. Implications of the study are that: a more thorough structure about consumer purchase decisions should be provided and the relationship between product knowledge and information search quantity should be verified.

**Practical implications** – Practical implications pf the study are that the company must face competitive strategies from many countries and also the effect of consumer product knowledge on business competitive strategy.

**Originality/value** – The added value of this paper is to link between theory and practice, and explore the different country-of-origin image, product knowledge and product involvement on consumer purchase decisions.

**Keywords** Country of origin, Consumer behaviour, Purchasing, Insurance, Catering industry, Taiwan

**Paper type** Research paper

An executive summary for managers and executive readers can be found at the end of this article.

## I. Introduction

The year 1947, saw the establishment of General Agreement on Tariffs and Trade (GATT), which was dedicated to trade liberalization amongst membership nations. Because of many problems occurring in international economics and trade and non-tariff trade barriers issues, up to the 1970s and 1980s, the GATT functionality was replaced by the Word Trade Organization (WTO) in 1995. WTO with its four principles of equality, mutual benefits, transparency, and fair trade,

The current issue and full text archive of this journal is available at
**www.emeraldinsight.com/0736-3761.htm**

Journal of Consumer Marketing
23/5 (2006) 248–265
© Emerald Group Publishing Limited [ISSN 0736-3761]
[DOI 10.1108/07363760610681655]

requested global membership nations to open their market under a mutual beneficial foundation, allowing our national consumers to not only choose among products from our country, but also from all over the world.

According to information released by the Directorate-General of Budget, Accounting and Statistics (DGBAS), Executive Yuan, the overall product value in the service industry has an increasing percentage in the overall gross national product (GNP) of our country from the 1960s, and has exceeded 60 percent since 1995. Up to the 3rd quarter of 2004, the average weight of the overall product value was 68.77 percent, which exceeded the average percentage in the manufacturing industry. This also shows the significance of the service industry to our civil economy. In December 2000, since the inauguration of "the Financial Institution Merger Law" its performance in combining all financial products from banks, insurance, security, and trust has brought a new possibility to the insurance business. With the increased income of citizens and their higher standards in food preferences, the restaurant industry has grown considerably. Therefore, this study has chosen insurance and catering services as research objects.

論文寫作要領

Since Schooler (1965) first explored the national image in his research 1965, it has been verified that the national image has had an impact on consumer recognition, attitude, and buying intention. This shows that consumers seem to have a different product appraisal of products made by different countries. However, this type of research tends to focus more on the manufacturing industry or consumer products, and research concerning national image tends to focus more on certain types of service industries – see Lehmann's (1986) research on skiing vacation; Harrison-Walker's (1995) exploration of the medical services of the ophthalmology department; Yang's (1994) investigation of banking and catering services; and Tseng's (2001) study of Airline and Western Food Chain catering services. Bilkey and Nes (1982) reviewed papers concerning country-of-origin from 1965 to 1979, and discovered that the country-of-origin does have effects on product appraisal, the manufacturing industry and the consumers' product purchase decision. However, it is not certain that the country-of-origin has an influence on the customers' purchase decisions concerning insurance and catering services industries. This is the first motive of this study.

Chao and Rajendran (1993) point out that, when customers are making decisions, they search for more information before making their purchase. In relation to products, with the exception of considering national image of the country-of-origin, consumer product knowledge is an important element when purchasing. However, the effect of product knowledge on the consumer buying intention and information searching intention mostly relies on the manufacturer's products, rather than its service. This is also the motive of this study.

The purpose of this study includes:

- exploring the influence of the country-of-origin image, product knowledge, and product involvement on the consumer purchase decision in insurance and dining services; and
- researching the impact of the country-of-origin image and also the product knowledge on consumer purchase decisions under different product involvement of the consumers in insurance and catering services.

## II. Literature review

### 1. Country-of-origin and its image

#### (1) Definition and effect of country-of-origin

Saeed (1994) points out that country-of-origin means the country that a manufacturer's product or brand is associated with; traditionally this country is called the home country. For some brands, country-of-origin belongs to a given and definite country, such as IBM belongs to the USA and SONY is a Japanese brand. However, Ahmed *et al.* (2004) defines country-of-origin as the country that conducts manufacturing or assembling, which follows the definition stated by Saeed (1994). Saeed (1994) indicates that country of manufacture (COM) represents the last location/country of manufacturing or assembling one product. Therefore, Saeed (1994) defines country-of-origin as the COM. In addition, Roger *et al.* (1994) report there is no distinct difference between location of manufacture and location of assembly, and this causes no significant difference to customers concerning product appraisal.

Roth and Romeo (1992) assert that country-of-origin effect means customers' stereotypes of one specific country. According to the definition stated by Johansson and Thorelli (1985), a country's stereotype means people in a country (or specific people) have stereotypes and preferences for products of another country. However, Saeed (1994) perceives that country-of-origin effect means any influences or preferences caused by country-of-origin and/or COM.

#### (2) Country image

Country image first appeared in a research paper written by Nagashima in 1970. He defines the term as:

> Consumer holds particular picture, reputation, and stereotype towards products of a specific country. This image is formed by the country's representative product, political and economic background, and historic tradition variables, which meHans overall country image (Nagashima, 1970).

In addition, Roth and Romeo (1992) assert that defining country image should clearly reflect its relation with product recognition. Therefore, they redefine country image as:

> Consumer forms his/her understanding to specific country based on his/her recognition of advantages and disadvantages of manufactured and marketed products from a specific country in the past (Roth and Romeo, 1992).

In short, country image means the consumer's general conscience for product quality manufactured from a specific country (Bilkey and Nes, 1982; Han, 1989).

#### (3) The role of country image in product evaluation

Hong and Wyer (1989) report that when customers hear any news or find any clues about country-of-origin, such as price or brand, the country-of-origin effect in the consumer recognition process should be observed from two sides. One is the halo effect, the other is the summary construct effect. When the consumer is not familiar with a specific country's product, then the country image would cause a halo effect, this would not only directly affect the consumer's trust in the product, but also it would indirectly affect the consumer's overall evaluation of the product (Erickson *et al.*, 1984; Johansson *et al.*, 1985). However, when the consumer is very familiar with a specific country's product, then he/she refers product associated information to the country and this causes a summary construct effect. This effect would indirectly affect his/her attitude towards this brand (Han, 1989).

#### (4) Measure of country image

Han and Terpstra (1988) referring to Nagashima's (1970) research, refine four factors from 14 measured items through factor analysis. The four factors are advanced technology, prestige, workmanship and economy. Furthermore, they place subjective concern serviceability and overall evaluation as the measure dimension of country image. Agarwal and Sikri (1996) review much literature; they summarize 24 items then narrow to 14 items to measure the country image. They adapt the factor analysis to refine three factors at least, which are industry technology, prestige and price as the measure dimension of the country image. According to Martin and Eroglu (1993), general tools and methods used for the country image measurement, can only measure the product image of a specific country but not the country image. So Martin and Eroglu (1993) propose that in finding effective and reliable measure tools for country image, country image or

An empirical study of insurance and catering services

*Long-Yi Lin and Chun-Shuo Chen*

Journal of Consumer Marketing

*Volume 23 · Number 5 · 2006 · 248–265*

product characteristic will be measured, and the researcher should have a clear definition for every questionnaire.

## 2. Product knowledge

*(1) Definition and classification of product knowledge*

Product knowledge plays an important role in the research of consumer behavior, therefore, it is an essential research subject in related fields. Brucks (1985) states that product knowledge is based on memories or known knowledge from consumers. Lin and Zhen (2005) assert that product knowledge depends on consumer's awareness or understanding about the product, or consumer's confidence about it. Based on a definition of Brucks (1985) about product knowledge, it can be divided into three major categories:

1  subject knowledge or perceived knowledge;
2  objective knowledge; and
3  experience-based knowledge.

However, Alba and Hutchinson (1987) indicate that product knowledge should contain two parts, which are:

1  expertise; and
2  familiarity with products.

*(2) Product knowledge measurement*

Wang (2001) summarizes much literature and reports that the index used to measure product knowledge by scholars include:

- The consumer's perception of how much he or she knows (Park and Lessig, 1981).
- The amount, type and organization of what the consumer has stored in his/her memory (Johnson and Russo, 1984).
- The amount of purchasing and usage experience (Marks and Olson, 1981).

Rudell (1979) uses an examination score to measure objective knowledge and applies a self-evaluation inventory to measure subjective knowledge. Lin and Zhen (2005) adopt the product knowledge definition stated by Brucks (1985) to measure product knowledge. The aim of the measurement of product knowledge is to measure the understanding and confidence level of notebook attribute and information, and a Likert seven-point scale was used.

*(3) The influence of product knowledge on information search behavior*

To understand consumer behavior, consumer knowledge is an important construct. This is because, before the consumer performs actual purchasing behavior, he/she most likely experiences two procedures:

1  Information search: this means when the consumer faces many consuming relevant questions, he/she requires relevant information to assist with his/her consuming decision. This type of search of appropriate information procedure is called information search (Solomon, 1997).
2  Information processing: includes consumer self selects to expose, notice, recognize, agree, accept, or retain. No matter how much knowledge the consumer has, it all affects his/her procedures concerning information search and information processing (Brucks, 1985).

Much evidence shows that product knowledge does have an impact on information processing to the consumer (Larkin *et al.*, 1980). For example, Zhu (2004) states that, in a RV leisure van research, when the consumer selects a product,

he/she usually rely on his/her product knowledge to evaluate it, and his/her product knowledge would also affect his/her information search procedure, attitude, and information search quantity. In addition, his/her level in product knowledge would determine consumer purchase decision, and indirectly affect his/her buying intention.

The relationship between product knowledge and information search has not yet generated any definite conclusion. Some scholars state that consumers' understanding in product knowledge has a positive correlation to information search quantity, such as Moore and Lehmann (1980), Punj and Staelin (1983), Selnes and Troye (1989), Alba and Hutchinson (1987). Some scholars assert that these two variables have a negative correlation, such as Brucks (1985), Newman and Staelin (1972). Therefore, when scholars face these two different conclusions, they submit another theory, i.e. that product knowledge and information search quantity has a U-shape correlation rather than simply a linear correlation, as Bettman and Park (1980) and Johnson and Russo (1984) assert.

## 3. Product involvement

*(1) Definition and concept of involvement*

The concept of involvement originated from social psychology. Krugman (1965) first brought and applied the involvement concept into marketing. He explains how low the involvement concept has a television commercial effect. With this low involvement concept, it not only brings a huge influence on advertisement, but also on marketing research concerning the consumer behavior theory. After this, involvement discussion gradually becomes part of the major stream in consumer behavior research.

Traylor (1981) defines involvement as a consumer's understanding or recognition of a specific product. The higher level the consumer consideration of the product is called high involvement and the lower level, low involvement. Zaichkowsky (1985) calls involvement personal demand, conception, and interest in the product. Engel *et al.* (1995) reports involvement as, under a specific environment, a consumer is stimulated by personal recognition and/or interest in the product. The higher the level, the higher of the involvement; the lower the level, the lower of the involvement.

*(2) Classification of involvement*

Depending on different involvement objects, involvement can be divided into advertising involvement, product involvement, and purchasing involvement. To understand the difference between these three involvements, they can further be divided into situational involvement, enduring involvement, and response involvement.

Krugman (1965) asserts that involvement with advertisement as understanding a consumer's involvement level or response after receiving advertising information based on a consumer's concern about advertising information. The involvement level ranges from absolute concentration to complete ignorance. Involvement with a product means consumer's concern and contribution to it (Cohen, 1983). Involvement with purchase refers to a consumer's self concern over purchase decision and purchasing activity (Slama and Tashchian, 1985). Enduring involvement reflects that an individual has given a response to specific behavior

**214**

論文寫作要領

An empirical study of insurance and catering services

*Long-Yi Lin and Chun-Shuo Chen*

**Journal of Consumer Marketing**

*Volume 23 · Number 5 · 2006 · 248–265*

environment. Houston and Rothschild (1978) indicate that enduring involvement originated from two sources, which are a consumer's personal subjective appreciation system in a product's meaning to a consumer or consumer's experience in using this product in the past. Bloch (1982) perceives that a situational involvement refers to when a consumer intends to reach outside goals about product purchasing or application, or has temporary concern about the product. After his/her goal is achieved, the situational involvement would immediately decrease. Arora (1982) demonstrates that, response involvement means combining situational involvement and enduring involvement, thus causing a mental condition about something.

*(3) Product involvement measurement*
Involvement is an abstract moderating variable, which cannot be measured directly. We should use involvement factor research and post-purchase conclusions to infer to it indirectly. Zaichkowsky (1985) adopts a semantic differential method and develops a set of inventory, which is known as personal involvement inventory. Chin (2002) refers to Zaichkowsky's (1985) personal involvement inventory to measure product involvement. After a reliability and validity examination, he contracts ten measurement items, and Likert's seven-point method was used.

## 4. Consumer purchase decision
*(1) Consumer behavior model*
There has been much research concerning consumer behavior; therefore, an explanation of many different consumer behavior models is extended. The EKB model was first presented by three scholars, Engel, Kollat and Blackwell, in 1968, and also a rather clear, complete, and systematic theory model concerning consumer behavior. The EKB model assumes that a consumer's decision processing is a consecutive processing which leads to solving problems, and which features considering decision processing as the center of combining interaction of relevant outside and inside elements.

The EKB model has three advantages (Yang, 2001), which includes:

1  *Thoroughness.* The EKB model contains fairly complete variables, which are capable of explaining entire processing of consumer behavior.
2  *It is process oriented.* The EKB model has rather relevant variables, which are collected with signs, are easier for researchers to confirm the relationship of variables, and also benefit hypothesis development and research result interpretation.
3  *The dynamic feature.* The EKB model combines many scholars and experts' opinions towards consumer behavior and performs many revisions; therefore, is considered as a fairly thorough consumer behavior model. The EKB model contains four major parts, which include: information involvement; information processing; decision processing; and variables of decision processing.

*(2) Consumer purchase decision*
Kotler *et al.* (1999) point out that, when a consumer makes a purchase decision behavior, there is a primary "stimulation-response" model and the black box concept in behavior science response. Through external stimulation sources, marketing and environment, it would further affect

consumer purchase decisions through the black box (including consumer feature and decision processing).

Engel *et al.* (1993) report that, the center concept of the EKB model means consumer purchase decision processing, which is also problem-solving processing to consumer decision processing and includes five stages: demand confirmation, search for information, evaluation of alternatives, purchasing, and purchasing result.

*(3) Information search intention and purchase intention measurement*
McQuarrie and Muson (1992) use Likert's seven-point method to measure information on search intention. Chin (2002) refers to McQuarrie and Muson's(1992) research and uses a Likert's seven-point method to measure information search intention. Dodds *et al.* (1991) use five questions, however, Klein *et al.* (1998) use six questions and both use Likert's seven-point method to measure it.

*(4) Major variables that influence consumer purchase decision*
Based on the above literature on consumer behavior and consumer purchasing behavior, this paper assumes that a consumer's purchasing behavior under his/her demand confirmation is ensured, rather than discussing how a consumer executes project evaluation and the after-purchasing result. Therefore, this paper selects and uses the following two elements:

1  Information search intention: summarizing consumer behavior and purchasing behavior from Nicosia (1968), Howard (1989), Engel *et al.* (1993), and naming relevant information/news parts as a search for information. When a consumer confirms his/her demand, he/she would start seeking relevant information. That means, a consumer reads about relevant product information through this news, compares differences among different products, and furthermore spends more time on product search (McQuarrie and Muson, 1992). In this processing when a consumer purchases a product, information search intention takes a large part. Therefore, this paper considers information search intention as the first element in affecting a consumer purchase decision.
2  Purchase decision: in evaluation of alternatives and purchase decision relation map, Kotler *et al.* (1999) indicate that between evaluation of alternatives and purchase decisions, they would first form buying intention. Fishbein and Ajzen (1975) verify that buying intention could be taken as an important index to predict consumer behavior. Therefore, this paper chooses buying intention as the second element that influences the consumer purchase decision.

## 5. The relationship between variables
*(1) The influences of the country-of-origin image on a consumer purchase decision*
Hsieh (1994) states that international co-operation has gradually become a major stream of modern business. A consumer no longer considers "location of manufacture" as a single source of reference information, he/she particularly perceives that country-of-origin image makes a great influence. Hong and Wyer (1989) report in their research, that the country-of-origin information does influence a consumer to evaluate the country's product quality. Moreover, Han (1990) and Papadopoulos and Heslop

An empirical study of insurance and catering services

*Long-Yi Lin and Chun-Shuo Chen*

Journal of Consumer Marketing

*Volume 23 · Number 5 · 2006 · 248–265*

(1993) point out that, country image does influence a consumer's purchase decision. Especially when the COM image appears negative, a consumer might have a negative image of that country's product. Lee (1999) and Tseng (2001) assert that country-of-origin brand does affect product and service and the purchasing intention. Therefore the country-of-origin brand and its country image do play a very important role when a consumer makes a decision and would affect a consumer's preference level and furthermore affect his/her purchasing intention and information search intention.

*(2) The influence of product knowledge on consumer purchase decision*

Research of consumer behavior and product knowledge plays a significant role. During his/her purchasing process, the amount of knowledge consumer has of about a product would not only affect his/her information search behavior (Brucks, 1985; Rao and Sieben, 1992), but also, at the same time, affect his/her information and decision-making processing. Furthermore, it influences the consumer purchasing intention. Zhu (2004) indicates that concerning the RV leisure van, when a consumer selects a product, he/she usually evaluates it based on his/her understanding of it, and his/her understanding would affect consumer information search processing, attitude, and information search quantity. A consumer's knowledge about a product would determine consumer purchase decisions, and would indirectly affect his/her purchase intention.

*(3) The influence of product involvement on the consumer purchase decision*

Friedman and Smith (1993) discover in their research concerning service that when consumer selects a service and his/her involvement increases, he/she will search for further more information. Goldsmith and Emmert (1991) report that product involvement plays an important role in consumer behavior. When his/her involvement level increases, the consumer will search for further information. Petty *et al.* (1983) adopt the Elaboration Likelihood Model (ELM) and discover that high product involvement, brand attitude and purchase intention have a much higher correlation than that of low product involvement. Neese and Taylor (1994) discover in their research concerning automobiles comparison advertisement that, under a different level of advertise information, high involvement of a product causes a distinctly positive purchase intention, whether in the advertising attitude, brand recognition, and brand attitude, than with a low involvement product.

*(4) The moderate effect of product involvement on the country-of-origin image, product knowledge and consumer purchase decisions*

Arora (1993) discovers in his comparative research between three kinds of service businesses, that medicine, beauty shop, and insurance verify that the involvement theory could be adapted in service marketing. He also states, the relationship between expected service quality and recognized quality under different levels of involvement would help constitution of service marketing strategy. Chin (2002) discovers that with high product involvement, a consumer would appear that have a higher level product information search intention, product evaluation, and purchase intention than from middle or low COM image.

Petty and Cacioppo (1981) present the ELM, which explains thoroughly and systematically the high/low involvement purchase behavior and its solutions. When a consumer considers purchasing a product which has a fairly high level (high product involvement), he/she will carefully evaluate product advantages and disadvantages. However, when a consumer owns product relevant or important information (high product knowledge), he/she will only concentrate on search and evaluate limited information, thus his/her information search intention is not high.

## III. Research methods

### 1. Conceptual structure

In the field of international marketing research, many scholars considered the country image and country-of-origin effect as important issues. Hong and Wyer (1989) discovered that when a consumer evaluates a foreign country product, he/she will mostly likely adopt a country-of-origin image as the most easy to obtain information. In a product, except for the country-of-origin image, a consumer would also consider product knowledge of some concern in purchasing. Brucks (1985) states that it does not whether matter the level of consumer knowledge is high or low, it all affects the consumer information search and information processing procedure. Rao and Monroe (1988) report that product knowledge would affect the relationship between consumer price and quality perception. Depending on the level of consumer product knowledge, it would affect him/her when evaluating product quality. With a different level of involvement, a consumer would have different purchase behavior, such as a different information processing method, different attitude, different level of information collection and purchase decision behavior. Zaichkowsky (1986) summarized scholars' research concerning product involvement and point out that product feature affects how a consumer perceives a product. Yang (2001) states that with a consumer of high product involvement, his/her decision processing feature would be extensive problem-solving (EPS). The consumer would carefully and widely evaluate and aggressively perform an information search before purchasing. However, to a consumer of low product involvement, his/her decision feature is the opposite, which belongs to limited problem-solving (LPS).

The aim of this research is to explore the effect of the country-of-origin image, product knowledge, and product involvement towards consumer purchase decision, and mainly to verify the effect of these three variables on consumer purchase decisions, and choose product involvement as the moderate variable between the country-of-origin image and product knowledge on the consumer purchase decision. Based on the reference of the scholastic stated above, the conceptual structure of this paper is developed and illustrated in Figure 1.

### 2. Hypothesis development

Manrai and Manrai (1993) find that when a country brings a rather positive country image to the consumer, then he/she would have a rather high quality perception and overall evaluation to a product manufactured in that country and furthermore would increase his/her purchase intention. Roth and Romeo (1992) state if a country is known for a rather

An empirical study of insurance and catering services

*Long-Yi Lin and Chun-Shuo Chen*

**Journal of Consumer Marketing**

*Volume 23 · Number 5 · 2006 · 248–265*

**Figure 1** Conceptual structure

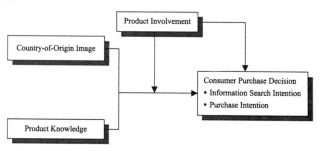

positive image, and this image is very important to product classification, a consumer would have a higher purchase intention to products from this country. Lee (1999) and Tseng (2001) discovered that the country-of-origin image does affect product and service and purchase intention. Wall *et al.* (1991) and Ahmed and Astous (1996) both assert product information search is essential to level of country-of-origin effect. Chin (2002) also discovers that with higher COM images, the consumer would have a higher intention of information search. Based on the above literature, the first hypothesis for this study is developed as follows:

*H1.* The country-of-origin image asserts a significantly positive impact on the consumer purchase decision.

*H1-1.* The country-of-origin asserts a significantly positive impact on the consumer information search intention.

*H1-2.* The country-of-origin asserts a significantly positive impact on the consumer purchase intention.

Brucks (1985) and Rao and Sieben (1992) point out that, during purchase processing, a consumer's knowledge of the product would not only affect his/her search behavior, but also affect his/her information treatment and decision-making processing, and would furthermore, affect his/her purchase intention. Zhu (2004) reports this in his research concerning the RV leisure van, when a consumer selects a product, he/she usually uses his/her understanding of the product to make evaluation. His/her understanding of a product would also affect consumer information search processing, attitude, and information search quantity. A different level of product knowledge would determine a consumer's purchase decision and would indirectly affect his/her purchase intention. Moore and Lehmann (1980) discovered that, in their empirical study, consumer product knowledge has a significantly positive impact on his/her effort in information search. According to the above literature it would conclude the second hypothesis for this study as follows:

*H2.* Consumer product knowledge has a significantly positive impact on consumer purchase decision.

*H2-1.* Consumer product knowledge has a significantly positive impact on consumer information search intention.

*H2-2.* Consumer product knowledge has a significantly positive impact on consumer purchase intention.

Krugman (1965) adopts involvement concept, and uses a low involvement concept to explain a television advertisement

effect. Friedman and Smith (1993) discovered in their research concerning service that, when a consumer selects service with an increasing involvement level, he/she will search for higher level information. Goldsmith and Emmert (1991) reveal that product involvement plays an important role in consumer behavior. With an increasing involvement level a consumer would search for higher level product information.

Petty *et al.* (1983) adopt the ELM and discover that, with high product involvement, the correlation between brand attitude and purchase intention is significantly higher than that with low product involvement. Neese and Taylor (1994) discover that, in an automobile comparison advertisement with different information advertisement load, a product of high involvement would have a much more positive influence on advertisement attitude, brand loyalty, and brand attitude, than that with a product of low involvement. Based on the above literature, the conclusion of a third hypothesis for this study is inferred as follows:

*H3.* Product involvement has a significantly positive impact on consumer purchase decision.

*H3-1.* Product involvement has a significantly positive impact on consumer information search intention.

*H3-2.* Product involvement has a significantly positive impact on consumer purchase intention.

In his research concerning three kinds of service businesses, doctor, beauty shop, and insurance, Arora (1993) verifies that the involvement theory can be applied to service marketing. Ahmed and Astous (1995) discovered that the country-of-origin would have a larger influence than the COM under high product involvement. In addition, when a product appears at a higher involvement level, a consumer would also notice other information, such as brand and price; therefore, the manufacture and country-of-origin effect would simultaneously decrease. Ahmed *et al.* (2004) also point out that the country-of-origin would affect a purchase decision when a consumer evaluates low product involvement. But, if there are any outside clues, then the country-of-origin effect would decrease.

Mitchell (1981) reports in his research that at a higher product involvement level, a consumer will aggressively search for relevant information and furthermore evaluate the product. Otherwise, on a lower product involvement level, the consumer might be reluctant to make an effort on product selection and evaluation. This finding matches the conclusion revealed by Swinyard (1993). Chin (2002) discovers that at a

發
表
論
文
範
本

Journal of Consumer Marketing

*Volume 23 · Number 5 · 2006 · 248–265*

high product involvement level, a consumer would have a higher information search intention, product evaluation, and purchase intention for high, than that for a middle or low country-of-manufacture image. Therefore, according to the above literature the fourth hypothesis for this study is inferred as follows:

*H4.* Country-of-origin image has a significantly positive impact on the consumer purchase decision on a different product involvement level.

*H4-1.* With an increasing product involvement level, the country-of-origin image has a significantly positive impact on the consumer information search intention.

*H4-2.* With an increasing product involvement level, the country-of-origin image has a significantly positive impact on the consumer purchase intention.

Petty and Cacioppo (1981) assert that when a consumer has higher concern to purchasing product (high product involvement), he/she would carefully examine product advantages and disadvantages. However, when a consumer has relevant or important product information (high product knowledge), he/she would only concentrate on searching and evaluating limited information, thus his/her intention in information search is not high. Rao and Sieben (1992) report that in purchase processing, a consumer's understanding of a product would not only affect his/her information search behavior, but also his/her information treatment and decision-making processing, and furthermore affect consumer purchase intention. Moore and Lehmann (1980) discover in their empirical study that consumer product knowledge has a positive influence on consumer's effort in information search. Friedman and Smith (1993) found, in their research concerning service, that when consumer selects service, with increasing involvement level, he/she would search for higher level information. Goldsmith and Emmert (1991) state that on an increasing involvement level a consumer will search for higher level information when he/she performs product selection. Petty *et al.* (1983) adopt the ELM and discover that, with a high product involvement level, brand attitude and purchase intention would have a significantly higher correlation than that with low product involvement. According to the above literature the fifth hypothesis for this study is inferred as follows:

*H5.* Product knowledge has a significantly positive impact on the consumer purchase decision under different product involvement level.

*H5-1.* With increasing product involvement level, consumer product knowledge has a stronger impact on the consumer information search intention.

*H5-2.* With increasing product involvement level, consumer product knowledge has a stronger impact on the consumer purchase intention.

## 3. Operational definition and variables measurement
### (1) Country-of-origin image
By adopting references from Saeed (1994), Nagashima (1970), and Roth and Romeo (1992) this paper defines and measures the country image, and also considers the overall country image and product image. This study defines the country-of-origin image as a consumer's overall recognition to a country-of-origin and perception level on the product quality of a specific service.

Han and Terpstra (1988) refer to Nagashima's (1970) research, employ factor analysis refines four factors from selected 14 measure items, thus advanced technology, reputation, skill and economics, additional subjective concerns about service and overall evaluation as dimensions used to measure country image. In country image measurement, this paper adopts methods used by Martin and Eroglu (1993) and Nagashima (1970), refers to and makes some revisions to Chen&s (2000) research. Country-of-origin image measurement includes eight dimensions, which are:

1 economics development level;
2 political and democratic level;
3 industrialization level;
4 living standard;
5 technology developing level;
6 product quality;
7 self-confident level for owning this product; and
8 product reliability.

When a seven-point Likert scale is employed to measure a respondent's opinions; 1 represents absolutely disagree and 7 means absolutely agree.

### (2) Product knowledge
In adopting the reference from Brucks (1985) and Park and Lessig (1981) for their definition about consumer's subjective knowledge, this paper defines product knowledge as a consumer's awareness or understanding level of a specific service.

In product knowledge measurement, Rudell (1979) uses examination scores and a self-measure scale to measure subjective knowledge. Lin and Zhen (2005) adopt the reference from Brucks (1985) for his definition of product knowledge. They use a seven-point Likert scale to measure a consumer's understanding level about product attribute and information of laptop. Measurement of product knowledge relating to insurance and catering service in this paper is used to measure the level of consumer understanding, and cumulative experience after enjoying a meal and the purchase of insurance. A seven-point Likert scale is used to measure a respondent's opinions about insurance and catering services; 1 means very little and 7 means very much.

### (3) Product involvement
By adopting the reference from Cohen (1983) and Zaichkowsky (1986) study for their definition of product involvement, this paper defines product involvement as a consumer's subjective self-perception of product importance and his/her involvement level concerning a specific service.

To measure product involvement, Zaichkowsky (1985) mainly adopts a semantic differential scale and develops a set of scales that measures product the involvement of the consumer, which is called personal involvement inventory. Also, Chin (2002) adopts a reference from Zaichkowsky (1985) study about personal involvement inventory, after reliability and validity tests, he contracts to ten items, using Likert's seven-point scale method. In this paper, a multiple dimension is used to measure a consumer's product involvement level. Based on personal involvement inventory submitted by Zaichkowsky (1985) and revised by Chin (2002), this study selects six measure items to measure a consumer product involvement level. Using

An empirical study of insurance and catering services

*Long-Yi Lin and Chun-Shuo Chen*

Journal of Consumer Marketing

*Volume 23 · Number 5 · 2006 · 248–265*

Likert's seven-point scale method to measure a respondent's opinion, 1 means absolutely disagree and 7 means absolutely agree.

*(4) Consumer purchase decision*
In adopting the reference from Solomon (1997) and McQuarrie and Muson (1992) study for their definition of information search intention, this paper defines information search intention as information search efforts consumer would spend on a specific service.

McQuarrie and Muson (1992) adopt Likert's seven-point scale method to measure information search intention. Chin (2002) adopts reference from McQuarrie and Muson (1992) study, and uses Likert's seven-point scale method to measure information search intention. This study, as far as selecting information search intention items, mainly adopts references from McQuarrie and Muson (1992) and Chin (2002) studies, which include four items and use Likert's seven-point scale method to measure a respondent's opinion. Amongst that, 1 means absolutely disagree and 7 means absolutely agree.

Consumer purchase intention means the possibility and probability of a consumer's willingness to purchase a specific product (Dodds *et al.*, 1991). This study adopts reference from Dodds *et al.*'s (1991) study and defines purchase intention as the possibility of a consumer's willingness to purchase a specific service.

Dodds *et al.* (1991) use five questions, however, Klein *et al.* (1998) use six questions, and adopt Likert's seven-point scale method to measure a consumer purchase intention. As far as selecting purchase intention items, this study mainly adopts reference from the Dodds *et al.* (1991) and Klein *et al.* (1998) studies, which include two measure items. Likert's seven-point scale method is used to measure a respondent's opinion, 1 means absolutely impossible and 7 means absolutely possible.

### 4. Questionnaire design
The questionnaire design in this paper includes five major parts, which are: country-of-origin image, product knowledge, product involvement level, and consumer purchase decision (including information search intention and purchase intention), and a respondent's basic information.

In order to measure the country image in this study the perspectives of Martin and Eroglu (1993) are adopted, and Chen's (2000) measure method is referred and revised. The questionnaire on product knowledge measurement, which is developed based on referring the studies of Brucks(1985) and Lin and Zhen (2005), mainly measures consumer's understanding and perception level, memory storage level, and after-purchase or after-use experience about product in insurance and catering services.

As far as selecting the dimension of product involvement measurement, this study adopts multiple dimensions to measure consumer product involvement level. The personal involvement inventory developed by Zaichkowsky in 1985 is adopted, referring Chin's (2002) measurement items, this study selects six items to measure the consumer's product involvement level. As far as measuring a consumer's purchase decision, including consumer information search intention and purchase intention, this study mainly takes reference from the McQuarrie and Muson (1992) and Chin (2002) studies

concerning information search intention and items selection. In addition, this study mainly takes reference from Dodds *et al.* (1991) and Klein *et al.* (1998) concerning measuring purchase intention and item selection.

A respondent's basic information includes whether he/she had purchased insurance or catering services, current residence, gender, age, career, educational background, and average monthly income.

### 5. Sampling design
*(1) Country-of-origin selection*
The research target in this study is the consumer of insurance and catering service. The insurance service takes reference from information on the web site of the Life Insurance Association of the ROC and the Non-life Insurance Association of the ROC. The catering service takes reference from a study of Wu (2001). Wu (2001) reports that, since the end of the Ching Dynasty, the catering service in Taiwan has been greatly influenced by China and the USA, such as the Taiwanese most favorite fast food culture is mainly American-style food. Furthermore, Chinese catering culture, such as dumplings and noodles are greatly preferred by Taiwanese consumers. Therefore, we choose countries that have interactions with Taiwan in either culture or economics as the target of the country-of-origin image in this study, which is Taiwan, China, and the USA.

*(2) Sampling targets*
This study chooses the Taipei area as a sampling area, and the sampling target is general consumers above 18 years old. Taipei area includes Taipei county and Taipei city. We choose Tamsui in Taipei county as the sampling location for considering economic progress in recent years, there are many sightseeing spots, convenient traffic, and large crowds in this location. This study choose downtown Taipei City as the sampling location with the consideration that many head quarters of financial and insurance company are located there and also it is convenient for getting to the source of communication and information, higher income and consumption levels, and frequent interactions of social activities; therefore, this location has more opportunities to interact with catering and insurance services.

*(3) Sampling method and sample size*
To consider the convenience and efficiency of this sampling, the study employs convenience sampling of non-probability. For data collection and questionnaire distribution personal interviews are adopted. The distribution and collection of questionnaire was done by the researcher.

According to four principles presented by Roscoe (1975), this study picks two items as reference standards. Therefore, sample size determination in this study includes:
1 appropriate sample size is 30 to 500;
2 performing multivariate analysis, sample size must exceed many times the variables in the research, and te times or above would be most appropriate.

Except for this, using simple random sampling to evaluate sample size, and inferring effective sample size would be more than 385. Based on these principles, this study calculates the appropriate sample size would be approximately 385 (Yen, 1996). In reference to these conditions, this study has distributed a total of 400 questionnaires. Among that, for this study picks Tamsui in Taipei county as sampling location, and considering difference of population only; therefore,

An empirical study of insurance and catering services

*Long-Yi Lin and Chun-Shuo Chen*

Journal of Consumer Marketing

*Volume 23 · Number 5 · 2006 · 248–265*

distribute 100 questionnaires in Tamsui area and 300 in Taipei area.

*(4) Pre-test*

To make sure of the reliability of the questionnaire used in this study to meet the requirement of research design, as well as sampling convenience, we performed a pre-test in Tairei subway Tamsui station before formal interviews to determine if reliability of questionnaire met the requirements. During the pre-tests, a total of 55 questionnaires were distributed, and 50 effective questionnaires were collected. The result shows that Cronbach's $\alpha$ value of every variable is more than 0.8 as shown in Table I, which it means that there is high consistency in variable measurement in this study.

## 6. Data collection and analysis method

This study chooses Taipei subway Tamsui station in Tamsui, and Taipei train station in Taipei City as sampling locations. The sampling time was from 8 a.m. to 6 p.m., including weekdays and holidays and consisted of interviewing people who come in and out of the station, asking them to answer the questionnaire, and collecting primary data.

The SPSS 10.0 version and LISREL 8.5 version is used for data analysis and comparison. Using Cronbach's $\alpha$ value to examine if the measure of variables in this paper meets the requirements of consistency, using factor loading and $SMC_S$ value to examine structure validity and convergent validity, and using stepwise regression analysis to test hypothesis.

## IV. Data analysis

### 1. Sample description

A total of 400 questionnaires were distributed in this study. After canceling 31 un-completed questionnaires, 369 effective questionnaires were collected; the effective return rate was 92.25 percent. According to the result of the questionnaire analysis, respondents who live in Taipei county and Taipei City are very close, which is 42.9 percent and 51.5 percent respectively. Female respondent (59.3 percent) is more than male respondent (40.7 percent). The respondents' age mainly lie between 20-29 years old (33.3 percent), and their education level mainly lies at college level (61.2 percent). The respondent's career background mainly lies in two major categories, business (30.4 percent) and student (16.5 percent), and personal average monthly income mainly lies at more than NT$45,000 (28.2 percent) and less than NT$15,000 (23.3 percent).

**Table I** Reliability of questionnaire of pre-test and formal investigation

| Variables | Pre-test Cronbach's $\alpha$ value | Formal investigation Cronbach's $\alpha$ value |
|---|---|---|
| Country-of-origin image | 0.8250 | 0.8715 |
| Product knowledge | 0.8463 | 0.9061 |
| Product involvement | 0.9313 | 0.9410 |
| Information search intention | 0.8658 | 0.8866 |
| Purchase intention | 0.8359 | 0.8261 |

### 2. Reliability and validity analysis

The purpose of reliability is to examine the level of non-error in measurement, which means to examine the consistency of measurement. This study adopts Cronbach's $\alpha$ as a tool for reliability examination. Based on suggestion of Guielford (1965), the bigger in Cronbach's $\alpha$ value, the higher internal consistency is. If $\alpha$ value is bigger than 0.70, then it shows reliability of measurement is fairly high.

The examination result of this study shows that, no matter whether during pre-test or formal investigation, Cronbach's $\alpha$ value in every variable is higher than 0.8, as shown in Table I, which means high reliability. It also shows that every variable has a fairly good internal consistency.

Validity means the measuring tool can measure the level of intended-to-measure object. The content validity, construct validity, and convergent validity were used in this paper to examine the validity of the questionnaire.

Content validity is performed based on the researcher's professional ability to judge subjectively if the selected scale can measure the researcher's intended-to-measure feature correctly. The dimensions and items explored in this study are based on relevant theory. This inventory or measuring item was used by many scholars both locally and globally. In addition, we carried out a pre-test and did some revision before setting out the questionnaire. Therefore, the questionnaire as a measuring tool used in this study should meet the requirement of content validity.

This study applies further confirmatory factor analysis to examine the construct validity and convergent validity of this questionnaire. The results are shown in Table II.

Chang (2001) and Chiu (2003) point out that, when the factor loading of measuring questions in a research are all higher than 0.5, it means the overall questionnaire quality is good and has a better construct validity. This study shows, according to the figures in Table II, factor loading of every question as being higher than 0.5. This means that the questionnaire used in this study performs a better construct validity.

In addition, Horng and Shen (2003) explain that, when SMCs is higher than 0.5, then a questionnaire has a convergent validity. This study shows that, based on figures in Table II, the average SMCs of variables, except for the country-of-origin image, is higher than 0.5. Although, the average SMCs of country-of-origin image is merely 0.46, but is also very close to 0.5. Therefore, it also means that the questionnaire used in this study performs convergent validity.

### 3. Correlation analysis

This study adopts Pearson's correlation coefficient analysis and its result is shown in Table III. With the judgment of the figures of correlation coefficients, we can examine correlation level of these variables. According to the figures shown in Table III, we find clearly the relationship between constructs in this study shows a highly positive correlation.

### 4. Hypothesis testing

The data collected in this study adopt stepwise regression analysis to verify the hypothesis. A total of 16 stepwise regression models were developed to test hypothesis. The hypothesis testing result is shown as Tables IV and V.

論文寫作要領

An empirical study of insurance and catering services

*Long-Yi Lin and Chun-Shuo Chen*

Journal of Consumer Marketing

*Volume 23 · Number 5 · 2006 · 248–265*

**Table II** Validity of formal questionnaire

| Variables | Questions | SMCs | Average SMCs | Factor loading |
|---|---|---|---|---|
| Country-of-origin image | 1 | 0.31 | 0.46 | 0.55 |
| | 2 | 0.40 | | 0.63 |
| | 3 | 0.36 | | 0.60 |
| | 4 | 0.54 | | 0.73 |
| | 5 | 0.44 | | 0.66 |
| | 6 | 0.60 | | 0.77 |
| | 7 | 0.52 | | 0.72 |
| | 8 | 0.54 | | 0.74 |
| Product knowledge | 9 | 0.68 | 0.66 | 0.82 |
| | 10 | 0.51 | | 0.72 |
| | 11 | 0.77 | | 0.88 |
| | 12 | 0.68 | | 0.82 |
| | 13 | 0.68 | | 0.83 |
| Product involvement | 14 | 0.65 | 0.73 | 0.81 |
| | 15 | 0.82 | | 0.91 |
| | 16 | 0.82 | | 0.90 |
| | 17 | 0.77 | | 0.88 |
| | 18 | 0.68 | | 0.82 |
| | 19 | 0.65 | | 0.81 |
| Consumer purchase decision | 20 | 0.71 | 0.71 | 0.84 |
| | 21 | 0.71 | | 0.84 |
| | 22 | 0.72 | | 0.85 |
| | 23 | 0.57 | | 0.76 |
| | 24 | 0.74 | | 0.86 |
| | 25 | 0.80 | | 0.80 |

**Table III** Average, standard deviation, and correlation coefficient of constructs

| Variables | 1 | 2 | 3 | 4 | 5 |
|---|---|---|---|---|---|
| 1 Country-of-origin image | 1.00 | | | | |
| 2 Product knowledge | 0.256 | 1.00 | | | |
| 3 Product involvement | 0.312 | 0.516 | 1.00 | | |
| 4 Information search intention | 0.252 | 0.447 | 0.482 | 1.00 | |
| 5 Purchase intention | 0.234 | 0.451 | 0.432 | 0.664 | 1.00 |
| Average | 14.36 | 7.69 | 10.28 | 25.4 | 23.85 |
| Standard deviation | 1.78 | 1.94 | 2.00 | 5.55 | 5.86 |

*(1) Testing of information search intention*

- *The impact of country-of-origin image on information search intention.* Based on the testing result from model 2 in Table IV, the explanatory power of model 2 is 6.2 percent (8.1 percent-1.9 percent), and *p* value that determinates the good of fitness is $0.000 < 0.01$, which means it reach statistical significance. This also means that that country-of-origin image does significantly influence the consumer information search intention, and the regression coefficient is 0.77, which shows that the country-of-origin image has a significantly positive impact on the consumer information search intention. Therefore, *H1-1* is strongly supported.
- *The impact of product knowledge on information search intention.* According to the testing result from model 3 in Table IV, the explanatory power of model 3 is 19.5 percent (21.4 percent-1.9 percent), and the *p* value that

determinates the good of fitness is $0.000 < 0.01$, which shows it reaches statistical significance. This also means that, product knowledge does cause a distinct effect on consumer information search intention, and the regression coefficient is 1.26, which shows that product knowledge has a significantly positive impact on consumer information search intention. Therefore, *H2-1* is strongly supported.

- *The impact of product involvement on information search intention.* Based on the testing result from model 4 in Table IV, the explanatory power of model 4 is 23.1 percent (25 percent-1.9 percent), and the *p* value that determinates the good of fitness is $0.000 < 0.01$, which shows it reaches statistical significance. This also means that, product involvement has a distinct effect on consumer information search intention, and the regression coefficient is 1.33, which shows that product involvement has a significantly positive impact on consumer information intention. Therefore, *H3-1* is strongly supported.
- *The moderate effect of product involvement under the influence of country-of-origin image on information search intention.* According to the testing result from model 6 in Table IV, the explanatory power of model 6 is 0.3 percent (26.4 percent-26.1 percent), and the *p* value that determinates the good of fitness is $0.000 < 0.01$, which shows it reaches statistical significance. This also means that, country-of-origin image and product involvement have an interactive relationship, and the regression coefficient is 0.0342, which shows that as product involvement level increases, country-of-origin image has a greater influence to

An empirical study of insurance and catering services

*Long-Yi Lin and Chun-Shuo Chen*

Journal of Consumer Marketing

*Volume 23 · Number 5 · 2006 · 248–265*

Table IV Stepwise regression analysis (reactive variable: information search intention)

| Explanatory power | Model 1 | Model 2 | Model 3 | Model 4 | Model 5 | Model 6 | Model 7 | Model 8 |
|---|---|---|---|---|---|---|---|---|
| Gender | ✓ | ✓ | ✓ | ✓ | ✓ | ✓ | ✓ | ✓ |
| Age | ✓ | ✓ | ✓ | ✓ | ✓ | ✓ | ✓ | ✓ |
| Education level | ✓ | ✓ | ✓ | ✓ | ✓ | ✓ | ✓ | ✓ |
| Income | ✓ | ✓ | ✓ | ✓ | ✓ | ✓ | ✓ | ✓ |
| Career | ✓ | ✓ | ✓ | ✓ | ✓ | ✓ | ✓ | ✓ |
| Country-of-origin image | | ✓ Regression coefficient: 0.77 | | | ✓ | ✓ | | |
| Product knowledge | | | ✓ Regression coefficient: 1.26 | | | | ✓ | ✓ |
| Product involvement | | | | ✓ Regression coefficient: 1.33 | ✓ | | ✓ | ✓ |
| Country-of-origin image × product involvement | | | | | ✓ | ✓ Regression coefficient: 0.0342 | | |
| Product knowledge × product involvement | | | | | | | | ✓ Regression coefficient: 0.0694 |
| $F$ | 7.145* | 16.213* | 49.868* | 60.969* | 42.964* | 43.548* | 73.456* | 41.240* |
| $R^2$ | 0.019 | 0.081 | 0.214 | 0.250 | 0.261 | 0.264 | 0.286 | 0.312 |
| $\Delta R^2$ | 0.019 | 0.018 | 0.014 | 0.017 | 0.011 | 0.014 | 0.054 | 0.007 |
| Adj-$R^2$ | 0.016 | 0.076 | 0.210 | 0.246 | 0.255 | 0.258 | 0.283 | 0.304 |
| Overall model $p$ value | 0.000 | 0.000 | 0.000 | 0.000 | 0.000 | 0.000 | 0.000 | 0.000 |

Note: * $p < 0.01$

**Table V** Stepwise regression analysis (reactive variable: purchase intention)

| Variables | Model 9 | Model 10 | Model 11 | Model 12 | Model 13 | Model 14 | Model 15 | Model 16 |
|---|---|---|---|---|---|---|---|---|
| Gender | ✓ | ✓ | ✓ | ✓ | ✓ | ✓ | ✓ | ✓ |
| Age | ✓ | ✓ | ✓ | ✓ | ✓ | ✓ | ✓ | ✓ |
| Education level | ✓ | ✓ | ✓ | ✓ | ✓ | ✓ | ✓ | ✓ |
| Income | ✓ | ✓ | ✓ | ✓ | ✓ | ✓ | ✓ | ✓ |
| Career | ✓ | ✓ | ✓ | ✓ | ✓ | ✓ | ✓ | ✓ |
| Country-of-origin image | | ✓ Regression coefficient: 0.76 | | | ✓ | ✓ | | |
| Product knowledge | | | ✓ Regression coefficient: 1.34 | | ✓ | ✓ | ✓ | ✓ |
| Product involvement | | | | ✓ Regression coefficient: 1.21 | ✓ | ✓ | ✓ | ✓ |
| Country-of-origin image × product involvement | | | | | | ✓ Regression coefficient: 0.0355 | | |
| Product knowledge × product involvement | | | | | | | | ✓ Regression coefficient: 0.0934 |
| $F$ | 12.91* | 17.943* | 55.865* | 47.039* | 33.529* | 33.860* | 63.392* | 67.737* |
| $R^2$ | 0.034 | 0.087 | 0.234 | 0.204 | 0.216 | 0.218 | 0.257 | 0.270 |
| $\Delta R^2$ | 0.034 | 0.032 | 0.031 | 0.018 | 0.012 | 0.011 | 0.054 | 0.023 |
| Adj-$R^2$ | 0.031 | 0.082 | 0.230 | 0.200 | 0.210 | 0.211 | 0.253 | 0.266 |
| Overall model $p$ value | 0.008 | 0.000 | 0.000 | 0.000 | 0.000 | 0.000 | 0.000 | 0.000 |

Note: * $p < 0.01$

consumer information search intention. Therefore, *H4-1* is strongly supported.

- *The moderate effect of product involvement under the influence of product knowledge on information search intention.* Based on the testing result from model 8 in Table IV, the explanatory power of model 8 is 2.6 percent (31.2 percent-28.6 percent), and the $p$ value that determinates the good of fitness is $0.000 < 0.01$, which shows it reaches statistical significance. This also means that, product knowledge and product involvement have an interactive relationship, and the regression coefficient is 0.0694, which shows that as the product involvement level increases, product knowledge has a greater influence to consumer information search intention. Therefore, *H5-1* is strongly supported.

### (2) Testing of purchase intention

- *The impact of country-of-origin image on purchase intention.* Based on the testing result from model 10 in Table V, the explanatory power of model 10 is 5.3 percent (8.7 percent-3.4 percent), and the $p$ value that determinates the good of fitness is $0.000 < 0.01$, which shows it reaches statistical significance. This also means that the country-of-origin image does cause a distinct effect on consumer purchase intention, and the regression coefficient is 0.76, which shows that country-of-origin image asserts a significantly positive influence on the consumer purchase intention. Therefore, *H1-2* is strongly supported. According to previous testing, we examined the *H1-1* is strongly supported; therefore, from the combination of these two testing result, *H1* is strongly supported.
- *The impact of product knowledge on purchase intention.* According to the testing result from model 11 in Table V, the explanatory power of model 11 is 20 percent (23.4 percent-3.4 percent), and the $p$ value that determinates the good of fitness is $0.000 < 0.01$, which shows it reaches statistical significance. This also means that that country-of-origin image does cause a distinct effect on consumer purchase intention, and the regression coefficient is 1.34, which shows that product knowledge causes a significantly positive influence on consumer purchase intention. Therefore, *H2-2* is strongly supported. According to previous testing, we examined the *H2-1* is strongly supported; therefore, from the combination of these two testing results, *H2* is strongly supported.
- *The impact of product involvement on purchase intention.* Based on the testing result from model 12 in Table V, the explanatory power of model 12 is 17 percent (20.4 percent-3.4 percent), and the $p$ value that determinates the good of fitness is $0.000 < 0.01$, which shows it reaches statistical significance. This also means that, country-of-origin image does cause a distinct effect on consumer purchase intention, and the regression coefficient is 1.21, which shows that product involvement causes a significantly positive influence to consumer purchase intention. Therefore, *H3-2* is strongly supported. According to previous testing result, we found *H3-1* is strongly supported; therefore, from the combination of these two testing results, *H3* is strongly supported.
- *The moderate effect of product involvement under the influence of country-of-origin image on information search intention.* Based on the testing result from model 14 in Table V, the

explanatory power of model 14 is 0.2 percent (21.8 percent-21.6 percent), and the $p$ value that determinates the good of fitness is $0.000 < 0.01$, which shows it reaches statistical significance. This also means that, there is an interactive effect between country-of-origin image and consumer purchase intention, and the regression coefficient is 0.0355, which shows that, as product involvement level increases, country-of-origin image would cause a significantly positive influence on consumer purchase intention. Therefore, *H4-2* is strongly supported. According to previous testing result, we examined *H4-1* is strongly supported; therefore, from the combination of these two testing result, *H4* is strongly supported.

- *The moderate effect of product involvement under the influence of product knowledge on information search intention.* According to the testing result from model 16 in Table V, the explanatory power of model 16 is 1.3 percent (27 percent-25.7 percent), and the $p$ value that determinates the good of fitness is $0.000 < 0.01$, which shows it reaches statistical significance. This also means that, these is an interactive effect between country-of-origin image and consumer purchase intention, and the regression coefficient is 0.0934, which shows that, as product involvement level increases, country-of-origin image would cause a significantly positive influence on consumer purchase intention. Therefore, *H5-2* is strongly supported. According to previous testing result, we found *H5-1* is strongly supported; therefore, from the combination of these two testing result, *H5* is strongly supported.

## V. Conclusion and suggestion

### 1. Conclusion

The verification of the hypotheses in this paper leads to five conclusions:

1. country-of-origin image has a significantly positive influence on consumer purchase decision;
2. consumer product knowledge has a significantly positive influence on consumer purchase decision;
3. product involvement has a significantly positive influence on consumer purchase decision;
4. country-of-origin image has a significantly positive influence on consumer purchase decision under different product involvement levels; and
5. product knowledge has a significantly positive influence on consumer purchase decision under different product involvement levels.

### 2. Management implication

#### (1) Theory implication

- *Provide a more thorough structure about consumer purchase decision.* In research concerning consumer purchase behavior, the past literature has used product evaluation, purchase intention, or re-purchase intention as research variables. This study focuses more on overall perspectives, and adds information search intention as one of important variables in consumer purchase decision, and develops more thorough and well-structured consumer purchase decision structure, complement part of the disadvantages in past theoretical structure.

- *Verify the relationship between product knowledge and information search quantity.* Moore and Lehmann (1980) discovered in their empirical study that consumer product knowledge has a significantly positive influence on consumer information search efforts. Newman and Staelin (1972) report that information search quantity has a negative relation with product experience level. Therefore, it shows that, scholar's opinion on relationship between product knowledge and information search quantity is not yet clearly defined. This study verifies that, product knowledge has a significantly positive relationship with information search intention. Therefore, it clarifies part of doubts and debates.

*(2) Practical implication*

- *Company must face competitive strategies from many countries.* Country-of-origin image does affect consumer purchase decision. The rise of the World Trade Organization (WTO) facilitates consumers to see and enjoy products from many different countries. Therefore, when company promotes their products to the global market, except for considering a product's brand image, they must also consider the country-of-origin image then develop the most appropriate competitive strategy. As far as the country-of-origin image is concerned, in a company's short-term marketing strategy, if a country has a good image, then its company would benefit from international marketing. Otherwise, if this country does not have a good image, then a company's marketing strategy should focus on the attribute of a product's features. Execution of a series of marketing activities helps a consumer to better understand the advantages of a product, in order to change a consumer's product evaluation principles. Other than this, a company can also adopt a strategy alliance or other strategies to decrease negative influences caused by a bad country image.
- *The effect of consumer product knowledge on business competitive strategy.* When a company uses consumer product knowledge to develop proper competitive strategy, it is similar to a two-sided knife. If used properly, then its marketing strategy is like a sharp knife, which can easily win a share of mind and encourage a consumer to purchase a product. Consumer product knowledge has a distinct positive influence on a consumer's information search intention; therefore, he/she must first have a certain level of product knowledge then search for a wider range of relevant information. Therefore, a company's developing marketing strategy should be fair to all consumers and expose a proper amount of relevant product information. Only if a company assists consumer to absorb its product information, will it raise the consumer purchase intention.

### 3. Limitation

Although this research attempts for a more planned and objective design, and has come to a concrete conclusion, it still has somehow in perfectly performed during the research process. There are three limitations in this study list as follows:

1 Unable to infer to national consumers: this study adopts convenience sampling and the sampling area is restricted in Taipei area. From the perspective of statistical theory, samples may lack generalization power, and may not be suitable to infer to general national citizens or other consuming groups.

2 Unsuitable to infer to other service area: this study only performs research based on insurance and catering services. Although it obtains concrete conclusion the research result may be unsuitable to infer to other types of services.

3 Explanatory power of some empirical model is relative low: this study adopts stepwise regression analysis to test hypothesis, but the explanatory power of *H4-1, H4-2, H5-1,* and *H5-2* is relative low. Therefore, it becomes a restriction of statistics theory in this study.

### 4. Suggestion

*(1) Suggestions to manufacturers*

When manufacturers export their products to other countries, they should first examine the evaluation of consumers in these countries to the product's country-of-origin image, then develop an appropriate marketing strategy, in order to actually attract consumer attention and increase their purchase intention. Moreover, when manufacturers attempt to promote a service product, they should first explore relevant product information through many kind of media or marketing activities, in order to prevent consumers stepping backwards and lose a great deal of business opportunities for consumer's personal mental factors, such as self-contained and fear.

This study discovers that, consumer product knowledge is an important factor in influencing their purchase intention. Therefore, when manufacturers attempt to develop a marketing strategy and project, they must first understand the consumer's attitude in dealing with relevant product information, in order to increase marketing strategy effect.

*(2) Future research suggestion*

This study only performs research based on two items of services, insurance and dining. Future research can be chosen in different service items for comparing differences of other service items. Moreover, the country-of-origin in this study only chooses Taiwan, Mainland China, and the USA. For future research, it can include other countries or measure other countries directly for comparing differences of other countries. Besides, it is advisable to study services in different industries, and compare differences of these researches.

### References

Agarwal, S. and Sikri, S. (1996), "Country image: consumer evaluation of product category extension", *International Marketing Review*, Vol. 13 No. 4, pp. 23-9.

Ahmed, S.A. and Astous, A.D. (1995), "Comparison of country of origin effects on house and organizational buyers' product perception", *European Journal of Marketing*, Vol. 29 No. 3, pp. 35-51.

Ahmed, S.A. and Astous, A.D. (1996), "Country-of-origin and brand effects: a multi-dimensional and multi-attribute study", *Journal of International Consumer Marketing*, Vol. 9 No. 2, pp. 93-115.

Ahmed, Z.U., Johnson, J.P. and Boon, L.C. (2004), "Does country of origin matter for low-involvement products", *International Marketing Review*, Vol. 21 No. 1, pp. 102-20.

An empirical study of insurance and catering services

*Long-Yi Lin and Chun-Shuo Chen*

Journal of Consumer Marketing

*Volume 23 · Number 5 · 2006 · 248–265*

Alba, J. and Hutchinson, J.W. (1987), "Dimensions of consumer expertise", *Journal of Consumer Research*, Vol. 13 No. 4, pp. 411-5.

Arora, R. (1982), "Validation of an s-o-r model for situation, enduring, and response components of involvement", *Journal of Marketing Research*, Vol. 19 No. 11, pp. 505-16.

Arora, R. (1993), "Consumer involvement in service decisions", *Journal of Professional Service Marketing*, Vol. 9 No. 1, pp. 49-58.

Bettman, J.R. and Park, C.W. (1980), "Effects of prior knowledge and experience and phase of the choice process on consumer decision processes: a protocol analysis", *Journal of Consumer Research*, Vol. 7 No. 3, pp. 234-48.

Bilkey, W.J. and Nes, E. (1982), "Country of origin effect on product evaluation", *Journal of International Business Studies*, Vol. 8, Spring/Summer, pp. 89-99.

Bloch, P.H. (1982), "Involvement beyond the purchase process: conceptual issues and empirical investigation", in Mitchell, A.A. (Ed.), *Advances in Consumer Research*, Vol. 9, Association for Consumer Research, Ann Arbor, MI, pp. 413-47.

Brucks, M. (1985), "The effect of product class knowledge on information search behavior", *Journal of Consumer Research*, Vol. 12 No. 1, pp. 1-16.

Chang, S.-S. (2001), *Research Method*, Tsuan Hai Press, Taichung (in Chinese).

Chao, P. and Rajendran, K.N. (1993), "Consumer profiles and perception: country-of-origin effects", *International Marketing Review*, Vol. 10 No. 2, pp. 22-39.

Chen, C.-L. (2000), "The influence of country image on product evaluation and purchase decision", Masters degree thesis, Graduate School of International Business, Ming Chuan University, Taipei.

Chin, C.-W. (2002), "The impact of the image of manufacturer's origin country consumer purchase behavior – take Taiwan and mainland China metropolitan as an example", Masters degree thesis, Graduate School of Business an Operations Management, Chang Jung Christian University, Tainan City.

Chiu, H.-Z. (2003), *Multivariate Statistical Analysis: SAS/STAT Application Method*, 1st ed., Chi-Bon Culture Press, Taipei.

Cohen, J.B. (1983), "Involvement and you: 100 great ideas", in Bagozzi, R.P. and Tybout, A.M. (Eds), *Advances in Consumer Research*, Vol. 10, Association for Consumer Research, Provo, UT, pp. 32-9.

Dodds, B.K., Monroe, K.B. and Grewal, D. (1991), "Effect of price, brands and store information on buyers' product evaluation", *Journal of Marketing Research*, Vol. 28, August, pp. 307-19.

Engel, J.F., Blackwell, R.D. and Kollat, D. (1995), *Consumer Behavior*, 8th ed., The Dryden Press, Harcourt Brace College Publisher, Chicago, IL.

Engel, J.F., Blackwell, R.D. and Miniard, P.W. (1993) in Miniard, P.W. (Ed.), *Consumer Behavior*, 7th ed., Dryden Press, Chicago, IL.

Erickson, G.M., Johansson, J.K. and Chao, P. (1984), "Image variables in multi-attribute product evaluation: country of origin effects", *Journal of Consumer Research*, Vol. 11 No. 2, pp. 694-9.

Fishbein, A.J. and Ajzen, L. (1975), *Belief, Attitude, Intention, and Behavior: An Introduction to Theory and Research*, Addison-Wesley, Reading, MA.

Friedman, M.L. and Smith, L. (1993), "Consumer evaluation process in a service setting", *Journal of Service Marketing*, Vol. 7 No. 2, pp. 47-61.

Goldsmith, R.E. and Emmert, J. (1991), "Measuring product category involvement: a multitrait-multimethod study", *Journal of Business Research*, Vol. 23 No. 4, pp. 363-71.

Guielford, J.P. (1965), *Fundamental Statistics in Psychology and Education*, 4th ed., McGraw-Hill, New York, NY.

Han, C.M. (1989), "Country image: halo or summary construct?", *Journal of Marketing*, Vol. 26, May, pp. 222-9.

Han, C.M. (1990), "Testing the role of country image in consumer choice behavior", *European Journal of Marketing*, Vol. 24 No. 6, pp. 24-40.

Han, C.M. and Terpstra, V. (1988), "Country-of-origin effects for uni-national and bi-national", *Journal of International Business Studies*, Vol. 19 No. 2, pp. 235-55.

Harrison-Walker, L.J. (1995), "The relative effects of national stereotype and advertising", *The Journal of Services Marketing*, Vol. 9 No. 1, pp. 47-59.

Hong, S. and Wyer, R.S. Jr (1989), "Effects of country of origin and product attribute information on product evaluation: an information processing perspective", *Journal of Consumer Research*, Vol. 16 No. 2, pp. 175-85.

Horng, S.-C. and Shen, C.-H. (2003), "The relationship between market driven organizational learning and new product success", *Journal of Management*, Vol. 20 No. 3, pp. 515-45.

Houston, M.J. and Rothschild, M.L. (1978), "Conceptual and methodological perspectives in involvement", *Research Frontiers in Marketing: Dialogues and Directions*, American Marketing Association, Chicago, IL, pp. 184-7.

Howard, J.A. (1989), *Consumer Behavior in Marketing Strategy*, Prentice-Hall, Englewood Cliffs, NJ.

Hsieh, W.-L. (1994), "The effect of production origin and brand origin on consumer behavior", Masters degree thesis, Graduate School of Business, National Taiwan University, Taipei.

Johansson, J.K. and Thorelli, H.B. (1985), "International product positioning", *Journal of International Business Studies*, Vol. 16 No. 3, pp. 57-75.

Johansson, J.K., Douglas, S.P. and Noanka, I. (1985), "Assessing the impact of country of origin on product evaluation: a new methodological perspective", *Journal of Marketing Research*, Vol. 22, pp. 388-96.

Johnson, E.J. and Russo, J.E. (1984), "Product familiarity and learning new information", *Journal of Consumer Research*, Vol. 11 No. 1, pp. 542-50.

Klein, J.R., Ettenson, R. and Morris, M.D. (1998), "The animosity model of foreign product purchase: an empirical test in the People's Republic of China", *Journal of Marketing*, Vol. 62 No. 1, pp. 89-100.

Kotler, P., Ang, S.H., Leong, S.M. and Tan, C.T. (1999), *Marketing Management: An Asian Perspective*, 2nd ed., Prentice-Hall, Englewood Cliffs, NJ.

Krugman, H.E. (1965), "The impact of television advertising learning without involvement", *Public Opinion Quarterly*, Vol. 29, Fall, pp. 349-56.

Larkin, J., McDermott, J., Simon, D.P. and Simon, H.A. (1980), "Expert and novice performance in solving physics problem", *Science*, Vol. 208 No. 14, pp. 335-42.

Lee, C.-F. (1999), "The influences of product involvement, brand equity, and market characteristics in evaluating and

論文寫作要領

choosing brand", Masters degree thesis, Graduate School of Business Administration, National Cheng Kung University, Tainan City.

Lehmann, D.R. (1986), "Measuring images of foreign products", *Columbia Journal of World Business*, Summer, pp. 105-8.

Lin, L.-Y. and Zhen, J.-H. (2005), "Extrinsic product performance signaling, product knowledge and customer satisfaction: an integrated analysis – an example of notebook consumer behavior in Taipei city", *Fu Jen Management Review*, Vol. 12 No. 1, pp. 65-91.

McQuarrie, E.F. and Muson, J.M. (1992), "The Zaichkowsky personal involvement inventory: modification and extension", in Wallendorf, M. and Anderson, P. (Eds), *Advances in Consumer Research*, Vol. 14, Association for Consumer Research, Provo, UT, pp. 36-40.

Manrai, L.A. and Manrai, A.K. (1993), "Positioning European country as brands in a perceptual map: an empirical study of determinants of consumer perception and preference", *Journal of Euromarketing*, Vol. 2 No. 3, pp. 101-29.

Marks, L.J. and Olson, J.C. (1981), "Toward a cognitive structure conceptualization of product familiarity", in Monroe, K. (Ed.), *Advances in Consumer Research*, Vol. 8, Association for Consumer Research, Ann Arbor, MI, pp. 145-50.

Martin, I.M. and Eroglu, S. (1993), "Measuring a multi-dimensional construct: country image", *Journal of Business Research*, Vol. 28 No. 3, pp. 191-210.

Mitchell, A.A. (1981), "Dimensions of advertising involvement", in Monroe, K.B. (Ed.), *Advances in Consumer Research*, Vol. 8, Association for Consumer Research, Ann Arbor, MI.

Moore, W.L. and Lehmann, D.R. (1980), "Individual differences in search behavior for a nondurable", *Journal of Consumer Research*, Vol. 7 No. 3, pp. 296-307.

Nagashima, A. (1970), "A comparative made in product image survey among Japanese businessmen", *Journal of Marketing*, Vol. 41, July, pp. 95-100.

Neese, W.T. and Taylor, R.D. (1994), "Verbal strategies for indirect comparative advertising", *Journal of Advertising Research*, Vol. 34 No. 2, pp. 56-69.

Newman, J.W. and Staelin, R. (1972), "Pre-purchase information seeking for new cars and major household appliances", *Journal of Marketing Research*, Vol. 9 No. 3, pp. 249-57.

Nicosia, F.M. (1968), *Consumer Decision Process, Marketing and Advertising Implication*, Prentice-Hall, Englewood Cliffs, NJ, p. 156.

Papadopoulos, N. and Heslop, L. (1993), *Product-Country Image: Impact and Role in International Marketing*, International Business Press, London.

Park, C.W. and Lessig, V.P. (1981), "Familiarity and its impact on consumer decision biases and heuristics", *Journal of Consumer Research*, Vol. 8 No. 2, pp. 223-30.

Petty, R.E. and Cacioppo, J.T. (1981), *Attitude and Persuasion: Classic and Contemporary Approaches*, Wm C. Brown, Dubuque, IA.

Petty, R.E., Cacioppo, J.T. and David, S. (1983), "Central and peripheral routes to advertisements effectiveness: the moderating role of involvement", *Journal of Consumer Research*, Vol. 10 No. 2, pp. 135-46.

Punj, G.N. and Staelin, R. (1983), "A model of consumer information search behavior for new automobiles", *Journal of Consumer Research*, Vol. 9 No. 4, pp. 366-80.

Rao, A.R. and Monroe, K.B. (1988), "The moderating effect of prior knowledge on cue utilization in product evaluation", *Journal of Consumer Research*, Vol. 15 No. 2, pp. 253-64.

Rao, A.R. and Sieben, W.A. (1992), "The effect of prior knowledge on price acceptability and the type of information examined", *Journal of Consumer Research*, Vol. 19 No. 2, pp. 256-70.

Roger, T.M., Kaminski, P.F., Schoenbachler, D.D. and Gordon, G.L. (1994), "The effect of country-of-origin information on consumer purchase decision process when price and quality information are available", *Journal of International Consumer Marketing*, Vol. 7 No. 2, pp. 73-109.

Roscoe, J.T. (1975), *Fundamental Research Statistics for the Behavior Science*, 2nd ed., Rinehart and Winston, New York, NY.

Roth, M.S. and Romeo, J.B. (1992), "Matching product and country image perceptions: a framework for managing country-of-origin effects", *Journal of International Business Studies*, Vol. 23 No. 3, pp. 477-97.

Rudell, F. (1979), *Consumer Food Selection and Nutrition Information*, Praeger, New York, NY.

Saeed, S. (1994), "Consumer evaluation of products in a global market", *Journal of International Business Studies*, Vol. 25 No. 3, pp. 579-604.

Schooler, R.D. (1965), "Product bias in the general American common market", *Journal of Marketing Research*, Vol. 2, November, pp. 394-7.

Selnes, F. and Troye, S.V. (1989), "Buying expertise, information search and problem solving", *Journal of Economic Psychology*, Vol. 10 No. 3, pp. 411-28.

Slama, M.E. and Tashchian, A. (1985), "Selected socioeconomic and demographic characteristics associated with purchasing involvement", *Journal of Marketing*, Vol. 49, pp. 72-82.

Solomon, M.R. (1997), *Consumer Behavior: Buying, Having and Being*, 2nd ed., Allyn and Bacon, Canberra.

Swinyard, W.R. (1993), "The effect of mood, involvement, and quality of store experience on shopping intention", *Journal of Consumer Research*, Vol. 20 No. 2, pp. 271-80.

Traylor, M.B. (1981), "Product involvement and brand commitment", *Journal of Advertising Research*, Vol. 21 No. 6, pp. 51-6.

Tseng, J.-Y. (2001), "A study of the influence of country-of-brand and brand equity on consumers' purchase intention", Masters degree thesis, Graduate School of Management Sciences, Aletheia University, Taipei.

Wall, M., Liefeld, J. and Heslop, L.A. (1991), "Impact of country-of-origin cues on consumer judgments in multi-cue situations: a covariance analysis", *Journal of the Academy of Marketing Science*, Vol. 19 No. 2, pp. 105-13.

Wang, W.-M. (2001), "The study of virtual community and experience, internet proficiency, product knowledge and information search cost on consumer perceived risk: an example of PC game soft", Masters degree thesis, Graduate School of Business Administration, National Central University, Chungli.

Wu, Z.-H. (2001), "Origin of Taiwan's dining development", paper presented at the The First Taiwan Sightseeing Development Convention.

An empirical study of insurance and catering services

*Long-Yi Lin and Chun-Shuo Chen*

Journal of Consumer Marketing

*Volume 23 · Number 5 · 2006 · 248–265*

Yang, S.-C. (1994), "The country image effect on the purchase intention of service products", Masters degree thesis, Graduate School of International Business, National Taiwan University, Taipei.

Yang, W.-S. (2001), "The study of relationships between the involvement levels and related factors of purchasing decision of the mobile phone consumers", Masters degree Thesis, Graduate School of Management of Business, National Chiao Tung University, Hsinchu.

Yen, Y.-Z. (1996), *Statistics*, 5th ed., Shan Ming Press, Taipei.

Zaichkowsky, J.L. (1985), "Measuring the involvement construct", *Journal of Consumer Research*, Vol. 12 No. 3, pp. 341-52.

Zaichkowsky, J.L. (1986), "Conceptualizing involvement", *Journal of Advertising*, Vol. 15 No. 2, pp. 4-14.

Zhu, P.-T. (2004), "The relationship among community identification, community trust, and purchase behavior- the case of RVs communities", Masters degree thesis, Graduate School of International Business, National Dong Hwa University, Shoufeng.

## About the authors

Long-Yi Lin, also known as Nicholas Lin and is an Assistant Professor of the Graduate School of Management Sciences of Aletheia University in Taipei, Taiwan. Long-Yi Lin obtained his PhD from National Taipei University, Taipei, Taiwan. He majored in marketing management and second majored in organizational management. Before teaching in graduate school, Long-Yi Lin worked for Hey-Song Corporation, which is the biggest soft drinks manufacturer in Taiwan. During 33 years working career, he worked very hard and was fortunate to have many good chances of being in charge of many important works, in the role of personnel manager, general affairs manager, sales promotion manager, purchasing manager, plant manager, business planning director, and marketing director. These working experiences in practice contribute greatly to his teaching career. Reading and studying is Long-Yi Lin' favorite pastime. He has translated 21 English books into Chinese for text book and business use. He has also published more than 100 articles in business newspapers in Taiwan.

Chun-Shuo Chen obtained the MBA degree from Aletheia University in Taiwan. Chun-Shuo Chen is now living in Tamshui.

## Executive summary and implications for managers and executives

*This summary has been provided to allow managers and executives a rapid appreciation of the content of the article. Those with a particular interest in the topic covered may then read the article in toto to take advantage of the more comprehensive description of the research undertaken and its results to get the full benefit of the material present.*

### Country of origin and its image

There is plenty of evidence to indicate that consumers evaluate products differently depending on their country of origin (COO) or country of manufacture (COM). Most of the research into this area has concentrated on manufacturing, industry or consumer products. Lin and Chen's aim is to investigate the influence of COO on information search and consumer purchases within the insurance and catering sectors, where little previous study has been carried out.

Extant literature suggests that the distinction between COO and COM often becomes blurred and sometimes merge into a single construct. Consequently, COO can refer to either or both.

COO image is formed through such as economic development, political background, level of industrialization, technology development, historical factors and tradition. This image gives rise to stereotypes that consumers relate to in order to evaluate products from a given country. Many observers argue that a damaging COO image exerts a more powerful influence on consumers, who then extend negative perceptions to goods produced in that country. Essentially, COO image influences a consumer's trust and evaluation of a product - particularly when the consumer has no prior knowledge of the product itself. This is also likely to influence evaluation of a brand.

### Product knowledge and product involvement

In addition to COO image, it is accepted that consumers generally search for additional information before making purchase decisions. This makes product knowledge an important factor. However, indications are that influence of such knowledge has previously tended to be more significant in relation to products than services.

Product knowledge has attracted different definitions and some analysts have subdivided the concept into categories such as objective knowledge and experienced based knowledge. Effectively, however, product knowledge refers to the consumer's level of awareness and understanding about a product and has been measured by the amount of purchase, usage and information stored in the memory.

Lin and Chen also consider the effect of product involvement, which relates to the importance that consumers attach to the product and their level of interest in it. Correlation exists between interest and involvement levels. This concept is also sometimes subdivided, this time into advertising involvement, product involvement and purchasing involvement. In addition to COO image, the authors investigate the effect of product knowledge and product involvement on information search and purchase decisions in the aforementioned service industries. The relationship between the factors is also analyzed.

A structured questionnaire was distributed to consumers in the Taipei area of Taiwan and 369 were properly completed and selected as part of the survey. Taiwan, China and the US were chosen for COO image mainly because the other two countries have significantly influenced catering in Taiwan.

The results indicated that all three factors exert a significant influence on information search and purchase intention. This substantiated earlier claims that consumers evaluate products based on their knowledge and understanding of them. Likewise, findings here also indicated support for the notion that consumers with higher levels of product involvement would search for more information to help their purchase decision. Previously, it had also been claimed that such consumers had a more positive attitude towards brands and advertising connected to them.

An empirical study of insurance and catering services

*Long-Yi Lin and Chun-Shuo Chen*

Journal of Consumer Marketing

*Volume 23 · Number 5 · 2006 · 248–265*

Lin and Chen also explored the relations between the different factors and concluded, for instance, that the effect of COO increases when the consumer's interest or involvement in the product is higher. However, earlier investigation revealed that consumers with higher levels of product involvement would also seek information relating to other attributes such as brand or price. This served to dilute the effect of COO and COM on information search.

Findings also indicated an interactive relationship between product involvement and product knowledge. The authors conclude that as product involvement increases, the influence of product knowledge on both information search and purchase decision becomes greater. Previous studies have not been conclusive in this area. In one example, consumers with high product knowledge were found to be less inclined to search for additional information. This suggests that firm conclusions should not yet be drawn about the relationship between these factors.

Some analysts argue that consumer purchase decision contains two stages: information search that includes evaluation of alternatives; and buying intention. Following their study, Lin and Chen conclude that information search has an important influence on the purchase decision.

## Implications

In view of the influence of COO image, the authors advise companies to adopt an appropriate strategy when marketing their products in different parts of the world. If the COO image is positive, then marketers should strive to exploit this to their advantage by incorporating COO attributes in their advertising strategies. Conversely, when a COO image is negative it is much wiser to focus on the product itself and promote it through a range of marketing activities that highlight the product features most likely to appeal to the consumer. An effective campaign can also successfully deflect attention from and reduce the harmful effects of a negative COO image.

It is additionally recommended that companies would benefit by making more effort to better inform consumers about their products. Apart from the influence on purchase intention, consumers equipped with higher levels of knowledge about a specific product are less likely to be apprehensive about using it. The informing process can be achieved using various media channels. Such a strategy may also help companies acquire an insight into how the consumer processes product information, which the authors believe could be particularly useful and informative.

Lin and Chen point out that the localized nature of their investigation means that any conclusions do not necessary apply nationally. Likewise, generalizations cannot be drawn about other service sectors since the study concentrated only on insurance and catering. In addition to expanding such issues, further research could also include other countries to further the knowledge about the effect of COO image.

*(A précis of the article "The influence of the country-of-origin image, product knowledge and product involvement on consumer purchase decisions: an empirical study of insurance and catering services in Taiwan". Supplied by Marketing Consultants for Emerald.)*

發表論文範本

# Tourism Review

# A study on the influence of purchase intentions on repurchase decisions: the moderating effects of reference groups and perceived risks

**Long-Yi Lin**
*Assistant Professor, Graduate School of Management Sciences, Aletheia University, Taipei, Taiwan*
**Yeun-Wen Chen**
*General Manager, Olé Travel Service Co. Ltd, Taipei, Taiwan*

**Recipient of Emerald Group Highly Commanded Award 2010 in UK**

Tourism Review, Vol. 64 No. 3, 2009,
© Emerald Group Publishing Limited, 1660-5373

論文寫作要領

# Tourism Review

**Tourism Review**
ISSN 1660-5373
© 2009 Emerald Group Publishing Limited

*Co-Editors*
**Prof Dr Christian Laesser**
University of St Gallen, Dufourstrasse 40a,
9000 St Gallen, Switzerland
E-mail: christian.laesser@unisg.ch

**Prof Dr Thomas Bieger**
University of St Gallen, Dufourstrasse 40a,
9000 St Gallen, Switzerland
E-mail: thomas.bieger@unisg.ch

*Publisher*
**Valerie Robillard**
E-mail: vrobillard@emeraldinsight.com

**Tourism Review is indexed and abstracted in:**
Associate Programs Source Plus
Cabell's Directory of Publishing Opportunities in Marketing
CIRET
Current Abstracts
Hospitality and Tourism Index
Vocational Studies Complete

This journal is also available online at:
**Journal information**
www.emeraldinsight.com/tr.htm
**Table of contents**
www.emeraldinsight.com/1660-5373.htm

**Online journal content available worldwide at**
**www.emeraldinsight.com**

**Emerald Group Publishing Limited**
Howard House, Wagon Lane,
Bingley BD16 1WA,
United Kingdom
Tel +44 (0) 1274 777700
E-mail emerald@emeraldinsight.com

INVESTOR IN PEOPLE

**Regional offices:**

**For Americas**
Emerald Group Publishing Inc., One Mifflin Place,
119 Mount Auburn Street, Suite 400, Harvard Square,
Cambridge, MA 02138, USA
Tel +1 617 576 5782
E-mail america@emeraldinsight.com

**For Asia Pacific**
Emerald, 7-2, 7th Floor, Menara KLH, Bandar Puchong Jaya,
47100 Puchong, Selangor, Malaysia
Tel +60 3 8076 6009; Fax +60 3 8076 6007
E-mail asia@emeraldinsight.com

**For Australia**
Emerald, PO Box 1441, Fitzroy North, VIC 3068, Australia
Tel/Fax +61 (0) 3 9486 2782; Mobile +61 (0) 4315 98476
E-mail australasia@emeraldinsight.com

**For China**
Emerald, 7th Xueyuan Road, Haidian District, Room 508,
Hongyu Building, 100083 Beijing, People's Republic of China
Tel +86 108-230-6438
E-mail china@emeraldinsight.com

**For India**
Emerald, 301, Vikas Surya Shopping Mall, Mangalam Place,
Sector -3, Rohini, New Delhi - 110085, India
Tel +91 112 794 8437/8
E-mail india@emeraldinsight.com

**For Japan**
Emerald, 92-5 Makigahara, Asahi-ku, Yokohama 241-0836,
Japan
Tel/Fax +81 45 367 2114
E-mail japan@emeraldinsight.com

**For African enquiries**
E-mail africa@emeraldinsight.com

**For European enquiries**
E-mail europe@emeraldinsight.com

**For Middle Eastern enquiries**
E-mail middleeast@emeraldinsight.com

**Customer helpdesk:**
Tel +44 (0) 1274 785278; Fax +44 (0) 1274 785201;
E-mail support@emeraldinsight.com
Web www.emeraldinsight.com/customercharter

**Orders, subscription and missing claims enquiries:**
E-mail subscriptions@emeraldinsight.com
Tel +44 (0) 1274 777700; Fax +44 (0) 1274 785201

Missing issue claims will be fulfilled if claimed within six months
of date of despatch. Maximum of one claim per issue.

Hard copy print backsets, back volumes and back issues of
volumes prior to the current and previous year can be ordered
from Periodical Service Company.
Tel +1 518 537 4700
E-mail psc@periodicals.com
For further information go to www.periodicals.com/emerald.html

**Reprints and permission service**
For reprint and permission options please see the abstract page
of the specific article in question on the Emerald web site
(www.emeraldinsight.com), and then click on the Reprints and
permissions link. Or contact:
Copyright Clearance Center- Rightslink
Tel +1 877/622-5543 (toll free) or 978/777-9929
E-mail customercare@copyright.com
Web www.copyright.com

**Emerald is a trading name of Emerald Group Publishing
Limited**

Printed by Apple Tree Print, Ashfield House, Ashfield Road,
Balby, Doncaster DN4 8QD

Awarded in recognition of
Emerald's production
department's adherence to
quality systems and
processes when preparing
scholarly journals for print

Emerald Group Publishing
Limited, Howard House,
Environmental Management
System has been certified by
ISOQAR to ISO14001:2004
standards

發表論文範本

# A study on the influence of purchase intentions on repurchase decisions: the moderating effects of reference groups and perceived risks

Long-Yi Lin and Yeun-Wen Chen

Long-Yi Lin is Assistant Professor, Graduate School of Management Sciences, Aletheia University, Taipei, Taiwan. Yeun-Wen Chen is General Manager, Olé Travel Service Co. Ltd, Taipei, Taiwan.

**Abstract**

**Purpose** – The purpose of this paper is to focus on the influence of purchase intentions on repurchase decisions, and also to examine the moderating effects of reference groups and perceived risks.

**Design/methodology/approach** – The travelers on Taiwan tourist trains were surveyed. Convenience sampling was used to collect primary data. A total of 1,200 questionnaires were distributed and 1,155 effective samples were collected. The effective return rate was 96 percent. Regression analysis was used to test hypotheses.

**Findings** – The paper finds that; purchase intentions will have a positive effect on repurchase decisions: the higher the informational reference group influence, the greater the positively moderating effect between purchase intentions and repurchase decisions; the higher the value-expressive reference group influence, the greater the positively moderating effect between purchase intentions and repurchase decisions; and the higher the psychological risk, the greater the negatively moderating effect between purchase intentions and repurchase decisions.

**Research limitations/implications** – Limitations of the study are: the research targets the travelers on tourist trains. Consequently, it is less efficient in external validity due to the limited scope; the conceptual limitation needs to be elaborated more; and, since the research adopts the cross-sectional research method without longitudinal section study it may be limited in the generalization. The moderating effects of reference groups and perceived risks have been examined on the inconsistency between purchase intentions and repurchase decisions in the study.

**Practical implications** – In tourism, reference group influence can provide the opportunity for individuals to communicate with group members in sharing the experiences of a destination and selection of a particular purchasing decision. The sole moderating effect of psychological risk has been verified among three dimensions. Therefore, the measurement and enhancement are critical for marketers to handle future business.

**Originality/value** – The extra value of the paper is to combine theory and practice together, and verify the moderating effects of reference groups and perceived risks between purchase intentions and repurchase decisions.

**Keywords** Consumer risk, Perception, Purchasing, Consumer behaviour, Taiwan

**Paper type** Research paper

## I. Introduction

Taiwan Railway Administration has managed the island's railroads exclusively for more than a century; however, the trains have primarily served as a means for traditional transportations instead of tourism. Until February 2001, Hualien Tourist Train launched a new journey directly from Taipei to Hualien on a daily basis, and a dining carriage was specially included with facilities to serve beverages, light refreshments and repasts during the trip.

Received: 4 March 2009
Accepted: 22 April 2009

DOI 10.1108/16605370910988818

Followed by Hot Spring Princess in August, it brought in new business-class cabin with oversized sightseeing windows, complete with 360-degree spacious and swivel seats for their Taipei to Jhihben route. Later, Kenting Star began to run the west trunk line from Taipei to Fangliao in October with an extra entertainment carriage featuring a mini karaoke bar. Within a year, three different categories of tourist trains were successfully created offering a variety of tour packages, by using integrated marketing to link up government, tourism industries as well as travel agencies.

Formosa Star – the deluxe presidential class cabin with six-star on-board service saw the introduction in October 2004 on a round-island four- and three-day jaunt. Color-painted and business-class carriages symbolize the Taiwan spirit and fervent atmosphere. Well-trained and experienced personnel were stationed in every carriage and professional tour guides were on-hand to provide comprehensive introduction at every scenic spot. Services on-board include baggage-handling, wide selection of delicious and sumptuous meals, selection of choice champagne, red wine, gourmet coffee and delectable local dessert specialties. Luxury hotel accommodation at every destination, the views of beautiful scenery spot and cultural relic leaves tourist's with unforgettable memories that rival Euro Star and Oriental Express.

Rail travel offers flexible numbers and options. It is a market ripe for development. Nevertheless, with a new shining star in the offering – Taiwan High Speed Rail –as a strong competitor run the west trunk line in 2007, a huge, but traditional, railroad company intended to develop and promote the higher-based products surely faces great challenge in seeking the right consumers. However, for seizing this brand-new and profitable market, the tourism industry is anxious to accomplish a blue ocean strategy through empirical research to discover the travelers' purchasing motivations, attitudes and behavioral intentions.

Understanding and knowing customers are never easy. The buyer's characteristics and decisions process lead to certain purchase decisions. A consumer's buying behavior is influenced by culture, social, personal, and psychological factors. Moutinho (1987) emphasized travel decisions are very much affected by forces outside the individual, including the influences of other people. The forces that other people exert are called social influences including:

- role and family influences;
- reference groups;
- social classes; and
- culture and subculture.

Reference groups may interact and overlap. They can be classified in terms of different criteria. Among several types of reference groups, there are three types of influences (informational, utilitarian, and value-expressive) have been identified (Park and Lessig, 1977). To take adequate actions in the field of tourism marketing, both seeking the opinion leaders and finding out which influence affects travel behavior are quite essential. This is the first motivation that initiates us to discuss this subject.

Schiffman and Kanuk (2004) indicated consumers must constantly make decisions regarding what products or services to buy and where to buy them. Meanwhile, due to the outcomes (or consequences) of such decisions are often uncertain, the consumers perceive some degree of risk in making a purchase decision. Roselius (1971) mentioned about how buyers often face the dilemma of wanting to purchase a product, and yet they hesitate to buy because it involves taking the risk of suffering some type of loss including time loss, hazard loss, ego loss and money loss.

Bloch et al. (1986) pointed out people usually get very involved with a purchase decision when they perceive significant financial risk, functional risk, or social risk. Pires et al. (2004) emphasize that differences in perceived risk were associated with whether the intended purchase was a good or service and whether it was a high or low-involvement product. Semeijn et al. (2004) concluded that by choosing among different brands, and depending on the degree of involvement with each product, consumers make trade-offs between the risks of losses they may incur when purchasing the product and the value they expect.

Since the concepts of perceived risk, brand and price need to receive further attention in hospitality research because of their significant impact on customers' decision-making processes (Kwun and Oh, 2004), in tourism, travelers' attitude toward tourist trains may be inversely related to the psychological risk associated with the complicated managing method by tour agencies, the financial risk associated with the higher price especially the penalty for the transaction being called off, and the functional risk associated with dissatisfied equipment and service on tourist trains, the empirical study may provide the ability to choose from a large number of risk reduction strategies in favor of travelers and marketers. This is the second motive that encourages us to explore this territory.

Purposes of this research include:

- study the effect of travelers' purchase intentions on repurchase decisions;

- research the moderating effect of different reference group between travelers' purchase intentions and repurchase decisions; and

- explore the effect of different perceived risks between travelers' purchase intentions and repurchase decisions.

## II. Literature review and hypotheses development

### 1. Purchase intentions and repurchase decisions

Dodds *et al.* (1991) proposed buyers' purchase intentions are their willingness to buy. The relationship between buyers' perceptions of value and their willingness to buy is positive. Blackwell *et al.* (2001) defined intentions are subjective judgments about how we will behave in the future. Purchase intentions represent what we think we will buy. In addition, purchase intent refers to a consumer's intention to purchase a product, or to patronize a service firm (Shao *et al.*, 2004). Past research has supported the link between service quality and purchase intent (Bitner, 1990; Boulding *et al.*, 1993). In addition, Kwun and Oh (2004) illustrated the importance of consumer value (e.g. brand, price and risk effects) as a powerful predictor of purchase intentions in both pre-and post-dining decision processes. Therefore, both higher service quality and higher consumer value will inadvertently lead to higher purchase intentions.

There are many types of consumer intentions. Besides purchase intentions, Blackwell *et al.* (2001) illustrated a special type of purchase intentions is repurchase intentions, which reflect whether we anticipate buying the same product or brand again. Shopping intentions indicate where we plan on making our product purchases. Spending intentions represent how much money we think we will spend. Search intentions indicate our intentions to engage in external search. Consumption intentions represent our intentions to engage in a particular activity. In more general terms, the strength of purchase intention as a surrogate measure of future behavior is a well-established phenomenon in the literature (Ajzen and Fishbein, 1980; Akhter and Durvasula, 1991; Akaah *et al.*, 1995). The extant literature on intentions has focused primarily on:

- determining which questions should be used to measure intentions; and

- assessing the strength of the intentions-behavior relationship (Armstrong *et al.*, 2000).

A decision is the selection of an option from two or more alternative choices. When a person has a choice between making a purchase and not making a purchase, a choice between brand X and brand Y, or a choice of spending time doing A or B, that person is in a position to make a decision. Consumers make three types of purchases: trial purchases, repeat purchases, and long-term commitment purchases. A repeat purchase usually signifies that the product meets with the consumer's approval and that he or she is willing to use it again and in larger quantities (Schiffman and Kanuk, 2004).

In executing a purchase intention, Kotler (2003) concluded the consumer might make up to five purchase sub-decisions: a brand decision, vendor decision, quantity decision, timing decision, and payment-method decision. Schiffman and Kanuk (2004) summarized various types of consumption and purchase-related decisions as:

- basic purchase or consumption decision;
- brand purchase or consumption decision;
- channel purchase decision; and
- payment purchase decision.

Repeat purchase behavior is closely related to the concept of brand loyalty.

Lim and Razzaque (1997) adopted repeat purchase rate to measure repeat purchase behavior. Repeat purchase rate is measured by the subject's indication of the likelihood, on a 11-point scale (from 0 to 10, with end labels "not at all likely" and "absolutely"), that he/she would purchase or act positively toward his/her most preferred brand under the stipulated situational circumstances.

In a repeat-purchase context, Chandon et al. (2004) proposed the product is more likely to be accessible in memory than it is for a first-time purchase. Nevertheless, measuring purchase intentions toward this product should further enhance its accessibility; thereby increasing the chances that consumer will make an additional purchase. Moreover, we expected that measuring purchase intentions would shorten the time until the first repeat purchase incidence because it makes intentions to repurchase more accessible in memory, relative to procrastination intentions.

LaBarbera and Mazursky (1983) found several longitudinal studies showed that consumers' prior repatronage intentions directly affect their subsequent repatronage intentions. Therefore, Bolton et al. (2000) concluded customers' repatronage intentions have a positive effect on their subsequent repatronage decisions. The following hypothesis is developed for this study.

> H1. Traveler's purchase intentions will have a positive effect on his/her repurchase decisions.

### 2. Reference groups

A reference group is broadly defined as an actual or imaginary institution individual or group conceived of having significant relevance upon an individual's evaluations, aspirations, or behavior (Lessig and Park, 1978). Moutinho (1987) pointed out any person or group – real or imaginary – that serve as a point of reference for an individual is said to stand as a reference group. It exerts a key influence on the individual's beliefs, attitudes and choices. Kotler (2003) indicated a person's reference groups consist of all the groups that have a direct (face-to-face) or indirect influence on the person's attitudes or behavior. Schiffman and Kanuk (2004) summarized a reference group is any person or group that serves as a point of comparison (or reference) for an individual in forming either general or specific values, attitudes, or a specific guide for behavior. From a marketing perspective, reference groups are groups that serve as frames of reference for individuals in their purchase or consumption decisions.

From the consumers' preference point of view, Cowan et al. (1997) recognized three reference groups – peer group, contrast group and inspirational group. Blackwell et al. (2001) concluded eight types of reference groups, including: primary, secondary, formal, informal, membership, inspirational, dissociative and virtual groups.

Concerning the types of reference group influences, Park and Lessig (1977) identified three important dimensions. Informational influence is based on the desire to make informed decisions. Utilitarian reference group influence is reflected in attempts to comply with the wishes of others to achieve rewards or avoid punishments. A third type of influence, value-expressive, is characterized by the need for psychological association with a person or group and is reflected in the acceptance of positions expressed by others. Blackwell *et al.* (2001) also proposed three primary types of influences that will affect individual's decisions, behaviors, purchases, and lifestyles. Besides informational influence and value-expressive influence, normative influence occurs when individuals alter their behaviors or beliefs to meet the expectations of a particular group.

Moutinho (1987) emphasized travel decisions are very much affected by forces outside the individual, including the influences of other people. In the consideration of major influences on individual travel behavior, the culture and reference group were first dealt with determinants of a broader nature. Furthermore, the positive influence of a reference group may take different forms, one of them is legitimizing decisions to use services and products that are adopted by the group. Darden *et al.* (1993) pointed out whether an employee identified with a full or part-time reference group could moderate a variety of job-connected relationships. It represents that reference groups have moderate effect on different jobs.

Since Bearden and Etzel (1982) investigated reference group influence on product and brand purchase decisions by examining the interrelationships among two forms of product use conspicuousness and three types of reference group influences (e.g. informational, utilitarian and value-expressive influence). Therefore, the social influences constructs we adopt the essences of both Park and Lessig (1977) and Bearden and Etzel (1982) to develop the hypotheses as follows:

*H2.* Different reference group influences will have a moderating effect between traveler's purchase intentions and repurchase decisions.

*H2-1.* The higher of informational reference group influence will have more positively moderating effect between traveler's purchase intentions and repurchase decisions.

*H2-2.* The higher of utilitarian reference group influence will have more positively moderating effect between traveler's purchase intentions and repurchase decisions.

*H2-3.* The higher of value-expressive reference group influence will have more positively moderating effect between traveler's purchase intentions and repurchase decisions.

### 3. Perceived risks

By Cox and Rich's (1964) description, risk is a function of the amount at stake and the subjective certainty of the outcomes. Cox (1967) mentioned the initial introduction from Bauer (1960) to the notion of risk as it is inconceivable that consumer can consider more than a few of the possible consequences of his actions, and it seldom is that he can even consider these few consequences with a high degree of certainty, meanwhile, the notion of perceived risk defined as consumer behavior involves risk in the sense that any action of a consumer will produce consequences which he cannot anticipate with anything approximating certainty, and some of which are likely to be unpleasant.

In extending perceived risk to different purchasing contexts, Dowling and Staelin (1994) proposed perceived risk is a situational and personal construct and risk is closely related to the level of uncertainty and likelihood of negative consequences of purchasing a good or service in terms of consumer's perception. In making a purchase decision, Schiffman and Kanuk (2004) indicated perceived risk is defined as the uncertainty that consumers face when they cannot foresee the consequences of their purchase decisions.

Oglethorpe and Monroe (1987) concluded consumer researchers define perceived risk in terms of uncertainty and consequences; perceived risk increases with higher levels of uncertainty and/or the chance of greater associated negative consequences. However, Mitchell (1999) pointed to the lack of a universally agreed definition providing researchers scope to use the definition appropriate to the research aims, however, suggested the weight of empirical research has favored a definition that has two components: the probability of a loss and the subjective feeling of unfavorable consequences (Cunningham, 1967).

Jacoby and Kaplan (1972) refined the initial specification of Bauer (1960) and suggested that perceived risk should be considered a multidimensional concept entailing multiple types of risks, including psychological, financial, performance, physical, and social risk. Mitchell (1992) classified six types of perceived risk for services as social, financial, physical, performance, time and psychological risk. By using a step-wise regression approach, Stone and Gronhaug (1993) testified six dimensions of risk (e.g. financial, performance, physical, psychological, social and time-related risks) will explain highly significant portion of overall risk and the result shows that 88.8 percent of the variance in overall risk is captured.

Schiffman and Kanuk (2004) concluded that the major types of risks that consumers perceive when making product decisions include:

1. *Functional risk*. This is the risk that the product will not perform as expected.

2. *Physical risk*. This is the risk to self and others that the product may pose.

3. *Financial risk*. This is the risk that the product will not be worth its cost.

4. *Social risk*. This is the risk that a poor product choice may result in social embarrassment.

5. *Psychological risk*. This is the risk that a poor product choice will bruise the consumer's ego.

6. *Time risk*. This is the risk that the time spent in product search may be wasted if the product does not perform as expected.

Measuring perceived risk can follow the methodology developed by Jacoby and Kaplan (1972) and refined and further tested by Peter and Tarpey (1975), the conceptualization is the probability of loss from the purchase of a brand and the subjective importance of that consequence. The operating definitions of six components and overall risk measures are described as:

1. *Financial risk*. The likelihood of suffering a financial loss due to hidden costs, maintenance costs or lack of warranty in case of faults.

2. *Performance risk*. The chances of the item failing to meet the performance requirements originally intended of the purchase.

3. *Physical risk*. The probability of the purchase resulting in physical harm or injury.

4. *Psychological risk*. The chances of the specific purchase being inconsistent with the personal or self-image of the consumer.

5. *Social risk*. The likelihood of the purchase resulting in others thinking of the consumer less favorably (external psychological risk).

6. *Convenience risk*. The probability of the purchase resulting in lost time in terms of delivery, fitting or customization, or in repair/down-time.

7. *Overall risk*. The likelihood that purchase of the item will result in general dissatisfaction of the consumer.

Perceived risk plays an important role in consumer decision-making (Stone and Gronhaug, 1993; Mitchell and Boustani, 1994; Erdem and Keane, 1996) and the higher the perceived risk, the more consumers must gamble in buying the product (Sweeney *et al.*, 1999). In consumer evaluations of store brands, Semeijn *et al.* (2004) leads to the conclusion that consumer attitude toward a store branded product are inversely related to the functional risk associated with the perceived difficulty for the retailer to produce that product, inversely related to the perceived psychological risk associated with the usage of the product, and inversely related to the perceived financial risk associated with quality variance in the product category.

Oglethorpe and Monroe (1987) indicated perceived risk increases with higher levels of uncertainty and/or the chance of greater associated negative consequences. Dowling and Staelin (1994) also related perceived risk closely to the level of uncertainty and likelihood of

發表論文範本

negative consequences of purchasing a good or service in terms of consumer's perception. Campbell and Goodstein (2001) proposed that perceived risk as an important situational factor that moderates the impact of congruity on evaluations.

Since psychological, financial and functional risks appear to discriminate effectively (Semeijn *et al.*, 2004), moreover, these risk constructs are further established through a focus and depth interview in advance from 30 tour agencies' representatives which are all members of Taiwan Railway Service Association and dominate main railroad business over the island. Therefore, the hypotheses are developed accordingly:

    *H3.*    Different traveler's perceived risks will have a moderating effect between his/her purchase intentions and repurchase decisions.

    *H3-1.*    The higher of traveler's psychological risk will have more positively moderating effect between his/her purchase intentions and repurchase decisions.

    *H3-2.*    The higher of traveler's financial risk will have more positively moderating effect between his/her purchase intentions and repurchase decisions.

    *H3-3.*    The higher of traveler's functional risk will have more positively moderating effect between his/her purchase intentions and repurchase decisions.

### 4. Influences between variables

*(1) The effect of purchase intentions on repurchase decisions.* A behavioral intention reflects a person's decision to perform the behavior (Fishbein and Ajzen, 1975). Many studies have found a positive correlation between purchase intentions and purchase behavior (Morwitz and Schmittlein, 1992). Therefore, purchase intentions are commonly used as a basis to forecast purchase behavior (Newberry *et al.*, 2003). Since several longitudinal studies show that consumers' prior repatronage intentions directly affect their subsequent repatronage intentions (LaBarbera and Mazursky, 1983), Accordingly, Bolton *et al.* (2000) found customers' repatronage intentions have a positive effect on their subsequent repatronage decisions.

Since the observed relationship between intentions and purchase is generally positive and significant (Gupta *et al.*, 2004), Chandon *et al.* (2004) expected that measuring purchase intentions not only increases the likelihood of the consumer's making a first time purchase from a category, but also increases the short-term likelihood that consumer will make a repeat purchase of a given product. In summary, the short-term effects of measuring purchase intentions increases the likelihood of repurchase incidences and accelerates repeat purchase incidence.

*(2) The moderating effect of reference groups between purchase intentions and repurchase decisions.* Blackwell *et al.* (2001) pointed out three types of influences (normative influence, expressive influence, and informational influence) affect individuals' decisions, behaviors, purchases, and lifestyles. Moutinho (1987) emphasized travel decisions are very much affected by forces outside the individual, including the influences of other people. The positive influence of a reference group may takes different forms, one of them is legitimizing decisions to use services and products that are adopted by the group.

Bearden and Etzel (1982) indicated a reference group concept has been used by advertisers in their effort to persuade consumers to purchase products and brands. The study investigated reference group influence on product and brand purchase decisions by using informational influence, utilitarian influence and value-expressive influence. The results supported hypothesized differences in reference group influence between publicly and privately consumed products and luxuries and necessities.

*(3) The moderating effect of perceived risks between purchase intentions and repurchase decisions.* Perceived risk theories have been applied in different consumer behavior contexts (Mitchell, 1999). Consumer purchase intentions can be examined as an outcome of the decision process (McGaughey and Mason, 1998), or by the relative value or risk presented by the purchase experience (Novak *et al.*, 2000). There are many possible

elements in a buying situation that may influence the perceptions of risk, the greater or more likely that the actual purchase experience differs from the purchase goals, the higher the perceived risk (Pires *et al.*, 2004).

Baron and Kenny (1986) distinguish between mediator variables that explain how or why certain effects occur and moderator variables which describe when such effects will occur. Campbell and Goodstein (2001) proposed that perceived risk as an important situational factor that moderates the impact of congruity on evaluations, when consumers perceive high risk associated with a purchase, the moderate incongruity effect is reversed such that the congruent is preferred to the moderately incongruent product. Being faced with a purchasing situation, Moutinho (1987) considered thata tourist has a certain degree of risk involved in the decision to be made, meantime, the degree of risk may vary with the costs involved in a decision and the degree of certainty that the decision will lead to satisfaction.

## III. Research methodology

### 1. Conceptual framework

Purchase intentions are often used to forecast sales of existing consumer durables and new consumer products. Buyer-intention surveys can also be useful in estimating demand for new products (Silk and Urban, 1978). Measuring purchase intentions for a product category can increase the likelihood of first-time purchasing (Fitzsimons and Morwitz, 1996). Marketers have generally accepted the reference group construct as important in at least some types of consumer decision making (Bearden and Etzel, 1982). Within the study of general framework, based on the research of Park and Lessig (1977), informational, utilitarian and value-expressive influences have been identified.

Mäser and Weimar (1998) characterized perceived risk as a function of uncertainty and found it to be a partial explanatory variable for the decision-making process of tourists. That is, the higher the perceived risk, the more information tourists search and the more rational their decision process. Jacoby and Kaplan (1972) suggested that perceived risk should be considered a multidimensional concept entailing multiple types of risks, including psychological, financial, performance, physical, and social risk. To understand how vacation tourists reduced risk, Moutinho (1987) proposed it is necessary to consider the major types of perceived risk as functional risk, physical, financial, social, and psychological risk. This study choose psychological, financial, and functional risks for finding how the traveler to be influenced in a purchase situation.

In tourism, repurchase decisions usually signify that the products meet with the tourists' approval and that they are willing to select and purchase them again from two or more choices. Kwun and Oh (2004) have reexamined the antecedents and consequences of the value-formation process by simultaneously considering pre- and post-purchase decisions in the restaurant management context. Peyrot and Van Doren (1994) pointed out the majority of consumer purchases are potential repeat purchases. Schiffman and Kanuk (2004) concluded repeat purchase behavior is closely related to the concept of brand loyalty, which most firms try to encourage because it contributes to greater stability in the marketplace. Hence, for gaining more long-term commitments from tourists, repurchase decisions are crucial to the tour business.

According to the research of motives and purposes described above, the conceptual framework of this study is presented in Figure 1.

### 2. Definitions and measurement of variables

*(1) Purchase intentions.* Dodds *et al.* (1991) proposed buyers' purchase intentions are their willingness to buy. Grewal *et al.* (1998) used a three-item scale (the probability of buying, the likelihood that I would purchase, the probability that I would consider buying) based on Dodds *et al.* (1991) to measure buyers' willingness to buy. The specific items were anchored at seven-point scales from "very low" to "very high".

This study defines purchase intentions as the likelihood that travelers will purchase tourist trains' products. The higher the score means the higher likelihood travelers will consider

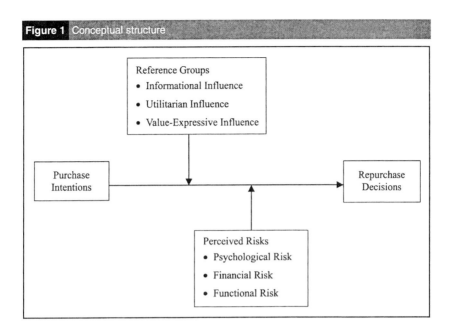

**Figure 1** Conceptual structure

buying tourist trains' products. Meantime, this research uses Likert seven-point scale to measure travelers' willingness to buy from "very low" to "very high". The scale is marked from one to seven points provided for each respondent to make selection. One point means highly disagree and seven points mean highly agree.

*(2) Reference groups.* Kotler (2003) indicated a person's reference groups consist of all the groups that have a direct (face-to-face) or indirect influence on the person's attitudes or behavior. Schiffman and Kanuk (2004) defined a reference group is any person or group that serve as a point of comparison (or reference) for an individual in forming either general or specific values, attitudes, or a specific guide for behavior. Base on the above research, this study defines reference group as any person or group that have a direct or indirect influence on traveler's attitudes or behavior.

Moreover, according to the fundamental research of Park and Lessig (1977), reference group influence was assessed and designed in three dimensions to reflect informational, utilitarian, and value-expressive influence. This paper defines informational influence occurs when a traveler actively seeks information from people viewed as knowledgeable or observes the behavior of acknowledged experts. Utilitarian reference group influence is reflected in compliance to group norms or standards to gain rewards or avoid punishments that may be forthcoming from the group. Value-expressive reference group influence is characterized by a traveler behaving in a manner that will improve his or her self-image or create the impression of attachment to the group.

Respondents were asked to answer five questions concerning their information influenced by certain reference group such as tour agencies, families, specialists, etc. Moreover, four-item preferences from families, social people, co-workers and others were designed to clarify the utilitarian influence. Similarly, four-item represents image, characteristic, respect and achievement from self as well as others were listed to measure the value-expressive influence. All individual items were operationalized as Likert seven-point bipolar highly agree (7)-highly disagree (1) statements. Scales were scored so that higher values represented greater influence of traveler's perception.

*(3) Perceived risks.* Bauer (1960) originally defined perceived risk as consumer behavior involves risk in the sense that any action of a consumer will produce consequences that he/she cannot anticipate with anything approximating certainty, and some of which are likely

to be unpleasant. In making a purchase decision, this study refers to the definition made by Schiffman and Kanuk (2004) to take perceived risk as the uncertainty that travelers face when they cannot foresee the consequences of their purchase decisions.

Peter and Tarpey (1975) made the operating definitions of psychological risk as the chances of the specific purchase being inconsistent with the personal or self-image of the consumer and financial risk as the likelihood of suffering a financial loss due to hidden costs, maintenance costs or lack of warranty in case of faults. Moreover, and Mitchell (1992) described financial risk as the risk that the service purchased will not attain the best possible monetary gain for the consumer; Schiffman and Kanuk (2004) also defined functional risk as the risk that the product will not perform as expected.

This paper aimed at the uncertainty and consequences that travelers should face when they were making their purchase decisions and defined three dimensions as:

1. *Psychological risk*. The chances of the specific purchase being inconsistent with the personal or self-image of the traveler.

2. *Financial risk*. The likelihood of financial loss that the specific purchase will not attain the best possible monetary gain for the traveler.

3. *Functional risk*. The probability that the specific purchase will not perform as expected.

Again, all individual items were operationalized as Likert seven-point bipolar highly agree (7)-highly disagree (1) statements. Scales were scored so that higher values represented greater influence of traveler's purchase intentions and repurchase decisions.

*(4) Repurchase decisions*. In the most general terms, Schiffman and Kanuk (2004) defined a decision is the selection of an option from two or more alternative choices. A repeat purchase usually signifies that the product meets with the consumer's approval and that he or she is willing to use it again and in larger quantities. Bolton *et al*. (2000) estimated models for two aspects of the repatronage decision:

1. the decision of whether or not to repurchase by measuring repatronage intentions; and

2. the decision of how much to use the service subsequent year by operationalizing repatronage usage intentions.

This study defines repurchase decisions as the selection that travelers are willing to purchase tourist trains' products again. The higher the score means the stronger decision travelers will repurchase tourist trains' products. Finally, this research also use a Likert seven-point scale to measure travelers' repurchase decision from "very low" to "very high". One point means highly disagree and seven points mean highly agree.

### 3. Design of sampling

The population of this study is on-board travelers who have bought one of tourist train's products. Questionnaires were distributed according to the ratio of seats available per week of four tourist trains as follows:

1. *Hualien Tourist Train*: daily, from Taipei to Hualien, round trip, 4,368 seats per week.

2. *Hot Spring Princess*: daily, from Taipei to Jhihben, round trip, 1,848 seats per week.

3. *Kenting Star*: daily, from Taipei to Fangliao, round trip, 1,498 seats per week.

4. *Formosa Star*: twice a week, from Taipei to Taipei, around the island, 240 seats per week.

Because of tourist trains' products being public ones available for travelers everywhere, this research adopts large sampling survey in an attempt to contain the populations all over the island.

This research targets at four tourist trains, calculates the number of sampling according to ratios of seats available per week offered by Taiwan Railway Administration. Convenience sampling method was used to collect primary data by interviewing respondents who took any of four tourist trains. Data collection was conducted by personal interview with travelers on the trains. A total of 1,200 questionnaires were distributed; with 660 (55 percent) on Hualien Tourist Train, 276 (23 percent) on Hot Spring Princess, 228 (19 percent) on Kenting Star, and 36 (3 percent) on Fomosa Star.

### 4. Questionnaire design and pre-test

The questionnaire used in this research was designed with reference to the dimensional questions proposed by Dodds *et al.* (1991), Grewal *et al.* (1998), Shao *et al.*(2004), Lessig and Park (1978), Bearden and Etzel (1982), Lim and Razzaque (1997), Koo (2003), Parasuraman *et al.*(1991), and Bolton *et al.*(2000). Questions have been modified to meet the current status of travelers on tourist trains. The questionnaire was divided into two sections. The first section consists of general questions regarding travelers' purchase behavior on tourist trains and the second part contains background information of the respondents.

After the questionnaire was completed, a pre-test was conducted on Hualien Tourist Train and Hot Spring Princess through convenient sampling. Since the seats of two trains took up 78 percent of the total 1,200 questionnaires distributed, it was considered representative. Distribution according to the ratio of two trains' seats, a total of 120 questionnaires were sent out, with 84 on Hualien Tourist Train, and 36 on Hot Spring Princess for verification of the reliability of the questionnaire.

Result of the pre-test yielded a purchase intentions variable Cronbach's $\alpha = 0.7869$; reference groups variable Cronbach's $\alpha = 0.8608$; perceived risks variable Cronbach's $\alpha = 0.9180$; and repurchase decisions variable Cronbach's $\alpha = 0.8637$. The total Cronbach's $\alpha = 0.9162$ indicated a high level of consistency in this research.

### 5. Data collection and analysis methods

This research was conducted through personal interviews with convenient sampling method. Questionnaires were distributed on four types of tourist trains with two of each train and totally eight assistants. Each interviewer has been trained in advance to be familiar with the purpose of this research, interview skills, actual rehearsal, and problems solving to ensure the accuracy of the results. While distributing the questionnaires, well-trained interviewers gave two ball pens, as a present, to each respondent to fill out readily for ensuring that the questionnaires could be completely answered and the ratio of effective samples could be increased. Furthermore, the whole survey was accomplished within three weeks specifically including working on weekdays, weekend and holiday to enhance the representation of all samples.

This research adopts SPSS10.0 software programs as tools for data analysis. The statistical methods were used as follows:

- *Descriptive statistical analysis*. This is distribution and percentage analysis for background information.

- *Reliability analysis*. This refers to credibility or consistence, meaning the accuracy or precision of a measurement tool.

- *Validity analysis*. This tests on the content validity and construct validity of this research.

- *Correlation analysis*, This uses Pearson coefficient analysis to verify the correlations of each dimension and analyze the relationships between dimensions.

- *Regression diagnostics*. This includes three basic assumptions of Normality test, Levene test and Independency test.

- *Regression analysis*. This is to verify *H1*, and *H2* and *H3* with multiple regression analysis.

## IV. Empirical analysis

### 1. Sample description

A total of 1,200 questionnaires were distributed for this research. After deducting 45 ineffective questionnaires, 1,155 effective samples were collected; resulting in a high response-rate of about 96 percent. The statistical results show a higher number of 666 (57.66 percent) are female as compared to 489 (42.34 percent) male travelers. This phenomenon may disclose some psychological needs for vacation of different genders. Females generally act as opinion leaders more actively with higher participation. The travelers' age has a broader range between 20 and 49 (81.56 percent) within 35.41 percent between 30 and 39. Education is mainly college/university (59.91 percent), whereas high school also shares 21.99 percent. The annual mean income spreads mostly on US$10,600 (40.1 percent) and US$17,650 (27.97 percent). It represents that travelers may own a higher disposable income but not necessarily related to the educational level. Occupations are widely ranged from commerce (47.27 percent), manufacturer (18.87 percent) to housewives and students (13.42 percent) etc. In marriage status, those who are married (62.16 percent) take up a higher percentage than those who are not married (37.84 percent).

### 2. Analysis of reliability and validity

The criterion of reliability is measured by Cronbach's $\alpha$ coefficient, when $\alpha = 0.70$ represents with high reliability of the questionnaire scale and $\alpha = 0.60$ means the reliability is acceptable (Cuieford, 1965). The overall internal consistent coefficients of the questionnaire are purchase intentions, Cronbach's $\alpha = 0.7869$; reference groups Cronbach's $\alpha = 0.9125$ (in which informational influence Cronbach's $\alpha = 0.7969$; utilitarian influence Cronbach's $\alpha = 0.8394$; value-expressive influence Cronbach's $\alpha = 0.8902$); perceived risks Cronbach's $\alpha = 0.8976$ (in which psychological risk Cronbach's $\alpha = 0.8540$; financial risk Cronbach's $\alpha = 0.8630$, functional risk Cronbach's $\alpha = 0.9437$); repurchase decisions Cronbach's $\alpha = 0.8755$. The values indicate that the overall consistency of the questionnaire used is at a high level.

Through literature review, questionnaire used in this research was designed with reference to the dimensional questions proposed by the scholars of the special field. Hence, the items of questionnaire are in accordance with content validity (Cooper and Emory, 1998). In the same time, principal component analysis was adopted to proceed with construct validity. According to the suggestion of Hair *et al.* (1998), the eigenvalue had to be higher than 1. Moreover, each item's absolute value of factor loading had better be higher than 0.6 after orthogonal by using varimax method. In this research, the factor lording of each item is higher than 0.6 within 0.632 to 0.929 and the eigenvalues are all higher than 2. Although the explanatory variance of informational influence and psychological risk are 55 percent and 56 percent respectively, the explanatory power is somewhat lower than 60 percent. Overall, the questionnaire used in this research has reached relatively good construct validity.

### 3. Correlations analysis

This research uses Pearson correlation coefficient to verify the relations between each variable/dimension. The correlation coefficient is shown as Table I. The informational influence and utilitarian influence are two dimensions with the highest correlation (correlation coefficient = 0.670) under 1 percent significant level; and the lowest ones are purchase intentions and functional risk (correlation coefficient = 0.049) under 10 percent significant level. From the matrix, we can realize that all significant correlation coefficients are positive. Since correlation between functional risk and repurchase decisions (correlation coefficient = 0.046, $p = 0.117 > 0.10$) can not reach the significance under 10 percent level, the explanation of these two variables should be careful. Normally we expect the correlation coefficients within independent variables are not high enough to present negative influences such as collinear phenomena. Because of the correlation coefficient of significance in each matrix reaches only from low to medium level, meanwhile, correlation between functional risk and value-expressive influence (correlation coefficient = 0.039, $p = 0.187 > 0.10$) is not significant, there should be no negative influence accordingly.

### 4. Testing hypotheses

*(1) The effect of purchase intentions on repurchase decisions.* First, we carried out regression analysis of the effect of purchase intentions on repurchase decisions. Data are summarized in Table II. In order to verify whether the residual errors are independent from

發表論文範本

**Table I** Pearson correlation analysis

| Dimensions | 1 | 2 | 3 | Variables 4 | 5 | 6 | 7 | 8 |
|---|---|---|---|---|---|---|---|---|
| 1. Purchase intentions | 1 | | | | | | | |
| 2. Informational influence | 0.437*** (0.000) | 1 | | | | | | |
| 3. Utilitarian influence | 0.253*** (0.000) | 0.670*** (0.000) | 1 | | | | | |
| 4. Value-expressive influence | 0.320*** (0.000) | 0.473*** (0.000) | 0.622*** (0.000) | 1 | | | | |
| 5. Psychological risk | 0.216*** (0.000) | 0.273*** (0.000) | 0.325*** (0.000) | 0.440*** (0.000) | 1 | | | |
| 6. Financial risk | 0.097*** (0.001) | 0.130*** (0.000) | 0.118*** (0.000) | 0.149*** (0.000) | 0.495*** (0.000) | 1 | | |
| 7. Functional risk | 0.049* (0.095) | 0.069** (0.019) | 0.053* (0.071) | 0.039 (0.187) | 0.255*** (0.000) | 0.610*** (0.000) | 1 | |
| 8. Repurchase decisions | 0.567*** (0.000) | 0.400*** (0.000) | 0.286*** (0.000) | 0.378*** (0.000) | 0.361*** (0.000) | 0.131*** (0.000) | 0.046 (0.117) | 1 |

Notes: $*p < 0.10$; $**p < 0.05$; $***p < 0.01$

**Table II** Regression analyses of three models

| Independent variable | Model 1 $\beta_i$ | t-value | Model 2 $\beta_i$ | t-value | VIF | Model 3 $\beta_i$ | t value | VIF |
|---|---|---|---|---|---|---|---|---|
| Intercept | 1.890 | 14.128* | 2.297 | 16.615* | – | 2.117 | 16.273* | – |
| Purchase intentions | 0.567 ($\beta_1$) | 23.399* | 0.314 | 8.124* | 2.710 | 0.424 ($\beta_5$) | 12.471* | 4.203 |
| Purchase intentions × informational influence | – | – | 0.186 ($\beta_2$) | 3.645* | 4.716 | – | – | – |
| Purchase intentions × utilitarian influence | – | – | − 0.030 ($\beta_3$) | − 0.630 | 4.025 | – | – | – |
| Purchase intentions × value-expressive influence | – | – | 0.201 ($\beta_4$) | 5.220* | 2.700 | – | – | – |
| Purchase intentions × psychological risk | – | – | – | – | – | 0.339 ($\beta_6$) | 9.835* | 2.205 |
| Purchase intentions × financial risk | – | – | – | – | – | − 0.006 ($\beta_7$) | − 1.515 | 3.540 |
| Purchase intentions × functional risk | – | – | – | – | – | − 0.036 ($\beta_8$) | − 0.922 | 2.840 |
| $R^2$ | 0.322 | | 0.368 | | | 0.380 | | |
| Adj-$R^2$ | 0.321 | | 0.366 | | | 0.378 | | |
| D-W | 1.675 | | 1.682 | | | 1.658 | | |
| F value | 547.535* | | 167.312* | | | 176.162* | | |
| Sample size $n$ | 1,155 | | 1,155 | | | 1,155 | | |

Note: *: $p < 0.01$

one another, the Durbin-Watson Statistic (D-W) was tested. In general, when the D-W is between 1.5 and 2.5; it means no auto-correlation existed between the residual errors (Wu and Lin, 2002). In this research the D-W = 1.675 shows that the figure is in conformity with the expectation of this item.

Purchase intentions can explain the 32.1 percent variable volume of repurchase decisions ($\bar{R}^2 = 0.321$, $R^2 = 0.322$, $F = 547.535$, $p = 0.000 < 0.01$) under 1 percent level and the model is interpretive. To test purchase intentions has influence on repurchase decisions, the results $\beta_0 = 0.567$, $t = 23.399$, $p = 0.000 < 0.01$ present statistically significant under

1 percent level and the positive direction of influence with the weight of 0.567. That is the traveler's purchase intentions have a positive effect on his/her repurchase decisions. Therefore, *H1* is strongly supported.

*(2) The moderating effect of reference groups between purchase intentions and repurchase decisions.* Second, we proceeded with multiple regression analysis. Data is summarized as shown in Table II. The model can explain the 36.6 percent variable volume of repurchase decisions ($\bar{R}^2 = 0.366$, $R^2 = 0.368$, $F = 167.312$, $p = 0.000 < 0.01$) under 1 percent level. The D-W = 1.682 is between 1.5 and 2.5 as stated before. In addition to D-W, Variance Inflation Factor Statistic (VIF) was used to test the collinear combination between independent variables, if VIF > 10, it exists collinear phenomenon probably (Chen, 2000). In this study all VIF values are minor than 10 that mean no collinear combination.

When purchase intentions served as a independent variable, $\beta_1 = 0.314$, $t = 8.124$, $p = 0.000 < 0.01$ show that purchase intentions has significant effect on repurchase decisions under 1 percent level and the direction of main effect is positive with the weight of 0.314. Followed by the analyses of three moderator variables, $\beta_2 = 0.186$, $t = 3.645$, $p = 0.000 < 0.01$ represent the interaction of purchase intentions and informational influence has significant effect on repurchase decisions under 1 percent level and the direction of interaction is positive with the weight of 0.186. Whereas, $\beta_3 = -0.030$, $t = -0.630$, $p = 0.529 > 0.10$ show insignificant statistically that indicates the interaction of purchase intentions and utilitarian influence has no association with repurchase decisions; that is, *p*-value exceeds 10 percent means the hypothesis is not supported. The third interaction of purchase intentions and value-expressive influence ($\beta_4 = 0.201$, $t = 5.220$, $p = 0.000 < 0.01$) also has significant effect on repurchase decisions under 1 percent level. Similarly, $\beta_4 = 0.201$ means the direction of interaction is positive with the weight of 0.201.

Overall, the result shows that the informational and value-expressive reference group influences will have more positively moderating effect between traveler's purchase intentions and repurchase decisions. Therefore, *H2-1* and *H2-3* are strongly supported. However, *H2-2* is not supported. Eventually, *H2* is partially supported.

*(3) The moderating effect of perceived risks between purchase intentions and repurchase decisions.* Third, the moderating effect of perceived risks between purchase intentions and repurchase decisions is tested by multiple regression analysis. From Table II, the model can explain the 37.8 percent variable volume of repurchase decisions ($\bar{R}^2 = 0.378$, $R^2 = 0.380$, $F = 176.162$, $p = 0.000 < 0.01$) under 1 percent level. The D-W = 1.658 is also between 1.5 and 2.5. All VIF values are minor than 10; therefore, there is no collinear phenomenon.

The main effect of purchase intentions ($\beta5 = 0.424$, $t = 12.471$, $p = 0.000 > 0.01$) has positively significant effect on repurchase decisions under 1 percent level with the weight of 0.424. Meantime, the interaction of purchase intentions and psychological risk ($\beta_6 = 0.339$, $t = 9.835$, $p = 0.000 > 0.01$) also has significant effect on repurchase decisions under 1 percent level and the direction of the interaction is positive with the weight of 0.339. However, Both the interaction of purchase intentions and financial risk ($\beta_7 = -0.066$, $t = -1.515$, $p = 0.130 > 0.10$) and the interaction of purchase intentions and functional risk ($\beta_8 = -0.036$, $t = -0.922$, $p = 0.357 > 0.10$) become insignificant statistically on repurchase decisions. Apparently, the last two moderator variables have no interaction effects on repurchase decisions at $p > 0.10$.

Therefore, the result shows the higher of psychological risk will have positively moderating effect between traveler's purchase intentions and repurchase decisions. Accordingly, *H3-1* is strongly supported, but *H3-2* and *H3-3* are not supported. Therefore, *H3* is partially supported.

### 5. Discussion

Some further discussions were made for discovering the essence of this research. First, regarding the explanatory power of two moderator variables, perceived risks ($\bar{R}^2 = 0.378$) is almost as interpretive as reference groups ($\bar{R}^2 = 0.366$). This means that two variables have the same good of fitness. None the less, as long as $\bar{R}^2 > 0.18$ in cross-section survey, the goodness of fit is qualified (Chow, 2002). Second, concerning the beta coefficients of three significant variables from model (2), the interaction of purchase intentions and informational influence ($\beta_2 = 0.186$), the interaction of purchase intentions and value-expressive influence ($\beta_4 = 0.201$) are not higher enough than purchase intentions ($\beta_1 = 0.314$). The same phenomenon appears in model (3), beta coefficient of purchase intentions and psychological risk ($\beta_6 = 0.339$) is lower than purchase intentions ($\beta_5 = 0.424$). It may represent that purchase intentions is the main factor to affect traveler's repurchase decisions while the interactions with some other variables also have moderating effects but not stronger than the direct effect itself.

Third, the interaction of purchase intentions and utilitarian influence cannot get up to the degree of conspicuousness ($p = 0.529 > 0.10$) under 10 percent level. One of the possible reasons may be due to the statements of the questionnaire are not understandable for respondents and another one may be the difficulty to discriminate between utilitarian influence and value-expressive influence. Meanwhile, the interaction of purchase intentions and financial risk ($p = 0.130 > 0.10$) and the interaction of purchase intentions and functional risk ($p = 0.357 > 0.10$) are also not significant under 10 percent level. The results have revealed some facts that traveler's consideration of financial loss such as the higher price and functional problem such as on-board facility and service are not as crucial as his/her psychological uncomfortableness such as never purchasing such product before.

Finally, due to samples have already bought one product and on the way to destination, therefore, For measuring the construct of their purchase intentions, a statement with definition of various categories of tourist trains' products such as ticket and hotel packages, Hualien two-day tour, Kenting three-day pass, . . . etc. was added in formal questionnaire to render a greater scenario for the answered items. Actually, each traveler only joined one itinerary, while lots of products were new. Therefore, no special logical problems were found in measuring the purchase intentions. Eventually, this article may have verified the gravity of moderating variables in a wider range of decision-making process from purchase intentions to the context of post-purchase behavior that overturns the majority of prior research.

## V. Conclusions and managerial implications

### 1. Conclusions

We established three models based on three purposes of our research and executing the pre-test of 120 questionnaires by regression analysis proved a high level of reliability and good construct validity. Moreover, we also tried to testify all the multiple relationships by using structural equation modeling, however, the results were difficult or even ambiguous to distinguish or identify those direct and indirect relationships. This provides a robust methodology for us to resolve all research issues by regression analysis.

Through the empirical analysis, this research derived the following conclusions:

- Traveler's purchase intentions have positive effect on their repurchase decisions: the strength of purchase intention is a surrogate to measure of future buying behavior. When a traveler knows clearly about what he or she thinks he will or she will buy, he or she will have much ability to coagulate his or her intention and hence has higher repurchase decision.

- Different reference group influence has positively moderating effect between traveler's purchase intentions and repurchase decisions: the finer explanation of reference group can be achieved through the analysis of different type of influence. If the scale of influence reaches the positive level, it means there is an acceleration effect to enhance purchase intentions and repurchase decisions. In this research, informational and value-expressive influences are significant.

- Different perceived risks have positively moderating effect between traveler's purchase intentions and repurchase decisions: The result shows the interaction of purchase intentions and psychological risk has positively moderating effect between purchase intentions and repurchase decisions.

*2. Managerial implications*

*(1) Implications for academics.* First, the moderating effects of reference groups and perceived risks has been examined on the inconsistency between purchase intentions and repurchase decisions in this study. It is no doubt to increase the different explanatory power by adding them to a conventional behavior-intention model originally developed by Fishbein and Ajzen (1975).

Second, in social influence constructs, the moderator variable-utilitarian influence is insignificant may represent that some consumers may be more sensitive to one or more of the other constructs. For example, they may be less concerned about the influences adopted in the model and willing to trade off another type of ones (e.g. normative or other influence). Hence, their purchase process may change and need for segmentation research to identify the different solutions.

Third, it is noticeable that perceived risk was the most important antecedent of perceived and compared values in both pre-and post purchase decisions. Furthermore, perceived risk appeared to be an important antecedent of customer values and behavioral intentions (Kwun and Oh, 2004). Many studies supported that psychological risk played an important role among other risks. For example, Murray and Schlacter (1990) found that consumers perceive service decisions to be riskier than product decisions, particularly in terms of social risk, physical risk and psychological risk. Stone and Gronhaug (1993) made further considerations of perceived risks for the marketing discipline and found that financial and psychological risk are the predominant risk dimensions, in the same time, psychological risk plays an important mediating function for other types of risk. In this study, there has been proved that psychological risk is a significant moderating variable to affect the traveler's intention to repurchase. Therefore, psychological risk is not only a critical component of perceived risks for service industry, but also served as a main, mediating or moderating variable.

Finally, since Chandon *et al.* (2004) proposed the product is more likely to be accessible in memory than it is for a first-time purchase and Bolton *et al.* (2000) concluded customers' repatronage intentions have a positive effect on their subsequent repatronage decisions, they encourage this study to explore a longer process of decision-making by using a greater scenario. A total amount of 1,200 questionnaires were used with an effort to reflect the actual decision processes of tourists. Certainly, we hope that they will prove more representative. In addition, this study attempts to grasp the repurchase behavior from the very beginning of purchase intentions to the final action of repurchase decisions challenges the traditional research. We sampled real world tourists who have just made, or in the process of making a purchase decision. The sampling method had the same spirit as empirical research from Sweeney *et al.* (1999) – "The role of perceived risk in the quality-value relationship: a study in a retail environment". Surely, we also hope that the result will prove more sensitive. Because buying a tour product always has to make a decision beforehand without foreseeing any consequences, knowing who are the opinion leaders as well as the risk reduction strategies are never easy, but relatively essential. Meantime, after all, only the repurchase behavior is what everybody expects and cares about. We hope the conceptual framework in this study can be applied to any service experience for future research in a broader way of thinking.

*(2) Implications for practitioners.* Three reference group influences were identified in the first phase of the study. From marketing and consumer behavior perspectives, these influences of reference groups may manifest in various types of tangible products and intangible services purchases by individuals. In tourism, these forms of influences can provide the opportunity for individuals to communicate with group members in sharing the experiences of a destination and selection of a particular purchasing decision. Three perceived risks were identified in the second phase of the study. Since the sole moderating effect of purchase intentions and psychological risk has been verified among three dimensions, therefore, the measurement and enhancement are critical for marketers to handle future business. For example, any chance of the specific purchase being inconsistent with the

發表論文範本

personal or self-image of the traveler such as the discomfort of first purchase, the worry from which tour agency to buy and the nervousness of unable to get the product during holiday or peak season should be highly taken care of. Nevertheless, more valuable discovery from the figures of three models may imply that the main purchase intentions are much more important than those interactions with other variables comparatively. It reacts the strength of purchase intentions remains its major position to measure the traveler's future behavior. Hence, purchase intentions should not be ignored in the tourism context because it is predictable.

### 3. Limitations and suggestions

*(1) Limitations.* Although the results of this study suggest important implications for reference groups in social influences of consumer behavior and on–the-spot unanticipated situations previously unexamined in this manner (tourist trains), there are limitations to address:

■ This research targets on the travelers of tourist trains, consequently, it is less efficient in external validity due to the limited scope. Hence, this research may be not suitable for the application to other industries.

■ More of conceptual limitation needs to be elaborated. As Bearden and Etzel (1982) indicated, the fact that three types of reference group influences were measured does not imply that all three should be present or absent in an individual case. In fact it would seem reasonable to find one type of influence operating and the others absent in a particular situation. Thus, it is reasonable to consider the hypotheses from the point of view of the presence or absence of any type of reference group influence. From that perspective, if this study considers the utilitarian influence may play a large role than either informational or value-expressive influence, the result will be strongly supported.

■ Finally, this research adopts the cross-sectional research method without longitudinal section study may be limited on its generalization. Therefore, data gained are only sufficient to understand the status of the research variables in a certain period of time.

*(2) Suggestions. These are as follows:.*

■ *Suggestions to managers.* There are many types of reference groups as well as their influences. However, consumers will differ in the degree to which they are influenced by referents while making product and brand purchase decisions. Apparently, which influence on the individual is most effective suggests a closer scrutiny among so many reference groups. Facing various risks, since consumers may have many goal-derived rationales for picking particular products that differ in their degree of risk, complexity, and other factors, therefore, a broader range of consumer needs, time pressures, other anticipated and unanticipated situational factors should be tested by marketing managers. For example, in everyday life it is common sense that people are more sensitive to financial aspects of risks, however, this research points out that only psychological risk is significant and must not be neglected. Moreover, because several risk-reduction strategies can be used by tourists such as expecting less from the product or service, regularly purchasing the same product, acquiring tourist information, purchasing the most expensive product, relying on government or consumer travel report and relying on tourist guarantees (Moutinho, 1987), hence, tourism industries should pay more attention to building risk-relief strategies through either of endorsement, brand loyalty, major brand image, private testing, store image, free sample, money-back guarantee, government testing, word of mouth, and so on.

■ *Suggestions for future studies.* In the research of the reference group construct, Childer and Rao (1992) pointed out that on the basis of a recent attempt at scale validation by Bearden *et al.* (1989), it appears that consumer perceptions of utilitarian and value-expressive influence are not easily distinguished empirically; these two components appear to represent the notion of normative influence and perhaps be combined. The contribution of this article to the literature is to re-testify the viewpoint in service industry through a larger sampling survey. For this reason, further research may use normative influence to replace utilitarian and value-expressive influences comparatively. In addition, risk was operationalized in this study primarily on three types of risk (e.g. psychological, financial and functional), Other types of risk (e.g. social, time and performance) may warrant future research to explore new risks affect the processing and evaluation between purchase intentions and repurchase decisions. We suggest that social risk would moderate congruity effects in the same way. Because psychological risk is the only one significant dimension among three risks, whereas, social risk is always regarded as an external psychological risk that may find out the likelihood of the purchase resulting in others thinking of the traveler less favorably. Furthermore, due to the less frequencies of special tourist trains (almost one day for one schedule only), time risk is another suggestion to be clarified whether the traveler will waste time, lose convenience or waste effort in purchasing a product redone. As Bearden and Etzel (1982) suggested earlier, situational variations and their impact on the complexity of studying reference group influences on purchase decisions also needed to address. Since perceived risks are very important situational variables, future effort may consider the extended behavioral intention model provided by Fishbein and Ajzen (1975) for examining various types of interactions between purchase intentions and purchase behavior (e.g. different reference group influences versus different perceived risks).

## References

Ajzen, I. and Fishbein, M. (1980), *Understanding Attitudes and Predicting Social Behavior*, Prentice-Hall, Englewood Cliffs, NJ.

Akaah, I., Korgaonkar, P. and Lund, D. (1995), ''Direct marketing attitudes'', *Journal of Business Research*, Vol. 34 No. 3, pp. 211-19.

Akhter, S. and Durvasula, S. (1991), ''Customers' attitudes toward direct marketing and purchase intention'', *Journal of Direct Marketing*, Vol. 5 No. 3, pp. 48-56.

Armstrong, J.S., Morwitz, V.G. and Kumar, V. (2000), ''Sales forecasts for existing consumer products and services: do purchase intentions contribute to accuracy?'', *International Journal of Forecasting*, Vol. 16 No. 3, pp. 383-97.

Baron, R.M. and Kenny, D.A. (1986), ''The moderator-mediator variable distinction in social psychological research: conceptual, strategic and statistical considerations'', *Journal of Personality and Social Psychology*, Vol. 51 No. 6, pp. 1173-82.

Bauer, R.A. (1960), ''Consumer behavior as risk taking'', in Hancock, R.S. (Ed.), *Dynamic Marketing for a Changing World*, American Marketing Association, Chicago, IL, pp. 389-98.

Bearden, W.O. and Etzel, M.J. (1982), ''Reference group influence on product and brand purchase decisions'', *Journal of Consumer Research*, Vol. 9 No. 2, September, pp. 183-94.

Bearden, W.O., Netemeyer, R.G. and Teel, J.E. (1989), ''Measurement of consumer susceptibility to interpersonal influence'', *Journal of Consumer Research*, Vol. 15, March, pp. 473-81.

Bitner, M.J. (1990), ''Evaluating service encounters: the effects of physical surrounding on employee responses'', *Journal of Marketing*, Vol. 54No. 2, pp. 69-82.

Blackwell, R.D., Miniard, P.W. and Engel, J.F. (2001), *Consumer Behavior*, 9th ed., Mike Roche, Grove City, OH.

Bloch, P.H., Sherrell, D.L. and Ridgeway, N.M. (1986), ''Consumer search: an extended framework'', *Journal of Consumer Research*, Vol. 13 No. 1, pp. 119-26.

Bolton, R.N., Kannan, P.K. and Bramlett, M.D. (2000), ''Implications of loyalty program membership and service experiences for customer retention and value'', *Journal of Academy of Marketing Science*, Vol. 28 No. 1, pp. 95-108.

Boulding, W., Kalra, W.A. and Zeithaml, V.A. (1993), ''A dynamic process model of service quality: from expectation to behavioral intentions'', *Journal of Marketing Research*, Vol. 30, February, pp. 7-27.

Campbell, M.C. and Goodstein, R.C. (2001), "The moderating effect of perceived risk on consumers' evaluation of product incongruity: preference for the norm", *Journal of Consumer Research*, Vol. 28 No. 3, December, pp. 439-49.

Chandon, P., Morwitz, V.G. and Reinartz, W.J. (2004), "The short- and long-term effects of measuring intent to repurchase", *Journal of Consumer Research*, Vol. 31 No. 3, December, pp. 566-72.

Chen, S.U. (2000), *Regression Analysis*, 3rd ed., Hua Tai Publishing Co., Taipei.

Childer, T.L. and Rao, A.R. (1992), "The influence of familial and peer-based reference groups on consumer decisions", *Journal of Consumer Research*, Vol. 19 No. 2, September, pp. 198-211.

Chow, W.S. (2002), *Multivariate Statistical Analysis: With Application of SAS/STAT*, Best-Wise Publishing Co., Taipei.

Cooper, D.R. and Emory, C.W. (1998), *Business Research Methods*, 6th ed., Richard D. Irwin, Homewood, IL.

Cowan, R., Cowan, W. and Swann, P. (1997), "A model of demand with interactions among consumers", *International Journal of Industrial Organization*, Vol. 15 No. 6, pp. 711-32.

Cox, D.F. (Ed.) (1967), *Risk Taking and Information Handling in Consumer Behavior*, Harvard University Press, Cambridge, MA.

Cox, D.F. and Rich, S.U. (1964), "Perceived risk and consumer decision making: the case of telephone shopping", *Journal of Marketing Research*, Vol. 1, November, pp. 32-9.

Cuieford, J.P. (1965), *Fundamental Statistics in Psychology and Education*, McGraw-Hill, New York, NY.

Darden, R.W., McKee, D. and Hampton, R. (1993), "Salesperson employment status as a moderator in the job satisfaction model: a frame of reference perspective", *The Journal of Personal Selling & Sales Management*, Vol. 13 No. 3, pp. 1-15.

Dodds, W.B., Monroe, K.B. and Grewal, D. (1991), "Effects of prices, brand and store information on buyers' product evaluations", *Journal of Marketing Research*, Vol. 28, August, pp. 307-19.

Dowling, G.R. and Staelin, R. (1994), "A model of perceived risk and intended risk-handling activity", *Journal of Consumer Research*, Vol. 21 No. 1, June, pp. 119-34.

Erdem, T. and Keane, M. (1996), "Decision making under uncertainty: capturing dynamic brand choice process in turbulent consumer goods", *Marketing Science*, Vol. 15 No. 1, pp. 1-21.

Fishbein, M. and Ajzen, I. (1975), *Belief, Attitude, Intention, and Behavior*, Addison-Wesley, Reading, MA.

Fitzsimons, G.J. and Morwitz, V.G. (1996), "The effect of measuring intent on brand-level purchase behavior", *Journal of Consumer Research*, Vol. 23 No. 1, pp. 1-11.

Grewal, D., Monroe, K.B. and Krishnan, R. (1998), "The effects of price-comparison advertising on buyers' perceptions of acquisition value, transaction value, and behavioral intentions", *Journal of Marketing*, Vol. 62 No. 2, pp. 46-59.

Gupta, A., Su, B.-C. and Zhiping, W. (2004), "An empirical study of consumer switching from traditional to electronic channels: a purchase-decision process perspective", *International Journal of Electronic Commerce*, Vol. 8 No. 3, Spring, pp. 131-61.

Hair, J.F., Anderson, R.E., Tatham, R.L. and Black, W.C. (1998), *Multivariate Data Analysis with Readings*, Prentice-Hall, Englewood Cliffs, NJ.

Jacoby, J. and Kaplan, L. (1972), "The components of perceived risk", *Proceedings of the 3rd Annual Conference of the Association for Consumer Research, Association for Consumer Research*, Chicago, IL, pp. 382-93.

Koo, D.-M. (2003), "Inter-relationships among store images, store satisfaction, and store loyalty among Korea discount retail patrons", *Journal of Marketing and Logistics*, Vol. 15 No. 4, pp. 42-71.

Kotler, P. (2003), *Marketing Management*, 11th ed., Pearson Education, Prentice-Hall, Upper Saddle River, NJ.

Kwun, J.W. and Oh, H. (2004), "Effects of brand, price, and risk on customers' value perceptions and behavioral intentions in the restaurant industry", *Journal of Hospitality & Leisure Marketing*, Vol. 11 No. 1, pp. 31-49.

LaBarbera, P.A. and Mazursky, D. (1983), ''A longitudinal assessment of customer satisfaction/dissatisfaction: the dynamic aspect of the cognitive process'', *Journal of Marketing Research*, Vol. 20, November, pp. 393-404.

Lessig, V.P. and Park, C.W. (1978), ''Promotional perspectives of reference group influence: advertising implications'', *Journal of Advertising*, Vol. 7 No. 2, pp. 41-7.

Lim, K.S. and Razzaque, M.A. (1997), ''Brand loyalty and situational effects: an interactionist perspective'', *The Journal of International Consumer Marketing*, Vol. 9 No. 4, pp. 95-115.

McGaughey, R.E. and Mason, K.H. (1998), ''The internet as a marketing tool'', *Journal of Marketing: Theory and Practice*, Vol. 6 No. 3, pp. 1-11.

Mäser, B. and Weimar, K. (1998), ''Travel decision making: from the vantage point of perceived risk and information preferences'', *Journal of Travel and Tourism Marketing*, Vol. 7 No. 4, pp. 107-21.

Mitchell, V. (1992), ''Understanding consumers' behavior: can perceived risk theory help?'', *Management Decision*, Vol. 30 No. 3, pp. 26-31.

Mitchell, V. (1999), ''Consumer perceived risk: conceptualization and models'', *European Journal of Marketing*, Vol. 33 No. 1/2, pp. 163-95.

Mitchell, V.W. and Boustani, P. (1994), ''A preliminary investigation into pre- and post-purchase risk perception'', *European Journal of Marketing*, Vol. 28 No. 1, pp. 56-71.

Morwitz, V.G. and Schmittlein, D. (1992), ''Using segmentation to improve sales forecasts based on purchase intent, which intenders actually buy'', *Journal of Marketing Research*, Vol. 29 No. 4, pp. 391-405.

Moutinho, L. (1987), ''Consumer behaviour in tourism'', *European Journal of Marketing*, Vol. 21 No. 10, pp. 5-25.

Murray, K.B. and Schlacter, J.L. (1990), ''The impact of services versus goods on consumers' assessment of perceived risk and variability'', *Journal of the Academy of Marketing Sciences*, Vol. 18, pp. 51-65.

Newberry, C.R., Klemz, B.R. and Boshoff, C. (2003), ''Managerial implications of predicting purchase behavior from purchase intentions: a retail patronage case study'', *Journal of Services Marketing*, Vol. 17 No. 6/7, pp. 609-20.

Novak, T.P., Hoffman, D.L. and Yung, Y.F. (2000), ''Measuring the customer experience in online environments: a structural modelling approach'', *Marketing Service*, Vol. 19 No. 1, pp. 22-42.

Oglethorpe, J.E. and Monroe, K.B. (1987), ''Risk perception and risk acceptability in consumer behavior: conceptual issues and an agenda for future research'', in Belk, R.W. and Zaltman, G. (Eds), *AMA Winter Marketers Educators' Conference*, American Marketing Association, Chicago, IL, pp. 255-60.

Parasuraman, A., Zeithaml, V.A. and Berry, L. (1991), ''Refinement and reassessment of the SERVQUAL scale'', *Journal of Retailing*, Vol. 67 No. 4, pp. 420-49.

Park, C.W. and Lessig, V.P. (1977), ''Students and housewives: differences in susceptibility to reference group influences'', *Journal of Consumer Research*, Vol. 4 No. 2, pp. 102-10.

Peter, J.P. and Tarpey, L.X. (1975), ''A comparative analysis of three consumer decision strategies'', *Journal of Consumer Research*, Vol. 2, June, pp. 29-37.

Peyrot, M. and Van Doren, D. (1994), ''Effect of a class action on consumer repurchase intentions'', *The Journal of Consumer Affairs*, Vol. 28 No. 2, pp. 361-79.

Pires, G., Stanton, J. and Eckford, A. (2004), ''Influences on the perceived risk of purchasing online'', *Journal of Consumer Behavior*, Vol. 4 No. 2, December, pp. 118-31.

Roselius, T. (1971), ''Consumer rankings of risk deduction methods'', *Journal of Marketing*, Vol. 35, January, pp. 56-61.

Schiffman, L.G. and Kanuk, L.L. (2004), *Consumer Behavior*, 8th ed., Pearson Education, Prentice-Hall, Upper Saddle River, NJ.

發表論文範本

Semeijn, J., Van Riel, A.C.R. and Ambrosini, A.B. (2004), ''Consumer evaluations of store brands: effects of store image and product attributes'', *Journal of Retailing and Consumer Services*, Vol. 11 No. 4, pp. 247-58.

Shao, C.Y., Baker, J. and Wagner, J.A. (2004), ''The effects of appropriateness of service contact personnel dress on customer expectations of service quality and purchase intention: the moderating influences of involvement and gender'', *Journal of Business Research*, Vol. 57 No. 10, pp. 1164-76.

Silk, S.J. and Urban, G.L. (1978), ''Pre-test market evaluation of new packaged goods: a model and measurement methodology'', *Journal of Marketing Research*, Vol. 15 No. 2, pp. 171-91.

Stone, R.N. and Gronhaug, K. (1993), ''Perceived risk: further considerations for the marketing discipline'', *European Journal of Marketing*, Vol. 27 No. 3, pp. 39-50.

Sweeney, J.C., Soutar, G.N. and Johnson, L.W. (1999), ''The role of perceived risk in the quality-value relationship: a study in a retail environment'', *Journal of Retailing*, Vol. 75 No. 1, pp. 77-105.

Wu, W.-Y. and Lin, Q.-H. (2002), *Marketing Research*, South-Western College Publishing, Cincinnati, OH.

## Corresponding author

Long-Yi Lin can be contacted at: longyi@ms12.url.com.tw

# 寬頻網路關係行銷結合類型、服務品質、關係品質與轉換成本對顧客忠誠之影響

林隆儀

真理大學管理科學研究所助理教授

徐稚軒

真理大學管理科學研究所碩士

陳俊碩

臺北大學企業管理學系博士班研究生

輔仁管理評論
第十六卷第一期抽印本
中華民國九十八年一月

*Fu Jen Management Review Vol. 16, No.1, January 2009*
*College of Management, Fu Jen Catholic University*
*Taipei, Taiwan, Republic of China*

輔仁管理評論

中華民國 98 年 1 月，第十六卷第一期，37-68

# 寬頻網路關係行銷結合類型、
# 服務品質、關係品質與轉換成本
# 對顧客忠誠之影響

林隆儀・徐稚軒・陳俊碩[*]

（收稿日期：97 年 2 月 21 日；第一次修正：97 年 8 月 19 日；
接受刊登日期：97 年 10 月 21 日）

## 摘要

　　本研究旨在探討寬頻網路業者使用的關係行銷結合類型、服務品質及關係品質與轉換成本對顧客忠誠的影響。以臺灣北部地區的寬頻網路消費者為研究對象，採用便利抽樣法蒐集初級資料，共發出 429 份問卷，收回有效問卷 407 份，有效問卷回收率為 95%。採用迴歸分析檢定研究假說，實證結果發現：(1)關係行銷結合類型對關係品質與轉換成本有顯著的正向影響，其中皆以結構性連結影響程度最大。(2)服務品質對關係品質有顯著的正向影響。(3)服務品質中的有形性、反應性、保證性、關懷性，對轉換成本皆有顯著的正向影響。(4)關係品質對顧客忠誠有顯著的正向影響。(5)損失績效成本對顧客的行為忠誠有顯著的正向影響；沉沒成本對顧客的態度忠誠與行為忠誠都有顯著的正向影響。

關鍵詞彙：關係行銷結合類型，服務品質，關係品質，轉換成本，顧客忠誠

# 壹・緒論

　　網際網路的興起造成人們生活上許多重大的改變。我國於民國九十年七月一日開放固網後，寬頻網路業者進入了競爭激烈的新時代，廠商爭取新顧客顯得更加困難，於是紛紛使出與顧客建立長期而穩固關係的行銷手法。近年來關係行銷逐漸受到重視，寬頻網路業者除了極力爭取新顧客之外，更把行銷焦點放在保留現有顧客上。因為瞭解影響顧客忠誠的主要原因，使得寬頻網路業者可以有效應用關係行銷策略，強化廠商與現有顧客間之關係，對於保留現有顧客及穩固廠商與顧客之間的關係大有助益。

　　Berry & Parasuraman (1991) 與 Berry (1995) 提出三種關係行銷結合類型，分別為財務性、社交性、結構性結合，並認為關係行銷結合類型的層次愈高，愈有助於增強企業競爭優勢。今天寬頻網路的使用已經相當普遍，但是在

[*] 作者簡介：林隆儀，真理大學管理科學研究所助理教授；徐稚軒，真理大學管理科學研究所碩士；陳俊碩，臺北大學企業管理學系博士班研究生。

寬頻網路接取業者關係行銷的相關文獻中,大多只探討關係行銷結合和顧客忠誠有密切關係,至於使用何種層級的關係行銷結合類型最能有效的和顧客連結的研究卻相對缺乏,例如 Lin, Weng & Hsieh (2003)、Hsieh, Chiu & Chiang (2005) 的研究都未指出哪一種關係結合類型與顧客的結合效果較佳,為深入探究及回答此一問題,乃激起本文研究此一題目的第一個動機。

Chaudhuri & Holbrook (2001) 認為提高顧客的購買忠誠,可以增加廠商的市場佔有率,而廠商的市場佔有率影響公司的營收至深且巨。因此培養顧客忠誠是廠商刻不容緩的重要議題,而影響顧客忠誠的因素相當廣泛,大多數廠商似乎都陷入滿意的迷思 (satisfaction trap) 之中,缺乏遠見,認為滿意和服務品質是保留顧客的唯一途徑。要打破這種迷思,行銷經理必須深入瞭解影響保留顧客的各種因素 (Burnham, Frels & Mahajan, 2003),其中轉換成本與顧客忠誠之間的關係扮演相當重要的角色,因為廠商若可以提高顧客的知覺轉換成本,表示顧客會因為轉換品牌或產品花費太多成本而減低其意願。因此提高顧客的轉換成本可以為企業帶來更高利潤 (朱博湧,2005)。過去有關轉換成本的研究,大多單獨探討轉換成本對顧客忠誠的影響,關於哪些因素可以有效提升顧客在轉換供應商時所知覺到的轉換成本之研究則相對缺乏,因此乃引發本文探討此一題目的第二個動機。

本研究的目的有三:(1)探討寬頻網路業者所使用的關係行銷結合類型,對消費者的知覺關係品質、轉換成本的影響;(2)研究寬頻網路之消費者所知覺的服務品質對消費者知覺關係品質與轉換成本的影響;(3)探討關係品質與轉換成本對顧客忠誠的影響。

# 貳‧文獻探討

## 一、關係行銷

關係行銷的概念率先由美國學者 Berry 於 1983 年在針對服務業的一項研究中所提出,此後便有許多學者針對關係行銷領域進行研究。Berry (1983) 在其服務業行銷的研究中,認為關係行銷為透過組織提供的多重服務,吸引、維持並提升顧客關係的一種策略。Berry & Parasuraman (1991) 指出關係行銷涉及吸引、發展及保持顧客關係。Shani & Chalasani (1992) 則認為關係行銷主要是透過家庭相關性產品及服務的提供,與消費者發展持續不斷的關係,目的是希望能藉由互惠與每一位顧客保持長期關係。

關係行銷與傳統交易式行銷分屬於行銷策略連續帶的兩端 (Gronroos, 1990)，代表企業實行關係行銷的程度高低，而不是只以有或沒有來分別。傳統交易式行銷爲單一銷售導向，重視間斷的顧客接觸、專注產品特徵，屬於一種短期交易；關係行銷主張留住顧客，重視持續性的顧客接觸、專注顧客的價值，屬於一種長期關係的建立與維護 (Payne et al., 2002)。Armstrong & Kotler (2000) 認爲關係行銷是指與顧客和其他利益團體創造、維持、增強彼此之間的價值關係之過程；他們也認爲關係行銷是針對長期關係，目標是傳送顧客長期的價值，而成功的指標是長期的顧客滿意與顧客忠誠。

Berry & Parasuraman (1991)、Berry (1995)、Armstrong & Kotler (2000) 皆指出，企業爲了培養顧客忠誠，所採用的關係行銷與顧客結合的類型可分成三種，並認爲關係行銷實現的層級愈高，表示顧客與公司之間的結合強度愈強，這三種類型分別是：(1)財務性結合：主要是以價格爲誘因來促使顧客購買公司的產品或服務，並以此維持顧客的忠誠，或給予長久和公司往來的顧客較低的價格或贈品，但這種由財務性動機而形成的關係結合所帶給企業的競爭優勢，通常都不易維持長久；(2)社交性結合：企業透過社會及人際關係的連結和顧客建立長久的關係，並且將顧客視爲不同的個體，針對不同的個體使用顧客化的服務以滿足不同的需求。相較於以價格優惠爲誘因的財務性結合，社交性的關係結合所能帶給企業的競爭優勢較高，因爲比較不容易被競爭對手取代；(3)結構性結合：結構性結合是指企業提供目標客戶群附加價值利益，強調透過將有價值且不易自競爭廠商取得的服務提供給顧客，以提高顧客的轉換成本。

Morris, Brunyee & Page (1998) 將關係行銷結合類型區分爲(1)法律性結合：主張以契約或條文明定供需雙方彼此之間的權力與義務；(2)結構性結合：主張在供需雙方作業系統間形成的正式連結；(3)社交性結合：主張在供需雙方間發展出的個人關係或社會關係。Hsieh et al. (2005) 在關係行銷結合類型對於網路購物者顧客忠誠影響的研究中，將關係行銷結合類型分爲財務性、社交性及結構性三種結合，並採用李克特七點尺度來衡量。Chiu et al. (2005) 和 Lin et al. (2003) 也分別在他們的研究中將關係行銷結合類型分爲財務性、社交性及結構性三種類型，並且都使用李克特七點尺度來衡量。

## 二、服務品質

服務具有無形性、不可分割性、可變性及易逝性等特性 (Kotler, 2000)，因此較難有一致性的衡量標準。但是服務的好壞主要還是以消費者實際感受到的服務，做為判斷服務品質好壞的依據，所以 Etzel et al. (2001) 認為服務品質是顧客將期望的服務與實際感受的服務相比較的結果。

服務品質泛指消費者接受服務後，是否再次購買的整體態度 (Bitner & Hubbert, 1994)。洪順慶 (2005) 將服務品質視為一種主觀而抽象的觀念，和顧客的感受息息相關，並將服務定義為包括所有產出不具有實體產品的活動，通常具有生產時同時消費的特色。Parasuraman, Zeithaml & Berry (1985) 認為服務品質是衡量顧客對服務品質的主觀知覺，也就是衡量顧客所知覺的品質。Parasuraman et al. (1988) 將服務品質定義為消費者對於企業整體優越程度的衡量，是一種態度，但不同於滿意，並且是由消費者對於服務期望與知覺之間的差距來判定。Gronroos (1984) 與 Lovelock (1991) 也認為服務品質代表顧客在消費過程中，實際所獲得的整體經驗與其先前對於該服務的期望之間所產生的知覺服務品質。

服務品質是顧客接受服務後的一種綜合感受，所以學者對服務品質的衡量構面的看法相當分歧，例如 Sasser et al. (1978) 主張從安全性、一致性、態度、完整性、調整性、可近性、及時性等七個構面來衡量服務品質。Lehtinen & Lehtinen (1982) 認為應該從提供服務者的實體品質、公司品質、服務提供者與接受者的互動品質來衡量服務品質。Parasuraman et al. (1985) 進行一項焦點團體訪談後發現，顧客在評量服務品質的好壞時大都使用相似的標準，他們並且提出影響服務品質的十項因素，用來衡量服務品質。Parasuraman et al. (1988) 在他們所發表有關服務品質的概念模型與衡量量表的研究中，提出 SERVQUAL 衡量量表，經過實證後將服務品質由上述的十個衡量因素，縮減為五個構面，分別為(1)有形性：是指顧客可看到的實體部分，包含實體設施、設備、服務人員的儀容與外表、文宣及其他溝通器材的外觀；(2)可靠性：指服務人員表現出來的可靠度與一致性，以及能正確提供其所承諾服務的能力；(3)反應性：指幫助顧客解決問題及提供迅速服務的意願；(4)保證性：指服務人員的知識和禮貌，即傳達給顧客的信任感與自信的能力；(5)同理心：指提供服務的人員能站在顧客的立場來考慮其所需的服務。SERVQUAL 衡量量表受到國內外學者的重視及討論，普遍被相關研究所引用。

## 三、關係品質

Crosby, Evans & Cowles (1990) 針對美國終身保險產業的研究認為，關係品質是買賣雙方關係強度的整體評價，此評價符合雙方的需求與期望，而這些需求與期望是以雙方過去成功或失敗的遭遇及事件為基礎。Hennig-Thurau &

Klee (1997) 認為任何買賣關係的基礎都建立在服務或產品的交易上，而關係品質如同產品品質的概念，可被視為滿足顧客關係需求上的適切程度。

關係品質的構面有許多學者提出不同見解，但是對於關係品質應包含那些基本構面，至今尚無一致的定論 (Smith, 1998)，例如 Crosby et al. (1990)、Lagace et al. (1991) 都認為關係品質可視為一個高階的建構，至少應該包含信任與滿意兩個構面。Hennig-Thurau & Klee (1997) 認為關係品質的構面，應該要加入承諾因素。Smith (1998) 綜合許多學者的看法，提出關係品質至少應包含滿意、信任及承諾三個構面；Crosby et al. (1990) 將關係品質區分為滿意與信任兩個構面。

Morgan & Hunt (1994) 在有關汽車業經銷商的一項研究中，認為信任和關係承諾是維持良好關係品質的重要條件。(1)信任：信任包含關係夥伴相信彼此會根據雙方的最佳利益來做決定。Crosby et al. (1990) 認為信任是一種信念，是顧客相信銷售人員值得依賴，並會以顧客的長期利益來行動。Morgan & Hunt (1994) 將信任界定為對交易夥伴的可靠及正直有信心的知覺。因此當彼此之間存在著信任時，顧客將會降低或消除一些不確定性的感覺，所以取得顧客的信任是維繫彼此買賣關係中的一個重要因素。(2)承諾：Dwyer, Schurr & Oh (1987) 指出承諾是指交易夥伴之間，對於關係的持續性之暗示或明白的誓約，並且認為承諾是買賣雙方彼此依賴的最高境界。Morgan & Hunt (1994) 認為交易夥伴相信現行關係相當重要，並會盡最大努力來維持這個關係。Hennig-Thurau & Klee (1997) 則將承諾定義為顧客對於關係長期維持的導向，不論是對關係的情緒連結或是基於保持關係，都能產生較高的利益。

Smith (1998) 使用李克特七點尺度來衡量關係品質中的滿意、信任與承諾，Crosby et al. (1990) 使用李克特七點尺度來衡量關係品質中的滿意與信任。Morgan & Hunt (1994) 使用李克特七點尺度衡量信任和承諾。Beloucif, Donaldson & Kazanci (2004) 使用李克特五點尺度來衡量關係品質中的滿意、信任與承諾。

## 四、轉換成本

轉換成本 (switching cost) 通常是指顧客從目前的供應商轉換到新的供應商所必須付出的一切成本。Lee, Lee & Feick (2001) 在探討法國的通訊產業時，將轉換成本定義為顧客轉換供應商時所發生的成本，當保留與原供應商繼續交易時這項成本就不會產生。Jones, Mothersbaugh & Beatty (2002) 將轉換成本定義為顧客從原先的供應商轉換至另一個供應商時，所知覺到的經濟成本與心理成本,因此轉換成本也可以被視爲一種在服務的關係中,顧客欲轉換供應商時將會遭遇到的轉換障礙。Burnham, Frels & Mahajan (2003) 研究信用卡和遠距離通訊兩個不同服務產業,認爲轉換成本爲顧客從原先的供應商轉換至其他供應商的過程中所產生的成本,然而轉換成本的發生必定是在轉換的過程中產生,而不是當顧客轉換供應商時就會立刻產生,且轉換成本並不只包含主觀的經濟成本,只要當顧客單純的認爲「不值得」轉換供應商時,他們就可能已經知覺受到某些東西的限制。

Lee et al. (2001) 認爲轉換成本可以分成交易成本及搜尋成本兩種類別,其中交易成本是指消費者轉換到另一家供應商所必須付出的時間與心力;而搜尋成本則是消費者爲了搜尋市場上其他供應商有關於價格或服務等相關資訊時,所必須花費的時間或精力的成本。Klemperer (1987) 將轉換成本分爲學習成本、交易成本、人爲轉換成本等三類。

Jones et al. (2002) 針對服務業提出了六個轉換成本的衡量構面,分別爲損失績效成本、不確定成本、轉換前之搜尋評估成本、轉換後之行爲成本、設置成本和沉沒成本,並且使用李克特七點尺度來衡量,他們的實證結果發現,沉沒成本和損失績效成本爲轉換成本中影響消費者再購買意願最主要的因素,其中沉沒成本是顧客認知爲了維持此一消費關係,所產生無法回收的時間、金錢與投資等成本。Maute & Forrester (1993) 認爲損失績效成本是指當與供應商的關係終止時,顧客所失去的原供應商回饋顧客之利益及補貼。

Burnham et al. (2003) 探討相關文獻及採用焦點群體訪談,發展出一種以多元尺度來衡量消費者的轉換成本的方法,包括經濟風險成本、評估成本、學習成本、建置成本、利益損失成本、財務損失成本、個人關係損失成本,以及品牌關係損失成本等八個因素,並且使用李克特五點尺度衡量之。Lee et al. (2001) 以法國行動電話爲例,探討消費者滿意和顧客忠誠之間是否會受到轉換成本的干擾,其中轉換成本的衡量便是使用單一的整體概念來衡量轉換成本,並且以李克特五點尺度來衡量。

# 五、顧客忠誠

在競爭激烈的市場中,要爭取新顧客並不容易,因此廠商對於提升現有顧客的顧客忠誠顯得格外重視,例如 Peppers & Rogers (1993) 就曾指出開發一位新客戶的成本是維持一位現有客戶成本的五倍。Oliver (1997) 將品牌顧客忠誠定義爲即使在不同的環境或各品牌激烈競爭下,競爭對手用盡努力吸引消費者,顧客仍然承諾未來會再次購買偏好品牌的產品或服務。他同時指出顧客忠誠可以分為知覺忠誠、態度忠誠、意欲忠誠與行為忠誠等四個階段 (Oliver, 1999)。

Prus & Brandt (1995) 指出，顧客忠誠代表顧客對於某品牌或公司維持長久關係的承諾，忠誠顧客是由態度與行為忠誠兩方面的組合來呈現，因此顧客忠誠的衡量可分為強調行為與強調態度兩方面。Chaudhuri & Holbrook (2001) 主張以行為及態度來衡量顧客忠誠。態度忠誠的重點在於了解消費者對產品與品牌的整體感覺，以及他們的購買意圖；行為忠誠則注重對促銷刺激所產生的反應，即對產品或品牌的購買行為而非態度 (Schiffman & Kanuk, 2006)。態度忠誠來自消費者就是喜歡某項產品或服務，而行為忠誠則是對某一產品或服務具有購買的慣性，因此要衡量顧客忠誠，除了需考慮行為忠誠之外，亦不可忽視消費者態度忠誠的重要性。

Javalgi & Moberg (1997) 認為行為忠誠通常是以購買次數來衡量，Bowen & Chen (2001) 也認為可以重複購買來衡量行為忠誠。而 Stum & Thiry (1991) 認為，企業若欲建立顧客忠誠，可從重複購買、購買產品和服務、推薦他人、對於其他競爭者的誘惑時之免疫性等四項指標衡量行為忠誠。Selnes (1993) 主張以顧客欲與供應商繼續維持關係之意願、顧客將供應商推薦他人之程度，衡量顧客的行為忠誠，並使用李克特六點尺度衡量之。Lee et al., (2001) 以重複購買、向他人推薦，衡量顧客的行為忠誠，使用李克特五點尺度衡量之。

Javalgi & Moberg (1997) 主張以顧客對於某品牌之偏好與傾向來衡量顧客的態度忠誠。Chaudhuri & Holbrook (2001) 主張以「我認為我對這個品牌是忠誠的」與「我願意以高於其他品牌的價格來購買它」，並且使用李克特七點尺度來衡量顧客的態度忠誠。而 Lee et al. (2001) 使用「當競爭者推出更好產品時，抵抗轉換至競爭者之能力」，使用李克特五點尺度來做為態度忠誠的衡量。陳建文和洪嘉蓉 (2005) 在針對 ISP 使用者的顧客忠誠研究中，有關於態度忠誠的衡量，採取「使用競爭者之抵抗力」、「我是忠誠顧客」、「願意持續使用該公司服務」、「注重新的加值服務及優惠方案」等題項，並使用李克特五點尺度來衡量。

另有學者主張顧客忠誠是指相對態度與再惠顧行為之間的關係 (Dick & Basu, 1994)，顧客忠誠最普遍的評估莫過於衡量顧客長期的印象與再惠顧形態 (Bloemer & Kasper, 1995)。Selnes (1993) 認為顧客忠誠是因為顧客滿意而產生，忠誠代表消費者對產品與服務的態度，為消費者實際購買行為的重要因素，其中口碑是指顧客願意將產品推薦給他人，顯示該顧客具有高度忠誠。

## 六、變數之間關係的相關研究

### (一)關係行銷結合類型對關係品質影響的相關研究

Lin et al. (2003) 在針對銀行業的研究中發現,想要和顧客建立長期的交易關係,財務、社交及結構三種關係行銷結合策略對於信任和承諾都有顯著的正向影響,也就是要提升顧客的信任和承諾,三種關係結合策略都是有效的方法。

Hsieh et al. (2005) 研究網路購物的消費者,探討網路拍賣業者是否也可以使用關係結合策略來提升顧客對廠商的承諾意願,他們將產品種類分為搜尋、經驗和信任三種類別,並將產品種類設定為干擾變數,研究結果發現不管產品種類為何,財務、社交及結構三種關係行銷結合類型都可以有效提升顧客對廠商的承諾。

Peltier & Westfall (2000) 研究保健機構與企業員工的福利管理者,發現顧客忠誠及關係強度以結構性結合的影響程度最大,社交性結合次之、財務性結合最小。Berry & Parasuraman (1991) 提出企業實施關係行銷結合的類型,可分為財務性結合、社交性結合、結構性結合三種類型,並且證實三種類型在連結顧客關係時,所產生的強度以結構性結合所造成的強度最高,其次分別為社交性、財務性。

### (二)關係行銷結合類型對轉換成本影響的相關研究

Berry & Parasuraman (1991) 所發展出來的關係行銷結合類型,所代表的是廠商可以用來與顧客建立關係連結的一種策略,當廠商和消費者之間經由結交、互動,便會產生一種經濟上、心理上、情緒上之依附關係。由轉換成本的定義可知,轉換成本代表的是消費者在轉換供應商時,知覺到某些障礙限制了顧客的轉換意願,而這些東西不外乎是結合了買方的財務、社會與心理上的風險所構成的搜尋成本、交易成本、學習成本、忠誠顧客折扣、顧客習慣、情感成本與知覺上的努力 (Fornell, 1992)。由此可知關係行銷結合類型所提供的財務性、社交性和結構性結合,會影響消費者在轉換供應商時的知覺轉換成本。

Hsieh et al. (2005) 也認為這三種關係行銷結合類型可以建立財務上或心理上的成本來避免消費者轉換供應商。他們認為財務性和社交性結合應該可以建立消費者的知覺轉換成本,因為當消費者轉換供應商時,消費者將會損失過去累積的紅利積點或對於熟客的某些特別待遇,社交性結合方式係指與顧客建立友誼等情感性關係,即公司的服務人員與顧客所發展如友誼、感情等之人際關係，或公司提供與顧客之間相互溝通，發展社交關係的方式 (Berry, 1995; Berry & Parasuraman, 1991)。

## (三)服務品質對關係品質影響的相關研究

Crosby et al. (1990) 針對終身壽險業所作的研究中發現，銷售人員的專業能力對關係品質有正向影響，表示銷售人員擁有優良的專業能力，顧客會對服務人員所提供之服務品質的保證感到有信心，亦即所知覺的服務品質保證會正向影響關係品質的優劣。Hennig-Thurau & Klee (1997) 也認爲可滿足顧客的服務或產品，應視爲高關係品質所不可或缺的條件。

周文賢與游信益 (2005) 研究網路銀行業的服務品質、關係品質與顧客忠誠的關係，實證結果發現服務品質中除了「個人化」與「線上服務人員」之外，其餘構面都會正向影響關係品質中的顧客滿意，而「線上系統品質」與「安全性」可提升關係品質中顧客信任的重要性。

## (四)服務品質對轉換成本影響的相關研究

Jones et al. (2002) 針對銀行業和髮型設計業的研究中，發現服務品質和人際關係對轉換成本有顯著的正向影響，並且證實服務品質和人際關係對轉換成本之損失績效成本與沉沒成本之間的關係，相較於其他轉換成本構面有最強烈的相關。

Aydin & Ozer (2005) 在探討影響顧客忠誠前提因素的研究中，發現土耳其的通訊產業影響顧客忠誠的因素包括知覺服務品質、信任和知覺轉換成本對顧客忠誠都有顯著的正向影響，同時也發現知覺服務品質和知覺轉換成本之間有顯著的正向影響，即當消費者知覺到愈高的服務品質時，其所知覺轉換成本程度也愈高。Fullerton (2005) 針對於零售服務產業所做的研究，探討服務品質和承諾之間的關係時，將承諾分爲繼續承諾和情感承諾兩個部分，實證結果發現男性服飾店服務品質對繼續承諾有顯著的正向影響，也就是說對男性服飾店的顧客而言，當其知覺到愈優良的服務品質，愈會提高其轉換供應商的知覺轉換障礙。

## (五)關係品質對顧客忠誠影響的相關研究

Crosby et al. (1990) 指出好的關係品質是顧客相信產品或服務提供者的誠實表現，顧客因爲對過去的績效感到滿意，並且瞭解未來可產生績效時，會有較高的再購買意願。Zeithaml & Bitner (1996) 也證實維持良好的關係品質，可增進顧客忠誠及願意支付溢酬等正面的行為意向,並且減少離去和散布不利訊息的負面行為意向。

周文賢與游信益 (2005) 針對網路銀行業顧客所做的研究,探討服務品質構面、關係品質對顧客忠誠間之關係,實證結果發現關係品質中的滿意和信任兩個構面都可提升顧客忠誠。

### (六)轉換成本對顧客忠誠影響的相關研究

Burnham et al. (2003) 針對信用卡及長距離通訊產業所做的研究發現,消費者知覺轉換成本愈高,其與原供應商繼續合作意願也愈高,因此轉換成本對繼續合作意願有顯著的正向相關。Jones et al. (2002) 針對銀行業和髮型設計業的研究中,也發現轉換成本對顧客的再購買意願有顯著的正向影響。

鄭士蘋與林其鋒 (2005) 的實證研究發現,對於台灣壽險業的顧客而言,轉換成本和顧客的轉換意願之間有顯著的負向影響,即當消費者知覺轉換成本高時,將會減低其轉換供應商的意願。

# 參‧研究方法

## 一、觀念性架構

本研究參考 Berry & Parasuraman (1991) 與 Berry (1995) 的分類方法,將關係行銷結合類型區分為財務性、社交性與結構性結合三種類型。本研究參考 Parasuraman et al. (1988) 所提出的服務品質五大構面,做為衡量申請寬頻網路之消費者所知覺的服務品質的構面。

Morgan & Hunt (1994) 強調信任和關係承諾是維持良好關係品質的重要條件,所以本研究採用 Morgan & Hunt (1994) 的看法以信任與承諾兩構面來衡量關係品質。Jones et al. (2002) 針對服務業提出衡量轉換成本的構面,包括損失績效成本、不確定成本、轉換前之搜尋評估成本、轉換後之行為成本、設置成本和沉沒成本,實證結果發現損失績效成本和沉沒成本為轉換成本中最主要的影響因素。因此本研究選擇以損失績效成本和沉沒成本,做為衡量轉換成本的主要構面。

顧客忠誠的衡量可分為行為忠誠與態度忠誠兩方面。許多學者在他們的研究中都以態度忠誠及行為忠誠做為衡量顧客忠誠的構面,如 Prus & Brandt (1995),Javalgi & Moberg (1997),Chaudhuri & Holbrook (2001),因此本研究採用 Chaudhuri & Holbrook (2001) 的看法，分別以態度忠誠與行為忠誠兩個構面來衡量顧客忠誠。

參考以上學者的觀點，以及參照以上有關各變數之間影響關係的文獻探討，發展出本研究的觀念性架構，如圖一所示。

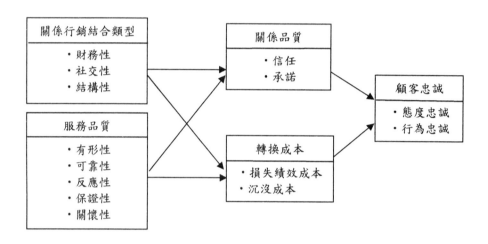

圖一　觀念性架構

# 二、研究假說

Lin et al. (2003) 在他們的研究中發現，銀行業使用三種關係行銷結合類型對信任和承諾都有顯著的正向影響。Hsieh et al. (2005) 研究網路購物消費者，探討網路拍賣業者是否也可以使用關係結合策略來提升顧客對廠商的承諾意願，研究結果證實三種關係行銷結合類型都可以有效提升顧客對網路拍賣業者的承諾。DuPont (1998) 的研究指出關係層級愈高，信任與承諾的程度也愈高，也就是說財務性結合對信任與承諾的影響最小，社交性結合的影響次之，結構性結合的影響最大。Peltier & Westfall (2000) 的研究也發現，顧客忠誠與關係強度以結構性結合的影響程度最大，社交性結合次之，財務性結合最小。因此可據以推論出本研究的研究假說 1 如下：

**H1：關係行銷結合類型對關係品質有不同程度的正向影響。**

　　**H1-1：廠商使用結構性結合方式最能提高顧客的信任，社交性結合的效果次之，財務性結合的效果最小。**

**H1-2：廠商使用結構性結合方式最能提高顧客的承諾，社交性結合的效果次之，財務性結合的效果最小。**

Berry & Parasuraman (1991) 指出關係行銷結合類型是廠商可用來與顧客建立關係連結的一種策略，其中所謂結合是廠商和消費者經由結交、互動所產生一種經濟上、心理上、情緒上之依附關係，在關係交換下，能夠使成員緊密的結合在一起 (Turner, 1970)。當廠商使用關係行銷結合策略提供顧客利益，使消費者在關係交換之下和供應商產生結合後，消費者對廠商便會產生一種經濟上、心理上、情緒上之依附作用，因此當消費者在轉換供應商時，會知覺到某些障礙限制了他們的轉換意願。Hsieh et al. (2005) 也認為關係行銷結合類型可以建立財務上或心理上的轉換成本，以避免消費者轉換供應商。Berry & Parasuraman (1991) 認為愈高層次的顧客結合類型，企業的持久性競爭差異化之潛力也愈大，因此愈高層次連結方式保留顧客的能力也愈高，對顧客的知覺轉換成本的影響也愈大。據此可推導出本研究的研究假說 2 如下：

**H2：關係行銷結合類型對顧客知覺轉換成本有不同程度的正向影響。**

**H2-1：廠商使用結構性結合方式最能提高顧客知覺損失績效成本，社交性結合的效果次之，財務性結合的效果最小。**

**H2-2：廠商使用結構性結合方式最能提高顧客知覺沉沒成本，社交性結合的效果次之，財務性結合的效果最小。**

Hennig-Thurau & Klee (1997) 認為可滿足顧客的服務或產品，應視為高關係品質所不可或缺的條件。Wong & Sohal (2002) 針對零售商店所做的研究發現，服務品質對關係品質有正向的影響。周文賢與游信益 (2005) 針對網路銀行業的關係品質及顧客忠誠之關係的研究中，也證實服務品質可以有效提升消費者的知覺關係品質。因此可據以推論出本研究的研究假說 3 如下：

**H3：消費者知覺服務品質對關係品質會有顯著的正向影響。**

**H3-1：消費者知覺服務品質的有形性、可靠性、反應性、保證性、關懷性對信任會有顯著的正向影響。**

**H3-2：消費者知覺服務品質的有形性、可靠性、反應性、保證性、關懷性對承諾會有顯著的正向影響。**

　　Jones et al. (2002) 針對銀行業和髮型設計業所做的研究，證實服務品質和人際關係對轉換成本都有顯著的正向影響。Aydin & Ozer (2005) 在探討影響顧客忠誠的前提因素研究中也發現，知覺服務品質和知覺轉換成本之間有顯著的正向影響，即當消費者知覺到愈高的服務品質時，其所知覺的轉換成本也愈高。Fullerton (2005) 針對於零售服務產業所做的研究，探討服務品質和承諾之間的關係時，將承諾分爲繼續承諾和情感承諾兩個部分，實證結果發現男性服飾店服務品質對繼續承諾有顯著的正向影響，也就是說對男性服飾店的顧客而言，當其知覺到愈優良的服務品質，愈會提高其轉換供應商的知覺轉換障礙。據此可推論出本研究的研究假說 4 如下：

**H4：消費者知覺服務品質對轉換成本會有顯著的正向影響。**

**H4-1：消費者知覺服務品質的有形性、可靠性、反應性、保證性、關懷性對損失績效成本會有顯著的正向影響。**

**H4-2：消費者知覺服務品質的有形性、可靠性、反應性、保證性、關懷性對沉沒成本會有顯著的正向影響。**

　　Zeithaml & Bitner (1996) 指出維持良好的關係品質，可增進顧客忠誠及願意支付溢酬等正面的行爲意向，並且減少離去和散布不利訊息的負面行爲意向。Boles et al. (2000) 也發現當顧客與銷售人員的關係較佳時，顧客有較高的再購買、引薦與推薦意願。周文賢與游信益 (2005) 的研究也發現，關係品質可提升顧客忠誠。因此可據以推導出本研究的研究假說 5 如下：

**H5：消費者知覺關係品質對顧客忠誠會有顯著的正向影響。**

**H5-1：消費者知覺關係品質對顧客的態度忠誠會有顯著的正向影響。**

**H5-2：消費者知覺關係品質對顧客的行爲忠誠會有顯著的正向影響。**

　　Jones et al. (2002) 針對銀行業和髮型設計業的研究中，發現轉換成本對顧客的再購買意願有顯著的正向相關。Lee et al. (2001) 以法國行動電話爲例，探討轉換成本對顧客忠誠的影響關係，研究結果發現高轉換成本會產生較高的忠誠度。Aydin & Ozer (2005) 在研究土耳其通訊產業時發現，消費者的知覺轉換成本和顧客忠誠有顯著的正向關係。Ibáñez et al. (2006) 針對歐洲家庭能源市場探討服務品質、滿意、信任與轉換成本對顧客忠誠的影響關係，研究結果也發現，顧客知覺轉換成本對顧客忠誠有顯著的正向關係。據此可推論出本研究的研究假說 6 如下：

**H6**：消費者知覺轉換成本對於顧客忠誠會有顯著的正向影響。

**H6-1**：消費者知覺轉換成本對於態度忠誠會有顯著的正向影響。

**H6-2**：消費者知覺轉換成本對於行為忠誠會有顯著的正向影響。

# 三、變數定義與衡量

## (一)關係行銷結合類型

本研究參考 Berry & Parasuraman (1991) 與 Berry (1995) 的見解將財務性結合定義為：寬頻網路業者提供現有顧客財務性的價格誘因，建立並提升與顧客之間關係的程度。將社交性結合定義為：寬頻網路業者藉由瞭解個別顧客的不同需要或提供顧客與顧客之間溝通管道，藉此提升與顧客之間關係的程度。將結構性結合定義為：寬頻網路業者藉由提供附加價值且不易自競爭廠商取得的服務，藉此提升與顧客之間關係的程度。並參考 Berry & Parasuraman (1991)、Berry (1995) 與 Lin et al. (2003) 所發展之關係行銷結合類型衡量量表，共計 11 題，以李克特七點尺度衡量之，分別代表非常不同意到非常同意。

## (二)服務品質

本研究將服務品質定義為：消費者對寬頻網路業者之期望與實際知覺到的服務，對整體的服務優異程度的主觀判斷，將從有形性、可靠性、反應性、保證性、關懷性等五個構面觀察服務品質。並參考 Parasuraman et al. (1991) 與 Javalgi & Moberg (1997) 所發展之服務品質衡量量表，共計 16 題，以李克特七點尺度衡量之，分別代表非常不同意到非常同意。

## (三)關係品質

本研究將關係品質定義為：寬頻網路業者與顧客維持良好關係的程度，將從信任與承諾兩方面觀察關係品質。將信任定義為：交易關係中顧客相信寬頻網路業者會以顧客的長期利益為考量，並認為其可以信任之程度。將承諾定義為：顧客渴望與寬頻網路業者繼續維持有價值關係之動機的程度。參考 Crosby et al. (1990)、Smith (1998) 與 Morgan & Hunt (1994) 所發展之關係品質衡量量表，共計 6 題，以李克特七點尺度衡量之，分別代表非常不同意到非常同意。

### (四)轉換成本

本研究將轉換成本定義為：消費者轉換寬頻網路業者時，本身知覺到所有因素會造成轉換障礙進而造成轉換困難的程度,將從損失績效成本及沉沒成本觀察顧客的轉換成本。將損失績效成本定義為：消費者與供應商的關係終止時,知覺所失去原供應商回饋顧客之利益及補貼的程度。將沉沒成本定義為：消費者轉換寬頻網路業者時,知覺其過去在建立、維持消費關係所產生無法回收的時間、金錢與投資成本的程度。參考 Jones et al. (2002)、Burnham et al. (2003) 與 Maute & Forrester (1993) 所發展之轉換成本衡量量表,共計 6 題,以李克特七點尺度衡量之,分別代表非常不同意到非常同意。

### (五)顧客忠誠

本研究將顧客忠誠定義為：消費者對寬頻網路業者所表現出正面積極的程度,將從態度忠誠與行為忠誠兩方面衡量顧客忠誠。將態度忠誠定義為：消費者在心理層面對於某一品牌的喜歡或偏好程度。將行為忠誠定義為：消費者對於某一品牌實際重複購買之程度。參考 Bowen et al. (2001) 與 Javalgi et al. (1997) 所發展之顧客忠誠衡量量表,共計 5 題,以李克特七點尺度衡量之,分別代表非常不同意到非常同意。

## 四、研究對象及資料蒐集方法

根據資策會 2006 年臺灣地區家庭寬頻用戶數統計資料顯示,臺灣地區家庭寬頻用戶數以北部地區,包括臺北縣市、基隆市、宜蘭縣、桃園縣、新竹縣市等五個地區,家庭寬頻用戶數佔臺灣地區家庭寬頻用戶數之 52%,達半數以上,用戶集中且具有代表性,因此本研究第一步選擇臺灣北部這五個地區申請寬頻網路之消費者為研究對象。

選購電腦產品之消費者較有可能使用寬頻網路服務,因此本研究第二步選擇在臺灣北部五個地區之 3C 賣場,利用結構性問卷訪問消費者,以人員訪問法蒐集初級資料。至於 3C 賣場的選擇,目前臺灣北部五個地區全國電子共有 126 家門市,燦坤 3C 共有 86 家門市,因此本研究選定以臺灣北部五個地區全國電子門市為調查地點,訪問時段涵蓋中午、下午、傍晚三個時段,以提高樣本的代表性,訪問有實際申請寬頻網路服務且有意願填寫之寬頻網路消費者。

問卷設計完成後,在臺北縣全國電子公司的門市進行前測,發出 50 份問卷,前測結果各變數之 Cronbach's α 值分別為關係行銷結合類型 0.9139,服務品質為 0.9509，關係品質為 0.9408，轉換成本為 0.8461，顧客忠誠為 0.8990，顯示問卷具有良好信度。正式問卷採用人員訪問的便利抽樣法進行調查，共發出 429 份問卷，並當場回收問卷。

# 肆‧研究結果與討論

## 一、樣本描述

　　本研究針對臺灣北部五個地區有申請寬頻網路之消費者進行問卷調查，按照五個地區寬頻網路用戶數比例分配樣本，共發出 429 份問卷，扣除無效問卷 22 份，共蒐集到有效樣本 407 份，有效樣本回收率為 95%。本研究的受訪者在性別分類上，男性消費者 (53%) 比女性消費者 (47%) 多；年齡主要集中於 21~30 歲 (56%)，其次為 31~40 歲 (34%) 的消費者；所得分布最多的是 19,999 元以下 (41%)，其次是 20,000-29,999 元 (26%) 的消費者；受訪者的職業以金融保險業 (20%) 族群最多，其次是一般服務業 (17%)。

## 二、信度與效度分析

　　信度分析是以 Cronbach's α 係數來判斷問卷的內部一致性與穩定性。周文賢 (2002) 提出的信度判定準則，α 係數高於 0.7 代表高信度，介於 0.7 與 0.35 間代表信度尚可，低於 0.35 則代表低信度。本研究各變數信度分析結果整理如表一所示，由表中數據可知，本研究各研究變數之 Cronbach's α 係數介於 0.7541 與 0.9462 之間，研究變數各構面之 Cronbach's α 係數介於 0.7472 與 0.8569 之間，皆高於 0.7，表示本研究問卷題項具有良好信度。

　　效度是表示量表能否真正量測出所想要測量的指標。本研究之問卷內容係參考過去學者的文獻與衡量題項，且經由前測後修定而成，因此應具有內容效度；此外本研究另以因素分析中的因素負荷量判定其建構效度，參考邱皓政 (2003) 的觀點，當衡量項目的因素負荷量高於 0.5 時，表示該測量問卷的品質良好，各項目的適切度高，具有良好的建構效度。本研究各研究變數題項因素負荷量皆高於 0.5，表示本研究問卷題項具有良好的建構效度。

　　區別效度需要求出所有潛在變數中，兩兩之間是否具有區別，也就是兩兩變數之間的檢定都必須具有統計顯著性，才能宣稱具有區別效度。本研究參考黃芳銘 (2004) 的觀點，求出兩兩變數間的相關係數矩陣與標準誤，並以 t 檢定檢測兩兩變數間是否有顯著的區別，檢測結果整理如表二所示。

表一　正式問卷信度分析結果

| 變數與構面 | | 衡量題數 | Cronbach's α 係數 | | |
| --- | --- | --- | --- | --- | --- |
| | | | 構面 | 變數 | 整體 |
| 關係行銷結合類型 | 財務性 | 3 | 0.7534 | 0.8880 | 0.9637 |
| | 社交性 | 3 | 0.8094 | | |
| | 結構性 | 5 | 0.8569 | | |
| 服務品質 | 有形性 | 3 | 0.7472 | 0.9462 | |
| | 可靠性 | 3 | 0.8402 | | |
| | 反應性 | 4 | 0.8507 | | |
| | 保證性 | 3 | 0.8245 | | |
| | 關懷性 | 3 | 0.7941 | | |
| 關係品質 | 信任 | 3 | 0.7894 | 0.8801 | |
| | 承諾 | 3 | 0.8186 | | |
| 轉換成本 | 損失績效成本 | 3 | 0.8077 | 0.8623 | |
| | 沉沒成本 | 3 | 0.7833 | | |
| 顧客忠誠 | 態度忠誠 | 2 | 0.8031 | 0.7541 | |
| | 行為忠誠 | 3 | 0.7958 | | |

表二　區別效度分析結果

| 比較變數 | 相關係數<br>(有考慮誤差) | 標準誤 | t 值 |
| --- | --- | --- | --- |
| 關係行銷結合類型－服務品質 | 0.74 | 0.03 | -8.76 |
| 關係行銷結合類型－關係品質 | 0.75 | 0.04 | -6.25 |
| 服務品質－關係品質 | 0.94 | 0.02 | -3 |
| 關係行銷結合類型－轉換成本 | 0.72 | 0.04 | -7 |
| 服務品質－轉換成本 | 0.86 | 0.03 | -4.67 |
| 關係品質－轉換成本 | 0.89 | 0.03 | -3.67 |
| 關係行銷結合類型－顧客忠誠 | 0.64 | 0.06 | -6 |
| 服務品質－顧客忠誠 | 0.75 | 0.05 | -5 |
| 關係品質－顧客忠誠 | 0.89 | 0.06 | -1.83 |
| 轉換成本－顧客忠誠 | 0.71 | 0.06 | -4.83 |

由表二的數據可知，關係品質與顧客忠誠此兩兩變數的比較符合 0.10 的顯著水準，亦即 t 檢定值小於-1.645，而其餘兩兩變數的比較皆符合 0.05 的顯著水準，亦即 t 檢定值小於-1.96 (Kim et al., 2008)，因此可以宣稱本研究兩兩變數間有顯著的區別，亦即量表具有區別效度。

# 三、相關分析與共線性檢定

本研究以 Pearson 積差相關分析檢視各研究變數之間的關聯性，各變數之間的相關分析表整理如表三所示。由表三的數據可知，各變數之間都呈現顯著正相關。

表三　　Pearson 積差相關分析表

| 變數 | 1 | 2 | 3 | 4 | 5 |
|---|---|---|---|---|---|
| 關係行銷結合類型 | 1.000 | | | | |
| 服務品質 | 0.648**<br>(0.000) | 1.000 | | | |
| 關係品質 | 0.615**<br>(0.000) | 0.832**<br>(0.000) | 1.000 | | |
| 轉換成本 | 0.568**<br>(0.000) | 0.740**<br>(0.000) | 0.730**<br>(0.000) | 1.000 | |
| 顧客忠誠 | 0.424**<br>(0.000) | 0.581**<br>(0.000) | 0.682**<br>(0.000) | 0.528**<br>(0.000) | 1.000 |

在進行複迴歸分析前，必須先檢測自變數之間是否有共線性的問題存在。要判斷研究中有無共線性之情況，一般可由變異數膨脹因子 (variance inflation factor, VIF) 來加以判別。Kamstra & Kennedy (1998) 指出若 VIF 值大於 10，就會有共線性的問題產生。

本研究若個別以信任、承諾、損失績效成本、沉沒成本為依變數，則自變數關係行銷結合類型與服務品質的所有構面其 VIF 值介於 1.62~3.72，皆小於 10；若個別以態度忠誠、行為忠誠為依變數，則自變數關係品質與轉換成本的所有構面其 VIF 值介於 2.10~2.98，皆小於 10，顯示本研究並無共線性的問題。

# 四、假説檢定

## (一)關係行銷結合類型對關係品質的影響效果

關係行銷結合類型對關係品質影響的迴歸分析整理如表四所示。由表四的數據可知，F=65.339，P=0.000＜0.01，財務性、社交性與結構性結合可解釋關係品質中之信任 32.2%的變異量，表示模式具有解釋能力，同時 D-W 值為 1.667，介於 1.5 至 2.5 之間，顯示殘差項之間無自我相關存在（邱皓政，2003）。財務性、社交性與結構性結合對信任皆呈現顯著的正向影響，而由 β 係數可知，結構性結合對信任的影響最大 (0.337)，財務性的結合次之 (0.209)，而社交性結合的影響則最小 (0.124)。根據以上檢定結果，結構性結合對信任的影響大於社交及財務性結合，但財務性結合對信任的相對影響力大於社會性結合，所以假設 1-1 未獲得支持。

再由表四數據可知，F=69.790，P=0.000＜0.01，財務性、社交性與結構性結合可解釋關係品質中之承諾 33.7%的變異量，表示模式具有解釋能力，同時 D-W 值為 1.651，顯示殘差項之間無自我相關存在。財務性、社交性與結構性結合對於承諾皆呈現顯著的正向影響，而由 β 係數可知，結構性結合對承諾的影響最大 (0.300)，財務性結合次之 (0.272)，而社交性結合的影響則最小 (0.115)。根據以上檢定結果，結構性結合對承諾的影響大於社交及財務性結合，但財務性結合對承諾的相對影響力大於社會性結合，所以假設 1-2 未獲得支持。假說 1-1 及假說 1-2 均未獲得支持，因此假說 1 未獲得支持。

表四　關係行銷結合類型對關係品質影響的迴歸分析

| 自變數 \ 應變數 | | 關係品質 | |
|---|---|---|---|
| | | 信任 | 承諾 |
| 關係行銷<br>結合類型 | 財務性 | 0.209** (0.000) | 0.272** (0.000) |
| | 社交性 | 0.124** (0.015) | 0.115** (0.023) |
| | 結構性 | 0.337*** (0.000) | 0.300*** (0.000) |
| F 值 | | 65.339*** | 69.790*** |
| P 值 | | 0.000 | 0.000 |
| $\overline{R}^2$ | | 0.322 | 0.337 |
| D-W 值 | | 1.667 | 1.651 |

## (二)關係行銷結合類型對轉換成本的影響效果

　　關係行銷結合類型對轉換成本影響的迴歸分析整理如表五所示。由表五的數據可知，F=57.895，P=0.000＜0.01，財務性、社交性與結構性結合可解釋轉換成本中之損失績效成本 29.6%的變異量，表示模式具有解釋能力，同時 D-W 值為 1.835，顯示殘差項之間無自我相關存在。財務性、社交性與結構性結合對損失績效成本皆呈現顯著的正向影響，由 β 係數可知，結構性結合對損失績效成本的影響最大 (0.345)，財務性結合次之 (0.159)，而社交性結合的影響則最小 (0.137)。根據以上檢定結果，結構性結合對損失績效成本的影響大於社交及財務性結合，但財務性結合對損失績效成本的相對影響力大於社會性結合，因此假設 2-1 未獲得支持。

　　再由表五數據可知，F=41.965，P=0.000＜0.01，財務性、社交性與結構性結合可解釋轉換成本中之沉沒成本 23.2%的變異量，表示模式具有解釋能力，同時 D-W 值為 1.837，顯示殘差項之間無自我相關存在。財務性、社交性與結構性結合對沉沒成本皆呈現顯著的正向影響，由 β 係數可知，結構性結合對沉沒成本的影響最大 (0.294)，社交性結合次之 (0.167)，而財務性結合的影響則最小 (0.112)。根據以上檢定結果， 結構性結合對 沉沒成本的影響大於社交及財務性結合，社交性結合對沉沒成本的相對影響力大於財務性結合，所以假設 2-2 獲得支持。假說 2-1 未獲得支持，假說 2-2 獲得支持，因此假說 2 獲得部分支持。

表五　　關係行銷結合類型對轉換成本影響的迴歸分析

| 自變數 ＼ 應變數 | | 轉換成本 | |
|---|---|---|---|
| | | 損失績效成本 | 沉沒成本 |
| 關係行銷結合類型 | 財務性 | 0.159*** (0.000) | 0.112** (0.047) |
| | 社交性 | 0.137*** (0.009) | 0.167*** (0.002) |
| | 結構性 | 0.345*** (0.000) | 0.294*** (0.000) |
| F 值 | | 57.895*** | 41.965*** |
| P 值 | | 0.000 | 0.000 |
| $\overline{R}^2$ | | 0.296 | 0.232 |
| D-W 值 | | 1.835 | 1.837 |

### (三)服務品質對關係品質的影響效果

服務品質對關係品質影響的迴歸分析整理如表六所示。由表六的數據可知，F=57.167，P=0.000＜0.01，有形性、可靠性、反應性、保證性及關懷性可解釋關係品質中之信任 61.5%的變異量，表示模式具有解釋能力，同時 D-W 值為 1.945，顯示殘差項之間無自我相關存在。服務品質的 5 個構面對信任的影響皆呈顯著的正向影響，因此假說 3-1 獲得強烈支持。

再由表六的數據可知，F=117.751，P=0.000＜0.01，有形性、可靠性、反應性、保證性及關懷性可解釋關係品質中之承諾 59%的變異量，表示模式具有解釋能力，同時 D-W 值為 1.757，顯示殘差項之間無自我相關存在。服務品質的 5 個構面對於承諾皆呈顯著的正向影響，因此假說 3-2 獲得強烈支持。假說 3-1 獲得強烈支持，假說 3-2 獲得強烈支持，所以假說 3 獲得強烈支持。

表六　服務品質對關係品質影響的迴歸分析

| 自變數 | 應變數 | 關係品質 | |
| --- | --- | --- | --- |
| | | 信任 | 承諾 |
| 服務品質 | 有形性 | 0.126*** (0.007) | 0.111** (0.022) |
| | 可靠性 | 0.266*** (0.000) | 0.178*** (0.003) |
| | 反應性 | 0.161*** (0.007) | 0.153** (0.013) |
| | 保證性 | 0.155*** (0.007) | 0.139** (0.019) |
| | 關懷性 | 0.180*** (0.001) | 0.290*** (0.000) |
| F 值 | | 57.167*** | 117.751*** |
| P 值 | | 0.000 | 0.000 |
| $\overline{R}^2$ | | 0.615 | 0.590 |
| D-W 值 | | 1.945 | 1.757 |

### (四)服務品質對轉換成本的影響效果

服務品質對轉換成本影響的迴歸分析整理如表七所示。由表七的數據可知，F=81.900，P=0.000＜0.01，有形性、可靠性、反應性、保證性及關懷性可解釋轉換成本中之損失績效成本 49.9%的變異量，表示模式具有解釋能力，同時 D-W 值為 1.756，顯示殘差項之間無自我相關存在。服務品質的 5 個構面中除可靠性外，其餘 4 個構面對損失績效成本皆呈顯著的正向影響，因此假說 4-1 獲得部分支持。

再由表七的數據可知，F=57.167，P=0.000＜0.01，有形性、可靠性、反應性、保證性及關懷性可解釋轉換成本中之沉沒成本40.9%的變異量，表示模式具有解釋能力，同時D-W值爲1.945，顯示殘差項之間無自我相關存在。服務品質的5個構面中除可靠性外，其餘4個構面對沉沒成本皆呈顯著的正向影響，因此假說4-2獲得部分支持。假說4-1及假說4-2均獲得部分支持，所以假說4獲得部分支持。

表七　　服務品質對轉換成本影響的迴歸分析

| 自變數 | 應變數 | 轉換成本 | |
|---|---|---|---|
| | | 損失績效成本 | 沉沒成本 |
| 服務品質 | 有形性 | 0.139*** (0.009) | 0.132** (0.023) |
| | 可靠性 | 0.053 (0.416) | 0.099 (0.162) |
| | 反應性 | 0.299*** (0.000) | 0.029** (0.162) |
| | 保證性 | 0.186*** (0.004) | 0.151** (0.033) |
| | 關懷性 | 0.122** (0.043) | 0.189*** (0.004) |
| F 值 | | 81.900*** | 57.167*** |
| P 值 | | 0.000 | 0.000 |
| $\overline{R}^2$ | | 0.499 | 0.409 |
| D-W 值 | | 1.756 | 1.945 |

## (五)關係品質對顧客忠誠的影響效果

關係品質對顧客忠誠影響的迴歸分析整理如表八所示。由表八的數據可知，F=26.548，P=0.000＜0.01，信任及承諾可解釋態度忠誠11.2%的變異量，表示模式具有解釋能力，同時D-W值爲1.905，顯示殘差項之間無自我相關存在。關係品質的信任與承諾對顧客態度忠誠皆呈顯著的正向影響，因此假說5-1獲得支持。

再由表八的數據可知，F=192.588，P=0.000＜0.01，信任及承諾可解釋行爲忠誠48.6%的變異量，表示模式具有解釋能力，同時D-W值爲1.631，顯示殘差項之間無自我相關存在。關係品質的信任與承諾對顧客行爲忠誠皆呈顯著的正向影響，因此假說5-2獲得強烈支持。假說5-1獲得支持，假說5-2獲得強烈支持，所以假說5獲得支持。

表八　關係品質對顧客忠誠影響的迴歸分析

| 自變數 | 應變數 | 顧客忠誠 | |
|---|---|---|---|
| | | 態度忠誠 | 行為忠誠 |
| 關係品質 | 信任 | 0.153** (0.029) | 0.399*** (0.000) |
| | 承諾 | 0.211*** (0.003) | 0.349*** (0.000) |
| F 值 | | 26.548*** | 192.588*** |
| P 值 | | 0.000 | 0.000 |
| $\overline{R}^2$ | | 0.112 | 0.486 |
| D-W 值 | | 1.905 | 1.631 |

## (六)轉換成本對顧客忠誠的影響效果

　　轉換成本對顧客忠誠影響的迴歸分析整理如表九所示。由表九的數據可知，F=13.164，P=0.000＜0.01，損失績效成本及沉沒成本可解釋態度忠誠 5.7%的變異量，表示模式具有解釋能力，同時 D-W 值為 1.917，顯示殘差項之間無自我相關存在。轉換成本中的損失績效成本對顧客態度忠誠呈現不顯著，但沉沒成本對於態度忠誠呈現顯著的正向影響，因此假說 6-1 獲得部分支持。

　　再由表九的數據可知，F=94.117，P=0.000＜0.01，損失績效成本及沉沒成本可解釋行為忠誠 31.4%的變異量，表示模式具有解釋能力，同時 D-W 值為 1.647，顯示殘差項之間無自我相關存在。轉換成本中的損失績效成本與沉沒成本對行為忠誠皆呈顯著的正向影響，因此假說 6-2 獲得強烈支持。假說 6-1 獲得部分支持，假說 6-2 獲得強烈支持，所以假說 6 獲得部分支持。

表九　轉換成本對於顧客忠誠影響的迴歸分析

| 自變數 | 應變數 | 顧客忠誠 | |
|---|---|---|---|
| | | 態度忠誠 | 行為忠誠 |
| 轉換成本 | 損失績效成本 | 0.061 (0.344) | 0.435*** (0.000) |
| | 沉沒成本 | 0.202*** (0.002) | 0.171*** (0.002) |
| F 值 | | 13.164*** | 94.117*** |
| P 值 | | 0.000 | 0.000 |
| $\overline{R}^2$ | | 0.057 | 0.314 |
| D-W 值 | | 1.917 | 1.647 |

# 五、討論

## (一)關係行銷結合類型對關係品質有不同程度的正向影響沒有獲得支持

　　本研究假說 1 沒有獲得支持的原因，可能是因為消費者較注重的還是價格上的優惠。社交性的結合期望的是和消費者能建立長久的關係，針對不同的個體使用客製化的服務以滿足不同的需求，例如銷售人員能記住每一位消費者的背景及喜好，不用等到消費者親自提及，所需求的產品與服務就已經準備好了，此舉通常能使消費者倍感窩心，以期建立長期性的良好關係。但本研究實證結果顯示，給予消費者較低的價格、贈品或紅利，其影響比社交性結合還要大。寬頻網路技術已漸趨成熟，每家廠商所能提供的產品與服務也都大同小異，消費者要比較的很自然就會落在價格上的差異了，只要另一家廠商的價格較優惠，消費者就會選擇此家廠商所提供的產品與服務，而不是選擇社交性結合較強的廠商。

## (二)關係行銷結合類型對轉換成本之損失績效成本有不同程度的正向影響沒有獲得支持

　　本研究的假說 2-1 沒有獲得支持的原因，可能是因為損失績效成本代表的是當顧客與供應商的關係終止時，顧客所失去的原供應商回饋顧客之利益及補貼 (Maute & Forrester, 1993)，消費者覺得所失去的財務性優惠比起社交性方面還要來得嚴重。當消費者在轉換供應商時，所感受到的立即損失即為與原本廠商所累積的優惠方案或紅利折扣方面，而較不注重所損失的社交性關係，因此使得本研究之結果呈現財務性結合對損失績效成本的影響大於社交性結合。

## (三)服務品質之可靠性對轉換成本有顯著的正向影響沒有獲得支持

　　Parasuraman et al. (1988) 所提出服務品質之可靠性是指服務人員表現出來的可靠度與一致性，以及能正確提供其所承諾服務的能力。本研究的假說 4-1 及 4-2 中服務品質之可靠性對轉換成本會有顯著的正向影響未獲得支持，可能是因為消費者對各家廠商服務品質之可靠性都深具信心或者根本都不具信心，導致服務品質之可靠性對轉換成本沒有顯著的正向影響。當消費者對各家廠商服務品質之可靠性都深具信心時，在轉換廠商時，消費者心目中對可靠性並沒有太大的差別感受，反之亦然。

## (四)轉換成本之損失績效成本對態度忠誠會有顯著的正向影響沒有獲得支持

Maute & Forrester (1993) 認為損失績效成本是指當與供應商的關係終止時，顧客所失去的原供應商回饋顧客之利益及補貼。由本研究假說 1 與假說 2-1 可知，消費者對財務性關係行銷結合類型比起社交性還要來得重視，消費者較關心的是價格、利益及補貼，但 Berry & Parasuraman (1991)、Berry (1995)、Armstrong & Kotler (2000) 皆指出，由財務性動機而形成的關係結合所帶給企業的競爭優勢，通常都不易維持長久，也就是說只要競爭對手可以在價格上提供更吸引消費者的低價，消費者便可能轉而投靠競爭者，而沒有所謂的忠誠可言，本研究假說 6-1 未獲支持的可能原因推測即為此一原因。

# 伍‧結論與建議

## 一、研究結論

關係行銷結合類型對關係品質有顯著正向影響。根據研究結果發現，關係行銷結合類型對關係品質有顯著的正向影響，雖然三種關係行銷結合類型對關係品質的影響程度順序與研究假說的推論並沒有完全相符，但是仍舊以結構性結合為最高，代表結構性結合是提升顧客對廠商的信任與承諾最有效的策略。

關係行銷結合類型對轉換成本有顯著的正向影響。根據研究結果發現，關係行銷結合類型對轉換成本有顯著的正向影響，雖然三種關係行銷結合類型對轉換成本的損失績效成本的影響程度與研究假說的推論並不完全一致，但三種關係行銷結合類型對轉換成本都有顯著的正向影響，表示關係行銷結合類型可以有效提升顧客的轉換成本。

服務品質對關係品質有顯著的正向影響。根據研究結果發現，服務品質對關係品質有顯著的正向影響，表示企業服務品質的好壞，可以決定顧客是否願意信任該企業及對該企業的承諾，雖然目前所有企業都強調服務品質，服務品質確實可以有效的提升顧客與企業之間的關係品質。

服務品質對轉換成本有顯著的正向影響。根據研究結果發現，除可靠性外，服務品質的其餘構面對轉換成本皆有顯著的正向影響，因此當消費者欲轉換供應商而考量到轉換成本時，企業的服務品質好壞，會成為消費者衡量轉換成本的一項重要因素，而當消費者感受到愈優良的服務品質，其知覺到的轉換成本也愈高。

　　關係品質對顧客忠誠有顯著的正向影響。根據研究結果發現，關係品質對於顧客忠誠有顯著的正向影響，表示當顧客對企業的信任與承諾程度愈高，愈願意持續對該企業表現忠誠行為。

　　轉換成本對顧客忠誠有顯著的正向影響。根據研究結果發現，轉換成本中的沉沒成本對顧客的態度忠誠；轉換成本中的損失績效成本與沉沒成本對顧客的行為忠誠皆有顯著的正向影響，因此對顧客而言，轉換成本的存在可以使顧客在轉換供應商時，因為受到轉換成本的限制而持續與該企業保持交易關係。

# 二、管理意涵

## (一)理論意涵

### 1.支持關係行銷結合類型的影響效果

　　Berry & Parasuraman (1991) 與 Berry (1995) 的研究指出，企業所採用的關係行銷可分成三種與顧客結合的類型，並認為關係行銷實現的層級愈高，表示顧客與公司的結合的強度也愈強。本研究實證結果證實，三種層級的關係行銷結合類型皆確實可以有效提升顧客的關係品質與轉換成本，而在影響程度方面，則和 Berry & Parasuraman (1991) 與 Berry (1995) 所提出的看法稍有不同，本研究結果發現，對於臺灣的寬頻網路業者的顧客而言，以結構性結合對關係品質與轉換成本的影響程度最大，但在社交性結合與財務性結合方面，則是以財務性結合的影響程度大於社交性結合。

### 2.彌補影響轉換成本因素的不足

　　根據 Burnham et al. (2003) 的看法，要打破「滿意的迷思」，行銷人員應該對各種影響顧客保留的因素進行深入瞭解，因此討論轉換成本可說是相當重要的一環，過去有關轉換成本的研究，大多是單獨探討轉換成本對顧客忠誠的影響，本研究嘗試在關係行銷的研究當中納入轉換成本，藉此瞭解轉換成本在關係行銷中的影響效果。根據本研究實證結果發現，三種關係行銷結合類型與服務品質的有形性、反應性、保證性與關懷性等因素，都可以有效的提升顧客的轉換成本，此一發現彌補了過去較少文獻探討哪些因素可以有效提升顧客在轉換時所知覺到的轉換成本，因此豐富了相關研究之文獻。

## (二)實務意涵及對廠商的建議

### 1.有效的運用不同層次的關係行銷結合類型

根據研究結果發現，不同的關係行銷結合類型對消費者有不同程度的影響，其中以結構性結合的影響力最大，因此廠商可提供附加價值服務，例如提供網路信箱、色情守門員或網路相簿等不同的加值服務來提升顧客對業者的信任與承諾，或經由提供這些加值服務使消費者因為不想轉換後失去這些加值服務，而建立起較高的轉換成本。財務性與社交性結合也都會正向影響關係品質與轉換成本，表示廠商可運用財務性的價格促銷或給予現有顧客較優惠續約價格；運用社交性結合，例如在顧客生日或特別節慶時給予賀卡，使顧客有受到個別重視的感覺等，都可以有效提升顧客對業者的信任、承諾與轉換成本，進而提升顧客忠誠。

經由實證結果發現，社交性結合的影響小於財務性結合，因此對廠商來說，在社交性結合方面的運用還有可發揮的空間，雖然目前廠商大多以價格方面的誘因來吸引或維持顧客，但財務性結合可以在短時間內刺激銷售量，就長期而言，在競爭激烈的市場中，只要競爭對手可以在價格上提供更吸引顧客的誘因，顧客便有可能興起轉換供應商的念頭。因此廠商可以加強社交性結合的手法，例如在重要節日時，親自以電話表達恭賀，或定期與顧客接觸，例如每隔一段期間便對顧客進行滿意度的訪問，使顧客有受到重視或有與眾不同的感覺，都可以使顧客感覺與業者有持續性的接觸。

### 2.致力追求顧客忠誠

本研究發現關係品質可以提升顧客之態度忠誠與行為忠誠，因此廠商希望爭取忠誠顧客，可加強建立與使用足以影響顧客關係品質的因素，此外轉換成本對顧客忠誠也是一個相當重要的因素，雖然損失績效成本也許無法提升顧客對某一企業真心的態度忠誠，但卻可提升顧客之行為忠誠，意即可以用來做為防止顧客轉換供應商的一個重要因素，所以廠商可以經由關係品質來提升顧客的態度忠誠，利用轉換成本來提升消費者的行為忠誠，由此兩方面同時提升顧客忠誠，以期望將顧客的流失率降到最低限度。

# 三、研究限制及後續研究建議

## (一)研究限制

本研究在研究設計上雖盡可能做到嚴謹與謹慎，研究結果雖然也獲得多項重要發現，但是在研究過程中難免受到一些限制，這些限制包括(1)抽樣範圍的限制：本研究僅針對臺灣北部五個地區進行便利抽樣調查，無法涵蓋整個臺灣地區寬頻網路消費者的意見與看法，研究結果可能僅限於臺灣北部地區消費者的看法，因此若欲推論至全臺灣各地區可能會有所偏誤。(2)研究結果一般化的限制：本研究僅針對寬頻網路產業進行實證研究，對於其他服務業是否也會有相同之結果，並無法得知，因此若欲將結果推論至其他產業時，外部效度可能會有所不足。(3)假說 6-1 的解釋能力偏低：假說 6-1 迴歸模型的解釋能力為 5.7%，該模型雖然具有解釋能力，但解釋能力有偏低的現象，是本研究美中不足之處。

## (二)後續研究建議

根據本研究實證結果提出下列二點建議，供後續研究者參考：(1)探討不同特性之消費者：後續研究者可以針對不同特性之消費者進行探討，例如平均上網時間、持續使用同一家寬頻網路業者服務的期間、實際有轉換經驗的消費者，或顧客滿意程度不同的消費者，對轉換成本不同的認知等，進一步探討這些因素的影響效果。(2)研究不同產業：本研究只針對寬頻網路的消費者進行研究，後續研究者可以將此模型運用於其他服務產業並加以比較，期使模型更具有一般化的能力。

## 參考文獻

朱博湧，「鎖住客戶，獲利關鍵」，遠見雜誌，第 229 期，2005 年，頁 32-34。

周文賢，「多變量統計分析－SAS/STATISTICS 使用方法」，臺北：智勝文化事業有限公司，2002 年。

周文賢、游信益，「網路銀行服務品質、關係品質、與顧客忠誠之研究」，企業管理學報，第 65 期，2005 年 6 月，頁 31-60。

邱皓政，「社會與行為科學的量化研究與統計分析」，臺北：五南圖書出版有限公司，2003 年。

洪順慶，「行銷管理」，臺北：新陸書局股份有限公司，2005 年。

陳建文、洪嘉蓉，「服務品質、顧客滿意度與忠誠度關係之研究－以 ISP 為例」，電子商務研究，第 3 卷第 2 期，2005 年 7 月，頁 153-172。

黃芳銘，「結構方程模式理論與應用」，臺北：五南圖書出版有限公司，2004 年。

鄭士蘋、林其鋒，「人際關係、轉換成本、和行銷變數對壽險服務業顧客轉換意圖影響之研究」，管理學報，第 22 卷第 3 期，2005 年 6 月，頁 377-389。

論
文
寫
作
要
領

Armstrong, G. & P. Kotler, "Marketing: An Introduction", 5th Edition, New Jersey: Prentice Hall, 2002.

Aydin, S. & G. Ozer, "The analysis of Antecedents of Customer Loyalty in the Turkish Mobile Telecommunication Market", *European Journal of Marketing*, Vol. 39(7), 2005, pp. 910-924.

Beloucif, A., B. Donaldson & U. Kazanci , "Insurance Broker-Client Relationships: An Assessment of Quality and Duration", *Journal of Financial Services Marketing*, Vol. 8(4), 2004, pp. 327-342.

Berry, L. L. & A. Parasuraman, "Marketing Service- Competing Through Quality", New York: The Free Press, 1991.

Berry, L. L., "Relationship Marketing, Emerging Perspectives on Services Marketing", Chicago: American Marketing Association, 1983.

Berry, L. L., "Relationship Marketing of Services-Growing Interest, Emerging Perspectives", *Journal of the Academy of Marketing Science*, Vol. 23(4), 1995, pp.236-245.

Bitner, Mary Jo & Amy R. Hubbert, "Encounter Satisfaction Versus Overall Satisfaction Versus Quality: The Customer's Voice. In Service Quality: New Directions in Theory and Practice", Eds. Roland T. Rust and Richard L. Oliver. Thousand Oaks. CA: Sage, 1994.

Bloemer, Josee & Han D. P. Kasper, "The Complex Relationship between Customer Satisfaction and Brand Loyalty", *Journal of Economic Psychology*, Vol.16, 1995, pp. 311-329.

Boles, J. S., H. C. Barksdale & J. T. Johnson, "How Salespeople Build Quality Relationships: A Replication and Extension", *Journal of Business Research*, Vol. 48(1), 2000, pp.75-81.

Bowen, J. T. & S. L. Chen, "The Relationship between Customer Loyalty and Customer Satisfaction", *International Journal of Contemporary Hospitality*, Vol. 13(4 ), 2001, pp.213-217.

Burnham, T. A., J. K. Frels & V. Mahajan, "Consumer Switching Costs: A Typology, Antecedents, and Consequences", *Journal of the Academy of Marketing Science*, Vol. 31(2), 2003, pp. 109-126.

Chaudhuri, A. & M. B. Holbrook, "The Chain of Effects from Brand Trust and Brand Affect to Brand Performance: The Role of Brand Loyalty", *Journal of Marketing*, Vol. 65(2), 2001, pp. 81-93.

Chiu H. C., Y. C. Hsieh, Y. C. Li & M. Lee, "Relationship Marketing and Consumer Switching Behavior", *Journal of Business Research*, Vol. 58(12), 2005, pp.1681-1689.

Crosby, L. A., K. R. Evans & D. Cowles, "Relationship Quality in Service Selling: An Interpersonal Influence Perspective", *Journal of Marketing*, Vol. 54(3), 1990, pp. 68-81.

Dick, Alan S. & Kunal Basu., "Customer Loyalty: Toward an Integrated Conceptual Framework", *Journal of the Academy of Marketing Science*, Vol. 22(2), 1994, pp. 99-113.

DuPont, R., "Relationship Marketing: A Strategy for Consumer-Owned Utilities in a Restructured Industry", *Management Quarterly*, Vol. 38(4), 1998, pp.11-16.

Dwyer, F. R., P. H. Schurr & S. Oh, "Developing Buyer- Seller Relationships", *Journal of Marketing*, Vol. 51(2), 1987, pp. 11-27.

Etzel, Michael. J., Bruce J. Walker & William J. Stanton, "Marketing Management", 12th Edition, McGraw-Hill, Irwin, 2001.

發表論文範本

Fornell, C., "A National Customer Satisfaction Barometer: The Swedish Experience", *Journal of Marketing*, Vol. 56(1), 1992, pp. 6-16.

Fullerton, G., "The Service Quality-Loyalty Relationship in Retail Services: Does Commitment Matter? ", *Journal of Retailing and Consumer Services*, Vol. 12(2), 2005, pp. 99-111.

Gronroos, C., "A Service Quality Model and Its Marketing Implications", *European Journal of Marketing*, Vol. 18(4), 1984, pp. 36-44.

Gronroos, C., "Relationship Approach to Marketing in Service Context: The Marketing and Organizational Behavior Interface", *Journal of Business Research*, Vol. 20(1), 1990, pp. 3-11.

Hennig-Thurau, Thorsten & Alexander Klee, "The Impact of Customer Satisfaction and Relationship Quality on Customer Retention: A Critical Reassessment and Model Development", *Psychology and Marketing*, Vol. 14(8), 1997, pp. 764-797.

Hsieh, Y. C., H. C. Chiu & M. Y. Chiang, "Maintaining a Committed Online Customer: A Study Across Search- Experience-Credence Products", *Journal of Retailing*, Vol. 81(1), 2005, pp. 75-82.

Ibáñez, V. A., P. Hartmann & P. Z. Calvo, "The Antecedents of Customer Loyalty in Residential Energy Markets: Service Quality, Satisfaction, Trust and Switching Costs", *The Service Industries Journal*, Vol. 26(6), 2006, pp. 633-645.

Javalgi, R. & C. R. Moberg, "Service Loyalty: Implications for Service Providers", *Journal of Service Marketing*, Vol. 11(3), 1997, pp. 165-179.

Jones, M. A., D. L. Mothersbaugh & S. E. Beatty, "Why Customers Stay: Measuring the Underlying Dimensions of Services Switching Costs and Managing Their Differential Strategic Outcomes", *Journal of Business Research*, Vol. 55(6), 2002, pp. 441-450.

Kamstra, M. & P. Kennedy, "Combining Qualitative Forecasts Using Logit", *International Journal of Forecasting*, Vol. 14, 1998, pp.83-93.

Kim, J., J. D. Morris & J. Swait, "Antecedents of true brand loyalty", *Journal of Advertising,* Vol. 37(2), 2008, pp. 99-117.

Klemperer, P., "The Competitiveness of Markets with Switching Costs", *The Rand Journal of Economics,* Vol. 18(1), 1987, pp. 137-150.

Kotler, P., "Marketing Management", 10th Edition, New Jersey: Prentice Hall, 2000.

Lagace, R. R., R. Dahlstrom & J. B. Gassenheimer, "The Relevance of Ethical Salesperson Behavior on Relationship Quality: The Pharmaceutical Industry", *Journal of Personal Selling and Sales Management,* Vol. 11(4), 1991, pp.39-47.

Lee, J., J. Lee & L. Feick, "The Impact of Switching Costs on the Customer Satisfaction-Loyalty Link: Mobile Phone Service in France", *The Journal of Services Marketing*, Vol. 15(1), 2001, pp. 35-45.

Lehtinen, U. & J. R. Lehtinen, "Service Quality: A Study of Quality Dimensions", Unpublished Working Paper, Helsinki: Service Management Institute, Finland OY, 1982.

Lin, N. P., C. M. Weng & Y. C. Hsieh, "Relational Bonds and Customer's Trust and Commitment-A Study on the Moderating Effects of Web Site Usage", *The Service Industries Journal*, Vol. 23(3), 2003, pp. 103-124.

Lovelock, C., "Service Marketing", 3rd Edition, New Jersey: Prentice-Hall, 1991.

Maute, M. F. & W. R. Forrester, "The Structure and Determinants of Consumer Complaint Intentions and Behavior", *Journal of Economic Psychology*, Vol. 4(2), 1993, pp. 219-247.

Morgan, R. M. & S. D. Hunt, "The Commitment-Trust Theory of Relationship Marketing", *Journal of Marketing*, Vol. 58(2), 1994, pp.20-38.

Morris, M. H., J. Brunyee & M. Page, "Relationship Marketing in Practice-Myths and Realities", *Industrial Marketing Management,* Vol. 27(4), 1998, pp. 359-371.

Oliver, R. L., "Satisfaction, a Behavioral Perspective on the Consumer", New York: McGraw-Hill, 1997.

Oliver, R. L., "Whence Consumer Loyalty", *Journal of Marketing*, Vol. 63, 1999, pp.33-44.

Parasuraman, A., V. A. Zeithaml & L. L. Berry, "A Conceptual Model of Service Quality and Its Implications for Future Research", *Journal of Marketing*, Vol. 49(4), 1985, pp. 41-50.

Parasuraman, A., V. A. Zeithaml & L. L. Berry, "SERVQUAL: A Multiple-Item Scale for Measuring Customer Expectations of Service", *Journal of Retailing*, Vol. 64(1), 1988, pp.12-40.

Parasuraman, A., L. L. Berry & V. A. Zeithaml, "Understanding Customer Expectations of Service", *Sloan Management Review*, Vol. 32(3), 1991, pp.39-48.

Payne, A., M. Christopher & D. Ballantyne, "Relationship Marketing-creating Stakeholder Value", First Edition, London: Butterworth-Heinemann, 2002.

Peltier, J. W. & J. Westfall, "Dissecting the HMO-Benefits Managers Relationship: What to Measure and Why", *Marketing Health Service*, Vol. 20(2), 2000, pp. 4-13.

Peppers, D. & M. Rogers, "The One to One Future: Building Relationships One Customer at a Time", Second Edition, New York: Doubleday, 1993.

Prus, A. & D. R. Brandt, "Understanding Your Customers", *Marketing Tools,* Vol., 2(5), 1995, pp.10-14.

Sasser, W. E., R. P. Olsen & D. D. Wyckoff, "Management of Service Operations", Boston: Allyn & Bacon, 1987.

Schiffman, L. G. & L. L. Kanuk, "Consumer Behavior", Ninth Edition, New Jersey: Pearson Prentice Hall, 2006.

Selnes, Fred, "An Examination of the Effect of Product Performance on Brand Reputation, Satisfaction and Loyalty", *European Journal of Marketing*, Vol. 27(9), 1993, pp.19-35.

Shani, D. & S. Chalasani, "Exploiting Niches Using Relationship Marketing", *The Journal of Services Marketing*, Vol. 6(4), 1992, pp.43-52.

Smith, B., "Buyer-seller Relationship: Bonds, Relationship Management, and Sex-Type", *Canadian Journal of Administrative Sciences*, Vol. 15(1), 1998, pp.76-92.

Stum, D. & A. Thiry, "Building Customer Loyalty", *Training and Development Journal*, Vol. 45(4), 1991, pp.34-36.

Turner, R. H., "Family Interaction", New York: John Wiley, 1970.

Wong, A. & A. Sohal, "An Examination of the Relationship between Trust, Commitment and Relationship Quality", *International Journal of Retail and Distribution Management*, Vol. 30(1), 2002, pp.34-50.

Zeithaml, V. A. & M. J. Bitner, "Service Marketing", New York: McGraw-Hill, 1996.

# The Impacts of Relationship Marketing Bond Types of Broadband Network, Service Quality, Relationship Quality and Switching Cost on Customer Loyalty

LONG-YI LIN, CHIH-HSUAN HSU, CHUN-SHUO CHEN [*]

## ABSTRACT

This study takes ISP's consumer in north Taiwan as the research target, tries to explore the influence of relationship marketing bond types of broadband network, service quality and relationship quality, switching cost on customer loyalty. The convenience sampling method was used to collect the primary data. A total of 429 questionnaires were distributed, 407 effective samples were collected and the effective response rate was 95%. The regression analysis was used to test the hypothesis. The results were list as follow: (1) Relationship marketing bond types have significant positive influence on relationship quality and switching cost, where the structure bond is the most influencer. (2) Service quality has significant positive influence on relationship quality. (3) Service quality has significant positive influence on switching cost except the reliability. (4) Relationship quality has significant positive influence on customer loyalty. (5) Loss performance cost has significant positive influence on customer behavior loyalty, and sunk cost has significant positive influence on both customer attitude and behavior loyalty.

Keywords: relationship marketing bond types, service quality, relationship quality, switching cost, customer loyalty

[*] Long-Yi LIN, Assistant Professor, Graduate School of Management Sciences, Aletheia University. Chih-Hsuan HSU, MBA, Graduate School of Management Sciences, Aletheia University. Chun-Shuo CHEN, Doctoral Student, Department of Business Administration, National Taipei University.

# 老年經濟安全保障、理財知識與逆向抵押貸款意願之研究

林隆儀

臺北大學企業管理學系副教授

商懿匀

臺北大學企業管理學系博士班研究生

輔仁管理評論

第二十二卷第二期

中華民國一○四年五月

*Fu Jen Management Review Vol. 22, No. 2, May 2015*
*College of Management, Fu Jen Catholic University*
*Taipei, Taiwan, Republic of China*

# 老年經濟安全保障、理財知識與
# 逆向抵押貸款意願之研究

林隆儀‧商懿勻[*]

（收稿日期：103年08月26日；第一次修正：103年09月19日；
第二次修正：103年11月14日；接受刊登：103年12月29日）

**摘要**

　　近年來臺灣人口結構已邁入高齡化，老年經濟安全保障相關議題逐漸受到重視。本研究探討老年經濟安全保障與理財知識對逆向抵押貸款借款意願的影響。以大臺北地區土地銀行擁有房屋的客戶為研究對象，採便利抽樣方式進行問卷調查。研究結果顯示：(1)老年經濟安全保障對逆向抵押貸款借款意願有顯著的影響；(2)理財知識對逆向抵押貸款借款意願有顯著的影響；(3)老年經濟安全保障與理財知識的交互作用對逆向抵押貸款借款意願有顯著的影響；(4)涉入在老年經濟安全保障對逆向抵押貸款借款意願影響有顯著的干擾效果；(5)涉入在理財知識對逆向抵押貸款借款意願影響有顯著的干擾效果；(6)涉入在老年經濟安全保障與理財知識的交互作用對逆向抵押貸款借款意願影響有顯著的干擾效果。並提出相關的管理意涵及後續研究的方向。

*關鍵詞彙：老年經濟安全保障，逆向抵押貸款，理財知識，涉入*

# 壹‧緒論

　　21世紀全球人口結構高齡化，將對人類的社會制度產生重大衝擊。近年來臺灣人口結構已漸邁入高齡化的社會現象，依據內政部戶政司2013年12月的統計資料[1]，顯示65歲以上高齡人口占總人口比率由2004年的9.48%上升至2013年的11.53%。政府在高齡化加速發展的趨勢下，產生財政及福利支出的經濟衝擊及挑戰，已無法因應長者經濟安全保障的需求。因此，年長者如何增加資金來源，提升退休後所得收入，重視年長者的經濟保障，便成為一重要課題。

　　國人在「有土斯有財」的傳統觀念影響下，擁有自有住宅率高。依據行政院主計處統計資料[2]，顯示我國2012年家庭自有住宅比率達85.8%，顯示我國屬高自有住宅率國家。美國已實施多年之「逆向抵押貸款（Reverse Mortgage, RM）」制度，讓62歲以上擁有房屋所有權之住屋者，抵押其住屋予銀行、保險公司等金融機構而獲得貸款收入，再由金融機構按月支付一定數額的養老金給申請抵押貸款的年長者，一直延續到抵押人離世，之後其抵押的房地產即交由抵押

---
[*] 作者簡介：林隆儀，國立臺北大學企業管理學系副教授；商懿勻，國立臺北大學企業管理學系博士班研究生（通訊作者）。
[1] 中華民國內政部戶政司。網址：http://statis.moi.gov.tw/micst/stmain.jsp?sys=100
[2] 中華民國行政院主計處。網址：http://www.stat.gov.tw/ct.asp?xItem=34949&ctNode=538&mp=4

權人金融機構。游欣霓（2007）研究中指出辦理逆向抵押貸款對提高退休後所得確實會有影響；石決（2005）的研究認為老年經濟安全保障係指退休時所領取的各種養老金至少要達到退休前薪資所得60%至70%的所得替代率，方能享受有品質的退休生活。綜言之，本研究擬探討臺灣在高自有住宅率情形下，實施「逆向抵押貸款」，是否影響老年經濟安全保障的問題。

Lusardi & Mitchell（2005）研究分析顯示大部分美國年長者的理財知識不足，大多數皆無完整退休規劃。臺灣也是類似情形，林左裕、楊博翔、徐偉棋（2009）的研究指出，大多數年長者無完善退休規劃，亦未能達到經濟上的獨立自主，有愈來愈多人必須仰賴政府救助津貼以因應日常生活所需。由於年長者的理財知識不足、無退休規劃，以致生活窮困等老年經濟安全的議題，將成一受矚目的焦點。

借款人申辦貸款時，除了利率、借款額度的因素外，理財知識（Financial Literacy）與金融知識（Financial Knowledge）均是借款人考慮申辦貸款的重要因素。借款人擁有較豐富的理財金融知識時，愈能獲得財務的需求。另一個影響借款意願強度的概念是涉入（Involvement），當涉入程度高時，借款人的意願也高。Arora（1993）研究亦證實涉入程度可以運用到服務行銷的領域，並進一步指出若能了解涉入對期望的服務品質與認知品質之間的關係，將有助於服務行銷策略之擬定。

本研究將以大臺北地區土地銀行擁有房屋所有權的客戶為研究對象，利用問卷調查，探討老年經濟安全保障、理財知識與逆向抵押貸款意願之研究。基於上述討論，本研究目的可分述如下：(1)探討老年經濟安全保障對逆向抵押貸款借款意願的影響。(2)探討理財知識對逆向抵押貸款借款意願的影響。(3)探討老年經濟安全保障與理財知識交互作用對逆向抵押貸款借款意願的影響。(4)研究涉入在老年經濟安全保障對逆向抵押貸款借款意願影響的干擾效果。(5)研究涉入在理財知識對逆向抵押貸款借款意願影響的干擾效果。(6)研究涉入在老年經濟安全保障與理財知識交互作用對逆向抵押貸款借款意願影響的干擾效果。

# 貳・文獻探討

## 一、老年經濟安全保障

老年經濟安全問題，包括退休問題、家庭結構變遷問題與人口老化等的問題（詹宜璋，1998）；方明川（1995）以保險經濟觀點檢視老年經濟安全問題發現，長者不但需有維持自己及扶養家屬生計之能力，亦應擁有估算老年生活成本之財務規劃，同時更需在意外事故發生前預存準備才行；乃因長者退休之後經濟收入少，醫療費用相對提高，長者應如何獲得經濟支援才能過安定有尊嚴的生活，是長者人權中最重要的一環（許皆清，2000）。

20世紀初工作權、經濟權、社會福利權等長者人權的理想，應與國家政策緊密的結合，特別是勞動政策與社會福利政策等，其基本精神都是希望滿足民眾的基本生活需求（王雲東，2005）；吳老德（2000）認為長者人權應包括下列三項：(1)長者應有維持基本生活水準之所得；(2)長者應有地點、設計及價格適當之居住環境；以及(3)長者應有依個人意願參與勞動市場的機會。石泱（2005）的研究則認為老年經濟安全保障係指退休時所領取的各種養老金至少要達到退休前薪資所得60%至70%的所得替代率，方能享受有品質的退休生活；所以衡量老年經濟安全保障應視各種老年經濟安全保障制度是否完善、可否達到理想的所得替代率。

老年經濟安全保障之衡量：許皆清（2000）以健康照顧、經濟安全、居住安養、生活調適等四個構面共29個題項，採問卷調查來衡量長者生活需求；王雲東（2006）則以基本人權、參與、照護、自我實現與尊嚴等五個構面共29個題項，採問卷調查來衡量長者人權受保障的程度。

# 二、理財知識

## (一)理財知識的定義及分類

Lusardi（2008）認為理財知識（Financial Literacy）可分為基礎理財知識與進階理財知識二種。美國理財知識教育委員會（The US Financial Literacy & Education Commission）將理財知識定義為對於錢財目前與未來的使用和管理，能夠作理智判斷與採取有效行動（Basu, 2005）；Noctor, Stoney & Stradling（1992）認為理財知識係指對於錢財的使用和管理，做理智判斷與決策的能力；Schagen & Lines（1996）延伸其定義指出具有理財知識者應擁有理財的能力與態度如下：(1)對錢財管理的主要觀念有相當的了解；(2)知悉金融機構、金融體系與服務的運作；(3)對一般與特定的理財事務具有分析與綜理的能力；(4)對理財事務的管理態度是肯定、負責的。

Widdowson & Hailwood（2007）的研究認為理財知識的定義範圍廣泛，包含的要素分析如下：(1)基礎的數學技能，例如債務的利率、投資報酬率等基本計算能力；(2)明瞭特定財務決策的收益與風險，包括借款、消費、融資和投資；(3)基本財務觀念的了解，包含報酬與風險之間的取捨，不同投資與各類金融商品的主要屬性，資產分散的優點和貨幣的時間價值；(4)知道何時尋求專業建議及如何詢問，並明瞭專家所給予的意見。

理財知識的分類，依據Chen & Volpe（1998）經由個人理財知識程度的測試，將得分之平均分數比例區分為：(1)超過百分之八十，代表具有相當高的理財知識；(2)百分之六十至七十九，代表具有中等的理財知識；(3)百分之六十以下，則具有相對低的理財知識。該研究設計涵蓋個人理財的主要項目，測試的內容包括一般知識、儲蓄和借款、保險和投資等。

Worthington（2006）指出與理財知識有關的文獻可分為兩大類，一為試圖解釋各種不同模式的理財知識，如複利或單利的利息計算、通貨膨脹的影響及風險分散的觀念等；第二種是嘗試評估不同理財知識改善方案的功效；雖然這兩個主流的研究以往是被視為分別獨立的，但實際上兩者是密切且相關的，因為其評估方案的目的就是在於改善理財知識。

## （二）理財知識的重要性

大多數家庭對於退休後生活的事前準備是覺得不足夠的（Lusardi & Mitchell, 2005），其主要原因在於理財知識的普遍不足，在面臨退休之際，大部分是沒有存款且面臨重大財務困難（Lusardi & Mitchell, 2007）。由此可知，理財知識對消費者的財務決策影響很大，其辦理理財知識的研究調查對象，是針對51至56歲財產累積幾乎已達頂點的受測者，檢驗他們多項財務決策，包括房屋抵押貸款、汽車貸款及信用卡、退休準備等基本金融知識，研究中指出對理財知識的忽視，可能會帶來許多嚴重後果，包含不良借款行為等。

Noctor, Stoney & Stradling（1992）、Lusardi & Mitchell（2007）的研究皆指出了解理財知識為金融消費者理財規劃應具備的知識，包括如何規劃借款及退休準備，其中：(1)借貸規劃：金融消費者因財務需求進行借款要善加規劃，需避免不當的借款行為及膨脹自己的所得能力；(2)退休規劃：為避免年長退休欠缺收入，退休規劃應在年輕時即需籌備，若退休後收入不足因應支出，年長者應善用既有的財產取得收入，因應退休生活。

理財知識對消費者金融服務的重要性在於，每位消費者每日都會面臨到基本財務決定的制定，包含該如何花錢及省錢？如何計劃預算？到哪裡去投資？財務的風險如何處理？需要舉債多少以支應開銷？要採取何種舉債方式等？這些決定有些複雜，皆需要具備基本的理財知識（Widdowson & Hailwood, 2007）。而理財知識對金融體系穩健與效率重要性，於Widdowson & Hailwood（2007）的研究發現，理財知識對金融體系穩健與效率的影響很明顯，影響方式有下列幾種：(1)理財知識在一定的範圍內會協助家庭財務更加審慎，相對就能減少銀行等金融機構的貸款風險；(2)理財知識的增長導致消費者更小心謹慎的過濾投資及金融商品，因此促進金融機構創新回應消費者的需求，使金融體系效率提升；(3)理財知識較先進的社會，期待金融機構能加強市場紀律，尤其是對特定金融機構及其商品的風險要嚴格審議。相對地，嚴格的市場紀律要求金融機構及高規格的金融服務需審慎管理風險；(4)消息靈通的投資決策是基於進階理財知識，期望經由時間導致更有利可圖的資源配置，以反應更挑剔的方式來平衡報酬與風險，如此有助潛在的高成長率，可減低經濟週期性波動，及為長期金融穩定的優勢。

## (三)理財知識的衡量

Worthington（2006）主張衡量理財知識的變數可區分為五個構面，第一個構面是有關性別、居住區域、種族背景（語言）和年齡；第二個構面為檢視受測者的就業狀態；第三構面則是關於受教育的程度及受教育的類別；第四構面則攸關家庭結構；最後的構面則是關於家庭的收入、投資和負債；研究的方式是採取電話訪問調查，評估尺度為-2分到2分的五點尺度；分數愈大，理財知識相對愈高。

Chen & Volpe（1998）則是採用問卷調查法衡量理財知識，其問卷設計範圍包含一般知識、儲蓄和借款、保險和投資等項目，設計的題項包含個人財務知識的複選題，對理財影響的看法、意見，及人口統計資料－教育程度、種族、語言及工作經驗等，只是調查整體平均答對率僅約53%，調查中發現非主修商科的學生和女性、三十歲以下經驗不豐富之低階工作人員等，理財知識的程度較差，由此可知，美國大學學生對理財知識的認識不足，導致無法作出明智財務決策；衡量尺度即是問卷的分數，分數愈大，理財知識相對愈高。

# 三、涉入

涉入（Involvement）的概念，最早起始於社會心理學領域，Krugman（1965）為首位將涉入的研究導入行銷領域的學者，以低涉入的概念解釋電視廣告效果。此低涉入的概念，對以消費者行為理論為中心的行銷研究，產生重大影響。Traylor（1981）認為涉入是產品對消費者的意義層次或是其重要程度，層次或程度愈高為高涉入，愈低為低涉入。Zaichkowsky（1985）則將涉入定義為個人基於本身的需求、價值觀和興趣，而對關切事物所感覺到的攸關程度。Engel, Blackwell & Kollat（1995）將涉入定義為在某特定情境下，由某一刺激所激發而知覺到的個人重要性與興趣的水準。水準愈高為高涉入，反之為低涉入。

Zaichowsky（1986）依涉入對象的不同，可將涉入分為廣告涉入、產品涉入與購買涉入三大類。敘述如下：(1)廣告涉入：Krugman（1965）指出廣告涉入（Involvement with Advertisement）主要是根據消費者對於廣告訊息的關心程度，來了解消費者的涉入水準或於接觸廣告訊息時所產生的心理反應狀態，從集中精神的注意，到鬆懈地視而不見。在不同的廣告涉入程度之下，消費者對廣告的理解與所引發的態度都將產生差異；(2)產品涉入：產品涉入（Involvement with Product）是指消費者對產品的重視與投入程度（Cohen, 1983）。從對產品完全投入的自我認同，到不屑一顧的漠不關心。基本上，產品認知是消費者對商品認知的一種主觀的狀態，而這種認知的狀態會受到各種內、外在因素所影響；(3)購買涉入：Engel Blackwell & Kollat（1995）認為購買涉入（Involvement with Purchase）是指消費者對購買活動的關注程度，主要在探討當消費者處於特定購買情境時，所考慮的個人關聯性或重要性，對購買決策產生的影響；亦有學者認為購買涉入是指購買決策及購買活動所引起消費者的自我收關程度（Slama & Tashchian, 1985）。

在理性思考下，消費者會花較多的時間考慮並蒐集相關的資訊，此即為高涉入購買決策；反之，則為低涉入購買決策。而涉入程度的差異，將對消費者的行為模式有著顯著的影響，在消費者決策過程中，對某一產品的辨識能力及行為過程的深度、複雜性及範圍廣泛程度，在購買行為中會被涉入的程度及知覺風險的特性所共同影響（Celsi & Olson, 1988）。Schoell & Guiltinan（1993）的研究即顯示，依據消費者涉入程度的不同，可將其購買決策歷程分為高涉入及低涉入程度者兩類。

涉入的衡量，一般可就：(1)單一構面：即對涉入的前因僅就單一指標來考慮與衡量，例如以自我收關程度來判斷涉入（Bloch, 1982），另外有研究認為涉入的前因是以認知（Wright, 1973）、規範重要性（Traylor, 1981）或自我觀念（Bloch, 1982）等單一構面來定義；(2)多重構面：Rothschild（1979）建議以價格、購買週期的長短、選項的相似性及知覺性風險四個變項來衡量消費者心理涉入。Laurent & Kapferer（1985）則認為以重要性／興趣、誤購風險性、風險可能性、愉悅性及象徵性等五個構面來衡量涉入剖面（Involvement Profile），而不要僅以單一構面來衡量，才能完整地描述消費者對產品之涉入程度。

Zaichkowsky在1985年以語意差異法發展出一套衡量消費者對產品涉入程度的量表，稱之為個人涉入量表（Personal Involvement Inventory, PII），用以衡量消費者對產品涉入的程度，其主要的衡量構面為：(1)產品對消費者的重要性；(2)產品對消費者的價值；(3)產品對消費者的需求；(4)產品對消費者的興趣等，利用七點尺度語意差異法，衡量消費者的涉入程度，將所測得的分數加總，即為消費者個人的涉入分數，以此表示涉入的程度。

## 四、逆向抵押貸款借款

逆向抵押貸款主要是一種金融產品，讓退休長者可將住宅部分房地產權益轉化為年金所得或一筆活用的信用額度。借款人不需按期償付貸款，同時可續住該住宅直到離世、搬家或房地產轉售，之後其抵押的房地產即予以處分償付貸款，一旦貸款本息超過抵押房地產的出售價碼，抵押品的賣方或承貸者，最多只能拿到房地產出售的總價值，償付貸款不夠的部分可向保險公司求償，因為，逆向抵押貸款的有關費用已包含償還貸款不足的保險（Wang, Valdez & Piggott, 2009; Ahlstrom, Tumlinson & Lambrew, 2004; Reed & Gibler, 2003）。

然而，逆向抵押貸款之所以稱之為「逆向」，係因其有別於一般貸款的現金流量模式，一般貸款為申貸者按時支付一筆金額予以承貸者用以償還債務；而逆向抵押貸款則是反向地由承貸者按時支付一定的金額給申貸者，其支付額的產生則由轉化房屋所有權而來（Ong, 2008）。因此，逆向抵押貸款將可活化不動資產的流動性，同時協助申貸者獲取日常消費資金來源（Hancock, 1998; Rowlingson, 2006）。

申辦一般房屋抵押貸款容易因為所得太低，資格不符而被拒絕，但逆向抵押貸款只要申貸者符合申貸資格，金融機構便會核准給予貸款或核准給予一筆信用額度，且承貸者並不會要求年長屋主按期償付貸款，唯有在年長屋主離世或搬家時，貸款才算到期（黃泓智、吳文傑、林左裕、鄭雅丰，2008）。

老年人口於經濟研究領域中，常被歸類為「擁有富裕資產之低收入者（Asset-Rich But-income-Poor）」，因此，透過逆向抵押貸款提供的新型態融資選擇，不但可提升不動產的變現性與增強資金使用的多樣性（Hancock, 1998; Rowlingson, 2006）。Reed & Gibler（2003）也認為逆向抵押貸款的規劃是讓擁有房屋但欠缺收入的年長屋主能利用房屋價值取得實質資金，且在無需出售房地產的情況下，獲取定時定額的生活費及緊急支出；在美國逆向抵押貸款的制度創立之前，年長屋主利用房屋價值取得可用資金的唯一選擇是辦理傳統的房屋抵押貸款或將房屋出售，而傳統的房屋抵押貸款必需依約定按期還款，對於收入相對有限的長者而言，具有困難與擔憂，逆向抵押貸款借用房屋權益借款概念，讓屋主可同時續住該住宅中並獲得實質資金協助，提升生活品質（Fratantoni, 1999），因此，逆向抵押貸款是降低年長者貧困程度最有效的方案。儘管逆向抵押貸款可產生上述的利益，但往往因年長者了解程度不足，使得推廣的情形不如預期，因此，要明瞭哪一種逆向抵押貸款的商品對特定年長族群最有利是很重要的，最好是能增加年長屋主現有的福利，而且能改善可用資金情形以因應未來經濟衝擊。

Ahlstrom, Tumlinson & Lambrew（2004）認為逆向抵押貸款允許年長者使用房屋權益借款，而無需搬家或出售房地產，借款的款項可用來修繕房屋、付稅、貼補收入、付長期看護費及其他支出；逆向抵押貸款通常對完全擁有房屋權益或房貸抵押債務極低的屋主較有利，因貸款的數額是以房屋可出售的價值為主要依據。

將房屋做為老年社會福利保障的一環，由辦理逆向抵押貸款的金融機構來負擔年長屋主養老金的一些責任；逆向抵押貸款可協助年長者運用自己的資產取得生活所需的費用，減輕政府的社會福利財務支出（張金鶚，2009）。Ong

（2008）的研究認為人口快速老化對社會安全福利、全民健康照顧等的政府支出大幅增加，政府財政的持續性及未來世代的責任分擔，在工業化國家中自然成為重要關切的政策；因此，年長屋主的房屋價值可利用逆向抵押貸款來減緩所得太低及減少依賴政府社會福利計畫（Wang, Valdez & Piggott, 2009; Fratantoni, 1999）。

大多數年長者都擁有財產卻收入不足，使得晚年生活貧困，其主要原因在於年長者想要將財產留給下一代，致使他們「生時貧困，死後富有」（Living Poor To Die Rich）；Rowlingson（2006）建議年長者對財產要採取務實平衡的態度，應適度透過逆向抵押貸款改善晚年生活水準。由於逆向抵押貸款主要是一種金融產品（Wang, Valdez & Piggott, 2009）且逆向抵押貸款無追索權，所以美國大部分逆向抵押貸款的承貸者會要求第一順位抵押權，作為對申請貸款財產的保全措施（Reed & Gibler, 2003）；如果借款人發生借款契約所約定的情況，例如，借款人搬出已辦理逆向抵押貸款的房屋或往生，則借款人或其繼承人必須負責償還貸款，假如是出售已辦理逆向抵押貸款的房屋來還款，賣屋的價值比應償還的貸款多，則借款人或其繼承人可取回；若賣屋的價值比貸款少，則借款人或其繼承人可不用負責。

黃泓智、吳文傑、林左裕、鄭雅丰（2008）的研究認為人口老化及低生育率已是全世界各國共同的現象，平均壽命隨著經濟發展所帶來醫療及居住環境之改善而快速延長中，退休準備不足成為一個嚴重且急迫的議題，具有高可取得性的逆向房屋抵押貸款是除了國民年金、企業退休金、個人儲蓄等一般之退休來源之外的一個新的選擇。

## 五、逆向抵押貸款之衡量

對於逆向抵押貸款的推行，應視為政府重視及因應老年化社會之必要社會福利政策指標；王健安（2009）的研究在「社會福利分析」中：(1)以退休前薪資水準為「所得替代率」之基礎，當比率設定在比照先進國家的70%，且逆向抵押貸款是唯一退休後收入來源的假設下，反推回承作逆向抵押貸款之條件大致是「65歲長者終期壽命預估為85歲，在3%利率水準下，持有原始房價大約在1,000萬（貸5成）左右」。若以原始房價約500萬來看，月領之逆向抵押貸款加計其他公勞保退休金等，總計仍可達到經建會建議之理想替代率70%之目標。(2)以「逆向抵押貸款對長期照護保險之助益」來分析，其中逆向抵押貸款支應10%的醫療照顧費用並無問題，但是對於其他85%-90%屬生活照顧費用方面，不管是在「公部門」長期照護社會保障制度，或是在「私部門」保險公司現所銷售的「長期看護險」，逆向抵押貸款只能作為提升老年長期照護品質的「補充品（Complement）」或「選項」之一；所得替代率及對長期照護保險之助益即為逆向抵押貸款衡量項目，評估尺度就是需達到所得替代率的七成以上及足以支應醫療照顧費用。

　　林左裕、楊博翔、徐偉棋（2009）在「逆向房屋抵押貸款在臺推行之可行性研究」研究中，設計的問卷調查內容認為申請逆向房屋抵押貸款的意願主要受下列因素影響：(1)教育程度：教育程度愈高，對申請逆向房屋抵押貸款的意願有顯著正向關係，評估尺度分為六個等級來衡量；(2)購買保險：有購買理財型保險對有意願申請逆向房屋抵押貸款有顯著正向影響，評估尺度分為是或否來衡量；(3)資產持有：資產持有以股票、債券或基金為主者，可認為較具有金融商品投資經驗及風險負擔能力，對於申請逆向房屋抵押貸款有顯著正向影響，評估尺度分為是或否來衡量；(4)富裕程度：愈富裕愈無意願申請逆向房屋抵押貸款之可能，原因是退休後的生活準備可能很周全，評估尺度分為五個等級來衡量。(5)傳承遺產：認為父母有傳承其名下房屋給後代的義務，則對於申請逆向房屋抵押貸款之意願有顯著負向影響，評估尺度分為必要或不必要來衡量；(6)是否分居：父母較傾向與子女分居，享受獨立生活空間，較有意願於年老之時申請逆向房屋抵押貸款，評估尺度分為是或否來衡量。

# 參・研究方法

## 一、研究架構

　　本研究旨在探討老年經濟安全保障、理財知識及涉入的干擾效果對逆向抵押貸款借款意願的影響。根據研究目的與上述之文獻探討，本研究的架構如圖一所示。而為探討各變數間的影響關係並驗證假設，將採問卷設計的方式來進行。

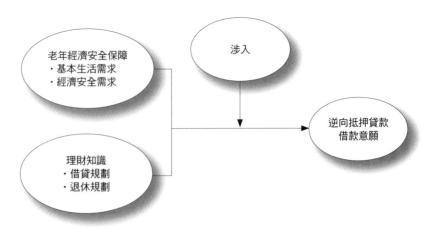

圖一　本研究觀念性架構

## 二、研究假說

### (一)老年經濟安全保障對逆向抵押貸款借款意願的影響

　　逆向抵押貸款可為長者針對目前擔保品（房屋）評定價格的最高可貸成數，申貸者可安心地將資產抵押換得定期領取之貸款年金，進行月領養老年金的估算，提供具自主性的現金流量使用，自定給付期間長短及給付金額的穩定性，來支付每月生活開銷，用以維持長者尊嚴並保持老年生活經濟的穩定與自主性（Wang, Valdez & Piggott, 2009; Ahlstrom, Tumlinson & Lambrew, 2004; Reed & Gibler, 2003）。Ong（2008）指出因逆向抵押貸款的實施使年長屋主的基本生活獲得改善，甚至提升其經濟品質，對逆向抵押貸款的借款意願具有正向的影響；黃泓智、吳文傑、林左裕、鄭雅丰（2008）的研究亦指出年長者為使經濟安全的保障更完整，申貸逆向抵押貸款確實具有正向影響使晚年生活更具尊嚴與自主性。

　　逆向抵押貸款能為長者建構更具規劃性的老年經濟安全保障，以彌補現行國民退休金之替代率不足的缺憾，是逆向抵押貸款成為長者老年退休金準備的重要融資工具之一（Wang, Valdez & Piggott, 2009; Fratantoni, 1999），同時亦可提升房產資源的優化配置，提前變現多重運用，使家庭財富最大化，亦提升晚年經濟生活品質與經濟資金需求的多樣性（Ong, 2008; Rowlingson, 2006）。林左裕、楊博翔、徐偉棋（2009）的研究亦證實改善老年生活品質及穩定日常經濟消費支出可強化逆向抵押貸款的意願並具有正向的關聯性。基於上述推論，本研究的研究假說1如下：

　　假說1：老年經濟安全保障對逆向抵押貸款借款意願有顯著的正向影響。

　　　假說1-1：基本生活需求對逆向抵押貸款借款意願有顯著正向影響。

　　　假說1-2：經濟安全需求對逆向抵押貸款借款意願有顯著正向影響。

### (二)理財知識對逆向抵押貸款借款意願的影響

　　全球人口老化現象攀升，子女沒有足夠時間與能力照顧家中長者，於是長者自身的理財知識與資源配置能力將成為退休後生活品質與資金來源的保障，緩解養老資源不足的難題，調整家庭養老負擔，化解老齡化危機的重要工具（Piggot, Sherris & Mitchell, 2006）。逆向抵押貸款的政策實施，將住宅與養老保險、社會保障與「養房防老」的概念重新整合，開拓新的金融營運範疇，為長者退休後的生活、子女經濟負擔與家庭氣氛注入更加穩定可靠的投資管道（Mitchell , Piggot, Sherris & Yow, 2006）。Noctor, Stoney & Stradling（1992）、Lusardi & Mitchell（2007）的研究皆指出了解理財知識為金融消費者理財規劃應具備的知識，其中應包括如何規劃借款及退休準備兩部分；Piggot, Sherris & Mitchell（2006）的研究指出年長者理財知識的提升，對逆向抵押貸款的借款意願有正向影響；Eschtruth, Sun & Webb（2006）的研究也證實有退休借貸規劃的長者屋主，對逆向抵押貸款的借款意願有正向的影響幫助。有鑑於此，本研究推論：

假說2：理財知識對逆向抵押貸款借款意願有顯著的正向影響。

假說2-1：借貸規劃對逆向抵押貸款借款意願有顯著正向影響。

假說2-2：退休規劃對逆向抵押貸款借款意願有顯著正向影響。

## (三)老年經濟安全保障與理財知識的交互作用對逆向抵押貸款借款意願的影響

理財知識為金融消費者理財規劃應具備的投資要件，包括如何規劃借款及退休準備等，為避免退休後欠缺收入來源，退休規劃應提前籌備（Wang, Valdez & Piggott, 2009）；因應高齡社會的到來，國人更應當提早為退休後的生活進行規劃，確保老年生活的品質與經濟自主性（Ong, 2008; Hancock, 1998; Rowlingson, 2006）。

逆向抵押貸款較傳統理財方式（包括抵押貸款與信託），更具有自我養老保障的成分，其將房產的殘餘價值轉換為現金，活化資金的運用與廣度，為晚年退休時光提供足夠的經濟支持與尊嚴。雖然國人受限於傳統財產（與不動產）繼承的刻板觀念，對於逆向抵押貸款的接受度，仍處推廣試辦階段。但林左裕、楊博翔、徐偉棋（2009）研究卻發現教育程度愈高（具較高理財知識）對申辦逆向抵押貸款意願具有顯著正向關係；其中有意願進一步了解逆向抵押貸款者，對老年經濟安全之準備具有強化的作用，由以上的論述可知，老年經濟安全保障與理財知識在年長者有意願申請逆向抵押貸款時，具有相互影響的關係，兩者的交互作用對逆向抵押貸款借款意願確實會有影響。本研究提出假說3如下：

假說3：老年經濟安全保障與理財知識的交互作用對逆向抵押貸款借款意願有顯

著的正向影響。

## (四)涉入在老年經濟安全保障對逆向抵押貸款借款意願影響的正向干擾效果

逆向抵押貸款運作方式，較一般抵押貸款與信託更具風險與不確定性，因逆向抵押貸款的承辦業務性質與申辦人身心狀況較具複雜性，例如，申辦者實際壽命與預期壽命的差異性等，使逆向抵押貸款須具備更多元性來因應不同申辦人的需求，因此，逆向抵押貸款隸屬涉入程度較高的金融產品，申辦者事前會盡可能的對於貸款方案有全盤的了解與研究，以降低內在的不確定感（Aldlaigan & Buttle, 2001; Foxall & Pallister, 1998）；其中申辦者對產品的涉入程度愈高，對購買銀行金融理財服務的意願亦愈高；Weinrobe（1987）的研究亦指出長者退休後收入會減少，而年齡愈大愈貧窮的屋主，因為想求得經濟安全的保障，所以愈有意願申請逆向抵押貸款；因此，年長者為擁有較高之經濟安全保障，當然會有意願申請逆向抵押貸款，而逆向抵押貸款屬於涉入程度較高的金融產品，因此，涉入就會產生正向干擾效果。本研究提出假說4如下：

假說4：涉入在老年經濟安全保障對逆向抵押貸款借款意願有顯著的正向干擾效果。

假說4-1：涉入在基本生活需求對逆向抵押貸款借款意願有顯著的正向干擾效果。

假說4-2：涉入在經濟安全需求對逆向抵押貸款借款意願有顯著的正向干擾效果。

## (五)涉入在理財知識對逆向抵押貸款借款意願影響的正向干擾效果

Lin & Chen（2006）研究指出產品涉入在產品知識對消費者購買決策有正向干擾效果；林左裕、黃泓智、楊博翔（2009）研究分析發現教育程度愈高（具較高理財知識），愈有意願申請逆向抵押貸款，其可歸因於教育程度愈高之受訪者，其願意接受新金融商品的程度愈高。該研究的調查問卷中有意願申請逆向抵押貸款的受訪者，其中有34%擁有碩士或博士學位。因此，擁有較高理財知識的消費者，為提升生活品質及分擔日常支出而申請逆向抵押貸款（林左裕、楊博翔、徐偉棋，2009），在逆向抵押貸款屬於涉入程度較高的金融產品，因此，涉入就會產生正向干擾效果。本研究提出假說5如下：

假說5：涉入在理財知識對逆向抵押貸款借款意願有顯著的正向干擾效果。

假說5-1：涉入在借貸規劃對逆向抵押貸款借款意願有顯著的正向干擾效果。

假說5-2：涉入在退休規劃對逆向抵押貸款借款意願有顯著的正向干擾效果。

### （六）涉入在老年經濟安全保障與理財知識的交互作用對逆向抵押貸款借款意願影響的正向干擾效果

林隆儀、曾席璋（2007）研究指出涉入在品牌策略與企業形象的組合對消費者購買意願有正向干擾效果；Chou, Chow & Chi（2006）亦指出年長者愈想改善或維持老年經濟安全，愈有意願申請逆向抵押貸款，而且教育程度較高（擁有較高理財知識）的借款人比較容易接受逆向抵押貸款的想法，也是較有意願申請逆向抵押貸款；老年經濟安全保障與理財知識在年長者有意願申請逆向抵押貸款時，具有互相影響的情形，兩者的交互作用對逆向抵押貸款借款意願會有正向的影響；林左裕、楊博翔、徐偉棋（2009）研究亦指出愈想加強老年經濟安全，而且發現教育程度愈高（擁有較高理財知識），愈有意願申請逆向抵押貸款。由以上學者的論述可知老年經濟安全保障與理財知識的交互作用對逆向抵押貸款借款意願有正向的影響，加上涉入對銀行金融理財服務購買意願有正向干擾效果，因此，涉入在老年經濟安全保障與理財知識的交互作用對逆向抵押貸款借款意願有正向干擾效果。本研究提出假說6如下：

假說6：涉入在老年經濟安全保障與理財知識的交互作用對逆向抵押貸款借款意願的影響具有顯著的正向干擾效果。

## 三、變數操作性定義

本研究探討的變數有老年經濟安全保障、理財知識、涉入及逆向抵押貸款借款意願等四部分。茲就研究變數內詳細說明如下：

## (一)自變數

　　1.老年經濟安全保障：政府對年長者基本生活、經濟安全得到保障的程度。

　　　(1) 基本生活需求：年長者的基本食衣住行、活動空間以及基本支出能得到保障。

　　　(2) 經濟安全需求：年長者退休後收入減少，因此，需要持續的經濟援助才能有安定生活的保障。

　　2.理財知識：金融消費者在現代社會因應借貸、退休規劃應具備的知識。

　　　(1) 借貸規劃：金融消費者因財務需求進行借款要善加規劃，需避免不當的借款行為及膨脹自己的所得能力。

　　　(2) 退休規劃：避免年長退休欠缺收入，退休規劃應在年輕時即需籌備，若退休後收入不足因應支出，年長者應善用既有的財產取得收入因應退休生活。

## (二)干擾變數

　　涉入：消費者對金融服務主觀認知的重視與投入程度，消費者對產品的涉入程度愈高，即代表其主觀認知的重視與投入程度愈高。

## (三)因變數

　　逆向抵押貸款借款意願：提升老年生活品質及分擔日常生活支出，而願意接受逆向抵押貸款的程度。

## 四、問卷設計

　　老年經濟安全保障本研究的問卷設計，包括五大部分，第一部分為衡量受訪者對老年經濟安全保障的基本生活需求與經濟安全需求的認同程度；第二部分為衡量受訪者對理財知識的借貸規劃與退休規劃的認同程度；第三部分為衡量受訪者對逆向抵押貸款涉入程度的高低；第四部分為衡量受訪者對逆向抵押貸款的借款意願；最後一部分則是受訪者的個人資料。

　　在老年經濟安全保障的衡量問項是參考許皆清（2000）、王雲東（2006）的問卷並加以適度修改，將老年經濟安全保障衡量構面分為：(1)基本生活需求；(2)經濟安全需求，利用兩個構面來衡量老年經濟安全保障，其中衡量基本生活需求有5個題項，衡量經濟安全需求有5個題項，總計有10個題項。

　　在理財知識的衡量問項是參考Chen & Volpe（1998）、黃春智（2008）、林芳姿（2010）的問卷並加以適度修改，將理財知識衡量構面分為：(1)借貸規劃；(2)退休規劃，利用兩個構面來衡量理財知識，其中衡量借貸規劃的構面有5

個題項，衡量退休規劃的構面有5個題項，總計有10個題項。

在涉入方面，衡量構面參考Zaichkowsky（1985）的涉入量表，並參考Lin & Chen（2006）、陳漢杰（2005）的問卷並加以適度修改，衡量涉入有5個題項。

在逆向抵押貸款的借款意願方面，衡量問項是參考林左裕、黃泓智、楊博翔（2009）的問卷並加以適度修改，衡量逆向抵押貸款借款意願有6個題項。

## 五、資料蒐集與分析方法

本研究採用人員指導的問卷訪問法（Personal Administered Questionaires），由土地銀行行員親自發放問卷與回收問卷。依據本研究之研究目的及所推論的研究假說，利用SPSS統計套裝軟體進行資料分析方法如下：

(1) 敘述性統計分析：分析受訪者之基本背景資料，藉以了解樣本之情形。

(2) 信度與效度分析：信度分析採用Cronbach's α值來衡量，數值愈高則表示其信度愈高。效度分析以「內容效度」與「建構效度」做為衡量問卷效度的工具。

(3) 相關分析：本研究以Pearson相關分析確認各變數間的相關性。

(4) 迴歸分析：本研究採用階層迴歸分析來檢定研究假說。

# 肆·研究結果分析

## 一、樣本結構

本研究以臺北市及新北市地區擁有房屋的民眾，發出問卷450份，結果收回425份問卷，回收率為94.4%，扣除資料不全與填寫錯誤的無效問卷15份，有效問卷共計410份，有效回收率為91.1%。依據問卷調查的統計結果顯示，受訪者的男女比例為45.4%和54.6%，年齡以30-40歲最多（35.6%）[3]，婚姻狀況以已婚較多（69.8%），有養育子女較多（65.9%），教育程度以大專程度最多（65.3%），職業以金融保險業最高（35.4%）。

---

[3] 逆向抵押貸款制度政策，係專為62歲以上擁有房屋所有權之長者進行解決養老生活經濟問題所提供的貸款制度，並普遍推廣運用於已開發國家之高齡社會（Aged Society）中，例如：美國、日本與澳洲等國。依據2014年內政統計年報之資料顯示，我國自1993年開始進入高齡化社會（Aging Society）（65歲以上占總人口比率突破7%），預估至2025年增為14%以上，達國際慣例所稱高齡社會，保守估計由高齡化社會轉變為高齡社會約需32年。檢視我國政府於2013年才首次推行試辦方案，欲打破國人不動產傳承的刻板思維，需透過政府積極推廣與具政策性且附有公共福利色彩之誘因。因此，因應高齡社會的到來，推估1974-1984年間出生的民眾（現年30-20歲）將會是未來邁入高齡社會的主要年齡層，此階段民眾將面對更沉重的人口老化問題，因此，該年齡階層者之思維轉變與接受度將會是逆向抵押貸款制度政策未來是否得以在我國普及運用的關鍵參考指標。可參考內政統計年報，網址：http://sowf.moi.gov.tw/stat/year/y02-01.xls

## 二、信度分析及效度分析

本研究採用Cronbach's α值作為衡量信度之量測工具。根據Guielford（1965）提出Cronbach's α係數的信度準則，α值愈大顯示構面內各問項間的相關性愈大，亦即內部的一致性愈高；當α > 0.70即代表高信度，而α > 0.60代表問卷中問項信度已可接受。本研究檢測結果皆大於0.70，顯示本研究各變數內部一致性仍相當良好。

表一　本研究變數／構面的信度分析

| 衡量變數 | 衡量變數之構面 | 題項 | Cronbach's α值 | | |
| --- | --- | --- | --- | --- | --- |
| | | | 構面 | 變數 | 整體 |
| 老年經濟安全保障 | 基本生活需求 | 1～5 | 0.955 | 0.917 | 0.884 |
| | 經濟安全需求 | 6～10 | 0.964 | | |
| 理財知識 | 借貸規劃 | 11～15 | 0.963 | 0.867 | |
| | 退休規劃 | 16～20 | 0.963 | | |
| 涉入 | | 21～25 | - | 0.963 | |
| 逆向抵押貸款借款意願 | | 26～31 | - | 0.898 | |

本研究所探討的構面與衡量項目，均根據相關的理論推演而來，且已有多數國內、外學者曾使用過的量表或衡量項目，再經多次修改後定案，因此，本研究所使用的衡量工具應能符合內容效度之要求。本研究以因素分析方法中的主成分分析，利用直交轉軸法（Orthogonal Rotation），以因素負荷量來驗證各個變數的建構效度，因素特徵值（Eigenvalue）需大於1，且以最大變異數（Varimax）法做直交轉軸後，因素負荷量絕對值需大於0.4，解釋能力達40%，表示整體測量問卷的品質良好，各題的適切度均高，具有建構效度（周文賢，2004）。本研究問卷效度分析如表二。

表二　問卷效度分析

| 變數／構面 | | 題號 | 因素負荷量 | 特徵值 | 解釋變異量（%） |
| --- | --- | --- | --- | --- | --- |
| 老年經濟安全保障 | 基本生活需求 | 1 | 0.999 | 4.377 | 87.549 |
| | | 2 | 0.691 | | |
| | | 3 | 0.999 | | |
| | | 4 | 0.690 | | |
| | | 5 | 0.998 | | |
| | 經濟安全需求 | 6 | 0.994 | 4.454 | 89.071 |
| | | 7 | 0.748 | | |

| | | 8 | 0.994 | | |
|---|---|---|---|---|---|
| | 經濟安全需求 | 9 | 0.732 | 4.454 | 89.701 |
| | | 10 | 0.985 | | |
| 理財知識 | 借貸規劃 | 11 | 0.997 | 4.450 | 89.000 |
| | | 12 | 0.740 | | |
| | | 13 | 0.997 | | |
| | | 14 | 0.732 | | |
| | | 15 | 0.993 | | |
| | 退休規劃 | 16 | 0.998 | 4.453 | 89.067 |
| | | 17 | 0.721 | | |
| | | 18 | 0.998 | | |
| | | 19 | 0.743 | | |
| | | 20 | 0.994 | | |
| | 涉入 | 21 | 0.992 | 4.443 | 88.854 |
| | | 22 | 0.747 | | |
| | | 23 | 0.992 | | |
| | | 24 | 0.732 | | |
| | | 25 | 0.979 | | |
| | 逆向抵押貸款借款意願 | 26 | 0.649 | 3.982 | 66.374 |
| | | 27 | 0.684 | | |
| | | 28 | 0.748 | | |
| | | 29 | 0.675 | | |
| | | 30 | 0.665 | | |
| | | 31 | 0.563 | | |

由表二的分析結果顯示，本研究各題項的因素負荷量皆大於0.4，且各構面的因素特徵值皆在2以上；因此，整體而言，本研究問卷除具備內容效度外，同時亦可宣稱具有良好的建構效度。

## 三、相關分析

相關係數（Coefficient of Correlation）是用以檢驗兩個變數線性相關的統計技術，其數值為一標準化分數，介於-1或+1之間，不受變數特性的影響；相關係數值愈接近正負1時，表示變數項的關聯情形愈明顯，+1或-1的相關係數稱為完全正或負相關。

本研究採用Pearson相關係數分析確認各變數與構面的關聯性，包括基本生活需求、經濟安全需求、借貸規劃、退休規劃、涉入與逆向抵押貸款借款意願。

相關分析如表三所示。

表三　變數／構面的Pearson相關分析

| 變數／構面 | 基本生活需求 | 經濟安全需求 | 借貸規劃 | 退休規劃 | 涉入 | 逆向抵押貸款借款意願 |
|---|---|---|---|---|---|---|
| 基本生活需求 | 1 | | | | | |
| 經濟安全需求 | 0.316** | 1 | | | | |
| 借貸規劃 | 0.005 | 0.026 | 1 | | | |
| 退休規劃 | 0.086 | 0.095 | 0.045 | 1 | | |
| 涉入 | 0.148** | 0.199** | 0.038 | 0.064 | 1 | |
| 逆向抵押貸款借款意願 | 0.221** | 0.232** | 0.093 | 0.115* | 0.644** | 1 |

** 在顯著水準為0.01時（雙尾），相關顯著。

* 在顯著水準為0.05時（雙尾），相關顯著。

# 四、假說檢定

本研究所蒐集的資料採用階層迴歸分析，其檢定結果整理如表四所示。

## (一)老年經濟安全保障對逆向抵押貸款借款意願的影響

由表四中模式一的檢定結果可知，其對逆向抵押貸款意願的解釋能力為45.0%（$R^2 = 0.450; \triangle R^2 = 0.450; F = 66.119$），判定模型合適性的$p < 0.01$，具有統計顯著性。共線性統計量的VIF 值皆小於10，符合迴歸分析無共線性需求（Kennedy, 1992），可知共線性不明顯，並不會影響本研究中有關統計數據的精確性與結果解釋。

其中基本生活需求之β係數為0.112，$t = 2.868$，$p < 0.05$，具有統計顯著性，表示基本生活需求對逆向抵押貸款借款意願有顯著的正向影響，故假說1-1獲得支持；經濟安全需求的β係數為0.088，$t = 2.220$，$p < 0.1$，具有統計顯著性，顯示經濟安全需求對逆向抵押貸款借款意願有顯著的正向影響，假說1-2亦獲得支持。

表四、階層迴歸分析（依變數：逆向抵押貸款借款意願）

| 自變數 | 模式一 | 模式二 | 模式三 | VIFs |
|---|---|---|---|---|
| 主效果 | | | | |
| 基本生活需求 | $0.112^{**}(2.868)$ | $0.124^{***}(3.212)$ | $0.133^{***}(3.427)$ | 1.228 |
| 經濟安全需求 | $0.088^{*}(2.220)$ | $0.074^{*}(1.891)$ | $0.070^{*}(1.790)$ | 1.239 |
| 借貸規劃 | $0.076^{*}(2.059)$ | $0.080^{*}(2.231)$ | $0.097^{*}(2.649)$ | 1.094 |
| 退休規劃 | $0.098^{*}(2.623)$ | $0.153^{***}(4.123)$ | $0.152^{***}(4.113)$ | 1.123 |
| 涉入 | $0.601^{***}(15.802)$ | $0.569^{***}(15.304)$ | $0.577^{***}(15.514)$ | 1.137 |
| 雙因子交互作用 | | | | |
| 基本生活×借貸規劃 | | $0.106^{*}(2.612)$ | $0.101^{*}(2.494)$ | 1.336 |
| 基本生活×退休規劃 | | $0.068^{*}(1.825)$ | $0.070^{*}(1.880)$ | 1.137 |
| 經濟安全×借貸規劃 | | $0.073^{*}(1.849)$ | $0.075^{*}(1.908)$ | 1.261 |
| 經濟安全×退休規劃 | | $0.071^{*}(1.911)$ | $0.078^{*}(2.097)$ | 1.132 |
| 基本生活×涉入 | | $0.122^{**}(3.174)$ | $0.123^{***}(3.202)$ | 1.209 |
| 經濟安全×涉入 | | $0.098^{*}(2.577)$ | $0.121^{**}(3.082)$ | 1.263 |
| 借貸規劃×涉入 | | $0.098^{*}(2.550)$ | $0.107^{*}(2.778)$ | 1.208 |
| 退休規劃×涉入 | | $0.065^{*}(1.767)$ | $0.067^{*}(1.816)$ | 1.105 |
| 三因子交互作用 | | | | |
| 經濟×理財×涉入 | | | $0.084^{*}(2.170)$ | 1.238 |
| F | $66.119^{***}$ | $32.101^{***}$ | $30.424^{**}$ | |
| $\triangle$F | $66.119^{***}$ | $6.411^{***}$ | $4.711^{**}$ | |
| $R^2$ | 0.450 | 0.513 | 0.519 | |
| Adjusted $R^2$ | 0.443 | 0.497 | 0.502 | |
| $\triangle R^2$ | 0.450 | 0.063 | 0.006 | |

註：$^{*}$：$p < 0.10$；$^{**}$：$p < 0.05$；$^{***}$：$p < 0.01$

## (二)理財知識對逆向抵押貸款借款意願的影響

同表四模式一的檢定結果顯示，借貸規劃的β值為0.076，t = 2.059，p < 0.1，具有統計顯著性，顯示借貸規劃對逆向抵押貸款借款意願有顯著的正向影響；退休規劃的β值為0.098，t = 2.623，p < 0.1，具有統計顯著性，表示退休規劃對逆向抵押貸款借款意願有顯著的正向影響。因此，假說2-1、假說2-2獲得支

持。

## (三)老年經濟安全保障與理財知識的交互作用對逆向抵押貸款借款意願的影響

本研究進一步檢定老年經濟安全保障與理財知識對逆向抵押貸款借款意願的交互作用，首先將所有變數進行中心化（Centering）後，再進行分析以避免共線性的問題產生（Aiken & West, 1991）。由表中數據可知，模式二可解釋逆向抵押貸款借款意願51.3%的變異量（$R^2 = 0.513$；$\triangle R^2 = 0.063$；$F = 32.101$；$p < 0.01$），VIF值皆為小於10，符合無共線性需求（Kennedy, 1992）。

依據表四中模式二之分析結果顯示，基本生活需求與借貸規劃的交互作用的β值為0.106，$t = 2.612$，$p < 0.1$；基本生活需求與退休規劃的交互作用之β值為0.068，$t = 1.825$，$p < 0.1$；經濟安全需求與借貸規劃的交互作用的β值為0.073，$t = 1.849$，$p < 0.1$；經濟安全需求與退休規劃的交互作用的β值為0.071，$t = 1.911$，$p < 0.1$。根據結果得知，老年經濟安全保障與理財知識的交互作用對逆向抵押貸款借款意願有顯著的正向影響。故研究假說3獲得支持。

## (四)涉入在老年經濟安全保障對逆向抵押貸款借款意願影響的干擾效果

探討涉入程度在老年經濟安全保障對逆向抵押貸款借款意願的干擾效果分析，其檢定結果如模式二所示，基本生活需求與涉入干擾的β值為0.122，$t = 3.174$，$p < 0.05$；經濟安全需求與涉入干擾的β值為0.098，$t = 2.577$，$p < 0.1$。

根據結果得知，基本生活需求和經濟安全需求在涉入的干擾下對逆向抵押貸款借款意願有顯著的正向影響，研究假說4-1、假說4-2獲得支持。

## (五) 涉入在理財知識對逆向抵押貸款借款意願影響的干擾效果

將涉入在理財知識對逆向抵押貸款借款意願的干擾效果進行迴歸分析，其檢定結果如模式二所示，涉入程度在借貸規劃對逆向抵押貸款借款意願的干擾效果之β值為0.098，$t = 2.550$，$p < 0.1$；退休規劃對逆向抵押貸款借款意願的影響，涉入的干擾效果之β值為0.065，$t = 1.767$，$p < 0.1$。根據結果得知，涉入在理財知識對逆向抵押貸款借款意願的影響有顯著的正向干擾效果，研究假說5-1、假說5-2亦獲得支持。

### （六）涉入在老年經濟安全保障與理財知識的交互作用對逆向抵押貸款借款意願影響的干擾效果

在探究涉入程度在老年經濟安全保障與理財知識的交互作用對逆向抵押貸款借款意願的干擾效果時，首先將所有變數進行中心化後，再進行分析以避免共線性的問題產生（Aiken & West, 1991）。由表四中數據可知，模式三整體可解釋逆向抵押貸款借款意願51.9%的變異量（$R^2 = 0.519$；$\triangle R^2 = 0.006$；$F = 30.424$），判定模型合適性的$p < 0.01$，具有統計顯著性，VIF值小於10，符合無共線性需求，並不會影響研究中統計數據的精確性與結果解釋（Kennedy, 1992）。

如模式三所示，涉入程度在經濟安全保障與理財知識的交互作用對逆向抵押貸款意願的影響中，其干擾β值為0.084，$t = 2.170$，$p < 0.1$。根據結果得知，涉入在老年經濟安全保障與理財知識的交互作用對逆向抵押貸款借款意願影響的正向干擾效果。研究假說6亦獲得支持。

# 伍・結語與建議

## 一、研究結論

本研究探討老年經濟安全保障、理財知識、涉入與逆向抵押貸款借款意願的關係，經實證分析結果，整理歸納而獲致下列的結論：

### （一）老年經濟安全保障對逆向抵押貸款借款意願有顯著正向的影響

本研究實證結果顯示，老年經濟安全保障對逆向抵押貸款借款意願確有顯著正向的影響，且老年經濟安全保障的二個構面對逆向抵押貸款借款意願皆呈現正相關，其中以基本生活需求影響程度較高（β = 0.112 > 經濟安全需求之β值0.088），代表年長者在老年經濟安全保障之中，比較在意的是基本生活能獲得實質改善，其原因可能是絕大多數年長者較無完善退休規劃，未能達到經濟上的獨立性，使得退休後的生活品質往往不如預期；再加上我國國人又普遍受「有土斯有財」的傳統觀念影響，使得大多數長者雖然擁有不動產卻在退休後無固定收入與缺乏流動資金的使用，漸漸無法支付往後的基本日常生活開銷與後續龐大的醫療健康費用等等，導致生活品質逐漸下滑，也讓愈來愈多長者晚年必須仰賴政府救助津貼得以應付日常生活基本所需。如同知名的馬斯洛需求層級理論（Maslow's hierarchy of needs）所示（Maslow, 1943），生理需求為人類最基本的需求之首，唯有先滿足其基本生活需求之後，方有可能再往下一個層級邁進與追求，此亦可解釋為何基本生活需求的滿足為長者們晚年普遍最在意的議題之因。

## (二)理財知識對逆向抵押貸款借款意願有顯著正向的影響

本研究實證結果顯示，理財知識對逆向抵押貸款借款意願確有顯著正向的影響，且理財知識的二個構面對逆向抵押貸款借款意願皆呈現正相關，其中以退休規劃影響程度較高（$\beta = 0.153 >$ 借貸規劃之$\beta = 0.080$），代表年長者重視理財知識之中，最在意的是計畫理財以求穩定退休生活、退休金不夠時要設法增加收入。

## (三)老年經濟安全保障與理財知識的交互作用對逆向抵押貸款借款意願有顯著正向的影響

本研究實證結果顯示，老年經濟安全保障與理財知識的交互作用對逆向抵押貸款借款意願有顯著正向的影響，其中以基本生活需求與借貸規劃的交互作用對逆向抵押貸款借款意願影響程度最大（$\beta = 0.106$），而基本生活需求與退休規劃的交互作用對逆向抵押貸款借款意願影響程度最小（$\beta = 0.068$）。

## (四)涉入在老年經濟安全保障對逆向抵押貸款借款意願影響有顯著正向的干擾效果

本研究實證結果顯示，涉入在老年經濟安全保障對逆向抵押貸款借款意願影響中，會產生干擾的效果，其中以涉入對基本生活需求的影響較大（$\beta = 0.122$），所以對逆向抵押貸款借款意願影響的干擾效果較強。

## (五)涉入在理財知識對逆向抵押貸款借款意願影響有顯著正向的干擾效果

經研究結果顯示，涉入在理財知識對逆向抵押貸款借款意願影響中，會產生干擾的效果，其中以涉入對借貸規劃的影響較大（$\beta = 0.098$），所以對逆向抵押貸款借款意願影響的干擾效果較強。

## (六)涉入在老年經濟安全保障與理財知識的交互作用對逆向抵押貸款借款意願影響有顯著正向的干擾效果

本研究實證結果顯示，涉入在老年經濟安全保障與理財知識的交互作用對逆向抵押貸款借款意願影響中，確實會產生正向的干擾效果（$\beta = 0.084$），表示申貸者對於逆向抵押貸款的瞭解與投入程度愈高，並有意改善或提升老年經濟安全保障時，愈有意願申請逆向抵押貸款，其中逆向抵押貸款為新金融性商品，教育程度愈高亦可幫助申貸者更加快速地瞭解與接受其商品內容，因此，教育程度較高（擁有較高理財知識）的借款人更較容易接受逆向抵押貸款的想法；老年經濟安全保障與理財知識在年長者有意願申請逆向抵押貸款時，具有互相影響的情形，兩者的交互作用對逆向抵押貸款借款意願會有正向的影響。

## 二、管理意涵

### (一)探討老年經濟生活與理財知識符合社會之需求

因應高齡社會的到來，國人健康狀況與平均壽命的延長，長者自身的理財知識與資源配置能力將成為晚年生活品質與資金來源的最佳保障（Piggot, Sherris & Mitchell, 2006）。老年經濟安全保障即在強調對年長者基本生活、經濟安全的保障；理財知識中的借貸、退休規劃，對年長者退休後的經濟狀況至為重要（Noctor, Stoney & Stradling, 1992; Lusardi & Mitchell, 2007），然而逆向抵押貸款提供具自主性的現金流量使用，自定給付金額的穩定性，用以維持長者尊嚴並保持老年生活經濟的穩定與自主性（Wang, Valdez & Piggott, 2009; Ahlstrom, Tumlinson & Lambrew, 2004; Reed & Gibler, 2003）。涉入程度是指對重要事務，會花較多時間考慮並蒐集較多相關的資訊；對現今社會上經濟狀況弱勢的年長者而言，在思考如何解決日常生活費用時，其實就是老年經濟安全保障與理財知識在涉入干擾的情況下，形成對逆向抵押貸款需求的影響。

### (二)逆向抵押貸款可為年長者增加收入來源，保障退休生活品質

逆向抵押貸款的實施可使老年經濟安全保障的措施更完整；此論點與本研究探討老年經濟安全保障影響逆向抵押貸款借款意願的模式相符。逆向抵押貸款是將住房與養老結合的一種特殊金融工具，因應全球人口老化現象攀升，逆向抵押貸款改變國人既定財產（不動產）傳承的思維，推廣「以房養老」理念，提升長者資源配置的活用性，開拓新的金融營運範疇，成為長者退休後的生活品質與資金來源的保障，緩解養老資源不足的難題，調整家庭養老負擔，化解老齡化危機的重要工具（Piggot, Sherris & Mitchell, 2006）。

### (三)提供逆向抵押貸款推廣策略的參考

逆向抵押貸款將房屋和養老保障緊密地結合在一起，對年長又相對貧弱的

長者提供一種全新概念的養老的途徑，因其具有強烈的公共福利色彩，得以強化社會保障功能，使得逆向抵押貸款不單只是簡單的融資行為，更能體現出全新的福利資助政策。

推廣逆向抵押貸款，可為長者建構更具規劃性的老年經濟安全保障，以彌補現行國民退休金之替代率不足的缺憾，使逆向抵押貸款成為長者老年退休金準備的重要融資工具之一（Wang, Valdez & Piggott, 2009; Fratantoni, 1999），同時可提升房產資源的優化配置，提前變現多重運用，使家庭財富最大化亦提升晚年經濟生活品質與生活資金需求的多樣性（Ong, 2008; Rowlingson, 2006）。其中逆向抵押貸款強調「以房養老」的理念，亦可鼓勵中青年者努力賺錢購屋，作為日後養老之用，亦能刺激國內房屋市場之交易，達到雙贏的局面。

## 三、研究建議

本研究之建議，可供政府、承辦金融機構與後續研究者參考。(1)政府透過中介機構來共同開發及提供學習理財知識。成立專責管理單位提升年長者有關逆向抵押貸款的理財知識以利推展逆向抵押貸款；(2)建議政府在預算可容忍範圍下，參酌美國施行的經驗，適度放寬申請資格，以免政府照顧弱勢的美意淪為口號；(3)建議承辦金融機構定期舉辦說明會協助提升年長者理財知識，回應年長者經濟安全需求的創新金融商品，以利逆向抵押貸款的推展。

對後續研究的建議：(1)擴大研究樣本的範圍：本研究母體為大臺北地區土地銀行擁有房屋的客戶，因此建議未來研究者可以擴大研究樣本的範圍；(2)規範研究樣本的對象：未來研究樣本的對象應該加以妥善規範，以期增加研究的客觀與貢獻性；(3)後續研究議題的探討：目前國內對於「逆向抵押貸款」的相關研究已有逐漸增加的趨勢，影響逆向抵押貸款的借款意願尚有其他變數，因此建議後續研究者持續探討此一議題，期待研究可更為完備。

## 參考文獻

方明川，「個人年金保險新論」，臺中：作者發行，1995年，頁29-30。

王健安，「臺灣以房養老財務及社會福利分析」，以房養老逆向抵押貸款方案研討會，臺北：中華民國住宅學會、政大臺灣房地產研究中心、經濟日報主辦，2009年12月。

王雲東，「2005年臺灣老人人權指標調查報告」，臺北：中國人權協會，2005年。

王雲東，「2000-2005年臺灣老人人權發展的現況與展期」，*應用倫理研究通訊*，第39期，2006年，頁15-32。

石泱，「老年經濟安全保障制度之探討」，*社區發展季刊*，第110期，2005年，頁260-274。

吳老德，「正義理論與福利國家」，臺北：五南圖書出版有限公司，2000年。

林左裕、楊博翔、徐偉棋，「逆向房屋抵押貸款在臺推行之可行性研究」，以房養老逆向抵押貸款方案研討會，臺北：中華民國住宅學會、政大臺灣房地產研究中心、經濟日報主辦，2009年12月。

林左裕、黃泓智、楊博翔，"It Is Time to Reverse! – the Feasibility Study of the Application of the Reverse Mortgage in Taiwan"，中華民國住宅學會第十七屆學術研討會，臺北：國立臺北大學主辦，2009年。

林芳姿，「臺北地區國小教師理財認知、退休理財規劃與理財行為之研究」，臺北市立教育大會歷史與地理學系碩士論文，2010年。

林隆儀、曾席璋，「品牌策略與企業形象對消費者購買意願的影響──涉入的干擾效果」，*真理財經學報*，第19期，2008年，頁79-122。

周文賢，「多變量統計分析」，第二版，臺北：智勝文化事業股份有限公司，2004年。

陳漢杰，「涉入、產品屬性評估與購買意願之相關研究──以銀行消費者購買理財服務為實證」，成功大學高階管理碩士在職專班碩士論文，2005年。

黃春智，「國中階段學生理財教育與理財知識之研究──以臺北縣市兩國中為例」，臺灣大學國家發展研究所碩士論文，2008年。

黃泓智、吳文傑、林左裕、鄭雅丰，"The Application of Reverse Mortgage in Aging Society"，*風險管理學報*，第10卷，第3期，2008年，頁293-314。

許皆清，「老人生活需求之研究──以臺南市松柏育樂中心松柏學苑為例」，中山大學中山學術研究所碩士論文，2000年。

張金鶚，「臺灣以房養老三方案模式提議」，以房養老逆向抵押貸款方案研討會，臺北：中華民國住宅學會、政大臺灣房地產研究中心、經濟日報主辦，2009年12月。

游欣霓，「以房養老制度在臺灣實施的可行性研究」，東吳大學國際貿易學系金融組碩士論文，2007年。

詹宜璋，「臺灣地區老年經濟安全之風險與保障」，中正大學社會福利學系博士論文，1998年。

Ahlstrom A., Tumlinson A. & J. Lambrew, "Linking Reverse Mortgage and Long-Term Care Insurance", The George Washington University, 2004.

Aiken, L. S., & S. G. West, "Multiple Regression: Testing and Interpreting Interactions", Newbury Park, CA: Sage Publications, 1991.

Aldlaigan, A. H. & F. A. Buttle, "Consumer Involvement in Financial Services: An Empirical Test of Two Measures", *The International Journal of Bank Marketing*, Vol. 19(6), 2001, pp.232-245.

Arora, R., "Consumer Involvement in Service Decisions", *Journal of Professional Service Marketing*. Vol. 9(1), 1993, pp.49-58.

5Basu, S., "Financial Literacy and the Life Cycle", White House Conference on Aging, 2005.

Bloch, P. H., "Involvement Beyond the Purchase Process: Conceptual Issues and Empirical Investigation", *Advances in Consumer Research*, Vol. 9, 1982, pp.413-417.

Celsi, R. L. & J. C. Olson, "The Role of Involvement in Attention and Comprehension Processes", *Journal of Consumer Research*, Vol. 15(2), 1988, pp.210-214.

Chen, H. & P. V. Ronald, "An Analysis of Personal Financial Literacy Among College Students", *Financial Service Review*, Vol. 7(2), 1998, pp.107-128.

Chou, K. L., Chow N. W. & I. Chi, "Willingness to Consider Applying for Reverse Mortgage in Hong Kong Middle-Aged Homeowners", *Habitat International*, Vol. 30(3), 2006, pp.716-727.

Cohen, J. B., "Involvement and You: 100 Great Ideas", *Advances in Consumer Research*, Vol. 10, 1983, pp.32-39.

Engel, J. F., Blackwell R. D. & D. T. Kollat, "Consumer Behavior", 8nd ed., The Dryden Press, Harcourt Brace College Publisher, 1995.

Eschtruth, Andrew D., Sun W. & A. Webb, "Will Reverse Mortgage Rescue the Baby Boomers?", Center for Retirement Research of Boston College, 2006.

Foxall, G. R. & J. G. Pallister, "Measuring Purchase Decision Involvement for Financial Services: Comparison of the Zaichkowsky and Mittal Scales", *International Journal of Bank Marketing*, Vol. 16(5), 1998, pp.180-194.

Fratantoni, M. C., "Reverse Mortgage Choices: A Theoretical and Empirical Analysis of the Borrowing Decision of Elderly Homeowers", *Journal of Housing Research*, Vol. 10(2), 1999, pp.189-209.

Guielford, J. P., "Fundamental Statistics in Psychology and Education", 4th ed., NY: Mcgraw. Hill Inc., 1965.

Hancock, R., "Can Housing Wealth Alleviate Poverty Among Britain's Older Population?", *Fiscal Studies*, Vol. 19(1), 1998, pp.249-272.

Kennedy, P., "A Guide to Econometrics", MA: Cambridge MIT Press, 1992.

Krugman, H. E., "The Impact of Television Advertising: Learning Without Involvement",

*Public Opinion Quarterly*, Vol. 29, 1965, pp.349-356.

Laurent, G. & J. N. Kapferer, "Measure Consumer Involvement Profile", *Journal of Marketing Research*, Vol. 22, 1985, pp.41-53.

Lin, Long-Yi & Chun-Shuo Chen, "The Influence of the Country-of-Origin, Product Knowledge and Product Involvement on Consumer Purchase Decisions: An Empirical Study of Insurance and Catering Services in Taiwan", *Journal of Consumer Marketing*, Vol. 23(5), 2006, pp.248-265.

Lusardi A. & O. S. Mitchell, "Financial Literacy and Planning: Implications for Retirement Wellbeing", Working Paper, Pension Research Council, Wharton School, University of Pennsylvania, 2005.

Lusardi A. & O. S. Mitchell, "Baby Boomer Retirement Security: The Role of Planning, Financial Literacy, and Housing Wealth", *Journal of Monetary Economics*, Vol. 54, 2007, pp.205-224.

Lusardi , A., "Financial Literacy: An Essential Tool for Informed Consumer Choice?" February, 2008, pp.8-11.

Maslow, A. H., "A theory of human motivation", *Psychological Review*, Vol. 50(4), 1943, pp.370-396.

Mitchell, O. S., Piggott J., Sherris M. & S. Yow, "Financial Innovation for an Aging World, Center for Pension and Superannuation", The University of New South Wales, 2006.

Noctor, M., Stoney S. & R. Stradling, "Financial Literacy, A Report Prepared for The National Westminister Bank", London, 1992.

Ong, R., "Unlocking Housing Equity Through Reverse Mortgage: The Case of Elderly Homeowners in Australia", *European Journal of Housing Policy*, Vol. 8(1), 2008, pp.61-79.

Piggot, J., Sherris, M., Mitchell O.S. & S. Yow, "Demographic Shift and Financial Risk", 2006.

Reed, R. & K. M. Gibler, "The Case for Reverse Mortgage in Australia-Applying the USA Experience", 2003.

Rothschild, M. L., "Advertising Strategies for High and Low Involvement Situations", Attitude Research Plays for High Stakes, J. C. Malongey ed., 1979.

Rowlingson, K., 'Living Poor to Die Rich'? Or 'Spending the Kids' Inheritance'? Attitudes to Assets and Inheritance in Later Life", *Journal of Social Policy*, Vol. 35(2), 2006, pp.175-192.

Schagen, S. & A. Lines, "Financial Literacy in Adult Life: A Report to the Nat West Group

Charitable Trust", Slough, Berkshire: National Foundation for Educational Research, 1996.

Schoell, W. F. & J. P. Guiltinan, "Marketing Essentials", Kluwer Academic Publisher Press, 1993.

Slama, M. E., A. Tashchian, "Selected Socioeconomic and Demographic Characteristics Associated with Purchasing Involvement", *Journal of marketing*, Vol. 49, 1985, pp.72-82.

Traylor, M. B., "Product Involvement and Brand Commitment", *Journal of Advertising Research*, Vol. 21, 1981, pp.51-56.

Wang, L., Emiliano A. V. & J. Piggott, "Securitization of Longevity Risk in Reverse Mortgages", *North American Actuarial Journal*, Vol. 12(4), 2009, pp.345-371.

Weinrobe, M., "An Analysis of Home Equity Conversion in the RAM Program", *Journal of the American Real Estate and Urban Economics Association*, Vol. 15(2), 1987, pp.65-78.

Widdowson, D. & K. Hailwood, "Financial Literacy and Its Role in Promoting a Sound Financial System", *Reserve Bank of New Zealand: Bulletin*, Vol. 70(2), 2007, pp.37-56.

Worthington, A. C., "Predicting Financial Literacy in Australia", *Financial Services Review*, Vol. 15, 2006, pp.59-79.

Wright, P. L., "The Cognitive Processes Mediating Acceptance of Advertising", *Journal of Marketing Research*, Vol. 10, 1973, pp.53-62.

Zaichkowsky, J. L., "Measuring the Involvement Construct", *Journal of Consumer Research*, Vol. 12, 1985, pp.341-352.

Zaichkowsky, J. L., "Conceptualizing Involvement", *Journal of Advertising*, Vol. 15, 1986, pp.4-14.

論文寫作要領

# The Influence of Old-Age Income Security and Financial Literacy on Willingness to Apply Reverse Mortgage: The Moderating Effects of Involvement

## LONG-YI LIN, YI-YUN SHANG[*]

## ABSTRACT

In recent years, Taiwan has entered the aging demographic, economic security issues related to the elderly gradually attention. The object of this research is to explore the influence of old-age income security and financial literacy on willingness to apply reverse mortgage. The research results were list as follow: (1) Old-age income security has a significantly positive influence on willingness to apply reverse mortgage. (2) Financial literacy has a significantly positive influence on willingness to apply reverse mortgage. (3) The interactions of old-age income security and financial literacy have a significantly positive influence on willingness to apply reverse mortgage. (4) The involvement has a significant moderating effect between the influences of old-age income security on willingness to apply reverse mortgage. (5) The involvement has a significant moderating effect between the influences of financial literacy on willingness to apply reverse mortgage. (6) The involvement has a significant moderating effect between the influence of the interactions of old-age income security and financial literacy on willingness to apply reverse mortgage, and proposed management implications and future research directions

Keywords: Old-Age Income Security, Financial Literacy, Reverse Mortgage, Involvement.

[*] Long-Yi Lin, Associate Professor, Department of Business Administration, National Taipei University.
Yi-Yun Shang, Ph D. Student, Department of Business Administration, National Taipei University.

# 參考文獻

司徒達賢，2001。策略管理新論——觀念架構與分析方法，智勝文化事業有限公司。

林隆儀，2000。臺灣中小型家族企業生產技術發展之研究：自販機製造業金雨公司之個案研究，產業管理學報，第二卷，第一期，頁75-102。

林隆儀，2000。郵寄問卷調查無反應偏差改善方法之效果——Meta分析，文大商管學報，第5卷，第1期，頁63-79。

林隆儀、黃營杉、吳青松，2004。不同聯盟型態之下經濟誘因與信任之相對重要性研究——以臺灣清涼飲料產業為例，交大管理學報，第24卷，第2期，頁1-35。

林隆儀、黃榮吉、王俊人譯，2005。V. Kumar, David A. Aaker and George S. Day著，Essentials of Marketing Research, 2$^{nd}$ Edition，臺北：雙葉書廊有限公司。

林隆儀、鄭君豪，2005。產品品質外在屬性訊號、產品知識與顧客滿意之整合分析——以臺北市筆記型電腦消費者為例，輔仁管理評論，第12卷，第1期，頁65-91。

林隆儀、許庭偉，2006。表演品質、服務品質、顧客滿意與顧客忠誠的關係之研究，行銷評論，第3卷，第4期，頁497-528。

林隆儀、方業溥，2006。行動商務應用對公司經營績效的影響——市場導向的干擾效果，電子商務學報，第8卷，第2期，頁271-294。

林隆儀、曾席璋，2008。品牌策略與企業形象對消費者購買意願的影響——涉入的干擾效果，真理財經學報，第19期，頁79-122。

林隆儀、胡瑋純，2009。服務品質、議題行銷及企業形象對購買意願的影響——顧客信任的干擾效果，真理大學管理學院，2009聯合研討會論文集。

林隆儀、張聖潔，2009。廣告訴求、廣告代言人、廣告態度與購買意願的關係，真理大學管理學院，2009聯合研討會論文集。

林隆儀、呂清鈺，2009。企業形象、關係行銷與信任對購買意願的影響——口碑的干擾效果，真理大學管理學院，2009聯合研討會論文集。

林隆儀、徐稚軒、陳俊碩，2009。寬頻網路關係行銷結合類型、服務品質、關係品質與轉換成本對顧客忠誠之影響，輔仁管理評論，第16卷，第1期，頁37-68。

林隆儀、陳俊碩，2010。來源國形象與品牌知名度的組合效果對消費者購買意圖的影響——產品涉入的干擾效果，聯大學報，第7卷，第1期，頁129-147。

林隆儀，2010。議題行銷的社會顯著性、活動持續度與執行保證對品牌權益的影響，輔仁管理評論，第17卷，第3期，頁31-54。

林隆儀，2010。促銷方式對私有品牌產品知覺品質的影響——促銷情境與產品類別特徵的干擾效果，中小企業發展季刊，第16期，頁51-78。

林隆儀、周佩琦，2010。服務品質、品牌形象、顧客忠誠與顧客再購買意願的關係——以臺北市銀行產業的顧客為例，中小企業發展季刊，第19期，頁31-59。

林隆儀，2010。創意＋特色，開啟農產品活路行銷之路，尚未發表論文。

林隆儀、李明真，2011。學校行銷策略與學校形象對家長選校決策的影響——知覺風險的干擾效果，聯大學報，第8卷，第2期，頁145-178。

林隆儀、商懿勻，2015。老年經濟安全保障、理財知識與逆向抵押貸款意願之研究，輔仁管理評論，第22卷，第2期，頁65-94。

吳萬益、林清河，2002。行銷研究，初版，臺北：華泰文化事業股份有限公司。

邱皓政，2006。量化與統計分析，第三版，臺北：五南圖書出版股份有限公司。

高明瑞、黃義俊、張乃仁、蔡依倫，2008。企業自然環境管理研究之回顧與展望，中山管理評論，第16卷，第2期，頁351-382。

許士軍，1990。管理學，臺灣東華書局股份有限公司。

商懿勻，2021。消費遠視症者之自我控制問題研究，崇越論文大賞參賽論文，論文編號10041。

楊雪倫校訂，2009。周海濤、李永賢、張衡翻譯，Robert K. Yin著，個案研究：設計與方法，五南圖書出版股份有限公司。

黃俊英，1997。行銷學，臺北：華泰文化事業股份有限公司。

黃俊英，1999。企業研究方法，臺北：臺灣東華書局股份有限公司。

黃俊英，2000。多變量分析，臺北：翰蘆圖書出版有限公司。

陳錦堂，2004。統計分析SPSS for Windows入門與應用，臺北：儒林圖書公司。

顏月珠，1996。統計學，三民書局股份有限公司。

瞿海源、畢恆達、劉長萱、楊國樞主編，2015。社會及行為科學研究法：質性研究法，臺灣東華書局股份有限公司。

Berg, Bruce L., 1995. Qualitative Research Methods for Social Sciences. 2nd Edition, Allyn & Bacon, USA.

Blech, G. E., R. J. Lutz and S. B. Machenzie, 1983. Attitude Toward the Ad as a Mediator of Ad Effectiveness: Determinates and Consequences, Advance in Consumer Research, 10(3), pp.352-539.

Bogdan, Robert, 1972. Participant Observation in Organizational Settings. Syracuse, NY: Syracuse University Press.

Cooper, Donald, and Pamela Schindler, 1998. Business Research Methods, 6th Edition, Boston: McGrow-Hill.

Feigl, H., 1958. The Scientific Outlook: Naturalism and Humanism, in H. Feigl and Mary Broadbeck, Eds., The Philosophy of Science, New York: Appleton-Century-Crofts.

Fox, J. H., 1958. Criteria of Good Research, Phi Delta Kappan, Vol.39 (March), pp.285-256.

Freiden, J. B., 1984. Advertising Spokesperson Effects: An Examination of Endorser Type and Gender on Two Audiences, Journal of Advertising Research, 24(5), pp.33-41.

Gilg, Andrew, Stewart Barr and Nicholas Ford, 2005. Green Consumption or Sustainable Lifestyles? Identifying the Sustainable Consumer, Futures, No. 37, pp.481-504.

Griffin, Ricky W., 2006. Fundamentals of Management, 4th Edition, New York: Houghton Mifflin Company.

Guielford, J. P., 1965. Fundamental Statistics in Psychology and Education, 4th ed., NY: McGraw Hill Inc.

Hofstede, Geert, 1980. Culture's Consequences, Beverly Hill, CA: Sage.

Kaikati, Jack G., 1987. Celebrity Advertising: A Review and Synthesis, International Journal of Advertising, 6(2), pp.93-105.

Kotler, Philip, and Kevin L. Keller, 2009. Marketing Management, 13th Edition, NJ: Prentice Hall.

Lee, Su-Yol, 2008. Drivers for the Participation of Small and Medium-Sized

Suppliers in Green Supply Chain Initiatives, Supply Chain Management: An International Journal, 13(3), pp.185-198.

Lin, Long-Yi, 2010. The Relationship of Consumer Personality Trait, Brand Personality and Brand Loyalty: An Empirical Study of Toys and Video Games Buyers. Journal of Product & Brand Management, 19(1), pp.4-17.

Lin, Long-Yi and Ching-Yuh Lu, 2010. The Influence of Corporate Image, Relationship Marketing, and Trust on Purchase Intention: The Moderating Effects of Word-of-Mouth, Tourism Review, 65(3), pp.16-34.

Lin, Long-Yi, 2011. The Impact of Advertising Appeals and Advertising Spokespersons on Advertising Attitudes and Purchase Intentions. African Journal of Business, 5(21), pp.8446-8457.

Lin, Long-Yi, 2011. The Influence of Service Quality, Cause-related Marketing, Corporate Image on Purchase Intention: The Moderating Effect of Customer Trust. International Journal of Research in Management, Vol.3 (November), pp.1-38.

O'curry, Suzanne and Michal Strahilevitz, 2001. Probability and Mode of Acquisition Effects on Choices Between Hedonie and Utilitarian Options. Marketing Letters, 12: 1, pp.37-49.

Oplatka, Izhar, and Jane Hemsley-Brown, 2007. The Incorporation of Market Orientation in the School Culture: An Essential Aspect of School Marketing, International Journal of Educational Management, 21(4), pp.292-305.

Platt, Jennifer, Case study in American Methodical Thought, Current Sociology, 40, 1992, pp.17-48.

Roscoe, J. T., 1975. Fundamental Research Statistics for the Behavioral Sciences, New York: Holt, Rinehart and Winston.

Schiffman, Leon G. and Leslie L. Kanuk, 2007. Consumer Behavior, 9th Edition, NJ: Pearson Education, Inc.

Stake, Robert, 2000. Case Studies. In Norman K. Denzin and Yvonna S. Lincoln (Ed.s), Handbook of Qualitative Research, pp.435-454, Thousand Oaks, CA: Sage.

Strahilevitz, Michal and John G. Myers, 1998. Donations to Charity as Purchase Incentives: How Well They Work May Depend on What You Are Trying to Sell. Journal of Consumer Research, February, pp.434-446.

Wilcox, J. B., 1977. The Interaction of Refusal and Not-at-Home Sources of Nonresponse Bias, Journal of Marketing Research, 14, pp.592-597.

Zeithaml, Valarie, A., 1988. Consumer Perceptions of Price, Quality, and Value: A Means-End Model and Synthesis of Evidence. Journal of Marketing, 52(July), pp.2-22.

參考文獻

國家圖書館出版品預行編目資料

論文寫作要領／林隆儀著．－－四版．－－臺北
市：五南圖書出版股份有限公司，2022.01
面；　公分
ISBN 978-626-317-515-0（平裝）

1.CST：論文寫作法

811.4　　　　　　　　　　110022294

1H68

# 論文寫作要領

作　　　者 — 林隆儀

發 行 人 — 楊榮川

總 經 理 — 楊士清

總 編 輯 — 楊秀麗

主　　　編 — 侯家嵐

責任編輯 — 吳瑀芳

文字校對 — 葉瓊瑄

封面設計 — 姚孝慈

出 版 者 — 五南圖書出版股份有限公司

地　　　址：106台北市大安區和平東路二段339號4樓

電　　　話：(02)2705-5066　　傳　　真：(02)2706-6100

網　　　址：https://www.wunan.com.tw

電子郵件：wunan@wunan.com.tw

劃撥帳號：01068953

戶　　　名：五南圖書出版股份有限公司

法律顧問　林勝安律師事務所　林勝安律師

出版日期　2010年 8 月初版一刷
　　　　　2011年 8 月初版二刷
　　　　　2016年 9 月二版一刷
　　　　　2019年 8 月三版一刷
　　　　　2022年 1 月四版一刷

定　　　價　新臺幣450元

# 經典永恆·名著常在

## 五十週年的獻禮 —— 經典名著文庫

五南，五十年了，半個世紀，人生旅程的一大半，走過來了。

思索著，邁向百年的未來歷程，能為知識界、文化學術界作些什麼？

在速食文化的生態下，有什麼值得讓人雋永品味的？

歷代經典·當今名著，經過時間的洗禮，千錘百鍊，流傳至今，光芒耀人；

不僅使我們能領悟前人的智慧，同時也增深加廣我們思考的深度與視野。

我們決心投入巨資，有計畫的系統梳選，成立「經典名著文庫」，

希望收入古今中外思想性的、充滿睿智與獨見的經典、名著。

這是一項理想性的、永續性的巨大出版工程。

不在意讀者的眾寡，只考慮它的學術價值，力求完整展現先哲思想的軌跡；

為知識界開啟一片智慧之窗，營造一座百花綻放的世界文明公園，

任君遨遊、取菁吸蜜、嘉惠學子！